Books of Merit

STANDING STONES

ALSO BY JOHN METCALF

New Canadian Writing 1969
The Lady Who Sold Furniture
Going Down Slow
The Teeth of My Father
Girl in Gingham
General Ludd
Selected Stories
Kicking Against the Pricks
Adult Entertainment
What Is a Canadian Literature?
Volleys (with Sam Solecki & W. J. Keith)
Shooting the Stars
Freedom from Culture
Acts of Kindness and of Love (with Tony Calzetta)
An Aesthetic Underground

STANDING STONES

The Best Stories
of John Metcalf

Introduction by Clark Blaise

Thomas Allen Publishers
Toronto

National Library of Canada Cataloguing in Publication

Metcalf, John, 1938–
    Standing stones : the best stories of John Metcalf / John Metcalf.

ISBN 0-88762-144-9

I. Title.

PS8576.E83S74   2004   C813'.54   C2003-906462-X

Editor: Patrick Crean
Cover design: Gordon Robertson
Cover image: Frantisek Staud/phototravels.net

"Single Gents Only" and "Polly Ongle" were originally published in the *Malahat Review*. "Girl in Gingham" and "Private Parts" appeared in *Shooting the Stars*, reprinted by permission The Porcupine's Quill, Inc. "The Eastmill Reception Centre" appeared in *Fiddlehead Magazine*. "Gentle as Flowers Make the Stones" and "The Years in Exile" were published in *Selected Stories* (McClelland and Stewart). "The Nipples of Venus" appeared in *Adult Entertainment* (Macmillan of Canada).

Published by Thomas Allen Publishers,
a division of Thomas Allen & Son Limited,
145 Front Street East, Suite 209,
Toronto, Ontario M5A 1E3 Canada

www.thomas-allen.com

  Canada Council
for the Arts

ONTARIO ARTS COUNCIL
CONSEIL DES ARTS DE L'ONTARIO

The publisher gratefully acknowledges the support of the Ontario Arts Council for its publishing program.

We acknowledge the support of the Canada Council for the Arts, which last year invested $21.7 million in writing and publishing throughout Canada.

We acknowledge the Government of Ontario through the Ontario Media Development Corporation's Ontario Book Initiative.

We acknowledge the financial support of the Government of Canada through the Book Publishing Industry Development Program (BPIDP) for our publishing activities.

08 07 06 05 04   1 2 3 4 5

Printed and bound in Canada

To Myrna

The object of art is to give life a shape.

— JEAN ANOUILH, The Rehearsal

CONTENTS

READING JOHN METCALF

by Clark Blaise

Y ou can read a collection of stories as you might a novel—only more so. The hero will have a dozen names and faces (or eight, in the case of *Standing Stones*) instead of one, and multiple traumas of birth and growing up. Like all mythic heroes, he is something of a self-made man; he realizes early he is not destined to stay where he was born or to accept the definitions that birth placed upon him. He defies his origins, which are mendacious and mincing. His earthly parents and their gods are abandoned early; he seeks new masters. They steal, they drink and they burn. Even in prison their freedom is alluring, a freedom that blasphemes the system. He yearns to violate standards he already despises, to get a tattoo, to behave irresponsibly, to get roaring drunk, sleep in and bail out. Throbbing American jazz and joyless English Methodism intersect in blues-y ways.

Montreal seems inevitable.

He can't rebel, of course, not then, or there—not in an England so spiritually crimped, so grim and War-pocked. If he stays, he's more likely to stew in his juices than subvert the system. He's not yet heard the Flaubertian advice to write like the devil but live like a bourgeois. From that agonized compromise, in fact, he will construct his life's body of work, but it will take a few moltings before getting there.

So far, the formula sounds familiar. Most anyone born into genteel poverty, castrating repression and Non-Conformist orthodoxy (the worst kind) will worship at the shrine of alternate gods. Why do Catholics in general, American Southerners and British Protestants in particular—at least those who survive—make such good writers? They carry the memories, the smell of the censer, the biscuit tins and flowered wallpaper, and their scabbarded antidote—the language (and in the case of Britain, the paintbrush as well) to confront it.

Our hero will be married here, divorced there, sometimes at rest but usually in need. He was born here, or over there, he has a few children, or none, boys or girls and he has had wives and girlfriends and years alone wondering if there will ever be marriage again. He finds her; she dies. She finds him; he escapes.

Heroes change continents but never leave home. They remain in their core connoisseurs of small, private spaces, the oxymorons of triumphant disappointment. Their heroes are scourges of bad food, spiritual poverty, hypocrisy, tarnished language and fraudulent claims. Even at their lowest, they will not yield to tasteless convenience. From multifarious assaults on their dignity they construct their prayers: Dear Lord, never let me forget. Give me the strength of memory, do not take from me the shank of shame, the wrath, the small triumphs, the secret victories, the glossary of vindication.

John Metcalf's work is a jeweler's art. Of course he loves the short story (and has done more for its celebration and preservation than anyone in Canada). Of course, his own potential novels are distilled into long stories, like "Polly Ongle," "Private Parts" and "Girl in Gingham." Unlike Rupert Brooke, he *is* "magnificently prepared for the long littleness of life."

Metcalf worships. He just had to find *his* church.

His worship is the deployment of language, the meticulous placement of words. In the honourable tradition of British empiricism, he is suspicious of all grandiloquence, all theories leading to grand syntheses. Fraud reveals itself in flaccid language; flaccidness inflates to cant and bombast. Or, as Yeats put it, only words are certain good. Words arranged as paragraphs, paragraphs shrunk to single words. He reminds me of a friend who once declared, "How hard it is to find something *plain!*" Plain is honest. Plain is good.

Words deployed like cut diamonds on black velvet trays.

Metcalf's worship asks us not to look to the altar or attend to the preacher. It directs us, rather, to the stained glass, the slants of colour and arrangement of shards separated by lead as though they were (and are) radioactive. A word like "dottle," say—crumbs of tobacco dribbling from a pipe onto a vest or jacket—evokes (for me, at least) a vanished, cloistered, unselfconscious eccentricity, a pre-industrial, cottage-bound, self-contained life; who ever knew it? A pre-*Depends*, pre-*Shout!* pre-*Nicoban* world. When "dottle" vanishes, so does a shelf of history; so does a wondrous life-form. Where else but here have I ever read it?

What separates Metcalf from nearly any stylist I know is that his "new" words are *old*. They relate to worlds that were; they are the rivets that align the visible with the remembered. No neologisms, no linguistic stretch marks.

You wouldn't know it, revisiting the miseries of bachelorhood and marginal employment in 1960s and '70s anglophone Montreal as presented in these stories, but those were magic times in that city and John Metcalf is their guide. The Québecois barely exist; the exotics are more likely to be Jews. One problem we young writers in Montreal faced in those years was our ambition to scoop it all up, to get it all in, against the ribbed crabbiness of the genre itself. The models of our beloved form were derived from Chekhov and Joyce and Hemingway, but the scope of our ambitions was novelistic at the very least. We were all packing for the long trip. Palpable and teeming, that was the life we knew and saw. A French-language novel of that same era, Réjean Ducharme's *L'avalé des avalées* (the swallower swallowed), captures that thirst. In English, only Hugh Hood with his twelve-volume *roman fleuve,* his collected stories and *Around the Mountain* managed to get it all in, the old-fashioned way. Metcalf was luckier than most of us. My model was Faulkner, but rattling around in the back of *his* head was the entire British literary canon, Milton to Wodehouse, Leavis and Connolly and the Angry Young Men.

Especially Wodehouse. What delicious sentences!

We can still revel in the echo of those decades. Alice Munro, a frequent visitor to Montréal in those years, and John Metcalf are the prime saboteurs of the conventional short story in Canadian writing. Time and again, their stories seem to end, that is, to approach the formal end of what could be a normal story, but the narrative voice won't let go. The voice still pleads for new understanding, for forgiveness and one more chance to get it right. It's the voice, not the form, that *is* the story. It's the voice that kidnaps the ending, that violates and compromises all that is neat and expected. "Polly Ongle" ends in Metcalf's longest sustained monologue, an address to the statue of José de San Martin in an Ottawa park. "Single Gents Only" concludes with a reading of "The Wind in the Willows" to a drunken roommate in a cold room under dreadful wallpaper. Or, most nakedly (without giving away the concluding sentences), at the close of "The Eastmill Reception Centre":

> You don't understand, do you, what it means for me to make these confessions? To *have* to make these confessions, to face the death I feel inside myself?
>
> Let me try to put this in a different way: Let me try to find words that perhaps you'll understand. Words! Understand! Good Christ, will it never end, this blathering!

It's the voice endlessly reflecting on the defects of its own storytelling, pulling it out from the fire while it's still plastic, as a glassblower or smithy might, reshaping it before it hardens. There are writers who prefer the oblong, the slightly wobbly, the plain and honest if not quite perfect, and . . . well, the *dottled*. The voice is never satisfied, it carries the story forward, or laterally, or backward at the last moment. The narrative is like a river plodding its way to the sea and the story-form is the ancient riverbed it effortlessly follows. But when the burden of meaning is too great, the voice punches out a new channel and the story spreads to become a delta.

You float down that river and come out in a different place, every time.

— *Clark Blaise*

STANDING STONES

After David had again wrested the heavy suitcase from his father's obstinately polite grip and after he'd bought the ticket and assured his mother he wouldn't lose it, the three of them stood in the echoing booking hall of the railway station. His mother was wearing a hat that looked like a pink felt Christmas pudding.

David knew that they appeared to others as obvious characters from a church-basement play. His father was trying to project affability or benevolence by moving his head in an almost imperceptible nodding motion while gazing with seeming approval at a Bovril advertisement.

The pink felt hat was secured by a hat-pin which ended in a huge turquoise knob.

Beyond his father's shoulder, looking over the paperbacks on the W. H. Smith stall, was a woman in a sari. David kept under observation the vision of the bare midriff and the ponderous hand of the station clock while pretending to listen to the knit-one-purl-one of his mother's precepts.

His father eventually made throat-clearing noises and David promptly shook his hand. He stooped to kiss his mother's cheek. Her hat smelled of lavender, her cheek, or possibly neck, of lily-of-the-valley. He assured her that the ticket was safe, that he knew where it was; that he'd definitely remember to let her know in the letter for which she'd be waiting if the train had been crowded; if he'd managed to get a seat.

The loudspeakers blared into demented announcement flurrying the pigeons up into the echoing girders. The onslaught of this amplified gargle and ricochet coincided with his mother's peroration, which seemed to be, from the odd phrase he caught, a general reworking of the Polonius and Mr. Micawber material, warnings against profligacy, going to bed late, burning the candle at both ends, debt, promiscuity, not wearing undershirts, and drink.

She gripped his hand.

He watched her face working.

As the metal voice clicked silent, she was left shouting,

"THE SECRET OF A HAPPY LIFE IS . . ."

Mortified, David turned his back on the gawping porter.

She continued in a fierce whisper,

". . . is to *apportion* your money."

He returned their wavings, watching them until they were safely down into the tiled tunnel which led to the car-park, and then lugged his case over to the nearest waste basket, into which he dropped the embarrassing paper bag of sandwiches.

With only minutes to go before his train's departure, the barmaid in the Great North-Western Bar and Buffet set before him a double Scotch, a half of best bitter, and a packet of Balkan Sobranie cigarettes. Flipping open his new wallet, he riffed the crisp notes with the ball of his thumb. The notes were parchment stiff, the wallet so new it creaked. Smiling, he dismissed the considerable change.

The Scotch made him shudder. The aroma of the Sobranie cigarettes as he broke the seal and raised the lid was dark, strange, and rich. He was aware of the shape and weight of the wallet in his jacket's inside pocket. Stamped in gold inside the wallet were words which gave him obscure pleasure: *Genuine Bombay Goat*. With a deft flick of his wrist, he extinguished the match and let it fall from a height into the ashtray; the cigarette was stronger than he could have imagined. He raised the half of bitter in surreptitious toast to his reflection behind the bar's bottles. Smoke curling from his nostrils, he eyed the Cypriot barmaid, whose upper front teeth were edged in gold.

———————

He sat in a window seat of the empty carriage feeling special, feeling regal, an expansive feeling as physical and filling as indigestion. He crossed his legs, taking care not to blunt the immaculate crease in his trousers, admiring his shined shoes. A mountain of luggage clanked past, steam billowed up over the window, a whistle blew. And then the carriage door opened and a toddler was bundled in from the platform followed by a suitcase and parcels and carrier-bags and its mother. Who hauled in after her an awkward stroller.

Doors slamming down the length of the train.

"Ooh, isn't the gentleman kind!" said the woman to the toddler as David heaved the suitcase up onto the luggage rack.

"And these?" said David.

From one of the carrier-bags, a yellow crocodile made of wood fell onto his head.

The toddler started to struggle and whine as the train pulled out. It was given a banana. It was pasty-looking and on its face was a sort of crust. Old food, perhaps. Possibly a skin disease. It started to mush the banana in its hands.

Turning away, David gazed out over the backs of old jerry-built houses, cobbled streets, cemeteries, mouldering buildings housing strange companies found in the hidden parts of towns visible only from trains: Victoria Sanitation and Brass, Global Furniture and Rattan, Allied Refuse. Clotheslines. The narrow garden strips behind the houses looking as if receding waters had left there a tide-line of haphazard junk.

The train cleared the neat suburbs, the gardens, the playing fields for employees, picked up speed, vistas of distant pitheads, slag-heaps, towering chimneys and kilns spreading palls of ochre smoke, all giving way to fields and hedges, hedges and fields.

Inside his head, like an incantation, David repeated:

The train is thundering south.

Beside the shape of the wallet in his jacket's pocket was the letter from Mrs. Vivian Something, the University's Accommodations

Officer. The tone of the letter brusque. He had not replied promptly as he had been instructed so to do and no vacancies now existed in the Men's Halls of Residence. Nor were rooms now available on the Preferred List. Only Alternative Accommodation remained.

274 Jubilee Street.

The morning sunshine strong, the train thundering south, the very address propitious, *Jubilee*.

As the train bore him on towards this future, he found himself rehearsing yet again the kind of person he'd become. What kind of person this was he wasn't really sure except that he'd known without having to think about it that it wasn't the kind of person who lived in Men's Halls of Residence.

Blasts on its whistle, the train slowing through a small country station.

Nether Hindlop.

On the platform, rolls of fencing wire, wicker crates of racing pigeons, holding a ginger cat in his arms, a porter.

But at the least, he thought, the kind of person who bestowed coins on *grateful* porters. He still blushed remembering how on his last expedition to London he'd tipped a taxi-driver a shilling and the man had said,

"Are you sure you can spare it?"

And later, even more mortifying, after a day in the Tate and National galleries, he had sat next to a table of very interesting people, obviously artistic, in a crowded café in Soho. He'd listened avidly as they chatted about Victor this and Victor that and he'd realized gradually that Victor must be Victor *Pasmore*. And as they were leaving, the man with the earring had paused by his table and said in a loud voice,

"So glad to have had you with us."

Even though he had been seared with shame and burned even now to think of it, he had in a way been grateful. He admired the rudeness and aggression and the ability to be rude and aggressive *in public*; the realm of books apart, he still considered it the most splendid thing that he had heard another person actually *say*.

But he found it easier to approach what he would become by defining what he was leaving behind. What he most definitely *wasn't* —hideous images came to mind: sachets of dried lavender, Post Office Savings Books, hyacinth bulbs in bowls, the *Radio Times* in a padded leather cover embossed with the words *Radio Times*, Sunday-best silver tongs for removing sugar-cubes from sugar-bowls, plump armchairs.

But *how*, he wondered, his thoughts churning deeper into the same old ruts, *how* did one change from David Hendricks, permanent resident of 37 Manor Way, ex-Library Prefect and winner of a State Scholarship, to something more . . . more raffish.

"Hold a woman by the waist and a bottle by the neck."

Yes.

Somerset Maugham, was it?

Not much of a point of etiquette in his own teetotal home, he thought with great bitterness, where wild festivities were celebrated in Tizer the Appetizer and where women were not held at all.

"*Whoopsee!*" cried the mother.

The toddler was launched towards him, was upon him. He looked down at his trousers. He tried to prise the clenched, slimy fingers from the bunched material.

"There," he said, "there's a good boy . . ."

"Not afraid of anything, *she* isn't!" said the woman proudly.

David blushed.

"Proper little tomboy, encha?"

David smiled.

And regarded his ruined knees.

———————

The house stood on a corner; the front of the house faced onto Jubilee Street, the side of the house faced the cemetery on the other side of Kitchener Street. From the coping of the low wall which bounded the cemetery, rusted iron stumps stuck up, presumably the remains of an ornamental fence cut down for munitions during the Second World War. In an aisle of grass between two rows of tombstones, a small dog bunched, jerking tail, its eyes anguished.

There were no facing houses on the other side of Jubilee; there was a canal, tidal the driver had told him, connecting with the docks. The tide was out. Seagulls screeched over the glistening banks of mud. The smell came from the canal itself and from the massive red-brick brewery which stood on its far side.

Most of the tiny front garden was taken up by an old motorbike under a tarpaulin.

"*Not* Mr. Porteous?" she said.

"No," said David, "I'm afraid not."

She held the letter down at a distance, her lips moving. Wiry hairs grew on the upper lip. He suddenly blushed remembering that her house had been described as Alternative Accommodation and hoping that she wouldn't be embarrassed or hurt.

Her gross body was divided by the buried string of the grubby pinafore. Her hair was grey and mannish, short back and sides with a parting, the sort of haircut he'd noticed on mentally defective women in chartered buses. The torn tartan slippers revealed toes.

"They didn't mark that down," she said.

"Pardon?"

"About the back double."

"Double?"

"With the Oxford gentleman."

"Oh," said David. "You mean . . . ?"

"Yes," she said. "They should have marked that down."

He manoeuvred his suitcase round the hatstand and bicycle in the gloom of the narrow passage and followed her ponderous rump up the stairs. Reaching for the banister, grunting, she hauled herself onto the dark landing.

Even the air seemed brown.

"This is the bathroom," she said, "and the plumbing."

He sensed her so close behind him that he felt impelled to step inside. The room was narrow and was largely taken up by a claw-foot bathtub. Over the tub, the height of the room and braced to the wall, bulked the monstrous copper tank of an ancient geyser.

She was standing behind him, breathing.

He began to feel hysterical.

The lower part of the tank and the copper spout which swung out over the tub were green with crusty verdigris; water sweating down the copper had streaked the tub's enamel green and yellow. Wet, charred newspaper half blocked the gas-burners in the geyser's insides.

"If you wanted a bath, it's a shilling," she said, slippers shuffling ahead of him, "with one day's warning."

Following her into the bedroom, he stared at the vast plaster elephant.

Two single beds stood on the brown linoleum. The wallpaper was very pink. Pinned on the wall between the beds was a reproduction cut from a magazine of Annigoni's portrait of Queen Elizabeth.

"You can come and go as you please—the key's on a string in the letterbox—but we don't have visitors."

David nodded.

"I don't hold with young ladies in rooms."

"No, of course," said David. "Quite."

His gaze kept returning to the elephant on the mantelpiece. Inside the crenellated gold of the howdah sat a brown personage in a turquoise Nehru jacket sporting a turban decorated with a ruby.

"Well . . ." he said.

Staring at him, doughy face expressionless, she unscrewed a Vicks Nasal Inhaler and, pressing one nostril closed, stuck it up the other.

He politely pretended an interest in the view.

Below him, a staggering fence patched with warped plyboard and rusted lengths of tin enclosed a square of bare, packed earth.

There was a bright orange bit of carrot.

On one of the sheets of tin, it was still possible to make out an advertisement for Fry's Chocolate.

In the middle of this garden sat a disconsolate rabbit.

When the sounds seemed to have stopped, he turned back to face the room. He looked round nodding judiciously, aware even as he was doing it that it was the sort of thing his father did. He had, he realized, no idea of how to conclude these negotiations.

"And this other person? The man from Oxford?"

"Mr. Porteous."

"He's . . . ?"

"We had a telegram."

"Ah," said David, "yes. I see."

"Cooked breakfast and evening meal included," she said, "it's three pound ten."

"Well," said David, contemplating the elephant, "that sounds . . ."

"And I'll trouble you," she said, "in advance."

———————

He shoved the empty suitcase under the bed.

The thin quilt, the sheets, the pillow, all felt cold and damp.

He thought of turning on the gas-fire but didn't have a shilling piece; he thought of putting a sweater on.

Jingled the change in his pocket for a bit, inspected the wallpaper more closely; the motif was lilac blossoms in pink edged with purple. It was five-thirty. He wondered at what time, and where, this evening meal was served, if "evening meal" meant tea in some form or dinner.

Voices.

Slap of slippers on lino.

He eased his door open a crack.

"*Evening Post.* Now that should serve her nicely, the *Evening Post.* Six pages of the *Post.* Read the newspaper, do you? Not much of a fellow for the reading. Scars, though! Now that's a different story entirely. Did I show you me scars?"

Through the banisters, an old man's head with hanging wings of white hair. Behind him, a stout boy in a brown dressing-gown.

The boy stood holding a sponge bag by its string; his calves were white and plump.

"Now there's a dreadful thing!" said the old man, who was scrabbling about on his hands and knees with the sheets of newspaper manufacturing a giant spill. "A dreadful thing! Two hundred homeless. Will you look at that! There, look, and there's a footballer. Follow the football, do you? Fill in the Pools? Never a drop of luck I've had. Spot the Ball? But a raffle, now! A raffle. I fancy the odds in a raffle. A raffle's a more reasonable creature than Spot the Ball."

He disappeared into the bathroom.

The front door slammed shaking the house.

Boots clumping.

Then the dreadful voice of Mrs. Heaney.

"PERCY?"

"WHAT?"

"PERCE!"

"Quick, now!" shouted the old man. "Quick! Holy Mother, she's in full flow!"

Matches shaking from the box, he secured one against his chest and then rasped it into flame. He set fire to the drooping spill.

"BACK, BOY! BACK!"

Body shielded by the door, face averted, he lunged blindly. The expanding sheet of light reminded David of war films. The old man's quavering cry and the explosion were nearly simultaneous.

Brown shoulders blocking the view.

Suddenly from below, at great volume, Paul Anka.

I'M JUST A LONELY BOY . . .

The old man was in the smoke stamping on the spill.

Ash, grey and tremulous, floated on the air.

———————

In front of Mrs. Heaney's place at the head of the table stood a bottle of Cream Soda.

The kitchen was silent except for the budgerigar ringing its bell and stropping itself on the cuttlefish. The cooked evening meal was a fried egg, a wafer of cold ham, a quarter of a tomato, and three boiled potatoes.

The slice of ham had an iridescent quality, hints of green and mauve.

In the centre of the oilcloth stood Heinz Ketchup, Crosse and Blackwell's Salad Cream, HP Sauce, Branston Pickle, OK Sauce, Daddy's Favourite, A1 Sauce, a bottle of Camp Coffee, and a punctured tin of Nestlé's Evaporated Milk.

Sliced white bread was piled on a plate.

The old man bobbed and fidgeted darting glances.

The fat boy was called Asa Bregg and was from Manchester and had come to university to study mathematics. Ken, who had acne and a Slim Jim tie and lots of ballpoint pens, was an apprentice at Hawker-Siddeley. Percy, presumably Mrs. Heaney's son, glimpsed earlier in overalls, was resplendent in a black Teddy-boy suit, white ruffled shirt, and bootlace tie. What forehead he had was covered by a greasy elaborate wave. He was florid and had very small eyes. The old man was addressed as "Father" but David was unable to decide what this meant.

Cutlery clinked.

Percy belched against the back of his hand.

The old man, whose agitation had been building, suddenly burst out,

"Like ham, do you? A nice slice of ham? Tasty slice of ham? Have to go a long way to beat . . ."

"Father!" said Mrs. Heaney.

". . . a nice slice of ham."

"Do you want to go to the cellar!"

Cowed, the old man ducked his head, mumbling.

The budgerigar ejected seeds and detritus.

David studied the havildar or whatever he was on the label of the Camp Coffee bottle.

Mrs. Heaney rose heavily and opened four tins of Ambrosia Creamed Rice, slopping them into a saucepan.

Percy said,

"Hey, tosh."

"Pardon?" said David.

"Pass us the slide."

"Pardon? The what?"

Percy stared.

"Margarine," said Ken.

"Oh! Sorry!" said David.

Crouched on the draining-board, the cat was watching the Ambrosia Creamed Rice.

The old man, who'd been increasingly busy with the cruet, suddenly shouted,

"Like trains, do you? Interested in trains? Like the railway, do you? Fond of engines?"

"Father!"

Into the silence, Asa Bregg said,

"I am. I'm interested in trains. I collect train numbers."

The old man stared at him.

Even Percy half turned.

Ken's face lifted from his plate.

Asa Bregg turned bright red.

"I'm a member of the Train-Spotters Club."

———————

Alone in the room that was his, David stared at the plaster elephant. He wondered how they'd got the sparkles in.

After the ham and Ambrosia Creamed Rice, he'd walked the neighbourhood—dark factories across the canal, bomb-sites, news agents, fish and chips, Primitive Methodist Church, barber, The Adora Grill, and had ended up in the Leighton Arms where in deepening depression he drank five pints of the stuff manufactured opposite his room, an independent product called George's Glucose Stout.

The pub had been empty except for an old woman drinking Babycham and the publican's wife, who was knitting and listening to *The Archers.*

At the pub's off-licence, as a gesture of some kind, he'd bought a bottle of cognac.

He arranged on top of the chest of drawers the few books he'd been able to carry, the standard editions of Chaucer and Spenser serving as bookends, and settled himself on the bed with Cottle's *Anglo-Saxon Grammar and Reader*. Skipping over some tiresome introductory guff about anomalous auxiliary and preterite-present verbs and using the glossary, he attempted a line of the actual stuff but was defeated by the conglomeration of diphthongs, thorns, and wens; he had a presentiment that Anglo-Saxon was not going to be his cup of tea.

Heavy traffic up the stairs, voices, a strange jangle and clinking. Mrs. Heaney appeared in the doorway and behind her a tall man with blond hair.

"This is Mr. Porteous," she said, "from Oxford."

"David Hendricks."

"How do you do? Jeremy Porteous. If I could trouble you?" he said, handing the tightly furled umbrella to Mrs. Heaney. He dropped the canvas hold-all on the floor and, slipping off the coiled nylon rope and the jangling karabiners and pitons, tossed them and the duffle coat onto the bed.

He glanced round.

"Splendid," he said. "Splendid. Now, in the morning, Mrs. . . . ah . . . Heaney, isn't it? . . . I think, *tea.*"

"About the rent, Mr. Porteous."

"A matter for discussion, Mrs. Heaney, if you'd be so kind, following breakfast. I've had rather a gruesome day."

And somehow, seconds later, he was closing the door on her.

He smiled.

"There's a person downstairs," he said, "called 'Father'. Seemed to want to know, rather insistently, if I enjoyed travelling by bus."

David grinned.

Advancing on the gas fire and elephant, Jeremy said, "There's a special name, isn't there, for this chocolate chap? The one on its neck?"

"Mahout," said David.

Seemingly absorbed, Jeremy moved back a pace the better to view the elephant. He had a slight limp, David noticed, and was favouring his right leg.

"Pardon?" said David.

"'A plate'," repeated Jeremy, "'of Spam'."

David wondered how it was possible to wear a white shirt in combination with an anorak smeared with mud and at the same time look as suave as the men in the whisky advertisements.

"What are you going to . . ." David hesitated ". . . read at university?"

"Actually," said Jeremy, "I'm supposed to be involved in some research nonsense."

"Oh!" said David. "I'm terribly sorry. I just assumed . . . What did you do at Oxford?"

"I spent the better part of my time," said Jeremy, still intent on the elephant, "amassing an extraordinarily large collection of photographs of naked eleven-year-old girls with their ankles bound."

David stared at the elegant back.

He could think of absolutely nothing to say.

The gas fire was making popping noises.

Desperate to break the silence, David said,

"Have you been climbing? Today, I mean?"

"Just toddling about on The Slabs at Llanberis. Are any of these free? I really must rest these shirts."

As he wrestled open a drawer in the chest, the mirrored door of the wardrobe silently opened, the flash of the glass startling him.

"Did you hurt your leg today?" said David, embarrassed still and feeling it necessary to ease the silence. "When you were climbing?"

"I hurt it," said Jeremy, dropping on his bed toothpaste, toothbrush, towel, and a large green book, "not minutes ago, and quite exquisitely, in what is probably referred to as the hall. On a sodding *bicycle*."

He added to his toiletries a pair of flannel pyjamas decorated with blue battleships.

"Good God!" he said, pulling back the quilt, patting further and further down the bed. "This bed is positively *wet*."

"Mine feels damp, too," said David.

"*Yours* may be damp," said Jeremy. "*Mine* is *wet*."

He hurled the rope and the climbing hardware into a corner.

"Wet!" he shouted, striking the bed with his furled umbrella, "*Wet! Wet! Wet!*"

He seemed almost to vibrate with rage.

He pounded on the lino with the umbrella's ferrule.

"*Can you hear me, Mrs. Heaney? Are you listening, you gravid sow?*"

He stamped so hard the room shook and the wardrobe door swung open.

"WET!"

He glared about him.

He snatched at the string between the beds.

It broke.

With a loud *clung*, the gas-meter turned itself off.

He stood beside the bed with his eyes closed, one arm still rigid in the air holding the snapped string as though he were miming a straphanger in the underground. Light glinted on the gold and onyx cuff-link. Slowly, very slowly, he lowered the arm. Opening his fingers, he let the length of string fall to the floor. Eyes still closed, he let out his pent breath in a long sigh.

He limped over to the window. He swept aside the yellowed muslin curtains. He wrenched the window high. He limped to the mantel. He hurled the elephant into the night.

David realized that he, too, had been holding his breath.

The edges of the curtains trembled against the black square.

David cleared his throat.

"Would you," he said, reaching under the bed, "would you like a drink?"

"Ummm?" said Jeremy, turning, wiping his hands with a handkerchief.

"A drink?"

"Ah, brandy!" said Jeremy. "Good man! It might help in warding off what these beds will doubtless incubate. Sciatica, for a start."

"Lumbago," said David.

"Rheumatoid arthritis," said Jeremy.

"*Mould*," said David.

Jeremy laughed delightedly.

Digging into his hold-all, he came up with a black case that contained telescoping silver drinking cups which, with a twist, separated into small beakers. He caught David's expression and said,

"Yes, a foible, I'm afraid, but I've always been averse to the necks of bottles. Equal in the eyes of God and all that sort of thing, certainly, but would one share one's toothbrush? Well, bung-ho!"

Along the rim of the beaker, David saw the shapes of hallmarks.

"'Lumbago'," said Jeremy. "Don't you find that certain words make you think of things they don't mean? 'Emolument', for example. Makes me think of very naked, very fat, black women. Something I read as a stripling about an African king's wives who were kept in pens and fed starchy tubers—so fat they couldn't get up—just rolled around—and *oiled* all over, rather like . . ." his hands sketched a shape ". . . rather like immense *seals* . . . What was I starting to say?"

"Lumbago," said David.

"Yes," said Jeremy. "I wonder why?"

There was a silence.

"So!" said Jeremy.

David nodded.

Jeremy held out his cup.

"What are you going to do?" said David.

"In the morning," said Jeremy, "we shall fold our tents. What was that woman called?"

"Mrs. Heaney?"

"No. The lodgings woman."

"The Accommodations Officer?"

"*She's* the one. Cornbury? Crownbury? We shall proceed against her."

"But I thought—well, from her letter, that there *wasn't* anywhere else."

"Nonsense."

"Are you just *allowed* to leave a . . . ?"

"*Who*," demanded Jeremy, "who got us into this—this *lazar-house* in the first place? The responsibility is purely hers. We shall question her judgment with indignation and bitterness."

"But . . ."

"With *voluble* indignation and bitterness. We shall demand reparations. *Silver*," he said, "is so comforting to the touch, isn't it?"

David held up the brandy bottle.

"Well," said Jeremy, "*yes.*"

"But you see . . ." said David.

"See what?"

"I paid her a week's rent."

"Always," said Jeremy, "try to *postpone* payment. On the other hand," he said judiciously, "never bilk."

"Well," said David, "now that you've . . . I mean, she's not likely to return my . . ."

"Life," said Jeremy, climbing into his pyjama bottoms, "is very much a *balancing*, a trading-off of this against that. It's a simple question, surely? The question is: Are you the sort of person who lives in a place like this? To which," he said, working a khaki sweater down over his pyjama top, "one hopes there can be but one reply."

He reassembled the bed and spread his duffle coat over the quilt and on the duffle coat spread two sweaters and his rope.

"I find sleep impossible," he said, "without *weight*."

Whistling "We Plough the Fields and Scatter," he went out with toothbrush and towel.

David sat on the bed enjoying the brandy, enjoying the weight and balance of the silver cup, savouring Jeremy's use of the word: *we*. Thinking about the amazing fluctuations of the long day, he decided that the flavour of events was exactly caught in the casual connective of biblical narrative: *And it came to pass . . .*

The wallpaper made him feel as if he were sitting inside a friendly pink cave.

He was, he realized, drunk.

Jeremy returned whistling the hymn about those in peril on the sea and started to work himself under the layers of bedding. He asked David to pass him the book, a large paper edition of *The Wind in the Willows* with illustrations by Ernest Shepard.

"I say," said Jeremy. "Would you . . . I mean, would it be a terrible imposition?"

"Would what?"

"Just to read a few paragraphs?"

"I haven't read this," said David, "since I was a child."

"Oh, but you should!" said Jeremy with great earnestness. "It never lets you down."

"From the beginning?"

"No," said Jeremy. "Let me think. Oh, this is *lovely*! There's the field mice singing carols to Ratty and Mole at 'Mole End'—that's always very nice. But . . . *I* know! Let's have the part where Ratty and Mole go to visit Toad. Remember? Where the motor-car wrecks Toad's caravan? Yes, here it is."

He passed over the book.

He closed his eyes, composed his hands.

"Most kind of you."

David began.

The old grey horse, dreaming, as he plodded along, of his quiet paddock, in a new raw situation such as this simply abandoned himself to his natural emotions. Rearing, plunging, backing steadily, in spite of all the Mole's efforts at his head, and all the Mole's lively language directed at his better feelings, he drove the cart backwards towards the deep ditch at the side of the road. It wavered an instant—then there was a heart-rending crash—and the canary-coloured cart, their pride and joy, lay on its side in the ditch, an irredeemable wreck . . .

Toad sat straight down in the middle of the dusty road, his legs stretched out before him, and stared fixedly in the direction of the disappearing motor-car. He breathed short, his face wore a placid, satisfied expression, and at intervals he faintly murmured "Poop-poop!"

The Mole was busy trying to quiet the horse, which he succeeded in doing after a time. Then he went to look at the cart, on its side in the ditch. It was indeed a sorry sight . . .

The Rat came to help him, but their united efforts were not sufficient to right the cart. "Hi! Toad!" they cried. "Come and bear a hand, can't you!"

David, turning the page, glanced over at Jeremy. His eyes were closed, his breathing deepening.

"Glorious, stirring sight!" murmured Toad, never offering to move. "The poetry of motion! The real *way to travel! The* only *way to travel! Here today—in next week tomorrow! Villages skipped, towns and cities jumped—always somebody else's horizon! O bliss! O poop-poop! O my! O my!"*

"O stop *being an ass, Toad!" cried the Mole despairingly.*

"And to think I never knew!" went on the Toad in a dreamy monotone.

David looked up.

With a long sigh, Jeremy had turned on his side.

His breathing deepened into a snore.

The coiled rope was balanced on the hump of his shoulder.

"All those wasted years," David continued, reading aloud in the pink bedroom, *"that lie behind me, I never knew, never even* dreamt! *But now—but now that I know, now that I fully realize! Oh what a flowery track lies spread before me, henceforth! What dust-clouds shall spring up behind me as I speed on my reckless way!"*

Jeremy's exhalations were a faint, breathy whistle.

David closed the book.

The edges of the curtains trembled against the black square of the open window.

He switched off the light.

He pulled the quilt up to his chin and lay in the darkness listening.

Somewhere far distant in the night, in the docks perhaps, perhaps slipping its moorings and preparing to move out down the river to the sea, a ship was sounding and sounding.

PRIVATE PARTS

A MEMOIR

PART ONE

1

One of my earliest sexual memories, more vivid and perhaps more important than any subsequent sexual memory, is of my Uncle Fred and the idiot. I must have been then six or seven years old, evacuated to my Uncle Fred's farm in what was then called Cumberland to escape the bombing of the Yorkshire industrial town in which my father worked. Auntie Lizzie even then seemed strange to me. She had what people called a "nutcracker" face, a nose and chin that threatened to meet, and the chin barbed with bristles. The countless farm cats fled under sofa and settle to escape her harsh caress. Her voice was so dreadful it could arrest the agricultural activities of men two and a half fields away. I learned years later that it was to escape Aunt Lizzie that my Uncle Fred trudged daily to the top field where he sat for hours smoking his pipe in a hen-hut. It was there that they found him face-down dead in the litter and hen shit.

Looking back now to those childhood times, I see their faces wrinkled and seamed, Uncle Fred always in corduroy worn smooth, Aunt Lizzie in faded pinafores and laceless, clopping shoes, her hands permanently reddened, the pair of them like illustrations in a history of rural life. They are, in later memory, like the crabbed, spiky drawings of Edward Ardizzone.

Whenever I think of them, words come to my mind of whose meanings I am not exactly sure, haunting words like "fustian" and "coulter," "stoup" and "flitch," words redolent of another age. It seems scarcely possible that as submarines cruised beneath the seas and tanks ground forward over the rubble of Europe, as Dresden burned and Hiroshima melted, my Uncle Fred and his day-labourers were leading-in the cornfields with scythes, stooking sheaves, and the women bringing dinner down to the field in cloth-covered baskets and bearing the earthenware pitchers of beer over the stubble. It is a scene that Brueghel painted.

Uncle Fred's farm lay in the lush dairy land of the Eden valley from which rose the wild and endless fells whose lower slopes were grazed by sheep but whose heights climbed to thinning bracken, boulders, bare rock, and the circling hawks.

That farm and farmyard enchanted me, the cathedral gloom of the vast barn where the silent tractor stood, its wheels nearly as high as my head, machines with spikes and tines and gleaming discs, the work bench with old biscuit tins with pretty ladies on the lids— tins full of nuts and bolts, washers, nails, screws, staples, cotter-pins, fuses, spark plugs, coils of special wire. I would rummage there for hours, bend things in the vice, pound nails. The feedshed, too, was gloomy but a warm gloom, rich with the smells of meal and bran, metal scoops in the rolled-down sacks, rolled down like Aunt Lizzie's lisle stockings, crusted paddles for stirring the mash.

I thought that lisle stockings, a word I'd heard Aunt Lizzie say, were somehow connected with Golden Syrup, a green and gold tin with a lion lying down on it and lots of flies buzzing around the lion and on the tin it said Tate and Lyle's Golden Syrup: "Hold your noise!" my Uncle often said when I spoke at table asking questions so I did not ask but I thought that stockings and syrup had some obvious connection that everyone understood in that world where bombs were falling and my father was being brave.

And I promised myself that when they'd finished evacuating me, I would go back to the bomb world where you could watch the soldiers marching and when I was there I would understand everything.

I loved my Uncle Fred but I was frightened of him too. He killed things and didn't care and he sometimes bellowed and slapped my head. He called Gyp, the one-eyed collie, "Bugger-Lugs" and when the cows leaned against him as he was milking, the milk *rin . . . rin . . . rin* in the pail, he called them "whoring buggers" and sometimes he did very long shouts when they kicked the pail over, shouts that always started "You would, would you, you shitarse! Get over you cock-struck twat, you . . ." I tried to learn them and practised them in bed.

But I was confused by this, too, because he never said interesting things near Auntie Lizzie, bad things, and he was a Methodist lay-preacher and on Sundays would put on a suit and shirt and tie, which on him looked as preposterous as a dress and hat looked on Aunt Lizzie, and conducted fervent services for small congregations in the parlours of neighbour farms.

When he was in a good mood, when he'd got the tractor mended, or the vet had been and it wasn't mastitis, he always used to sing the same song very loudly and sometimes he sang it over and over and sometimes he just hummed most of it but burst out with single lines of words.

> *From the oppressive power of sin*
> *My struggling spirit free;*
> *Perfect righteousness bring in,*
> *Unspotted purity;*

Then with a final heave on the wrench, a final twist of the screw-driver, or the last bash on the shackle pin, he'd stand back and bellow,

> *Speak, and all this war shall cease,*
> *And sin shall give its raging o'er:*
> *Love me freely, seal my peace,*
> *And bid me sin no more.*

But he frightened me also, because his jokes and tricks were rough and sometimes painful. He it was who always squirted me with milk when stripping the cows, who urged me to touch electric fences, who advised me to wash paint off my face with petrol drawn from the tractor so that I had to be taken to the doctor for ointment, who put salt instead of sugar on my porridge, who encouraged me to pick up the body of a fox he'd shot so that I stank for a week of its musk and suffered daily scrubbings in the tin tub in front of the fire with Aunt Lizzie's emery wash cloths.

Uncle Fred employed an idiot, the son of a widow woman who lived in the village. The idiot's name was Bobby. I was frightened of him because of his potato face and I could never understand anything he said. Uncle Fred employed him, I realize now, more from charity than for his usefulness. Mucking out the stables and balancing the wheelbarrow on its perilous trip to the midden took him all the day.

Bobby stank. He never changed his clothes. He always wore the same boots, green cord trousers, leggings, and khaki battledress top on which his mother had stitched all the buttons, crests, badges, and ribbons which the Italian prisoners of war who worked on my Uncle's and neighbouring farms had given him. They had taught him to march up and down the yard with his pitch-fork on his shoulder like a rifle and he liked to do that more than mucking-out and when Uncle Fred saw him he'd yell, "Get out of that, you girt softie! Get down the barn, you daft lummox!" and then he'd yell, "Move yourself, bollock-brains!" but the funny thing was that he called him all the same things when he was pleased with him, when the barn was finished early or he hadn't tipped over the wheelbarrow in the yard.

Uncle Fred's Italians slept in bunks in one of the barns. He called them all Albert. He was fond of them and they of him and after the war two of them refused repatriation and stayed on with him until he died. Uncle Fred had lent them a twelve-bore shotgun to shoot rabbits and they let me go with them. They shot thrushes and blackbirds, too, and ate them and Uncle Fred said foreigners were different.

I knew my Uncle was a man of power because he preached to other grown-ups on Sundays and told them what to do but I learned one day that he was so powerful that even Policemen obeyed him.

We were doing something to the tractor and I was holding a tin can of grease with a stick in it when into the yard cycled the Policeman.

"It has come to my attention, Mr. Moore," he said, "that you have given a shotgun to them Eyetalians."

"Is that right?" said my Uncle Fred.

"Them, they're the Enemy," said the Policeman.

"Is that right?" said my Uncle Fred again.

"You have supplied arms and ammunition," said the Policeman, "to the enemies of England."

"Mr. Moore?" said my Uncle. *"Mr. Moore!"* he shouted. "I've been Fred to you since your arse was wet, George Voules, so you bugger off and play blackouts or I'll be having a word with your mum."

And then the big Policeman got on his bike and my Uncle started to walk away and then he turned and shouted.

"At least they were *fighting* before they were taken!"

And then when the big Policeman was at the yard gate, my Uncle Fred shouted,

"Flat feet, my arse!"

Behind the farmhouse is an apple tree in full blossom. Not a simple apple tree—an apple tree explosive in blossom, such an apple tree as Samuel Palmer saw. Beside the tree, a brook runs down behind the house, across the bottom fields, through the bed of wild watercress, to join the River Eden. Its rock-strewn shallowness and sound widens near the apple tree into a silent pool. The sun is bright. It is not hot but Uncle Fred insists it is. He persuades Bobby to unlace his boots and paddle in the pool. He winks at me. The joke, the wink seems to say, is coming soon. Uncle Fred next persuades Bobby to take off all his clothes and play in the water. Bobby struggles awkwardly with buttons and sleeves and the second he is naked Uncle Fred snatches away the clothes and runs off shouting with laughter towards the yard.

Bobby is making his angry face and shouting angry-sounding things. He is pointing towards the yard and he is crying. I cannot understand a word. I feel guilty and sorry but it is one of Uncle

Fred's jokes and Uncle Fred is grown up and preaches and shouts at Policemen.

I am staring at Bobby's thing. It hangs down from a bush of black hair and it reaches nearly to his knee. It is as fat as my arm. His ball-bag is huge like the Hereford in the dark stall.

I stare and stare.

2

"When we hear the words *penis* and *vagina*, the pictures we have in our minds (known as *mental images*) tell us a lot about our true feelings," writes Dr. Ethel Fawce, author of *Sex and the Adjusted You*. "These *mental images*," she goes on, "can be approving or disapproving. Favourable female childhood images of the penis may be of: a banana, an ice cream cone, a mushroom, a musical instrument, or a Tootsie Roll." But what of me, whose *mental image* is of Bobby?

There's an essential rightness about this image for me, brought up as I was a hardcore Yorkshire Nonconformist. Not for me sly serpents whispering intelligences, the temptations of an Eve, but a subhuman figure in the Garden with a cock like a malignant growth.

The world of my parents and of most of the adults with whom I came in contact was pious, sour, and thin. They had married better not to burn—a fire soon damped. Gripeguts Wesley was their God.

I have a very early memory of myself, a tiny child, standing in the back garden of that Yorkshire manse gazing upon rows of crucifixes which were stuck in a special plot of earth near the door of the coal cellar. I made the crosses with kindling. Pinned to each cross was a worm. They wriggled for a long time, but then they just drooped, and then they went flat and brittle.

Poor Billy Blake, so misunderstood. To those choirs that sang in chapel and tabernacle, those grimy, mean, industrial towns of the north of England with their fortitude under the grey rain *were* Jerusalem.

My evacuation was of short duration.

When I came back I was given a gas-mask with a Mickey Mouse face on it.

Cod-liver oil in huge bottles was supplied free of charge to children; as with all else, my mother equated nastiness with virtue.

Our way of life was like the enactment of a set of improving proverbs. Early to bed and early to rise, we wasted not, we stitched in time, took care of the pence, made sure our hands were never idle, received the reward of virtue which is its own. "Cleanliness," as Wesley remarked in one of his sermons, "is indeed next to Godliness"— and ours was carbolic.

My mother's conversation was a compendium of homely cliché; our drink was Adam's ale or "the cup that cheers," all activities were powered by "elbow grease," all locomotion by "shanks' pony"; if at first we didn't succeed, we tried and tried and tried again; supper was always Hobson's choice.

At some ungodly hour in the morning, my mother daily holy-stoned the front doorstep and polished the brass door-knocker and the brass flap of the letter-box. If we were to set out on an infrequent journey, she would arise in the morning dark to prepare sandwiches because to eat in a restaurant was to waste money and she would then clean the oven and polish the toilet bowl, because, as she always said, were we to be killed in a car-crash or derailment, she wouldn't like people thinking she hadn't kept a clean house.

The war years with their strawberry jam made of turnips and their powdered eggs, were, for my mother, the happiest years of her life. The suffering was total. There was grim joy in her response to an inadequate diet and perpetual cold, to stretching out meagre scraps into meals and "making do." Something went out of her when rationing ended.

People in my world actually used such expressions as "Antichrist," "The Great Beast," and "Whore of Babylon." "Scarlet Woman" was sometimes Rome and "Whore of Babylon" was sometimes Rome and "Scarlet Woman" was sometimes not Rome but Mrs. Henderson who "carried on" with soldiers. The Book of Revelation is the source of much Nonconformist imagery; its threats of apocalyptic destruction appeal to the Nonconformist temperament. I naturally understood it to be an anti-Catholic diatribe. My world of missionary boxes, Sunday School, and sin was violent in its anti-Catholicism. Faith versus Good Works, the thirty-nine Articles, and the fallacy of Transubstantiation, were as ABC to me. But I soon penetrated this historical obfuscation and grasped that the essence of the wickedness was that Catholicism pretended to *forgive*. Which was not *only* wicked but *silly*. For God alone could forgive and the only person I knew who claimed to have been forgiven was a man who stood up in church and said so during one of my father's sermons but my father said later the man was drunk.

In my world, guilt was personal and permanent; atonement, though demanded, was understood to be a hollow gesture.

The world beyond my world was made up of drunkards, fornicators, lewd people, those who used the King's English incorrectly, backsliders, vulgar people, sots, adulterers, those who took the Name of the Lord in Vain, who ate things in the streets, were spendthrift, who used foul language, and who carried on.

I naturally imagined Rome to be the centre of these activities and even then envied the Allied troops who were actually there seeing it all.

———————

The abstract meanings of "the Flesh" did not have to be explained to me. The antithesis between Spirit and Flesh was in the very air I breathed. The Flesh existed to be subdued; this was accomplished by a wide range of prohibitions, silence, soap, whitened doorsteps at dawn, and whatever other mortifications my mother could invent.

The lewdest story my mother ever told, and that perhaps when I was fifteen or sixteen, was of standing beside a man in a bus queue during the war and chatting about the previous night's raid. The man said:

"I were that frightened, Mrs., you couldn't have got a needle up me bum."

What it was about this story that appealed to her I don't quite know; it couldn't have been the humour.

I retain vivid, pre-evacuation memories of our dog, Sandy, on whom I lavished all my love. My mother disliked dogs because she said they were dirty; my father said dogs were good for children and were not dirty; my mother said he didn't have to clean up after them or bear their habits; my father regarded her and then retired to the silence of his study. My mother could invest an apparently innocent word like "habits" with such intensity that even if her meaning was not clear to me her loathing nipped questions in the bud.

If Sandy, lying on her mat, raised a hind leg to lick what my mother called her "parts," she was immediately shooed out of doors.

One morning I noticed spots of blood on the kitchen floor. Sandy was not spanked for this which made me curious. At the same time, I noticed that her thing was more visible, red, swollen like a tulip.

I hoped it would heal up.

"It is her Time," said my mother mysteriously.

During her Time she was not allowed to go outside except on the leash but one day I forgot and she escaped to gambol with the next door mongrel. Later, I saw them on the lawn fighting, pumping, heaving, tongues lolling. I ran to find my mother who was vacuuming, somewhere on the third floor. By the time she arrived, Sandy and Rex were no longer fighting but were standing disconsolate in the middle of the lawn with their behinds mysteriously stuck together. Sandy, seeing us, tried to pull towards us but she was stuck to Rex and when she pulled, Rex yowled as if someone had stepped on his paw and Sandy whimpered. I knew they were in pain, there had been fighting, blood, and I didn't understand why my mother did not do whatever had to be done to help.

"It's too late," she said tonelessly.

This incident made me very anxious but I knew better than to ask questions: this, I somehow knew, was the World of the Flesh.

At exactly this time, it might have been that very week, I found a hedgehog in the garden and put it in a big cardboard box to keep as a pet. My mother would not allow it in the house because she said it was dirty. She shook a box of DDT over it until it was white. Next morning it was dead.

These events somehow fused in my mind.

——————

Much later than this, after I'd come back from being evacuated, I became aware of the other meaning of "self" and managed in a confused way to understand the nature of the Holy Ghost.

Every bath night, my mother washed me and then rinsed off all the soap and then washed my hair and when she'd finished, she'd hand me the cloth and say,

"Wash yourself."

When she returned to the bathroom minutes later, she would brutally towel me until I was bright red and then give me the towel, saying as she left the room,

"Dry yourself."

I understood the Trinity as being three people who were not actually people but parts of one person. I understood "yourself" in the commands to wash and dry as meaning one's thing, one's parts. The Holy Ghost was part of God and I felt I now knew *which* part.

And it was unfortunate that it was at precisely this time that I heard of something called The Sin Against the Holy Ghost. I was very anxious about this sin, not being able to discover its exact nature. All I could learn was that it was the worst sin of all, a sin too horrendous to even talk about. The one subject never talked about in my house was "that kind of thing" and it therefore seemed obvious that sex and The Sin Against the Holy Ghost were one and the same thing.

And I had done it.

Had miniature erections like the dog, seen Bobby naked and bestial, played with myself, said words, and given a girl called Marie a threepenny bit to let me watch her pee.

I knew myself to be unforgivable, of the damned, one from whom God's Face was averted for eternity.

This burden of guilt and conviction of sin tortured me for years —dirtiness, death, disapproval, impurity—and eventually became the front line of the ravaged battlefield of my adolescence.

(This will not do. The paragraphs flow too evenly, the sequence of statements rounds off the subject too neatly, leading too comfortably to the next asterisk and the beginning of another sequence of anecdote and reflection.

To reread these last paragraphs nauseates me. They remind me of cute stories of children mistakenly praying "Harold Be Thy Name," such anecdotes as grace the pages of *Reader's Digest*.

And what can you understand by my use of the word "tortured"? Did you think I mean—"troubled"?

The fault is mine. I have pictured my mother as a joyless puritan. But this is not the whole truth. The fault lies in my writing, feelings hidden behind humour, pain distanced by genteel irony. The truth is ugly and otherwise. My father was merely eccentric; my mother was mad.

Her mind festered. It was a pit of unimaginable filth—a contagion I did not escape. I hated her. I am happy she is dead.

Had I not been stronger, had I not battled her every day of my life, I could well have joined my brothers in institutions the world over, those who mutilated their genitals with shards of glass, or worse, the ones who came in judgement and cut off tits with butchers' knives, carved cunts with cleavers.)

As I grew older and sinned more, as my reading revealed to me a larger world than the loveless world of chapel and grey rain, I vowed that my life would be filled with laughter, beautiful women, warm flesh; my life would be lived in the sun.

It's a common enough story.

At eighteen I left home forever.

At twenty-one I emigrated to Canada.

3

At about the age of seven I had my first encounter with Art—an event central to this memoir and as dramatic as Paul's conversion on the Damascus Road.

Art played no part in the life of my parents or their society. The only occasion vaguely artistic was the annual performance of the *Messiah*; for this, professional soloists were imported and backed by several choirs combined. The music was supplied by a merging of brass bands. I remember a colliery band and the uniforms of the Fire Brigade.

The visual arts were not encouraged; even the old masters had too much thigh and breast about them for my mother's taste. There may have been the occasional *Laughing Cavalier* but walls were usually decorated with anonymous landscapes and calendars.

One morning my father had left the newspaper lying on the breakfast table. There was a photograph in it of a painting which had just been cleaned of the dinge and varnish of centuries and which revealed that the naked lady was not merely pointing her breast at the sky but was squirting from it a jet of milk which as it streamed across the canvas became stars in the Milky Way.

I asked my mother what the picture was in the paper for.

"It's a picture by an old painter that's in a museum."

"Is it beautiful?"

"Handsome is as handsome does," said my mother.

She took the paper away.

"Why is the lady . . . ?"

"If you ask me," she said, "and I don't mind who hears me say it, people who painted that sort of thing were no better than they should be."

She rattled the dishes in the sink.

"I wouldn't give *that sort of thing* house room."

She sniffed.

"I wouldn't give you tuppence for the lot of them."

But of all the arts, the theatre was the most wicked; the word "actress" carried much the same suggestiveness as the word "model" did a few years ago. Wesley had fulminated against the theatre in the spirit of his puritan forebears and the historical disapproval was still strong in the north. Not only was my family Methodist, the whole area was an ardent Methodist stronghold. The town in which we lived was only a few miles from Haworth Parsonage and the moors. Mrs. Gaskell in her *Life of Charlotte Brontë* described among the books at Haworth "some mad Methodist Magazines full of miracles and apparitions, and preternatural warnings, ominous dreams, and frenzied fanaticism . . ."

A later biographer, Margaret Lane, wrote: "On the Brontë children the effects of such intimacy with Methodism were various . . . On Anne it laid its most unhappy behest, infecting her with the morbid fear of personal damnation which darkened her youth . . . On Branwell the pressure of so much religious emphasis was to destroy belief."

And my intimacy with Methodism was more intimate than theirs.

I was once taken to a pantomime at Christmas in Leeds and I remember being removed tearfully halfway through because my mother said it was vulgar and full of "that sort of thing"; I had liked it very much indeed because one of the Broker's Men had played a trombone solo and with every note his trousers had fallen lower and lower and he was wearing red underpants with big flowers on them.

There existed, however, varieties of approved entertainment which were carried on in church halls and basements. Documentary films about wildlife, the postal service, or deep-sea fishing were sometimes shown; professional itinerants such as Grey Owl sometimes appeared; missionaries gave lectures with magic-lantern slides of lepers. These church halls also provided a fourth-rate circuit for professional monologuists, a profession surely now extinct.

I can remember the monologuist who brought the certainty of art into my life. I can even remember his name; it was Mr. Montague. A large, florid, middle-aged man wearing the kind of checked suit of which characters in English novels say, "No gentleman would wear a suit like that."

He came to our house for tea. He was a flamboyant and welcome change from the usual pursed and mealy visitors such as Sanitary Inspectors and Church Stewards. Across his paunch was a looped gold chain. His voice was boomy and fruity. He called my mother "Dear Lady" which I thought was very grand and he called my father "Sir" and he asked me if I found shaving painful. When offered a ninth or tenth scone, he patted the wide check of his waistcoat and said,

"Spare, Dear Lady, these grey hairs."

We later conducted him to the church hall. Everything was ordinary; the same boys and girls, the same ladies of the church who made much of me because I was my father's son, the same stage curtains that didn't quite close, a stage familiar to me because in dressing-gown and teatowel-headcloth I had trodden it as Third Shepherd or Orient King.

But Mr. Montague, when he appeared, was a Mr. Montague quite different from the Mr. Montague of the tea-table. He was wearing mutton-chop whiskers, violent eyebrows, and what must have been a smoking jacket. He did different people by moving about the stage in different voices. There was a lady's voice and a terrible, stern father's voice, and a younger man's voice. The story, I had been told, was called *The Barretts of Wimpole Street*. It seemed magical to me that when he was the father you could see quite clearly the non-existent lady he was speaking to and when he was the lady you could see him standing where he'd been before he'd moved to become the lady.

I was entranced. Any sense of being in an audience vanished. Only he and I existed. Suddenly he began to pace and shout terribly at the lady who was frightened too and I felt so frightened I felt sick. Then I was. On Miss Moseby. Then I fainted clear away.

I was carried out and revived and afterwards I was taken back to the closet where the hymn books and extra tea cups were stored and which he was using as a dressing room. Beads of sweat were standing on his face. I watched him peeling off the whiskers and wiping off the grease paint.

I don't remember his saying anything to me or my saying anything to him but I knew from that moment on that when I was grown up I would be like him, become other people, be applauded, be magical. I didn't know how this would happen or what had to be done to make it happen but standing in that cramped closet where his smell of sweat and vanishing cream was stronger than the smell of the maroon hymn books I was filled with certainty that happen it would.

4

Every five years or so my father was required to move to a new church and usually to a new circuit. Shortly after Mr. Montague, we moved from the north of England to the south, from baths pronounced "baths" to "barthes," a more gentle climate.

These years were marked by other transitions, from elementary to secondary school, to an intensification of the warfare with my mother, to the first counter-moves of my self-shaping.

Because my father was a Minister of Religion (the words I had to write on forms at school, or worse, say in front of the class) I was forced to demonstrate that I was not easy prey. I was perhaps the only boy in the schoolyard who never pulled a punch; I once tried to finish off a fallen opponent with a rock but some older boys grabbed me in time. Nor was this wickedness merely assumed; I seemed drawn towards all that was bad and sinful. The word "drunkard" had the same sort of allure for me that the word "buccaneer" might have for a normal child.

As complaints trickled in, fist-fights, raids on fruit trees, smoking, goldfish speared from an ornamental pond, my mother wept and prayed and assured me that I had been born for the gallows. At the end of each tearful session, she made me kneel with her and pray aloud for salvation.

In sexual terms, these years from nine to eleven were marked by an increase in masturbation and guilt. Sin had claimed me utterly. My most intense desire at that time was to be able to ejaculate. I have vague memories of group masturbation though this had no particular homosexual overtones. Certain older boys would demonstrate for those younger but much in the spirit of an old-timer passing on wisdom to a greenhorn.

My two most vivid memories of those years are both rather odd. One is of a boy called Malcolm, two or three years older than us, in the second form of the grammar school, who for a fee—candy, a penny, a general whipround—would demonstrate how when he came, sperm appeared not only from the tip of his organ *but from a hole in the side half-way up.*

When released from chores, homework, and other such nonsense, all the boys in my area took their bicycles and foregathered in a small wood about a mile from my house. There, by the ruins of an old house, we smoked cigarettes, practised throwing our sheath knives into trees, wrestled, gossiped, set fires, and swapped stolen merchandise. Malcolm smoked cheroots.

Regularly, about every three days, the local pervert appeared, much to our joy. What benefit he derived from these performances was beyond our comprehension but we were grateful to him.

The place where we played was in a clearing about half-way down a steep path. The top end of the path was close to the main road; the bottom end, screened by bushes, led out onto a quiet residential street. The path itself was a winding, beaten track, bumpy, crossed by tree roots, rutted. It was dangerous at speed and one of our more frightening games was to time bicycle runs down it.

The pervert's ritual was unchanging. He would trudge down the path wheeling his bicycle until he was about a hundred yards above us. Then he would prop his bicycle up on its little stand, turn his back, then turn again, mount, and pedal furiously down the steep hill. Just before he was level with us, he would swerve from the track onto the grass at high speed, coming to within five yards of us. By this time he was steering with one hand on the handlebars. In his other hand he gripped his member which he attempted to wave.

Then he would veer back onto the path and wobble down the hill to crash down through the bushes at the bottom and debouch onto Gladstone Avenue.

His progress was unsteady and hazardous, rather like the charge of an inept knight whose visor has suddenly obscured vision.

When he neared us, we'd shout,

"Let's have a look at it, then!" and "My sister's is bigger than that!"

And as he careered away from us almost out of control down the bumpy hill, he'd yell, "You bastards!" and then, faintly, *Rotten bastards*, and then the crash as he engaged the bushes.

5

Had there been any truth in the myths about masturbation, I and all the other boys I knew would have been blind, deaf, dumb, hairy as the Ainu, and so debilitated as to have needed hospitalization. We dismissed these bromides as fit only for Boy Scouts. It was, however, an article of faith among us that an emission was the equivalent in exertion to a ten-mile run. Some boys did a hundred miles a day.

We masturbated, not for fun, but from overwhelming need for release. At school, and by now I was in the first form of grammar school, boys masturbated at recess, lunch hour, during the welcome darkness of educational films, some even, driven by indescribable urges, during lessons. A glance revealed those so engaged, their faces red from exertion and frustration. It was difficult to sustain the necessary rhythm and increasing speed and concentration if some fool decided to pace the aisles or ask questions about the staple products of China.

Those who had achieved success were also immediately recognizable; their faces softened into that dreamy expression which I've noted in infants who are completing a bowel movement.

Masturbation was known as "wanking" or "wanking off"; one young master endeared himself to us by pretended pedantry. He affected not to know the meaning of "wank" and always addressed a boy called Stoughton, a frenzied self-abuser, in the following way:

"Stoughton. Your attention, please. Can you enlighten us as to the nature of the feudal levy? Or may I, as your chums appear to do, address you as 'Wanker'?"

This compulsive masturbation was not, as far as I can recall, related to any external object; it was not accompanied by sexual fantasies or even imaginings of sexual intercourse. It was more in the nature of a raging unscratchable itch.

Some idea of the state might be suggested by observing a colony of monkeys.

At home, and in privacy, apart from the usual masturbations before going to sleep and on awakening, we all devised more elaborate forms of gratification. Some boys coated their penises and hands with a rich soap lather which was pleasing but had one drawback; soap was likely to enter one's organ so that ejaculation was accompanied by a stinging pain much like getting soap in one's eye. Other boys used Vaseline but it was difficult to remove afterwards. Pond's Vanishing Cream and hand-lotions were other favourites.

But as time went by, these solitary acts *were* turned to focus on sexual images of the outer world. Our main source of these was a magazine which could be rented for three-pence per lunch-hour from a newsagent's near the school. The newsagent was called Mr. Albert. The magazine was called *Health and Efficiency* and featured photographs of ungainly nude people having picnics and playing ping-pong.

It was, perhaps, these images which drove us to the desire to stick our members *into* things. Vacuum cleaners were widely discussed and I went so far as to switch ours on one day when my mother was out shopping but the roar and pluck of it against the cloth of my trousers frightened me. One boy I knew described to me putting his organ into a thermos flask full of warm tea. He had done this while his member was only semi-erect but the warmth rising from the tea and the constriction, and what he described as a kind of suction, aroused him in a second and he was agonizingly trapped in the flask's narrow neck. His peril was doubled because his parents were upstairs, his sister playing just outside, and he was in the kitchen. Another boy in my class swore by oranges. Another inserted himself between the furry legs held tight of a younger brother's teddy bear. One boy who played in the wood every night claimed to have fucked a hen but everyone knew he was a liar.

My own invention was the cardboard core of a toilet roll liberally coated inside with Brylcreem. The only drawback was that the Brylcreem was cold and took some time to warm up. Ejaculations were so fearsome and overwhelming that I sometimes tottered about the bathroom close to fainting.

These acts of ferocious self-abuse were of course attended by agonies of guilt. Every night I knelt by my bed until I was cold and my knees hurt asking Jesus' forgiveness for my lies, impurity, smoking, foul language, and constant abuse of the Temple of the Holy Spirit. And every night after my prayers, warmed, reviewing the day, my mind would fill with the image of the hairy thatch of a lady ping-pong player and my hand would sidle down to grasp my heated member and guilt would temporarily be driven out in a fresh burst of sweaty friction.

It was something of a problem to know what to do with what eventually must have amounted to pints of sperm. I tried handkerchiefs but what would happen if I forgot to remove it from under my pillow one morning and my mother discovered this yellow, rigid rag? And besides it would have been difficult to explain the loss of a handkerchief every two or three days. Eventually I took to lifting the carpet round the edges and dribbling onto the felt underlay. My bedroom began to smell like the corridor of an extremely sleazy hotel. After some months the carpet and underlay were so tightly bonded that I began to worry about what possible explanation I could give when spring cleaning occurred.

6

Sexologists state that males reach a peak of sexual energy at about eighteen while females reach a peak of sexual desire in their thirties. Inaccurate, as usual. Boys achieve a peak of sexual energy at about thirteen or fourteen and by eighteen are, comparatively, quiescent, if not in decline. A boy of thirteen lives possessed and I use the word in its biblical sense. Such words as "desire" or "lust" are pallid counters for the raw actuality. *Frenzy* or *fever*, with their medical connotations, are more appropriate.

Everything in the physical world promoted excesses of deranged desire. Erections occurred without volition, induced by the vibrations of buses, store dummies being dressed in passing windows, the hair or an earring of the lady passenger in the seat in front. Washing hung out on a line sometimes proved unbearable. Even the texture of velvet, fresh-planed wood, or the curve of a highly glazed vase was enough to induce a voluptuous state necessitating a hasty trip to a locked bathroom.

We fought our way onto double-decker buses in order to be behind some particularly attractive woman in the hope that she might go upstairs and we could hang back on the platform perhaps to glimpse an ascending stocking seam, a froth of lacy slip or petticoat. We believed that women who wore highly shined shoes mirrored onto that polished surface visions of what was above and stared intently in the always disappointed hope.

The words, "Thank you. Come again," from shop assistants caused us to reel about the pavement in paroxysms of hysterical laughter.

We stood as close as possible over seated women in the hope of being able to peer down blouses; when free of homework we haunted parks and waste land at twilight in the hope of observing lovers engaged in sexual acts; in shops we asked to see items on high shelves; we peered at night through every lighted window. Housewives were stalked in the constricted aisles of G.R. Lumley and Son: Grocers, until the erection had to be concealed by stooping as if in consideration over the Huntley and Palmers Assorted Creams knowing that our naked lusts were marked on our brows for all to see. Being dragged through department stores by mothers where lingerie was flaunted and panties strewn about in casual heaps *while pretending to ignore it all* was anguish. Other boys' sisters and mothers were assessed; even grandmothers were eyed.

Ours was, of course, an all-male school. The girls' grammar school was about a mile away. We were forbidden to speak to them.

The sight of these maidens in their plum-pudding hats and blazers, serge skirts, ankle socks and brown oxfords drove us to the mindless frenzy of piranhas scenting blood. Our weekly trip to the nearby municipal baths was hallowed by the knowledge that the day before those very girls had used the same cubicles, hung their clothing on the same hooks, immersed their bodies in the same water. We could have drunk it, chlorine and all, in homage and desire.

The power of words need hardly be mentioned. The father of a boy who lived near me had a Navarre Society edition of the *Decameron* with sepia-tinted illustrations. Although I didn't like the boy, I cultivated him so that I could gaze at these pictures of wenches, breasts boiling over their bodices, seated on the knees of jolly friars. We gazed together transfixed with lust. The word itself, "bodice," was only just bearable; such a word as "nipple" was beyond endurance; the black letters on the white page blurred into an aura, an aureole of shimmering desire so intense that further reading was impossible and we would stare into space bereft of our wits.

Much of my early reading was merely the search for erotic incident. Two fragments lodge in my mind yet. One, "he toyed with her bubbies" was presumably from some eighteenth-century novel. The other, "she made him free of her narrow loins," was the first of many intense pleasures given me by Evelyn Waugh.

Nightly I crouched beneath the window-sill of my bedroom with my telescope trained on the bedroom window of a girl two houses away; once I saw her pick her nose.

I longed for a sister so that I could commit incest.

My masturbatory practices grew more fanciful and more desperate; I did it with a cylindrical pencil-case filled with warm porridge and violated my younger brother's kaleidoscope.

————————

On Sundays I walked with my mother to church. In the winter, she wore fur gloves; in the summer, white gloves of some sort of netting stuff. I was embarrassed to be seen with her and these white gloves, worn even in extremes of heat, served as a focus for all my hatred of her and our way of life. Those net gloves were everything from which I wanted to escape.

On Sundays she invariably smelled of lavender, a scent which even now makes me feel irritable, reminds me of piety and death.

At the close of each service, Holy Communion was celebrated. Although I always attended the sacrament I have never, in fact, partaken of it. During this most solemn rite I prayed with desperation to be forgiven my manifold sins and wickednesses. I evoked Christ's Passion, He who had died for *me*, but the harder I prayed the more my mind crowded with narrow loins, nipples, thighs, and buttocks. And although I was slowly coming to an active rejection of Christianity I felt nervous about receiving the sacrament because being in a state of sin something bad *might* happen and there was no point in going around *asking* for trouble. I had read in some anti-Semitic work of a woman in the Middle Ages who had contracted with some wicked Jews to steal a wafer by retaining it in her mouth until after mass and then handing it over to them; the Lord, however, caused the Host to turn to flesh and grow immediately to the roof of her mouth in a vast lump. My theory was that if you *hadn't* swallowed it you hadn't really *done* it so it was my practice to swallow the wine (that didn't count; it was nonalcoholic grape juice) but push the cube of bread into my cheek and flatten it. This slimy mess I then coughed later into my handkerchief or spat out unnoticed.

On the walk home, my mother, softened perhaps by Communion, would often take my unwilling hand with her netted glove and say,

"You're still my little boy, aren't you?"

7

At the end of my first year in grammar school came my first Annual Report and the subsequent Parent-Teacher Interview Evening. My report was mediocre but my main fear was what might be said.

It seems, looking back, that I lived in a world of constant guilt, anxiety, and self-loathing; they were my mother's handmaidens. When I was a small boy, she had even managed to make me assume guilt for the sufferings of the Eighth Army. I had been playing with an outdoor tap in the garden, enjoying the splash and sparkle of it, and she'd grabbed me from behind, shaking me and shouting,

"You *wicked* boy! You're wasting water while soldiers are *dying* in the desert."

Even at the victory celebrations when they lit a huge bonfire right in the middle of our street and the road melted and someone shot the grocer's shop a secret worm of guilt gnawed at my pleasure.

My anxiety extended from myself to a distrust even of the inevitable processes of nature.

I had been convinced that in my case sperm would never flow.

I had despaired of growing pubic hair.

I had thought it likely that when my voice broke it would later break back again.

I was consciously kind to a ginger-coloured boy called Probert who had an undescended testicle because I felt that there but for the Grace of God.

But, always, it was my mother who instilled in me the deepest sense of failure and despair. I can still hear her voice in its litany of sorrows:

"You're breaking my heart."

"You were born for the gallows."

"How can we love a boy who . . ."

"I'll try to find it in my heart to forgive . . ."

"You're breaking Jesus' heart . . ."

"I never thought a boy of mine . . ."

"You've let down everyone who loves you . . ."

When my mother returned in the evening from the Parent-Teacher Interviews, I was in bed reading. I heard her footsteps coming upstairs. She was wearing her Sunday clothes, a turquoise costume with a horrible turquoise hat which was bandaged with sort of turquoise net stuff and stuck through with a hat-pin with a big turquoise lump on it. She said nothing. She closed the door.

Her face was set; she had that deadly calmness about her which is more frightening and dangerous than rage. She opened her handbag, groped in it without taking her eyes from mine, and then dropped on the coverlet a copy of *Health and Efficiency*.

It lay on my stomach like a lead block. It had been confiscated from me during music the week before.

She pulled up the chair and sat beside the bed.

In a quiet, almost conversational voice, she started. She could scarcely credit that a boy of hers had deliberately set fire to another boy in the metal-work shop. Why had I not told her I had broken the bench drill? I had broken the drill by disobeying orders. Rules were made to be obeyed. Had I considered what would have happened had the broken drill-bit killed, maimed, or blinded another child? My father, impoverished as we were, would buy a new drill and a new apron for the boy whose apron was burned. Even if I did hate algebra so much, was it really manly to hide in the lavatories? Was that facing up to my responsibilities? Mr. Dodds had seemed evasive; was there anything I wished to tell her about geography? Anything I had not confessed? I would feel better if my conscience were clear. Her heart was sore that I had been detected smoking behind the bicycle sheds. Mastery of Latin could not be expected if I frittered away my time passing surreptitious notes. What was in the notes? Some lewdness, she had no doubt. And what wickedness could have possessed me to trace *that word* in the dust on Mr. Taylor's car?

I didn't deny doing that?

Did I know the meaning of that word?

Did I?

The true and unspeakable meaning of that word?

If I did not throw myself on God's mercy and mend my ways, if I did not apply myself to my studies, if I did not shun evil companions, and if my heart was not contrite, she had no doubt that I would end up as a common labourer with no future but the gallows.

All this, however, was of little importance.

The sacrifices that she and my father were making to give me a good education were nothing, merely duty done. She could bear the shame I had brought upon her and my father and my brother. She was, by now, used to such shame. She loved me deeply; my father loved me; my brother loved me; my uncles and aunts loved me. But it was obvious that there was no love in *my* heart. Actions speak louder than words. Was it not obvious from my actions that I did not return the love so freely given? If I loved others, then I would not wound them.

This *was* obvious, wasn't it?

My heart was a heart of stone.

That pain, that mother's sorrow, too, she could bear.

But it cut her to the quick—

She pointed to *Health and Efficiency* and tears started to roll down her cheeks. She was unable to express, heartbreak, inner wounds, shame, the defilement, the revulsion in her that *this*, this filth, this degradation, wallowing vile filthy nastiness, this lewd and sinful filth —did I *wish* to kill her? She would die of a broken heart. She could never raise her head again. She was heartsick that she'd lived to see this day.

For those who gave themselves to *this* there was no salvation. Christ Himself would shun them and condemn them to suffering eternal.

Her face was blotchy with tears. She gripped one of my hands in hers. Her grip was so fierce that the stone in her ring was cutting into my flesh. She brought her face closer to mine.

"If I had known," she said, "on the day that you were born what I now know, if I had known that that baby was to become what you *are*, do you know what I'd have done?

"Do you?

"Do you?"

Spittle was flecking my face.

"With joy in my heart," she said, "with *joy*, I'd have had you taken from my arms and put out for adoption."

Still gripping my hand, she knelt by the bed pulling me down towards her.

"Oh God," she prayed, "forgive me my sins and wickedness. I am weak but Thou art strong. Take from me this bitter cup. Make known unto me wherein I have transgressed that Thou shouldst punish me by making bitter unto me the fruit of my womb. Wreak upon *me*, Oh Lord, Thy wrath, but spare, I beseech Thee, this boy . . ."

There was a lot of this stuff and it went on for quite a long time. She was rocking herself backwards and forwards in its rhythms and pulling me with her. By the end of it, she'd reduced me to a shuddering, tear-racked hysteria. She eventually left me to my tears and the glow of the reading lamp.

In the doorway, she turned and half-whispered,

"Do you know what I'm going to do now?"

I shook my head.

"Do you?"

Her eyes moved from mine, glancing at the magazine.

"I'm going to wash my hands."

I cried until I could cry no more. I felt empty, exhausted, sick. I turned my pillow to the dry side. I hated myself. I looked with loathing through *Health and Efficiency* which had been left on the bed in accusation.

I stared at the roses on the wallpaper grouping them into different patterns.

Mournfully, I wanked myself to sleep.

8

When I was fourteen we moved again to a new church in a different circuit—this time not far from London. By now I could hardly contain my hatred of my mother and her comfortable world of teas, scones, Agatha Christie, and missionary boxes. The Night of the Annual Report was, in memory, the turning point though in fact the whole process must have been more complex, drawn-out, and guilt-sodden. But the feeling was hardening that if for the gallows

I was born then to the gallows I would go but I'd give the crowd a tune and a jig on the way to the Tyburn Tree.

It was with this move and in this new house that I started the daily practice of dipping my mother's toothbrush in the lavatory.

Between the years of twelve and fifteen I was building for myself a new identity. I did no more than pass at school; I was absorbed in more important tasks. My reading had always been wide and precocious but now I read so much and secretly late into the night that in school I was pale and lethargic and could hardly bring myself to go through the motions with Bunsen burners and balances and x and y and contour maps from which one was supposed to draw bumpy hills. My reading in non-fiction was mainly of rationalist history, theology, and studies of religious deviation. I devoured the works of H.G. Wells, Professor Joad, and the popular essays of Bertrand Russell. I became something of an authority on witchcraft, heresies major and minor, and the rites of the Copts. I was particularly pleased to discover that in Ethiopia, Judas Iscariot was worshipped as a saint.

I started to carry the fight to my mother by introducing the unspeakable under the guise of religious knowledge. At the tea-table, I would offer such topics as the derivation of the word "bugger" from "Bulgarian" explaining to her the Manichean background until my father cleared his throat for silence or my mother said, "Though I speak with the tongues of men and of angels, and have not charity, I am become as sounding brass, or a tinkling cymbal."

I read *The Voyage of the Beagle* because I understood that Darwin had totally undermined Christianity but the book was not helpful; *The Golden Bough*, equally heralded, was equally disappointing but it was enlivened by accounts of some sexual customs which I would never have imagined.

Father and Son by Edmund Gosse was a particular joy.

I also managed to irritate and hurt my mother by insisting on going to churches of other denominations; I presented this as a religious and ecumenical enthusiasm. I goaded her with a show of great interest in the Roman Catholic church and invented a priest called Father O'Neil with whom I claimed to be having fascinating conversations; I managed to intimate that Father O'Neil was bent on conversion.

One of my greater triumphs in the first months of that new church was with yaws. A missionary campaign was being carried on to collect money to relieve our African brothers. A missionary had shown a colour film at church of these disgusting raspberry-like sores and skin lesions. I looked yaws up in the library, as I looked up everything, and could scarcely contain my pleasure.

At the tea-table, I enquired as to the success of the campaign; my mother was out every night with a collecting box. The campaign, it seemed, was going well.

"I was reading about yaws today in the library," I said.

"Poor things," said my mother.

"In a book by Dr. Schweitzer."

(Actually a brief paragraph in a medical encyclopedia but the saintly Schweitzer was better for my purposes.)

"Some more tea?" said my mother.

"It seems," I said, "that yaws is a form of venereal disease."

A cup clinked on a saucer in the silence.

"What's venereal disease?" said my brother.

"Pass this to your father," my mother said to him.

"If unchecked," I said, "it has much the same effects as syphilis and . . ."

"Cake?" said my mother. "It's got raisins in it."

". . . and like syphilis is caused . . ."

"Would anyone like another cup of tea?"

". . . caused by a spirochete. A spirochete of the same family."

"I don't think," said my mother, "that the tea-table . . ."

"Dr. Schweitzer," I said, "didn't actually say if yaws was contracted in the same way as syphilis but if the spirochete . . ."

My father cleared his throat and I busied myself with a slice of cake.

She was badly shaken.

But it was fiction that sustained me and offered models of sub-version. And what a strange hodge-podge of books it was. I cannot remember even a fraction of them but I do recall the effects on me of *Tono-Bungay*, *Sons and Lovers*, *The Moon and Sixpence*, *Wuthering Heights*, *The Constant Nymph*, and the opening sections of *David Copperfield* and *Oliver Twist*.

My favourite poet was Keats, my favourite poem "The Eve of St. Agnes." I was bewildered that a poem so patently lubricious was endorsed for school consumption. Swinburne earned my allegiance with the lines:

> *Thou hast conquered, O pale Galilean; the world*
> *has grown grey from thy breath,*

sentiments which accorded exactly with my own.

I read the plays of Christopher Marlowe because I'd heard he was an atheist and was murdered in a pub; I identified strongly with Tamburlaine.

I haunted the local library in my quest for knowledge. Not only was it a very good library but I lusted after one of the younger librarians who had a nice smile and breasts which gave the impression of great solidity. I spent hours wondering how much they weighed, what one would feel like hot and unconfined.

It was in the library that I found one day a book called *The March of the Moderns* by the art historian William Gaunt. I have never seen or read the book since. It struck me with the radiance and power of revelation. The mundane world fell away; I was oblivious to the smell of floorpolish and damp raincoats, the click of the date-stamp, the passage of other browsers along the shelves. I read standing up until closing-time and then took the book home and finished it in bed.

It was like the Second Coming of Mr. Montague.

The book revealed to me a world where brilliant but persecuted people drank champagne for breakfast and were pissed by lunch, took lobsters for walks on leashes, shaved off half their moustaches, sliced off their ears and gave them to prostitutes, possessed women by the score, consorted with syphilitic dwarves, *lived* in brothels, and were allowed to go mad.

Somewhere in the sun, D.H. Lawrence was at it.

Hemingway was giving them both barrels.

Ezra was suffering for the faith in an American bin.

Painters everywhere were possessing their exotic Javanese models.

I, meanwhile, was in Croydon.

But Art was obviously the answer; it was just a question of finding my medium. The problem with the novel was that writing took a long time and nothing interesting had happened to me. I tried poetry for a time being particularly drawn to the Imagists because they were very short and seemed easiest to imitate. H.D. was one of my favourites. Painting, because of the models, attracted me the most but I couldn't draw anything that looked like anything; abstraction was the answer, of course, but secretly I thought abstraction not quite honest. I had a go at a few lino-cuts but gouged my hand rather badly. Drama was soured for me by memories of endless pageants and nativity plays where kids tripped over the frayed carpet and I had to say:

"I bring you tidings of Great Joy."

But I was not depressed.

I settled down to wait. I lived in the manse, ate scones, and went to school, but I was charged with a strange certainty that I was somehow different, chosen, special; my Muse, in her own good time, would descend and translate me from Croydon to that richer world where women and applause were waiting.

The calm of this new-found certainty soon began to fray; though I had no doubts about my calling it was bringing me no immediate relief; it was bringing me no closer to an actual girl. Being new to the area I had no friends. And I had no idea of how I could approach girls. I envied the boys at school who could indulge in easy badinage at the bus stop or tobacconist. For all its crudity, it seemed to work. I would have liked to say to the girls, as they did,

'Carry your bag, Miss?' or 'When are you going to wash your hair, then?' but it was not simple shyness or fear of rebuff which prevented me. I felt myself to be so other that had I offered such pleasantries, I knew they'd just stare or be frightened or call a policeman.

Girls obsessed me but apart from being shy I was also frightened of them. Not frightened of humiliation, though that would have been bad enough, but frightened of other things less realized, fears I was scarcely able to formulate—that contagion with which my mother had infected me. Although intellectually I rejected all her attitudes and ideas, I still somewhere felt the flesh to be sinful, obscene, disgusting. I'd once asked a boy who'd done it what it was like and he'd said, "hot and slimy"; this had only confirmed what I knew instinctively to be the truth. And jokes boys told about the smell of kippers. I feared, also, the disease they might carry; the word "lues" was more than a word I'd found in a dictionary; it was a physical horror. And then there was all this menstrual business. For all my lust and desire, some puritan cancer sat in my heart.

(A few years ago, I read a biography of Ruskin which recounted the debacle of his wedding night. Ruskin, intense, pure, and idealistic, was acquainted with the female form only through sculpture and paintings; his first sight of pubic hair brought him to the verge of nervous collapse; the marriage was annulled. His situation then and mine at fourteen and fifteen had much in common.)

Another thing troubled me for all my strange reading and precocity, something impossible to talk about with another boy however close, a type of ignorance impossible to admit to. I had studied diagrams of female apparatus many times, followed the arrows which pointed to the various parts, read the labels, but still did not really understand the lay-out. Much as in botany, it was simple to learn the diagrams of a cross-section of a stem, flower, or trunk, and label the neat pencil lines *stamen, carpels, vascular bundles* etc., but a completely different matter working from an actual specimen. My specimens always turned out quite differently from the way the book said they ought to be. How much worse, then, with girls where I couldn't even follow the diagram to start with. And the possible vagaries of an actual specimen didn't bear thinking about.

For some unremembered reason I had become convinced that within a small area were three orifices each capable of receiving a penis. *But only one was the right one.* I imagined dreadful scenes ranging from a contemptuous "That's my urethra, dear," to shrieks of protest and pain. Nor did I much like the sound of labia majors and labia minors which, medical works informed me, "covered and guarded" the entrance to the vagina. One presumably had to get past them first before even standing a chance of finding the right place.

It all made me very anxious.

I still pinned my hopes on Art; I bought a book called *Teach Yourself How to Draw in Pencil and Charcoal* and the largest size sketching pad that Reeves manufactured. I laboriously traced with tracing paper from the *Teach Yourself* book two nudes and some drawings of leaves and twigs. I transferred the tracings into the sketching pad and then hung about the local park and stared intently at things, pencil poised or measuring whenever girls went past. The impression I gave, alone and palely loitering by bench and drinking-fountain, was, I hoped, Byronic. What was supposed to happen was this: a girl, attracted by my artistic absorption and obvious sensitivity, would approach me and say,

"Are you an artist?"

A nod.

"Yes."

"Can I look at your picture?"

"If you like. They're only sketches."

She would be overcome. She admits she's always wanted to be drawn by a real artist. I offer to sketch her. She says she lives near and her dad's at work and her mum's out shopping. We are in her bedroom. She is rather shy at first.

This scenario never did take place; even the ducks which surged to everyone else in the hope of bread learned to ignore me.

9

And then I met Tony.

The circumstances of our meeting were comic; we were introduced by our mothers. Tony's mother attended my father's church. Tony had not been in Croydon when we first arrived because he had been away at boarding school but his parents had now brought him home because he'd been so terribly unhappy there. Tony, my mother assured me, was "such a nice boy." He would be a nice friend for me and a good influence. Any boy my mother considered "nice" was obviously a twit and an undesirable of the first water, and I have no doubt he felt the same way about me. When I first saw him, I saw an extremely handsome boy, dark, with black curly hair. He was wearing a suit; his manners were impeccable. When left alone, we sniffed around each other like rigid-legged dogs. I made the first move by offering him a Player's; he declined with thanks, taking out his own Craven A *and fitting one into an amber cigarette-holder*.

We were soon inseparable. In a rush of communion, we exchanged our most valued pieces of information. He told me about sexual acts between women and animals in the Roman gladiatorial shows. He explained that as human scent would not arouse an animal, the trainers had cloths which had been wiped over the parts of a female animal in heat and then sealed in airtight boxes. Just before the act was to take place, the cloth was rubbed on the woman so that the animal would think the woman of its own species. He spoke of donkeys and panthers. I told him the real name of "sucking off" was fellatio and gave him my copy of *The Picture of Dorian Gray*. I got *The March of the Moderns* from the library for him; he lent me a book called *Venus in Furs* which was really very boring but I liked it. I told him I'd never done it; he said he had done it in a rowing-boat with his cousin who was nineteen but then confessed he was lying.

We bought snuff together and tried it; it was horrible.

He told me he hadn't been withdrawn from the boarding school but expelled for writing an anonymous letter to the matron.

I confided in him my fears about the three holes and which was the right one and he said he was pretty sure there were only two. He said he had *seen* his cousin's in the rowing-boat but he couldn't tell about the labia majors and minors because it was just hairy but from the sound of it he thought they were probably part of being a virgin and were inside.

He said you couldn't catch it off a toilet seat.

He said he didn't believe anything anybody told him.

He said he'd even thought of doing it with his mother.

Tony's father and mother were interesting. His mother was tall and elegant, her face bony and beautiful. In some ways she was worse than my mother because she was extremely evangelical and used to request casual callers, the grocer's boy or the plumber, to kneel with her in prayer. She was earnest with strangers in buses and trains; she sang hymns a lot. It was Tony's opinion that she only had a few more years before they put her away for life. Tony's father was equally interesting. He was a rigid, trim, crisp man who had been a major in the war. He did not go to church at all and drank and made Tony call him "Sir" and called me "old chap." He also actually used words like "tiffin" and "chotapeg"; I think I recognized him even then as a character from a novel. Whenever I thought of him the words "patent leather" came to mind. He called my father "padre" which I think secretly pleased my father considerably.

Tony's father had a .38 revolver and a box of bullets hidden in a dresser drawer under his shirts. One afternoon we shot Tony's toolshed in the garden twelve times. Tony had suggested that we shoot it just once but we then decided with the strange logic of children that his father would be less likely to miss twelve bullets than one. We stained the fresh wood of the bullet holes with mud. We studied the illustrated instruction pamphlet in a box of his mother's Tampax; we stole two contraceptives from a big box full of them in his father's drawer and tried them on.

Tony was clever in all sorts of ways that I was not. He had rigged up an electrical device of wires under the stair-carpeting which caused a red light to flash in his bedroom if anyone was approaching;

invaluable, he explained, if one were smoking, wanking, or reading good stuff.

Tony stole more money than I did because his parents were richer but we shared equally.

We bought brushes and tubes of oil paint and painted abstract pictures in his bedroom. In our painty jeans and reeking of turpentine we sat about on Saturdays in coffee bars eyeing girls and hoping they'd think we were from the art school.

A girl we both knew at the church youth club had a penfriend in Yugoslavia who came that summer for a holiday. She was quite beautiful and her English was beautifully broken. We were both very attracted. One day we met her and she was wearing a kind of singlet thing that revealed her armpits. In these armpits were long tufts of brown hair. This aroused us immensely as it was the first time we'd seen such a thing. I was aroused and repelled. Tony said he'd like to put his mouth to her armpit, enclose all the hair, and suck it slowly, sweat and all. It was this wonderful quality of imagination in him I most admired.

Tony also introduced me to a new art form; he had a large collection of jazz records. He played for me Louis Armstrong, Bix, Muggsy Spanier, Kid Ory, Bunk Johnson, Johnny Dodds, Sidney Bechet, and Mezz Mezzrow. The music spoke to me immediately because its joy or sadness was easy to feel. I became a fervent convert. But the music had for us another great virtue; our parents detested it and churches and newspaper editorials thundered against it invoking the Fall of Rome. And better still it was played by Negroes who were perfectly all right as long as they were in Africa suffering from leprosy and yaws but otherwise not all right. And better than *that*, these were *wicked* Negroes who drank and whored, cut each other with razors, and died young.

We read *Shining Trumpets* by Rudi Blesh and *Mr. Jelly Roll* by Alan Lomax and countless other works of jazz hagiography. Our imaginations lived in New Orleans, Memphis, and Chicago; they were our Jerusalem and we swore pilgrimage.

Tony favoured trumpet men, King Oliver, Punch Miller, George Mitchell, Celestine, Bix, Bunk, Ladnier, and the always wonderful

Satchmo. The call sounded out over the privet hedges and rockeries into the decorous suburban streets until the telephones complained. I soon came to favour the pianists and bluesmen—Cripple Clarence Lofton, Jelly Roll, Speckled Red, Yancy, Meade Lux Lewis, and those massive women, Bessie Smith, Ma Rainey, and Bertha Chippie Hill.

To know anything of jazz in those days was like being part of an underground, a freemasonry which led to immediate trust and friendship; more accurately, it was like being an early Christian. We listened to the radio at dead of night to pick up faint stations from France and Hamburg which played jazz records; we learned by heart the scanty details of the musicians' desperate lives; we studied the matrix numbers of defunct race labels.

We were ravished by the American language. Ten-shilling notes became "bills" and then "ten-spots"; we longed to taste black-eyed peas, chitlins, collard greens, and grits; we would have given years of our lives to smoke a reefer, meet a viper.

Neither of us could play an instrument or read a note but Tony, always a purist, bought a cornet and carried it on our Saturday expeditions to coffee bars.

(Years later, when I first came to Canada, I fulfilled the vow that Tony and I had taken. I drove to New Orleans through the increasing depression of the southern States, illusions, delusions lost each day with every human contact, until I reached the fabled Quarter, and sat close to tears listening to the Preservation Hall Jazz Band— a group of octogenarians which as I entered was trying to play "Oh, Didn't He Ramble"; the solos ran out of breath, the drummer was palsied, the bass player rheumy and vacant. The audience of young Germans and Frenchmen was hushed and respectful. Between tunes, a man with a wooden leg tap-danced. I knew that if they tackled "High Society" and the clarinetist attempted Alphonse Picou's solo, he'd drop dead in cardiac arrest; the butcher had cut them down and something shining in me with them.)

Whenever I hear Freddie Keppard playing "Salty Dog," it brings to mind the party that Tony and I gave when we were fifteen. His parents had to go to a funeral in Scotland and had to be away for three days.

Tony assured them that he wouldn't be frightened alone in the house and would be good and not make things dirty and be sure to turn off the gas taps before going to bed. He suggested that I come to stay for the weekend. It seemed to reassure his parents knowing that he would be with a nice boy and that my parents would not be too far away.

We called the party, of course, a Rent Party. Such a party as we envisaged needed drink. Lots of it. We'd tasted sherry, and Scotch once, and been pale drunk on beer, but neither of us knew much about the subject except that drunkenness was an ultimate good and inseparable from the artistic life.

The problem was that we were too young to buy the stuff; all we'd ever managed was a bottle of Bulmer's cider and six beers from an off-licence run by a benevolent old man but his benevolence wouldn't stretch to what *we* had in mind. Tony had seven pounds and ten shillings; I didn't enquire where it had come from.

One of our older acquaintances from the El Toro Coffee Bar, one of the jazz fraternity, came to the rescue. He bought for us a large bottle of gin, six quarts of India Pale Ale, two bottles of Australian Ruby Port, six bottles of Newcastle Brown Ale, and a bottle of something from Cyprus.

Tony's father had recently bought a resplendent new radiogram —a large piece of furniture veneered in walnut which housed on one side a radio, speaker, and storage space for records, and on the other side a record player with a sprung turntable. Tony was strictly forbidden to even touch it.

We selected our records with care.

And there were girls. Tony, far more dashing than I with his amber cigarette-holder, good looks, and three-speed bike, had persuaded three girls he'd met at the municipal baths and the girl who worked after school and on Saturdays in the record shop. Other boys were bringing girlfriends.

As people arrived, more bottles were added to our stock.

My memory of the evening is not perfect.

Somehow, who knows how, miraculously, I ended up with the girl who worked in the record shop. She had blond hair in a pony-tail and she was wearing a black felt skirt with a big red heart on it and a black sweater. She was beautiful. I have forgotten her name. She was wearing black shoes like slippers, like ballet shoes.

We were dancing. The radiogram was playing "Skip the Gutter." The label on the sherry bottle said: Commercial Sherry; it was sweet and I liked it but I stopped drinking it when another boy said it was a ladies' drink. The ruby port was all right but the gin made me shudder; the India Pale Ale was nicer than the Newcastle Brown.

In the upstairs lavatory, Tony and I were pissing together, a wavering aim into the bowl.

Tony said, "I tell you, man, she's hotter than a Saturday Night Special."

In the back garden, a boy we didn't know got stuck and wounded in the monkey-puzzle tree.

A girl passed out: a voice kept saying *Loosen her clothes*. It might have been mine.

Somebody took the jazz record off and put on some waltzes. The light was out. I felt strong but unsteady; she whispered in my ear,

My mother told me
She would scold me
If a boy I kissed

She licked the inside of my ear.

Behind the settee, she whispered,

"I like it."

My arm was around her; she made some contortionist move and I was holding a hot, naked breast.

I summed the situation up in my mind with perfect clarity.

I said: *I am sitting holding the naked breast of a beautiful girl. She is hotter than a Saturday Night Special.*

I knew that all was not well. It was worse when I turned towards her, better if I kept both feet on the floor and my head straight.

"Salty Dog" was playing; I played the trumpet line in my head.

I let go of the breast.

I stumbled over another couple in the dark room. The only light was the green glow from the dials inside the radiogram. I knew the radiogram was near the door. I lurched towards that light and filled the glowing depth with noisy vomit.

10

By the end of my fifteenth year my conviction that I would never lose my virginity was becoming morbid. Tony by then had done it, or claimed to have done it, with a girl who worked at the confectionery counter in Marks and Spencers. By way of cheering me up, he said she was ugly; I said that you didn't look at the mantelpiece while stoking the fire.

I had attempted a couple of girls at the Methodist Youth Club and the girl who worked at MacFisheries. I had taken her to the cinema but every time I tried to touch her breast she had said "Cheeky!" until I'd become discouraged.

I brooded.

The idea of a prostitute grew in my mind. I knew myself to be the kind of person to whom women would always say, "Cheeky!" Mine was a hand which would always be slapped. I had no choice. My shyness, fear, and revulsion were overwhelmed by a kind of fatalism. I felt like a soldier in the trenches waiting for the officer to blow his whistle. The bombardment has stopped. A lark is singing. The whistle will blow and there will be nowhere to go but over the top and on in a steady walk towards whatever horror awaits.

Tony and I discussed the propriety of the services of a prostitute. He felt that it was all right so long as she was a personal friend. He instanced the cases of Toulouse-Lautrec and Van Gogh. Otherwise he felt that it was not all right. I asked him if he would, then, mind terribly introducing me to one of his prostitute friends in Croydon so that intimacy might blossom before I engaged her services. For two days we did not speak.

A remarkable chance came at the end of the school year. Three classes were to be marshalled into a trip to London to see Paul Scofield in a production of *Hamlet*.

The theatre was near Soho where prostitutes jostled one on every pavement, where barkers called the attractions of unnatural acts from every doorway, where pimps physically dragged resisting passers-by into bordellos. I determined that in the confusion of entering the theatre I would slip away and hide until the coast was clear and then make my way to Soho, gratify myself, return to the station at the appointed time, and claim to have got lost on the underground.

Tony simplified this. He advised going into the theatre and then simply getting up to go to the lavatory and walking out.

Everything played into my hands. The master-in-charge was one of the younger teachers and more casual than most; school uniform was not obligatory.

Tony gave me ten shillings and sixpence and I closed my Post Office Savings Accounts which gave me another two pounds, eleven shillings, and ninepence—the results of birthdays and the visits of uncles. I did not know how much it cost to do it but I'd decided to throw myself on her mercy and if I didn't have enough, to offer all I had just to have a look at it.

I did slip away and I did go to Soho. I spent an hour or more wandering about in Italian grocery shops looking at salami and strange-smelling foods, browsing in a second-hand bookshop, looking at the menus in the windows of dingy restaurants, staring at the displays of the purveyors of rubber goods and artificial limbs. There were no prostitutes to be seen; I wondered if there were some custom governing harlotry unknown to me—like half-day closing on Thursday in shops.

I read the postcard advertisements in a newsagent's window; I'd heard about that. I phoned a likely sounding one ("The Service of Miss Roche—Stimulating, Healthy, Once Tried Never Forgotten") but it turned out to be a Registered Nurse who administered colonic irrigation.

I also phoned a Miss Ponce de Leon but a man's voice said, "Piss off, sonny."

Finally, in Gerrard Street, a man in a doorway looked at me and I looked at him.

He said,

"You look like a fun-loving gentleman."

I said I was and he sold me membership in the White Monkey Club for seventeen shillings and sixpence. The White Monkey Club was at the top of a flight of uncarpeted stairs; it was about the same size as my former bedroom and had the same sort of smell. The barman, who wore lipstick and a grubby blouse, gave me a gin and orange; it came with membership. There were three other patrons, each with a gin and orange. A long time passed; the room was silent except for the barman filing his nails. Eventually a woman as old as my mother came in and danced about on the tiny stage to a record of "Pop Goes the Weasel." At the last, "Pop," she undid her bra and her tits fell down. And when I got back to the station there was hell to pay.

11

Ironically enough, it is to Billy Graham that I owe my first brush with a girl's private parts.

But that came at the end of the affair not the beginning.

After my failure in Soho I fell in love with a girl called Helen.

I had no alternative.

Squat in me somewhere sat that cold creature, my mother's gift, and the only possible resolution of my contradictory feelings was an extreme romanticism. Love elevated coupling, the beast with two backs, into the union of souls. As many a cynic has observed, romantic love is the result of unsatisfied desire and my romanticism was Provençal in its intensity.

Helen attended the local girls' grammar school and every day after school we sat on a corner on our bicycles talking. I wrote poems to her. And although I saw her every day, I wrote her letters. One poem I wrote to her was modelled on a poem called "Helen" by H.D.

Hers ran something like:

All Greece hates
the still eyes in the white face,

the lustre as of olives
Something, something
and the white hands

or it might have been "pale hands." Such is fame that I've never been able to find the poem since.

My version, with a fine disregard of history, ran:

All Greece loves
the dark eyes
in the white face

"My eyes aren't dark," she said when I gave her the poem.
"I know," I said, "but I'm writing it as if you're Helen of Troy."
"Oh," she said.

Helen thought Tony was nice and handsome but wasn't he a bit wild? I agreed that he was. Didn't I think that smoking made people's breath smell? I agreed that it probably did. Wasn't beer rather a working-class sort of drink and weren't Tony and I too young to go in the back parlour of the Quadrant? For two years I suffered indignities such as escorting her shopping on Saturday morning; for two years I trotted attendance on her like a small dog in the wake of a large bitch who is coming into heat but not yet ready and who encourages the entourage but snaps at too bold an advance.

Our sexual relationship had a curiously ritual quality; sexual favours were doled out in measured and mutually understood amounts like a recipe.

On walks, endless walks, hands were held.

After the weekly meetings of the Methodist youth club when I'd walked her home, kissing was permitted for a few minutes.

During a party, if she were in a good mood, a breast might be fondled for a limited amount of time.

On three or four occasions I put my hand under her skirt some three inches above the knee at which point she would say,

"We mustn't get carried away."

Her lips, to which I wrote poems, were thick and rather squashy and she wore a lot of lipstick and perfume and powder so that kissing her was a sort of meal in itself.

Every Thursday after the youth club meeting, I walked her home along tree-lined streets, stopping in the shadows just before her house to kiss her for the statutory five or ten minutes. This always gave me an erection like an iron bar. Then she always said:

"Goodness! Just *look* at the time!"

And then my erection and I would limp homewards until we reached a front garden far enough away from a street light and braced there on trembling legs I would wank in an agony of relief onto laurel, lilac, or hydrangea.

The leader of the youth club, a man in his thirties called Ernest Langley, an enthusiast and ping-pong player of note, was mad keen to organize an expedition to London to hear Billy Graham who was at that time saving England. I didn't want to go but Helen did so we went.

The whole experience filled me with rage. Massed choirs in white and black sang soft hymns and a smooth man played meretricious trombone solos. Helen thought he was wonderful; I agreed that he was. I would have liked to grip him by the neck and shake him fiercely while forcing him to listen to Jack Teagarden playing "A Hundred Years from Today" or "Stars Fell on Alabama."

In spite of myself, I was quite looking forward to Billy Graham himself; I enjoyed a good speech or performance whatever the subject. But even he was dismal. His timing was fair only, his gestures wooden, his brandishing of the Bible almost comic. He was too handsome; his suit too well cut. Evangelists need something of the maniac about them to be convincing. One could have imagined Billy Graham making hamburgers on the barbecue and feeding them to a gang of ill-mannered American kids who called him "Pop." One could not imagine Calvin, Wesley, Luther, Knox, or Savonarola being called "Pop" nor could one imagine them making hamburgers. Feeding *kids* onto a barbecue, yes; hamburgers, no.

Helen sang and prayed and cried a little; from time to time she gave my hand a tiny squeeze; at the end she went down to the front to be saved. I stayed where I was and waited for her; we agreed we had shared a wonderful experience. I agreed that the choir was indeed heavenly and that the trombone man was extraordinarily gifted. I secured the back seat in the coach. Ernest Langley led the coach in a few uplifting hymns as we rolled through London but it was late and as we settled to the long drive back to Croydon the overhead lights in the coach one after another were dimmed.

Helen was amazingly ardent. She gave me open-mouthed kisses usually reserved for the most special occasions. Emboldened, I sought a breast. Two buttons were somehow undone; feast after famine. As we slowed down to roll through Penge, I put my hand under her skirt and reached the statutory point, when, unmistakably, her thighs relaxed, softened, opened.

My wrist was bent at a painful angle and my finger trapped beneath some unyielding elastic and then somehow—miraculously —I felt dampness and *pubic hair*.

My mouth and throat were dry. Over the top of her head I stared at my dim reflection in the window of the coach. "I will never forget this moment," I said to my hammering heart. "We are just out of Penge and are now on the road to Beckenham just passing the Beckenham Public Library and I am sitting in seat number forty-two of a Wondertour Coach *and I am touching pubic hair*."

And then I realized that Helen was crying. In an immediate access of guilt I retrieved my hand. She was not sobbing; tears just rolled down her cheeks.

What was the matter? What had I done?

Nothing. Stop. Don't talk to me.

But as we approached Croydon all became brokenly clear. The beautiful service and feeling so wonderful, she'd been carried away. She'd never done such a thing. I was the first. It was awful. Billy Graham, Jesus, sin, salvation.

I assured her with complete sincerity that I believed she'd never done such a thing before; I assured her that of course I would not think any the worse of her; I declared my love for her to be undying.

But when I awoke in the morning, stretched in sunlight, punched up the pillow and stared at the familiar dressing-table and the thumb-tack print of the *Yellow Chair*, I felt a giddy lightness inside me, a swelling, the bobbing of clustered balloons, a freedom I hadn't felt since I'd met her.

No hank of hair owned *me*. It was only with the slightest twinge of guilt that I realized Helen and I were finished. The spell was broken. For two years I'd been chained by a wisp of hair, two years of servitude and indignities.

I worked up an anger against myself to still the little nag of guilt.

I, who was destined for great things, I, whom the Muse had claimed, had squandered two years of my valuable life on a girl with fat lips, on a girl who probably thought Ezra Pound was a kind of cake, on a girl *who had been genuinely moved by Billy Graham's trombonist.*

By the time I got up I felt so good humoured that instead of my usual coffee I condescended to eat one of my mother's gargantuan breakfasts.

12

The photographs left us largely silent. In most were two women and a man. One of the women was almost plump with a crease of fat at the waist, the other was scrawny. The man had a very large organ. The photographs illustrated all the possible positions for sexual intercourse and the modes of oral stimulation. The pictures had a curiously formal quality as the three performers were wearing black domino masks.

Tony had borrowed the photographs from an older boy we'd met at the record shop.

We didn't say much to each other as we studied them; they were somehow not erotic. Their effect was deadening.

I kept returning to one particular picture; it disturbed me profoundly. A mattress lay on the floor. On the mattress side by side lay the two women. At the extreme edge of the picture was a toe-cap, a shoe belonging perhaps to the man holding the spotlight above the scene. One woman held in her hand a long animal's horn, the tip of which she was inserting into the other woman's vagina. The animal's horn was about two and a half feet long and spiral in form, the horn perhaps of some kind of antelope. The face of the woman into whom this was being inserted was partially obscured by the domino mask but she seemed to be smiling.

PART TWO

1

The vision of Bobby naked remained important long after those years of early childhood. I must confess that during boyhood and youth I suffered from what "sexologists" call feelings of "penile inadequacy."

I had seen Bobby's naked, shivering form, the repulsive whiteness of those parts of his body not covered with hair. Features, build, pelt, Bobby resembled one of those "artist's impressions" of prehistoric man. His scrotum was the size of half a large grapefruit and his member equine.

I've heard it said that the cretinous are always vastly endowed in compensation, as it were, for their lack of mental development. Whether this is an old wives' tale or not I do not know.

Cleland makes use of the belief in *Fanny Hill*.

Louise, desiring to substantiate or disprove the notion, seduces an idiot flower-seller.

A waistband that I unskewer'd, and a rag of shirt that I removed, and which could not have covered a quarter of it, revealed the whole of the idiot's standard of distinction, erect, in full pride and display: but such a one! it was positively of so tremendous a size, that prepared as we were to see something extraordinary, it still out of measure, surpass'd our expectation, and astonish'd even me, who had not been used to trade in trifles. In fine, it might have answered very well the making a show of; its enormous head seemed, in hue and size, not unlike a common sheep's heart; then you might have troll'd dice securely along the broad back of it; the length of it too was prodigious . . .

Many men suffer from the secret fear that they are sexually inadequate, that other men's penises are bigger than theirs. I don't know where this belief comes from but it's a common anxiety. Possibly it stems from the child's impression of his father's organ—an instrument which compared to his own must seem impossibly vast. And the matter seems so important perhaps because of the early identification of "self" with penis.

Wash yourself.

Dry yourself.

That I chanced to see Bobby naked gave me a poor start in life and I suppose, on reflection, that anxiety has been the constant in my sexual career.

I had thought that particular anxiety stilled long ago, an anxiety of my boyhood and youth, an absurdity that marriage and fatherhood enabled me to smile over. But the other day my youngest daughter, who has the unpleasant habit of trailing me about the house from room to room, crept into the bathroom as I was urinating. She stood and watched.

Then she said in a congratulatory tone,

"You can make it come out of your finger!"

I shared this latest cuteness with my wife and we laughed together over her. But later, I found myself, not brooding exactly, but *thinking* upon it.

Finger?

Finger!

I read of somewhere, or was told about, saw perhaps—or did I imagine this?—I am not being coherent. I believe there exists a monograph by Sir Richard Burton on the nature of penises. As frequently happens to me, I find I can't distinguish between real and imagined events. A story told me or a story I've invented often becomes more real than an event I know to have occurred. And increasingly, I find myself doubting even those certainties.

You remember . . . says my wife. But I don't. And I say to her, *Didn't we* . . . ? and she says, *We never have been there.*

I've always admired Sir Richard Burton, admired that hawk-like face in the portrait by Lord Leighton. Master of thirty-five languages and their dialects, poet, translator, soldier, diplomat, explorer—such a book would be typical of his mind and interests.

This book (I don't pretend to know its title) suggests that there are two basic and distinct kinds of penis—one which when detumescent is small but grows proportionately very large when erect and one which when detumescent is relatively large and grows proportionately very little when erect. The first kind of organ is, according to Burton, typical of Caucasian peoples, the second typical of African, Semitic, and Hamitic peoples.

(The most interesting part of the research of Masters and Johnson was a confirmation of Burton's thesis though their findings were not, I think, linked to race. They reported that *the longer the limp penis the less its length increases in erection.* They noted the case of a 3½ inch limp penis which in erection increased by 120 percent!)

It would be a simple matter to discover whether the book exists or not but I'm no longer curious. I am persuaded that it does. I can see it quite clearly. A folio bound in red morocco illustrated with page after page of steel engravings of penises drooping from left to right, root to tip, and then, in comparison, standing right to left. And a commentary in Burton's rather ponderous prose.

It was, of course, privately printed.

———————

I've always taken a guilty pleasure in John Cleland. The following passage appeals to me.

> Curious then, and eager to unfold so alarming a mystery, playing, as it were, with his buttons, which were bursting ripe from the active force within, those of his waistband and fore-flap flew open at a touch, when out IT started; and now, disengag'd from the shirt, I saw, with wonder and surprise, what? not the plaything of a boy, not the weapon of a man, but a maypole of so enormous a standard, that had proportions been observ'd, it must have belong'd to a young giant. Its prodigious size made me shrink again; yet I could not, without pleasure, behold, and even ventur'd to feel, such a length, such a breadth of animated ivory! perfectly well turn'd and fashion'd, the proud stiffness of which distended its skin, whose smooth polish and velvet softness might vie with that of the most delicate of our sex, and whose exquisite whiteness was not a little set off by a sprout of black curling hair round the root, through the jetty sprigs of which the fair skin shew'd as in a fine evening you may have remarked the clear light aether through the branchwork of distant trees over-topping the summit of a hill; then the broad and blueish-casted incarnate of the head, and blue serpentines of its veins, altogether compos'd the most striking assemblage of figures and colours in nature. In short, it stood an object of terror and delight.

My wife says she thinks they look silly.

Modern research and scientific method claim to have established beyond doubt that the average male organ, fully erect, is approximately 6 inches in length. (All measurements taken along the upperside of the penis from the pubic bone to tip.) It is further claimed that the average circumference is 1⅝ inches. (All measurements taken one inch below the rim.)

I, personally, don't believe a word of this.

One of the first such studies was carried out in 1947 by the prominent sexologist Dr. Robert Latou Dickinson. He claimed the average size of the adult male penis, fully erect, to be within the range of 5½ to 6½ inches. He claimed the largest erect organ measured to date (i.e. 1947) to be 13¾ inches in length and 7 inches in circumference. He noted that many erect penises fell within the 10-to-12 inch range.

The recent studies of Dr. William H. Masters and Mrs. Virginia E. Johnson tend to confirm these findings.

Averages are, however, notorious.

Let us think logically.

Masters and Johnson measured "several hundred" penises; it is not enough. Let us imagine that they measured five hundred. Is it not possible that by chance they measured a majority of small ones? Or large ones? What would have happened to their average had they measured another two hundred, all of which, by chance, fell within the 10-to-12 inch range? Or, by chance, in the 2½-to-4 inch range?

These authorities are also disquietingly silent on the following point—were these all Caucasian organs?

And when they use the words "fully erect" can we, in fact, be sure that these penises *were* fully erect? Nervousness—indeed the very atmosphere of a clinic or hospital can produce profound physical reactions. Might not the very act of having one's penis *measured* inhibit full erection?

(This is no frivolous objection to the validity of the data. Doctors often find it necessary to test blood pressure two or three times because nervousness in patients produces inaccurate readings. I am reminded, also, of the time during the first year of my marriage when I had to undergo a fertility test. The instruction card stated that I must drink no liquids the night before, refrain from sexual expression, arise at 7 AM and produce a sperm sample which was to be delivered to the hospital no later than 8 AM.

I arose at 7 AM still bleary with sleep and stood in the bathroom trying to think of something erotic. All I could think of was breakfast. Eventually, however, I succeeded and stoppered the test-tube I had been given. After a hasty cup of coffee, I rushed the sample to the Montreal General by taxi and handed it to the technician. He held the tube up to the light and said,

"Is this all?"

This suggests, I think, the point I'm trying to make.)

And then again, we might ask ourselves what, precisely, Dr. Robert Latou Dickinson means when he claims 13¾ inches "as the largest erect organ measured to date." Surely, he can mean only "seen and measured by *him*." Why should we not assume organs in the nation greater in length and vaster in circumference *not* seen by Dr. Robert Latou Dickinson? How did he locate this specimen? Was an appeal made for the exceptionally endowed to come forward? And if so, where? Learned journals, after all, have a limited circulation.

Any logical examination of this evidence must also note that the data *in every study* are American. Conclusions should, logically, state that the average length, fully erect, of the adult male *American* penis is such and so. *American* circumference this and that.

It is not necessarily quibbling to suggest that the Canadian penis is a different penis. Not to mention the immigrant penis.

And while I have no particular wish to cast aspersions I do find myself wondering about the reliability and stability of these good doctors; devoting one's life to such measurement is a strange specialization to choose.

I cannot but regard this average of 6 inches as extremely suspect.

But whatever the truth may be—and does it really matter?—feelings of penile inadequacy are widespread. Even a casual glance through the correspondence columns of any sex magazine reveals the extent of this anxiety and its pathos. The following letter is not untypical.

I am 26 years old. My penis is only 3½ inches long when erect and about 2 inches long when flaccid. I have never masturbated —the one time I tried it didn't work. I tried intercourse once and think I reached orgasm. Sometimes when I have an erection it feels like I'm going to shoot out urine. I read in a magazine where a man took hormones every day and his penis increased in length. Would hormones help me?

"No, Mr. A.H. of Pennsylvania," was the curt reply, "you are too old."

The world over, men desire larger members. Certain African tribes suspend weights from their penises at puberty; others thrash their organs with bundles of nettle-like herbs in the hope the swelling will be permanent. The *Kama Sutra* recommends massage with a liquid made by boiling pomegranate seeds in oil. The Japanese, apparently more concerned with thickness than length, insert their penises into holes bored through heated bricks. Clinics in Switzerland give courses of treatment with vacuum developers; this treatment is used in conjunction with what is described as "double-handed milking massage" with theatrical cream "until the pain becomes unbearable."

Enlarging courses using the vacuum principle are marketed in the United States under the trade name *Megaphall.*

The Chinese are reported to do things with silver rings.

———————

Style betrays me.

An easily written kind of humour, five-finger exercise.

My heart isn't in it.

"Truth," as my mother always used to say, "will out."

It doesn't matter that all those endearingly innocent American authorities state that an average-sized organ is preferable to one larger than average. *It doesn't matter* that women claim to prefer organs in the normal range. *It doesn't matter* that the average length of the vagina in a sexually aroused woman is only 4½ inches. *It doesn't matter* that I'm married happily, the father of four children. I don't care what my wife and other women say, have said.

I have seen Bobby and I know what I know. I KNOW my thing is small. I know that hidden in all the trousers around me are huge organs. In every public convenience happy extroverts stand back from the urinals

cosseting with justifiable pride members which to me seem to fall into the
10-to-12 inch range while I fumble for it in my underpants, trying to
find it, winkling it out.

I wish I had a big one.

How neatly the rhetoric of that confession is managed! How prettily
worked its repetitions, its movements in and out of italic.

Lies. Mainly lies.

So much of my life is spent alone in silence creating illusions that
even when I set out to tell the truth I cannot escape the professional
gestures, the hands turned palms-and-backs to the audience, the
cuffs pulled wide to illustrate emptiness—then the sudden string
of flags.

I am not confessing here merely to "penile inadequacy" but to
the continuing power of that disapproval of and distaste for "self"—
for me—to the continuing power of those ghostly commands.

Wash yourself.

Dry yourself.

Why must in disappointment all I endeavour end?

2

Within a very short time of leaving home to go to university I was
relieved of my unlovely virginity by a kindly girl from Lancashire.
She lanced the infection, cleansed, and healed. And with her laughter and affection flowed away the accumulation of tortured images,
dogs strangely joined, dead hedgehogs, the lewd smile beneath the
domino.

I did not love her nor she me; we liked each other. For some years
after I came to Canada we exchanged Christmas cards and brief
messages until time passed and one of us moved or forgot or forgot
to care.

From the loss of my virginity onwards my sexual career was much as any other man's and of no particular interest to anyone but myself. Sex, thigh, and breast, which had seemed to shimmer and beckon like the gilded domes and minarets of an unattainable and mirage city were now, to my surprise, a fairly ordinary part of my life. Everything in the garden was lovely until anxiety intruded once again—this time in the form of a book.

I was about to say that the book was called—but its title, I find, is gone. And its author. Even its appearance. I *think* it had a yellow cover and was by Van de-somebody. Dutch-sounding name. But what I do remember very clearly was its insistence that women derived no pleasure from intercourse unless they attained orgasm and this depended on the stimulation of the clitoris.

To a neophyte as I was then, this insistence was disturbing. I didn't know if I had ever induced an orgasm, wasn't quite sure what one was. And the nature and location of the clitoris haunted me for years.

But the book was quite plain on the subject. It said:

"The shaft of the penis must at all times be kept in contact with the clitoris."

I thought about that sentence for a long time. The book was, after all, a manual and it was written by a doctor. I tried to reconstruct the various anatomies which I'd felt under bedclothes and covers and if the clitoris was where I thought it was supposed to be and if vaginas were where *they* were supposed to be, I was left with only two possible solutions to the problem this sentence posed: either I was deformed or I'd had the misfortune to have had sexual intercourse with four deformed girls.

I researched the clitoris: it was variously defined as "a miniature penis," "an external, erectile organ," and "a hooded member analogous to the male organ of generation." According to some authorities, it had erections and a kind of foreskin. Some authorities stated that it was the size of a pea, others the size of a large pea. Some just said it was "miniature." One authority stated that clitorises the size of the first joint of the thumb and which protruded through the outer lips were not uncommon.

When I first came to Canada, I bought a book in a United Cigar Store called *Clit Hunger* published by Nightstand Books but it was not illuminating.

The spontaneity of my sex life was ruined by my anxiety as I groped about trying to find this pea- or thumb-sized organ. It proved as elusive as a bird of paradise.

I never have actually *seen* one. I grudgingly admire direct men, those who milk their nursing wives into a cup of tea, or the explorers who take a flashlight to ladies' nether parts, but I am too shy, too unwilling to risk giving offence. My wife, too, is shy and sexually rather reserved—"modest," I suppose, would be the old-fashioned word and I have come to approve of modesty.

(Though now, if I ever think about the subject at all, I *would* like to see a thumb-sized one, just once, just look.)

And then after the Clitoris Anxiety and the Shaft and Clitoris Anxiety, both before and after marriage, came new Anxieties as the fashions changed.

The Simultaneous Orgasm Anxiety.

The Clitoral versus the Vaginal Orgasm Anxiety.

The Multiple Orgasm Anxiety.

It was all mildly depressing.

Marriages were breaking up around us; women were leaving their husbands for electric toothbrushes.

Now, of course, things are different. Most nights we're both too tired or I go to bed early while Mary is out canvassing for the NDP or I stay up writing while she goes to bed with a book. Saturdays are usually our day because of *Sunshine Saturday on ABC*. The two younger kids usually get up at about 6 AM and sit gazing at the blank TV screen waiting for the cartoons to start. Mary, who always wakes up before me, makes a jug of coffee and brings it into the bedroom. I always drink three cups. I am not sure whether or not she is aware that this pressure on my bladder stiffens my resolve.

We have no time for lengthy foreplay, by-play, toe-sucking, ice packs, orgasms simultaneous or multiple—we have exactly the amount of time that *Sunshine Saturday* allows before the next commercial and the demands for more toast or Wheaties and Jane trod on Peter's tractor and Peter took Jane's hockey cards and today *is* Saturday and if it's Saturday isn't Saturday allowance day?

3

Last night the Waldmarks came to dinner. These dinners are a ritual, an observance ritually celebrated every two or three weeks—at their house or ours—and last night I cooked three wild ducks. Gerry was one of the first friends I made when I came to Canada; we were post-graduate students together and for a year shared an apartment which was noted for its flow of girls, its spaghetti, and extraordinary gin-based drinks which Gerry invented on Fridays. The friendship still endures. The evening had progressed as it always does with talk of old friends, old times, and Gerry insisting that early in the morning he'll be off skiing, taking a much-needed break from work and Alice and children and then, red-faced with exertion, Gerry always tries to stand on his head and Alice cries out reminding him of his bad back, and his body wavers until he falls down. And then shouts of goodbye in the late street.

I woke early this morning as I often do if I've had too much brandy to drink the night before. Drink used to render me unconscious but now brandy seems to make my heart knock in my ears and I'm wakeful, drowsy, then stirred by sweating dreams and wake with unpleasant clarity. Mary was curled asleep, only her black hair visible on the pillow; I don't know how she doesn't suffocate. Her hair is touched now with grey which she used to dye but now does not; I asked her not to. The digital clock that I dislike clicked again and it was 6:03. I decided to get up and clean the dishes and the kitchen from the night before. It was still dark. I felt not too bad, slightly hung-over in spite of the aspirin, possibly still slightly drunk. It would get worse as the morning wore on. I eased out of bed, put on my bath robe and closed the bedroom door behind me.

My knitted slippers still make me feel silly.

The sleep of others seems sacred. Perhaps all too often I can only express my love by washing dishes, shopping, saying it with flowers. I am no Heathcliff. In certain moods of self-loathing I feel I have become what my mother would have called "a good provider."

I went into the kitchen and closed the door to contain the noise and faced the aftermath of duck.

I stared out across the sink into what would be the back garden when the blackness paled and looked at my reflection. I still felt odd —as though a few of the less essential wires in my head were loosely connected. On mornings such as these my body forces itself on my attention in ways it never did before. I started on the roasting pan scraping out dollops of congealed fat with a wooden spoon and plopping and smearing them onto an old newspaper. And something— wires disconnected, night thoughts, dreams perhaps—something about the duck fat, its opaqueness, its bland, dull surface, made me think of Gerry. Our friendship too was set, congealed. We all knew what must be avoided. We always talked about the past, things that happened twenty years and more ago, old wounds, old friends, old grievances, the two who were already dead, as though we could only be comfortable in mythology, in events upon which time had imposed some imaginable order. We seemed to live there more brightly than in our present, with more enthusiasm than we would in our imaginable future.

I drink too much, Gerry drinks too much, we all do; but morning always comes.

I am more aware than I was of my heart and its mechanisms. I still felt uncomfortable, aware of its beating in my temples. And in my troubled sleep I had dreamed again the same dream, always the same, precise in every detail. I don't know what it means; it needn't so far as I can see, mean anything. Each part is as significant as any other.

The dream is a dream of journey.

It always starts on a railway station in England during the war. I am standing by a slot-machine which dispenses Nestlé chocolate bars but there are, of course, no chocolate bars because the war is on.

The machine is dirty, its glass panel through which one might have seen the stacked bars is shattered, the brass handle you pull to get out the chocolate is tarnished almost black.

I am journeying to visit a friend. When I arrive in the town in which he lives I go to his house. My knock is not answered. The door is unlocked. I go in and find him hanging. The rope is brand new half-inch manila, almost yellow, stiff and varnished. His face is as I have always known it, calm, composed. There is no violence.

On the mantelpiece is an engraved invitation card with a deckle edge. It is an invitation to me from my younger brother to a civic reception in his honour.

I am in a taxi drawing up to the Town Hall. There is a red carpet, a footman. I am wearing evening dress. When I go in, I find porters in livery stacking chairs, stripping and folding linen tablecloths. They wear white, buttoned gloves. The reception, they tell me, ended an hour ago.

I am by a broken Nestlé chocolate bar machine again. Again another journey. Again the door is unlocked. Another friend hangs from a length of manila rope. Again the invitation card stands on the mantelpiece and again I am too late and find the liveried porters dismantling the festive chamber.

Sometimes in the dream I seem to be angry with my brother, sometimes I feel nothing. I wonder why he figures in this dream? I have not seen him since I left England and we never write. I did not even see him when my father died. I was not at home when the telegram arrived—I was in Eugene, Oregon, teaching a summer school session to afford whatever had to be afforded—repairs to the house, the car, the furnace, clothes for the children—and by the time phone calls from Mary traced me and air-line schedules had been checked, it was too late. And my father was buried.

In a file under F, in a file marked Father, I have all the letters he ever wrote me. There are seven. They were never sent from home but always from somewhere on an infrequent holiday. They all start off with depressing ordinariness. They are addressed to My Dear Boy and signed Your Loving Father.

One starts:

The weather here is fine. We are, praise God, in good health.

Another:

The Lord has granted us good weather.

But then come his typical outbursts of eccentricity:

Here they pretend not to know how to boil eggs. I have given the strictest instructions—I could not have been more explicit. I can only conclude that this is done to aggravate me.

Another said:

Your mother constantly remarks upon the views. I have requested her NOT to remark upon views but to no avail. I am not blind. She desires me to take photographs of these views; this I have refused to do. God has given us memories and if we cannot remember what we have seen then it is not memorable. I have explained this to her.
    There are many Germans.

How I wish I had known him.
    The bare branches of the lilac tree outside the window began to appear stark in the blue blackness. I searched for the Brillo pads; Mary always puts things in different places. Scraps of the skin of the duck proved almost impossible to remove.
    When my mother died, I did go back to England. It wasn't filial piety or respect. I think, secretly, I wanted to be sure. I wanted to see the coffin with my own eyes and hear the earth thudding onto the wood. What would her words have been? Laid to rest? Gone to her reward?
    The minister of the church she'd attended, a Heepish creature, asked me if I would read from the Scriptures; I gravely declined and

he hastened to understand my feelings. There were floral tributes and the singing of hymns. She had, an ancient uncle assured me, fought the good fight.

This time, ironically, my brother was away, somewhere in Greece on holiday, unreachable. It was left to me to dispose of immediate matters. She had been living in a small town in Kent. I wandered about that house for two days, touching, looking, feeling strange. It was all gone now, all finished.

The clothes neatly folded in all the drawers; the stink of lavender. Little silken bags of lavender. I gathered up all the little bags and burned them. The net gloves. Them too.

The same pictures from twenty-five years before when I'd left. The picture of Peter Pan she'd tried to keep hanging in my bedroom. *The Light of the World*—Christ with a lantern. Holman Hunt, was it? Anonymous landscapes. Few books—some volumes of popular devotion, the autobiography of a vet, a life of Wesley, Agatha Christie and Dorothy L. Sayers.

In her bedroom, on the dressing table, still the remembered objects of childhood. The ebony hairbrush. A strange little ebony pot with a screw top with a hole in the top which was for putting hair into from a comb or brush before throwing it away. An amazing object—obviously common thirty or forty years ago but now as oddly antique as a sand-shaker for drying letters. Formidable hairpins and hat-pins, brooches fussy with little coloured stones.

In a kitchen drawer, neat piles of *ironed* rags.

A bureau contained scissors, glue, and large scrap books in various stages of completion. They were haphazardly full of pictures of holly, mangers, Christmas trees, lanterns, candles, carol-singers, Pickwickian coaches and ostlers, etc. etc. all cut from Christmas cards and intended for the missions in Africa. I was struck by some of the pictures that had taken her fancy—one in particular, I recall. A kitten sitting in a shoe. Harsh people are often sentimental.

I wondered what tiny Ibo or Luba children would make of these strange images from a different world. I burned them all.

A large cupboard in the kitchen was chock full of patent medicines, strange bottles with nineteenth-century-looking labels. Most of them were laxatives and purgatives, infusions of strange bark and pods, extract of prune, and numerous bottles of something called Slippery Elm.

The only reminder in the house that my father had ever lived was a framed photograph of him which stood on an occasional table in the sitting room. And that photograph, significantly, posed him with the mayor and alderman in their robes in the year he'd been mayor's chaplain. The mayor was wearing his golden chain of office.

All my father's books, the books he'd written, his occasional writings, his sermons, not a thing remained. She'd managed to restore the home of her last years to the spinsterish order and purity of her dreams. Her bed was a single bed with a new eiderdown.

Even with my mother dead and me a father in my forties, I still could not imagine them doing "that sort of thing." could not imagine her thighs loosening or that angular body softening or hear her cry out in the dark bedroom. They still were giant figures on a glaring stage, their lives the myth of my life. I believed when a boy and believe now they did it twice. Me and my brother. And duty done, she—what? Something must have driven him to his eccentricities and silence. How could he be explained? He collected in his last years first editions of Conrad. Of all writers, *Conrad*. He remains a mystery.

I can imagine her voice in their dark bedroom, a voice little more than a chill whisper.

Or perhaps stolid silence.

Silence.

Silence.

After I had given all her personal effects to Oxfam before my brother could return, after I'd signed tedious documents with a disapproving lawyer disinheriting myself in my brother's favour, I found myself bored, irritable, and thinking insistently about Croydon. I still had time on my excursion ticket so I made the journey.

Croydon.

Though I've often been pissed by lunch and sometimes on champagne, I never did shave off half my moustache or take a lobster for a walk, live in brothels, or cut my ear off. I've never had syphilis either. But I did become a writer of sorts; not the writer that I'd dreamed of becoming in my Croydon adolescence; the Muse hovers but does not ravish me. I write short stories which are published in the little magazines and university journals. I have published two collections of these stories, one of which is still in print. Several stories have been anthologized. I wrote a novel about a boy's growing up. He was a rebel. It was remaindered in Classics book stores a year later for 99 cents. Reviewers have described my work as "sensitive" and "finely tuned explorations of loneliness and self-discovery." I have some small reputation in a minor genre in the parochial world of Canadian letters. Like many Canadian writers, I support myself by teaching in a university.

In the calendar I am designated as:

T.D. Moore (Ph.D.): Modern British Poetry (1003)
Moore (Ph.D.): Contemporary Fiction (2001)

In Croydon I walked around familiar streets. I looked at the exterior of my father's old church. A notice outside stated the minister's name and the hours of services and white, plastic letters asserted beneath:

God So Loved The World That He Gave His Only Begotten Son.
I went to the park where Helen and I had walked and held hands.
I looked into the library.

I tried to find a shop I'd loved as a boy, a shop that sold antique arms and armour, but the whole area had been torn down and in its place stood a complex of office-space, Odeon cinema, and bowling alley.

Tony and I had been smitten for a short time, perhaps between jazz and painting, with the idea of becoming diamond prospectors —pork-knockers they were called—in what was then British Guiana.

We read Peter Fleming and *Green Hell* and all the books about Colonel Fawcett. We drew bold lines from Georgetown into the uncharted interior. Like Sir Richard Burton, we would write our names large on the map's white spaces.

I did not try to find Tony. I made no enquiries of his life.

I wanted to remember him for always and ever as the boy who imagined sucking the hair in Eliska's armpit.

In my hotel room that night, lying on the bed with indigestion after eating something the hotel menu called Gooseberry Fool and drinking their coffee—I found my mind full of pictures of that Yorkshire manse where I'd pinned worms to crosses, full of memories of Mrs. Henderson, the Scarlet Woman, and Mr. Montague.

Nothing held me now in England; she was dead. My life was wholly in Canada with Mary and the children in Montreal—in what my brother, an historian of medieval matters, still calls the New World.

He phoned me after our father's funeral—some legal matter—and I invited him to visit us in Canada; I can hear his hesitant voice declining—family responsibilities, money, pressure of work—and then, "I really feel that the New World offers little that could engage my interests . . ."

I was lonely in that hotel bedroom, unsettled, and those ghosts called me, beckoned to me across forty years. And so I struggled with the telephone system and British Railways—two institutions obdurately inefficient and unchanged since my youth, and arranged to journey to that northern town.

It's a common experience—all adults must remember particular school teachers and meet them after childhood to find them shrunken, mild-mannered, ordinary, ordinary. That huge manse where I'd hidden in alcoves and played on the vast expanse of polished landings, that mansion with its many rooms, turned out to be a seedy Victorian house, certainly not small, but not the monstrous pile that I remembered. I stood looking at it and thought of asking if I might go round into the back garden—to do what? Look at my crucifix plot? Open the coal cellar door and peer down into the dark which had terrified me as a child? Little Pakistani children trundled up and down on their tricycles. I could not face the complexities of request or explanation.

I did find the Scarlet Woman. She must have been sixty-five or so, but looked older. I felt foolish. She turned out to be a lonely old woman who drank too much gin too early in the day.

"So you're the vicar's little boy!" she said, marvelling.

"I remember you. Yes, I do. Picked all my daffodils, you did, and put horse manure through my letter-box!"

I confessed that it sounded like me.

"Of course, the neighbourhood's gone down," she said, "what with those Pakis and their customs."

On every surface in her living-room stood framed photographs of her husband. Wedding pictures. The pair of them windswept on a seaside pier. A young man in uniform. A posed group of soldiers grinning like embarrassed boys.

He'd died in France, burned alive in his tank.

"Eh," she said, in that suddenly comfortable Yorkshire, "my Tom, he were a *lovely* lad."

We drank gin together all afternoon and I told her about a Canada I thought she might like to hear about, a Canada of skyscrapers, rivers wider than the eye could command, snow that buried cars in a single night, Red Indians, bears and timber wolves.

She cried when I had to leave and I hugged her and was glad I'd made the journey. And as I bent to kiss her goodbye, she said,

"Canada! Well, I never! Who'd a thowt it when tha was a little lad!"

I winced at the clatter of cutlery, held my breath and was silent in that silent kitchen waiting to hear movement from the bedroom. It was beginning to get light. I could see the bulk of our neighbour's house, the whiteness of the white fence that I'd have to paint again in the summer. The water in the sink was brown and greasy; horrid soft things nudged my hands in the water.

The glasses could go straight into the dishwasher.

Mary's life fascinates me; I love to observe all her drama and silliness. I often feel she's more *alive* than I am; sometimes I even feel I live *through* her. Her political rages and feuds amuse me though I try to disguise my amusement. Mary genuinely *believes* in justice and being fair and the dignity of man. She reminds me of Peter and Jane at bedtime when one or the other says it isn't *fair*! She accuses me of not caring about people and in the way she means it she's quite right. All that was long ago burned out of me.

"You're *cold*," she says. "You don't *care*."

And she's fiercely eccentric, too, in her own way, irrational, and I love that about her as well. She hasn't spoken to our neighbour in the back for six years. She's convinced he's a Peeping Tom. The story, according to her, is that when she was about eight months pregnant with Peter she was sitting on the lavatory one evening and the frosted bathroom window which looks out onto the back garden was open about an inch. She suddenly felt uncomfortable and looked up and there watching her she saw a pair of eyes.

How could she possibly identify our neighbour I wanted to know.

"I'd know those eyes anywhere!" she declared.

The other week the poor man was up on his roof in the ice and snow mending one of the wire stays of his TV aerial.

"Just look at him!" she said indignantly. "He'll do anything to peer in."

Gerry had spilled wine on the table-cloth and I decided to take it and the napkins downstairs and put them in the washing machine. The basement is finished as a large room for the kids but a part of it is partitioned off to enclose the furnace and the washer and drier and a part of that partition is closed off again to afford me a tiny dark room where I grade papers, read, and write my stories. Mary calls it my "study" but the word "study" or "office" is rather grandiose for what is as narrow as a stall; I generally call it my "room." And there, with as much silence as I can get between the washing machine and kids and the rush of the bloody furnace, I write my stories of "loneliness and self-discovery."

I coiled the garden hose and hung it back on its rack; it's Peter's favourite toy which he's been told numberless times not to touch. Someone had knocked over the plastic sack of Diamond Green

Combination Lawn Fertilizer. I dragged it upright and propped it up against the wall again. The huge box of Tide was empty and I had to rip the top off a new one. I made a mental note to speak to Peter about the hose.

Truth to tell, I'm not all that interested in the kids. When they don't irritate me, they bore me. Angela is now fourteen and sulky, Billy thirteen and apathetic. I'd have been content enough to leave it there but Mary decided she'd like more so we had Peter and Jane. I study Billy covertly. I assume that he must be as I was, that he lusts after girls and women and wanks himself senseless. But sometimes I have my doubts. As far as I can tell, he spends most of his time watching TV and when he isn't watching TV he's reading *Mad Magazine*. Perhaps he wanks while he watches. Angela spends most of her life behind a slammed bedroom door; other than play rock music, I don't know what she does in there. They are both too interested in money and Billy deposits every cent he can get in his bank account. If he isn't reading *Mad Magazine* or *TV Guide*, he's reading his bank book. It is impossible to talk to Angela; she pouts, flaunts, and sulks. She is currently enraged that I have refused to have installed in her bedroom a Princess phone on a separate line. My considered desire is to flog the living daylights out of her but Mary says she's going through a difficult time.

They're children from another world, a world in which I'm alien, the New World.

I watch them sometimes on their bicycles, observe their play; Jane is almost fat. Sometimes I chauffeur Angela and even Billy to *dances* for God's sake! and I think them lotus-eaters, children lacking any drive or purpose, softlings.

And as for me, I come from the Pre-TV, the age which in their ahistoric minds followed the Bronze or Iron.

I am probably as remote from them as my father was from me.

Would I wish on them *my* history and *its* history?

Sometimes, yes.

On that trip to Yorkshire after I'd seen my mother buried, I made a sentimental excursion to Haworth Parsonage; my motivation wasn't

literary. My father had taken me there once when I was a small child.
I enquired about a taxi in town and the man said:

"Tha's not American. Bus is nobbut a shilling."

The gravestones, slate and shining in the rain, crowd right up the
sides of the Parsonage. The children were buried there one by one;
the remaining sisters wrote among the ghosts. Emily's fevered imagination, its mad intensity, reminds me of some quality in my own
childhood; I read her book with recognition. It is the work of a virgin.
Would she have written it, I wonder now, if she'd married, married
and lived longer?

I walked among the gravestones, pausing now and then to trace
weathered lettering with my fingertips and then out and up onto the
moors. The heather was wet and springy and I shivered in my light
raincoat. I stood for a few minutes by an outcrop of rock where so
many years ago I'd stood with my father.

I, too, often feel I live my life among ghosts, that the stories I
write are exorcisms. The dead are all around me. I am too much part
of them.

Wash yourself.
Dry yourself.

It's as if I exhausted all my passion by the age of sixteen; nothing
since has compared with the drama and intensity of that battle of
wills, a titanic struggle fought against the backdrop of Hell.

And none of it now means anything I can understand; I no
longer believe in the fire and ice of Hell and sex is what happens on
Saturdays.

I watch Angela and her friends who lounge on our balcony and
lawn in the summer. I observe the loveliness of their young bodies.
Mary's breasts are fallen, disfigured with stretch-marks, her nipples
like plugs. I wonder what is going to happen to Angela, how *her* story
will unfold.

"Young girls with little tender tits."

Foals in an autumn field.

The wash was thumping about in the machine, water sloshing. My hangover was getting worse as I knew it would. Something vital in the washing-machine needed oiling. I groped through its rhythm and the pounding in my head for the rest of those lines, something I'd been teaching, "Young girls with little tender tits," teaching the term before, tried to remember the line that rhymed, remember . . .

Remember, imbeciles and wits
Sots and ascetics, fair and foul,
Young girls with little tender tits,
that Death is written over all.

I sat and waited in my room.

A year or so ago I was wandering about near Craig Street in an unfamiliar part of Montreal searching for a stationer's which was reputed to carry a make of fountain pen I wished to buy. Down a side-street, I found a store which was a cross between an army surplus and a chandler's. On some strange impulse, I bought a sextant. It was expensive and the moment I'd paid for it I felt silly and went to some trouble to smuggle it into the house. I hide it under papers in a drawer in my room.

As the washing-machine changed rhythm and the water drained away I took the sextant out. It sits in a mahogany box, the brass and glass nestled in green baize. I looked at it, at its telescope, index mirror, and horizon glass. I turned the clamp screw and the tangent screw enjoying the feel of the milled edges. I'm not quite sure how it's supposed to work.

THE EASTMILL RECEPTION CENTRE

After a year in the university's Department of Education, a year worn thin discussing the application of Plato to the Secondary Modern School and enduring my tutor, a mad dirndl woman who placed her faith in Choral Speaking, this was to be my first taste of the real world.

While Uncle Arthur was assembling a ring of the necessary keys, I stood looking down from his office window into the asphalt quadrangle where the boys were lounging and smoking, strolling, dribbling a football about. They all wore grey denim overalls and black boots.

"The wife and I," said Uncle Arthur, "were not blessed with issue."

I turned and nodded slowly.

"So in a sense—well, the way *we* feel about it—every last one of these lads is *our* lad."

I nodded and smiled.

Uncle Arthur was short and tubby and was wearing grey flannels and a grey sleeveless pullover. Strands of fine blond hair were trained across his reddened pate. He looked jolly. In the centre of the strained pullover was a darn in wool of a darker grey. It drew attention like a wart.

"Here's your keys, then. They're all tagged. And use them at *all* times. Artful as a barrel-load of monkeys, they are, and absconders is the *last* thing we want. One whistle with lanyard. There's your timetable. And a word of advice, a word to the wise. If you get yourself into difficulties, just you come to me. I'm House Father and it's what I'm here for. Comprendo?"

"Thanks," I said. "I'll remember that."

"Right, then . . ." said Uncle Arthur.

I glanced at my timetable.

"*Gardening?*"

"Oh, everyone takes a hand at gardening," said Uncle Arthur. "Very keen on gardening, the Old Man is. Doesn't know you're here, does he? The Old Man? You didn't phone from the station?"

"No," I said. "Was I supposed to?"

"Probably wiser," said Uncle Arthur, "yes, to wait till morning."

I nodded.

"*Mid*-morning," he added.

I looked at him.

"A nod's as good as a wink," he said, "if you get my drift."

"Oh, right," I said. "Of course."

"That's the ticket!" said Uncle Arthur. "Well, you come along with me, then, do the evening rounds, get the hang of things."

I followed him along the disinfectant- and polish-smelling corridor, down the echoing steel stairs, out into the warmth of the summer evening.

Pallid faces, cropped hair, army boots. I was the centre of much obvious speculation. I kept close to Uncle Arthur and endeavoured to look bored. I nodded as casually as I could at the faces which stared most openly.

We mounted the steps of the North Building. Uncle Arthur blew one long blast on his whistle and all motion froze. His glance darted about the silent playground.

"Nothing like a routine," he murmured, "to settle a lad down."

Two blasts: four boys ran to stand beneath us, spacing themselves about ten feet apart.

"House Captains," explained Uncle Arthur.

Three blasts: the motionless boys churned into a mob and then shuffled themselves out into four lines. He allowed a few seconds to elapse as they dressed ranks and then blew one long blast.

Silence was rigid.

As each boy, House by House, called out *Present, Uncle Arthur!* in response to his surname, Uncle Arthur ticked the mimeographed sheet. When numbers were tallied and initialled, Churchill House and Hanover moved off first to the showers.

"Never initial anything," said Uncle Arthur, "until you've double-checked personally. Best advice I can give you. I learned that in the Service and it's stood me in good stead ever since."

Stripped of their grey overalls, the boys looked even more horribly anonymous, buttocks, pubic hair, feet. I glanced down the line of naked bodies trying not to show my embarrassment and distaste. I looked down at Uncle Arthur's mauve socks in the brown open-work sandals. At the further end of the line, a mutter of conversation was rising. Uncle Arthur's whistle burbled, a sound almost meditative.

"Careful you don't lose your pea, Uncle Arthur," said one of the tallest boys.

All the boys laughed.

"It won't be *me*, lad," said Uncle Arthur, nodding slowly, ponderous work with his eyebrows, "it won't be *me* as'll be losing my pea."

I recognized this as ritual joke.

The laughter grew louder, wilder, ragged at the edges.

Order was restored by a single blast.

He advanced to a position facing the middle of the line.

Into the silence, he said,

"Cleanliness, Mr. Cresswell, as the Good Book says, is next to Godliness. So at Eastmill here it's three showers a day *every* day. We get lads in here that come from home conditions you wouldn't credit. Never had contact with soap and water, some of them. Last time some of this lot touched water was when they was christened. *If* they was christened. *Sewed* into their underclothes, some of them are. And dental decay? Horrible! Turns the stomach, Mr. Cresswell. Athlete's foot. Lice. Scabies and scales. Crabs of all variety. Crabs, Mr. Cresswell, of every stripe and hue."

He surveyed the silent line.

"Start with little things, you see, Mr. Cresswell, because little things lead to big things. That's something that in the Service you *quickly* learn. And talking of *little things*," he bellowed suddenly, his face flushing, "what are *you* trying to hide, lad? *Stand up STRAIGHT!*"

Half turning to me, he said from the side of his mouth,

"A rotten apple if ever I saw one. Attempted rape was the charge. Got off with interference."

I nodded and avoided looking at the boy.

In spite of all the showering, there was a close smell of sweat, feet, sourness.

While Uncle Arthur raked the naked rank with his flushed glare, I made a pretence of reading the mimeographed names on the clipboard. I found myself thinking of the strange civil service gentleman, somehow connected with the Home Office, who'd interviewed me a month earlier.

We like our chaps to have rubbed along a bit with other chaps.
Boxing, eh? The Noble Art, hmm?
Excellent. Excellent.

My role, he had informed me, would be both educational and diagnostic.

Uncle Arthur's keys clinked in the awful silence. He selected one, and the captain of Churchill stepped out of line to receive it. The boy unlocked a metal cupboard and took out a square ten-pound tin and an aluminum dessert spoon.

Upon command, the boys began to file past holding out a cupped hand and Uncle Arthur spooned in grey tooth-powder.

"Better than paste," he confided. "What's paste but powder with the water added?"

The boys were crowding round the racks of tagged toothbrushes, bunching round the six long sinks, dribbling water onto the powder, working it up in their palms with the brushes.

"What about the others?" I said. "The other boys?"

"They'll be at their exercises in the yard with Mr. Austyn. In the quadrangle. Stuart House and Windsor tonight. Anyone who goes on report, you see, the whole House suffers. Ginger them *all* up. Doesn't make the offenders popular. Discourages them as likes to think of themselves as hard cases."

A scuffle was starting around the last sink. The sounds of hawking, gobbing, gargling, were becoming melodramatic.

"Right! Let's have you!" bellowed Uncle Arthur. "Lather yourselves all over paying special attention to all crevices—and no skylarking!"

He turned on the showers and the dank room filled with steam. The pale figures slowly became ghostly, indistinct. Conversation was difficult above the roar of the water.

When the showers were turned off, the boys dried themselves, fixed the soggy towels round their waists, and formed a single line facing the far door. Uncle Arthur unlocked the door and the line advanced. The first boy stopped in front of us, stuck his head forward, contorted his features into a mocking grimace. I stared at him in amazement, fearing for him. Uncle Arthur inspected the exposed teeth and then nodded. Face after snarling face, eyes narrowed or staring, flesh-stretched masks, until the last white towel was starting up the stairs.

"Here's a tip for you just in passing," said Uncle Arthur as he double-locked the door and we followed them up, "a wrinkle, as you might say, that they wouldn't have taught you in the university. Tomorrow, in the morning showers, keep your eyes skinned for any lad as has a tattoo. Right? Then you have a read of his file. Right? Any young offender, as they're now called, any young offender that's got a tattoo, you be on the *qui vive* because sure as the sun shines you've got trouble on your hands. Right?"

I nodded.

"Most particularly," said Uncle Arthur, stopping, puffed by the stairs, "if it says 'Mother'."

There were forty beds in the dormitory, twenty on each side of the room. On each bed was a single grey blanket. Hanging from the end of each iron-frame bed was a grey cloth drawstring bag. The boys, now in pyjamas, stood at attention at the foot of the beds.

Uncle Arthur surveyed them.

Then nodded.

The boys opened the cloth bags, taking out rolled bundles of *Beano* and *Dandy*, *Hotspur*, *Champion*, and *The Wizard*.

"Providing there's no undue noise," said Uncle Arthur, "comics till nine."

I followed him down the sounding stairs and along another blank corridor until he stopped and said,

"Here we are, then—our home away from home."

The Common Room contained six shabby Parker-Knoll armchairs, two coffee tables, and a low bookcase stacked and heaped with pamphlets and old newspapers. In one of the armchairs sat a morose middle-aged man whose spectacles were wrapped at the bridge with a Band-Aid. By the side of his chair stood a wooden crate of beer. He was wearing slippers, his feet stretched out towards the electric fire where imitation flames flickered.

"Mr. Grendle," said Uncle Arthur, "our metal-work teacher. Our new English teacher, Mr. Cresswell."

"How do you do?" I said.

Mr. Grendle did not look up and did not reply.

"Well . . ." said Uncle Arthur.

The yellowing muslin curtains stirred in the breeze.

"Coffee," said Uncle Arthur, "tea," pointing to an electric kettle and some unwashed cups and spoons. "Ale you'll have to organize for yourself."

Mr. Grendle tapped out his pipe on the arm of the chair, swept the ash and dottle onto the floor, wiped his palm on his cardigan.

"Perhaps," said Uncle Arthur, "you'd better come along and see your room, get yourself settled in."

"*A scriber!*" said Mr. Grendle, staring at the imitation flames. "A scriber in the back. Or battered with a ball-peen hammer. That's how *I'll* end."

As we went out into the fading light of the summer evening, Uncle Arthur said,

"Get's a bit low, sometimes, does Henry. Since his accident."

"Accident?"

"Yes," said Uncle Arthur. "That's right. Now this is a view I've *always* been partial to."

We stood looking at the screen of trees, at the long gravel drive which turned down through tended lawns and shrubs to the Porter's Lodge, a single-storey brick building beside the gate in the tall mesh fence which was topped by angled barbed-wire.

Far below us, a man was wandering over the lawns spiking up scraps of paper.

"Often comes out for a constitutional around this time," said Uncle Arthur.

"Pardon?"

"The Old Man."

The figure disappeared behind a clump of rhododendrons.

"Well," said Uncle Arthur, consulting his watch, "no rest for the wicked, as they say. Time for me to relieve Mr. Austyn. Now over *here's* where you are, in the West Building."

My room was featureless. A red printed notice on the inside of the door said: Please Keep This Door Locked At All Times. On the iron-frame bed were two grey blankets. I hung up clothes in the small varnished wardrobe, stacked shirts and underwear in the varnished chest of drawers, stowed the suitcase under the bed. I set my small alarm-clock for six-thirty.

The toilet paper was harsh and stamped with the words: Not For Retail Distribution.

Lying in bed under the tight sheets, I found myself thinking of the boys in the dormitory, found myself wondering if the serials *I'd* read as a boy were still running in the comics, the adventures of Rockfist Rogan, the exploits of Wilson the Amazing Athlete. Was it *Hotspur* or *The Wizard*? I could feel the rough paper, smell the smell of the paper and print. I found myself wondering if the Wolf of Kabul with his lethal cricket-bat bound in brass wire was still haunting the Frontier.

And as I drifted into sleep, I remembered the name of the cricket-bat. The Wolf of Kabul. He'd called it "Clickee-baa."

Tick-tock of the clock.
Clickee-baa.

———————

When I entered the Staff Dining Room next morning with my tray,
one of the two men at the long table called,

"Do come and join us! Austyn. With a 'Y'. Sports and Geography."

He was tall and boyish, dressed in a white shirt and cricket
flannels.

"My name's Cresswell," I said, shaking his hand, "and I'm supposed to be teaching English."

"And my surly colleague," he said, "is Mr. Brotherton. Wood-
work."

I nodded.

"You're a university man, I understand?" said Mr. Austyn as I
unloaded my tray. "Something of a *rara avis* in Approved School
circles."

"Oh, I'm just a novice," I said.

"I, myself," he said, "attended Training College. Dewhurst. In
Surrey."

Mr. Brotherton belched.

"Well, look," said Mr. Austyn, rising, draining his cup, consulting his watch in a military manner, "time marches on. I'd better be
getting my lads organized. I'll look forward to talking to you later."

I watched him as he walked out. He was wearing white plimsolls.
He walked on his toes and seemed almost to bounce.

Mr. Brotherton explored his nose with a grimy handkerchief and
then started to split a matchstick with his horny thumbnail.

I drank coffee.

He picked his teeth.

"'I *attended* Training College'!" he said suddenly.

"Pardon?"

"I've 'attended' a symphony concert at the Albert Hall but it
doesn't mean I played first sodding violin."

"What do you mean by that?"

"You wouldn't likely think it," he said, getting to his feet and tossing a crumpled paper napkin onto the table, "but I was once a sodding cabinet-maker."

In the quadrangle, the boys, lined up House by House, were standing silent but at ease facing the steps of the North Building. It was five minutes to eight. Uncle Arthur and Mr. Austyn were supervising two House Captains who were positioning on the top step a record-player and two unhoused speakers. Uncle Arthur adjusted the height of the microphone stand. Not knowing what exactly to do, I sat on the low wall by the side of the East Building.

The microphone boomed and whined. One of the House Captains touched the needle of the record-player and a rasp sounded through the speakers. Mr. Grendle hurried out of the East Building bearing large plywood shields. He propped them against the low wall beside me and hurried back into the building. The outer shield said: STUART. A man I hadn't seen before strode up and down the lines rearranging a boy or two here and there to establish an absolute descending order of height.

Uncle Arthur looked at his watch.

He blew a single blast.

In a long shuffle of movement, the boys dressed ranks.

Mr. Austyn said something urgently to Uncle Arthur and Uncle Arthur turned to one of the House Captains, jabbing his finger in my direction.

The boy sprinted towards me.

"Is it these you want?" I said, fumbling together the awkward sliding shields.

"Oh, fucking hell!" said the boy, grabbing them from me, nearly dropping them, bumping me in his urgency.

"*Ssssss!*" said a voice behind me.

Turning, I saw Mr. Grendle on top of the East Building steps urging me in clenched pantomime to stand at attention.

Mr. Brotherton, his face expressionless, stood sentry on the top step of the South Building.

The whistle shrilled again; the boys stiffened; the shields, HAN-OVER, STUART, WINDSOR, and CHURCHILL, were steadied by the captains. Mr. Austyn lowered his outstretched arm as though applying a slow-match to a touch-hole. At this signal, the crouching boy lowered the needle onto the record. There was a loud prelimi-nary hissing before the music rolled forth. The awful volume and quality of sound brought to mind fairgrounds and gymkhanas. Uncle Arthur held wide the North Building's heavy door. The brass and massed choir worked their way through "Land of Hope and Glory."

Nothing happened.

The crouching boy put on another record.

The National Anthem blared.

At

Long to reign over us

the shadowed doorway darkened and a large man in a brown suit walked out past Uncle Arthur and stood before the microphone. His chest was massive. He seemed almost without a neck. He was wearing mirrored sunglasses. Stuck at the angle of his jaw was what looked like a small piece of toilet-paper. What could be seen of his face was red and purple.

As the Anthem concluded, the boy lifted off the hissing needle.

Our Father Which Art in Heaven

Hallowed Be Thy Name

said the Headmaster.

And stopped.

The silence extended.

And extended.

Mr. Austyn was quivering at attention.

The Headmaster cleared his throat. The head moved, the mir-rored lenses scanning the four ranks.

"If I find a boy," he said slowly, his voice heavy with menace, "*not* pulling together, I'm going to be very sorry for that boy. Very sorry indeed. But not half as sorry as that boy is going to be."

There was another long silence.

He brought out a packet of cigarettes and a box of matches and looked down at them and then put them back in his jacket pocket.

He then buttoned the jacket.

Uncle Arthur moved to his side and the microphone picked up the murmured prompting.

Thy Kingdom Come . . .

"What do you say, Arthur?" boomed the microphone.

The head and torso turned ponderously to the left; he seemed to be staring at the shield that said WINDSOR.

For ever he suddenly said *and ever. Amen* and his brown bulk broke from the microphone and strode past the taut white figure of Mr. Austyn into the shadows of the doorway and disappeared.

Roll-call followed.

Followed by morning showers.

My classroom was less than a quarter the size of a normal classroom and the twenty boys were jammed along the benches. There was somewhere, Uncle Arthur believed, a set of readers. I issued each boy with a sheet of paper and a pencil, and, as I had been instructed by Uncle Arthur, wrote on the blackboard:

When I grow up, I want to—

These papers were to be read by Dr. James, described by Uncle Arthur with a wink and a finger pressed to the side of his nose as "the old trick cyclist."

I watched the boys writing, watched the way the pencils were gripped or clasped. I curbed the use of the wall-mounted pencil-sharpener after a couple of boys had managed to reduce new pencils to one-inch stubs. I denied nine requests to go to the lavatory. At the end of the allotted time, I collected and counted the pencils and glanced through what Uncle Arthur had called the "completions."

They were brief, written in large, wayward script, and violent in spelling. Some of the papers were scored almost through. Deciphered, they expressed the wish "to be pleeceman," "to hav big musels," "to go Home," etc.

One paper was blank except for the name sprawled huge.

"Who's Dennis Thompson?"

A boy put up his hand. He looked about eleven or twelve.

"Why didn't you complete the sentence, Dennis?"

"Well, I don't do writing, do I?"

The accent was south London.

"Why's that?" I said.

"Well, I'm excused, aren't I?"

"Excused?"

Uncle Arthur bustled in. I was to meet the Old Man. Immediately. The boys were left with dire threats. I was hurried through the North Building and out of the rear door. The brown-suited figure was standing some two hundred yards distant with his back to us looking at the vast area given over to garden.

"Word to the wise," puffed Uncle Arthur, laying his hand on my arm, "sets great store, the Old Man does, by being called 'Headmaster'."

As we drew nearer, Uncle Arthur cleared his throat.

The Headmaster's hand was large and moist.

Uncle Arthur was dismissed.

The Headmaster returned to his contemplation of the large floral bank which spelled out:

EASTMILL RECEPTION CENTRE.

I stood beside him looking at the greyish plants of the lettering, the green and red surrounding stuff.

"The letters," he said, after a long silence, "of the display are Santalima Sage. A hardy perennial."

I nodded.

"The red," he said, pointing, "the green, the contrasting foliage, known as the filler, is called Alternamthera."

I nodded again and said,

"It's extremely impressive, Headmaster."

"A tender annual," he said.

"Pardon?"

"Alternamthera."

"Ah!" I said.

"I am proud of our record here at Eastmill, Mr. Cresswell. In eleven years, *three*—"

The mirrored glasses were turned upon me.

"—only *three* absconders."

I nodded slowly.

"Two," he said, "were caught before they'd gone five miles."

He paused.

"The third was apprehended in Pontypool."

There was a long silence.

We studied the floral display.

Eventually, he cleared his throat in a manner which I took to be a sign that the interview was concluded.

"Thank you, Headmaster," I said.

The long day bore on with three more "completions," lunch supervision, midday roll-call and showers. The cricket match between Windsor and Stuart with twenty boys on each side was interminable. The shepherd's pie and jam-roll with custard weighed upon me. Uncle Arthur, seemingly tireless, drove the boys on through the afternoon's hot sun. An occupied boy, he held, was a happy boy. As we stood joint umpires at the crease his public exhortations were punctuated by *sotto voce* asides:

"Don't ponce about, lad! Hit it square!"

Stole a Morris Minor.

"Come on, lad! That's not the spirit that won the war!"

Had half a ton of lead off of a church roof.

The game lasted for more than three hours.

After evening meal supervision, roll-call, and evening showers, I settled down in the empty Common Room with the files of those names I'd managed to remember. I'd scarcely got myself arranged, coffee, ashtray, cigarettes, when the door opened and I looked up at a man of about forty who was wearing a blue suit with a Fair Isle pattern pullover.

"Good evening," I said. "My name's Cresswell."

"James," he said, nodding his head almost as if ducking, and then plugged in the electric kettle.

"Not *Dr.* James?"

"Well, not really. It's a Ph.D. You're from a university. I did *try* to explain . . ."

He came over and sat facing me. The blue shoulders were dusted with dandruff. He began to fiddle with a tiny bottle of saccharine tablets, trying to shake out just one.

"I'm about to make a start on your files," I said.

"Were you interviewed by the Home Office?"

"For this job? I'm not sure really. Some sort of civil service character."

"They *all* call me 'Doc'," he said. "Even the boys."

I watched him trying to funnel saccharine tablets back into the bottle.

"Have you spoken to the Headmaster? Since you've been here?"

"Yes," I said. "This morning."

"Did he by any chance say anything to you about me? In any way?"

"No," I said. "He . . ."

"Or imply anything?"

He started nibbling at his thumbnail.

"No. He didn't say *anything*, really. Just warned me about boys absconding. He seemed to want me to look at his flower-bed-thing. Actually," I said, "he seemed rather *odd*."

"Odd!" said Dr. James. "*Odd*! The Headmaster—"

He got up and went to close the door.

"Files," he said, guiding the boiling water into his mug, "files and expert opinion are obviously the centre of any such organization as this. The heart. The very core."

He looked up, spectacles befogged by steam.

I nodded.

The teaspoon was stuck to the newspaper.

"The Headmaster," he said, "the Headmaster ignores my reports. He rejects all my recommendations. He deliberately undermines the efforts of all my work. Deliberately. And he openly influences the staff against me."

"Why?" I said.

Seating himself again, he took off his spectacles and stared at me with naked eyes.

"There have been countless ugly incidents. He's incapably alcoholic, but of course you must have realized that. And for all this, accountable to no one, of course, we have the Home Office to thank."

"But why would he undermine your . . . ?"

"Because he perceives me as a threat."

The naked eyes stared at me. He rubbed the spotty spectacles on the Fair Isle pullover.

"Threat in what way?"

"The man has no education whatever beyond elementary school. Yes! Oh, yes! But there's more you should know, Mr. . . . er . . ."

"Cresswell," I said.

"For your own protection."

He peered again towards the door.

"Before he became Headmaster, he was employed—I have access to the files—the man was employed by the City of Eastmill—"

He bent his head and hooked the springy wire side-pieces of the spectacles around the curves of his ears and looked up again.

"—employed as a *municipal gardener*."

"No!" I said.

He nodded.

"But how on earth . . ."

"Ask our masters at the Home Office."

"Good God!" I said.

He carried the mug of coffee to the door.

"Mention to no one," he said, "that we have spoken."

I settled down to read.

The files contained condensed case histories, I.Q. scores, vocabulary scores, reports from previous schools, reports from social workers and probation officers, family profiles, anecdotal records, recommendations. The files were depressingly similar.

Thompson, Dennis.

I remembered him, the London boy from the morning who'd claimed to be excused from writing, the waif's face, the dark lively eyes. Fifteen years of age. According to the scores he'd received in the *Wechsler-Bellevue, Stanford and Binet, Terman and Merrill*, etc., his achievements and intelligence were close to non-existent. His crime was arson. Three derelict row-houses in Penge had been gutted before the flames had been brought under control.

He claimed not to know why he had done it.

He said he liked fires.

———————

I soon lost my nervousness of these boys under my charge. As the days passed, I stopped seeing them as exponents of theft, rape, breaking and entering, arson, vandalism, grievous bodily harm, and extortion, and saw them for what they were—working-class boys who were all, without exception, of low average intelligence or mildly retarded.

We laboured on with phonics, handwriting, spelling, reading.

Of all the boys, I was most drawn to Dennis. He was much like all the rest but unfailingly cheerful and co-operative. Dennis could chant the alphabet from A to Z without faltering, but he had to start at A. His mind was active, but the connections it made were singular.

If I wrote CAT, he would stare at the word with a troubled frown. When I sounded out C-A-T, he would say indignantly: Well, it's *cat*, isn't it? We had a cat, old tom-cat. Furry knackers, he had, and if you stroked 'em . . .

F-I-S-H brought to mind the chip shop up his street and his mum who wouldn't never touch rock salmon because it wasn't nothing but a fancy name for conger-eel.

C-O-W evoked his Auntie Fran—right old scrubber *she* was, having it away for the price of a pint . . .

Such remarks would spill over into general debate on the ethics of white women having it off with spades and Pakis, they was heathen, wasn't they? Said their prayers to gods and that, didn't they? *Didn't they?* Well, there you are then. *And* their houses stank of curry and that. You couldn't deny it. Not if you knew what you was talking about.

These lunatic discussions were often resolved by Paul, Dennis's friend, who commanded the respect of all the boys because he was serving a second term and had a tattoo of a dagger on his left wrist and a red and green hummingbird on his right shoulder. He would make pronouncement:

I'm not saying that they are and I'm not saying that they're not but what I *am* saying is . . .

Then would follow some statement so bizarre or so richly irrelevant that it imposed stunned silence.

He would then re-comb his hair.

Into the silence, I would say,

"Right. Let's get back to work, then. Who can tell me what a vowel is?"

Dennis's hand.

"It's what me dad 'ad."

"*What!*"

"It's your insides."

"What is?"

"Cancer of the vowel."

The long summer days settled into endless routine. The violent strangeness of everything soon became familiar chore. Uncle Arthur left me more and more on my own. Showers and the inspection of teeth. Meal supervision. Sports and Activities. Dormitory patrol.

The morning appearances of the Headmaster were predictably unpredictable. The Lord's Prayer was interspersed with outbursts about what would happen if boys did not pull their weight, the excessive use of toilet-paper, an incoherent homily concerning the flotilla of small craft which had effected the strategic withdrawal of the British Army from Dunkirk, and, concerning departures from routine, detailed aphasic instructions.

Every afternoon was given over to Sports and Activities.

Cricket alternated, by Houses, with gardening. Gardening was worse than cricket. The garden extended for roughly two acres. On one day, forty boys attacked the earth with hoes. The next day forty boys smoothed the work of the hoes with rakes. On the day following, the hoes attacked again. Nothing was actually planted.

The evening meals in the Staff Dining Room, served from huge aluminum utensils, were exactly like the school dinners of my childhood: unsavoury stews with glutinous dumplings, salads with wafers of cold roast beef with bits of string in them, jam tarts and Spotted Dick accompanied by an aluminum jug of lukewarm custard topped by a thickening skin.

Uncle Arthur always ate in his apartment with the wife referred to as "Mrs. Arthur" but always appeared in time for coffee to inquire if we'd enjoyed what he always called our "comestibles."

Mr. Austyn, referred to by the boys as "Browner Austyn," always said:

May I trouble you for the condiments?

Between the main course and dessert, Mr. Brotherton, often boisterously drunk, beat time with his spoon, singing, much to the distress of Mr. Austyn:

Auntie Mary
Had a canary
Up the leg of her drawers.

Mr. Grendle drizzled on about recidivists and the inevitability of his being dispatched in the metal-work shop. Mr. Hemmings, who drove a sports car, explained the internal-combustion engine. Mr. Austyn praised the give and take of sporting activity, the lessons of co-operation and joint endeavour, The Duke of Edinburgh's Awards, Outward Bound, the beneficial moral results of pushing oneself to the limits of physical endurance.

But conversation always reverted to pay scales, overtime rates, the necessity of making an example of this boy or that, of sorting out, gingering up, knocking the stuffing out of etc. this or that young lout who was trying it on, pushing his luck, just begging for it etc.

The days seemed to be growing longer and hotter; clouds loomed sometimes in the electric evenings promising the relief of rain, but no rain fell. The garden had turned to grey dust; cricket-balls rose viciously from patches of bald earth. Someone stole tobacco; there was a fight in the South Building dormitory. Comprehension declined; pencils broke. Showerings and the cleaning of teeth measured out each day.

One afternoon at the end of my fifth week, I was in charge of thirteen boys, seven having been commandeered by Mr. Grendle to do something or other to his forge. At the shrill of my whistle, the boys halted outside Mr. Austyn's shed while I drew and signed for the necessary cricket gear.

I unlocked the gate in the wire-mesh fence, locked it behind us. The cricket bag was unpacked; two boys were detailed to hammer in the stumps. The rest stood in a listless group grumbling about bleeding sunstroke and bleeding running about all bleeding afternoon for bleeding nothing.

There were only three bails; I had signed for four, had watched them go into the bag.

"Bail?" repeated a boy in vacant tone.

"What's he mean, 'bail'?" said another voice.

"It's money what you have to pay to get out the nick."

"You stupid berk!" said another voice.

The laughter grew louder, jeering.

I shrilled on the whistle, confronted them.

"I will give you," I said, "precisely five seconds to produce the missing bail."

"What's he going on about?"

"If the bail," I said, "is *not* produced . . ."

A flat voice said,

"Oh fuck the fucking bail."

Lunging, I grabbed a handful of the nearest denim, swung the boy off his feet. He fell on one knee. I jolted him backwards and forwards ranting at him, at them.

"*Sir!*"

Dennis's voice penetrated.

"'Ere! Sir!"

The boy fell slack; he was making noises.

My hand was like a claw.

I wandered away from them, crossing the limed line of the boundary, and sat waiting for my heart to stop the thick hammering. The close-mown grass was parched and yellow. Beyond the mesh fence yards in front of me were thick woods a quarter of a mile deep before the beginning of the houses of the East Point subdivision. In the afternoon heat the trees were still. I watched the unmistakable dance of Speckled Wood butterflies over the brambles, dead leaves, and leaf-mould at the wood's dappled edge. As a child, I'd chased them with my green muslin net. I stared beyond them into the darkening, layered shade.

Time had passed without my noticing. The missing bail had appeared; the game had got under way without the usual squabbling; was now winding down to a merely formal show of activity.

Dennis wandered over, and, in a pretence of fielding, crouched down a few yards away from me.

"It's all right, Dennis," I said.

He nodded. He sat down.

"It's all right," I said again.

Soon all the boys were sprawled in the grass.

"Wish we could play in there," said Dennis, staring into the woods.

I lay back and closed my eyes listening to their voices.

You could make a house in a tree like on the telly. That family. They had this house . . .

You haven't got no hammer and you haven't got no nails. And you haven't got no bits of old wood neither.

What about Tarzan, then? He didn't have no hammer neither.

Red suns behind my closed eyelids glowed and faded.

'Ere! Know what I'd be doing right now if I was Tarzan? Do you? I'd be having a bunk-up, having a crafty one with Jane.

Get lost! With a face like yours, wanker, you'd be lucky to cop a feel off his bleeding monkey.

I sat up and forced the key around the double ring until it was free. I tossed it to Dennis.

"Be back here," I said, "in one hour. Understand?"

As I lay back in the grass, I heard their yells and laughter, the sounds of their passage through the undergrowth, sounds which grew fainter. Later, a thrush started singing.

At three o'clock, I walked back towards the four main buildings.

———————

Well, even that, I suppose, could do as an ending.

Of sorts.

Lacking in drama, some might say.

Pastel colours. Too traditional.

I know all about that.

. . . marred in its conclusion by an inability to transcend the stylistic manner of his earlier work . . .

If I were interested in finishing this story, in cobbling it up into something a bit more robust, it's here that I ought to shape the thing towards what would be, in effect, a *second* climax and denouement. It's at this point that I should make slightly more explicit the ideas which have been implicit in the detail and narrative matter, treating them not baldly *as ideas*, of course, but embodying them, in the approved manner, in incident. (As a story-writer, I'm concerned, needless to say, with feelings, with moving you emotionally, not sermonizing.) And what is it exactly, then, that I would wish to emerge a touch more explicitly were I interested in rounding the story off for your entertainment? Certainly nothing intellectually stunning. Platitudes, some might say. That the guard is as much a prisoner as those he guards; that the desire to conform, to fulfil a role, distorts and corrupts; perhaps, to extend this last, that the seeds of Dachau and Belsen are dormant within us all.

And how, in the approved manner, might I have effected these ends? Dramatically, perhaps. A confrontation with the deranged Headmaster, the mirrored sunglasses worn even in his dim room, the venetian blinds permanently shuttered.

David and Goliath.

Or, more obliquely, affectingly, by an encounter at a later date with the recaptured Dennis.

Simple enough to do.

But I can't be bothered.

It was while I was writing this story that something happened which disturbed me, which made the task of writing not only tedious but offensive.

What happened was this.

It was Open Evening at the public school my son and daughter attend. My wife and I dutifully turned out, watched the entertainment provided, the thumping gymnastics, the incomprehensible play written and performed by the kids in Grade Seven, renditions by the choir, two trios, a quartet, and the ukulele ensemble. We then inspected our children's grubby exercise books which we see every day anyway, admired the Easter decorations, cardboard rabbit-shapes with glued-on absorbent-cotton tails etc. Smiled and chatted to their teachers. A necessary evening of unrelieved dreariness.

And driving back home along the dark country roads replying to my children's back-seat interrogation—Which did you like best? The gymnastics? The choir? What about the play? Wasn't the play funny?—and assuring my wife that I wasn't driving too fast, that the road wasn't icy, I passed the township dump. The dump was on fire. I looked down on the scene for only a few seconds. Twisting above the red heart of the fire, yellow tongues of flame. In the light thrown by the flames, grey smoke piling up to merge with the darkness of the night. Two figures. And high in the night sky, a few singing sparks. Then the sight was gone.

At that moment, my heart filled with a kind of—it's a strange word to use, perhaps, almost embarrassing, but I *will* say it—filled with a kind of *joy*.

What disturbed me, upset me, was that the feeling was so violent, so total. No. No, that's not what upset me. In the aftermath of that feeling, what upset me was its *strangeness*, the realization that I'd felt nothing like it for so many years.

Since then, and during the time I've been trying to finish up this story, I've been thinking about Dennis, for there *was* a Dennis, though I have no idea now what his name was. Let's call him Dennis and be done with it. Those events, in so far as they're at all autobiographical, happened more than twenty years ago in a country which is foreign to me now. So. Dennis. I've been thinking about him. And me.

And the vision of fire at night.

Fire at night seen through winter trees.

Drifting into sleep or lying half-awake, I picture fire. And I'm filled with an envious longing. Though I ought to qualify "envious." As I qualify most things. This isn't making much sense, is it? But listen. This is difficult for me, too. I want to make clear, you see, that I'm in no way romanticizing Dennis. I think that's important.

I know his life quite intimately. Much to my parents' distress, I admired his local counterparts and played with them for much of my childhood. I can imagine the pacifier smeared with Tate and Lyle's Golden Syrup when he was a baby, the late and irregular hours as an infant. On the casually wiped oilcloth of the kitchen table, the buns with sticky white icing and the cluster of pop bottles. I can imagine him and his brother and sister like a litter of hot-bellied puppies squabbling, gorging, sleeping where they dropped oblivious to the constant blare of the TV and radio. I can see his sister, off to school in a party frock, his snot-blocked brother with the permanent stye. And as Dennis grew a little older, ragtag games that surged in the surrounding streets till long past dusk.

I know his mother, warm and generous but too busy and always too tired. Too soft with him, too, after his father died. Not a stupid woman but slow and easy-going. I can see her dressing herself up on Friday nights in a parody of her youth, a few too many at the local, and after the death of her husband, consoling herself with a succession of uncles who'd give Dennis a couple of bob to go to the pictures to get him out of the way.

And then the drift into playing where one should not play, railway-yards perhaps, bouncing on the lumber in timber-yards, the pleasures of being chased. And as the world of school closed against him—hand-me-downs, incomprehension, hot tears in the school lavatories—the more aggressive acts. Street lights shot out, bricks through windows, feuds in the parks, and running stone-fights with rival gangs across the bomb-sites where willow herb still grew. Webley air-pistols, sheath knives, an accident involving stitches. Shoplifting in Woolworth's. Padlocks splintered from a shed. And edging towards the adult world, packets of Weights and Woodbines bought in fives, beer supplied by laughing older brothers, and, queasily, the girl up his street they all had, the girl from the special school.

And, years past the year I knew him, I can see him in the pub he's made his local, dressed to kill, his worldly wealth his wardrobe, dangerous with that bristling code of honour which demands satisfaction outside of those whose eyes dare more than glance . . .

No. I'm not romanticizing Dennis.

I wonder what became of him. Did he become a labourer perhaps? Carrying a hod "on the buildings," as he'd say? Or is he one of an anonymous tide flowing in through factory gates? Difficult to imagine the Dennis I knew settling down to that kind of grind. More probably he's on unemployment or doing time for some bungled piece of breaking and entering.

Dennis.

I *did* see Dennis again after I'd left the Approved School that afternoon. I saw him after he'd been recaptured. I know I'm not organizing this very well. It's difficult for me to say what I want to say.

It happened like this. I'd got another job in Eastmill almost immediately in a Secondary Modern School. Dr. James—let's call him that anyway—got the information from my parents, whose address was on the application I'd filed at the Reception Centre. He phoned me at the school and told me that Dennis had been caught in London, had been held down naked over a table by Uncle Arthur and Mr. Austyn and savagely birched by our friend in the sunglasses, was in the Eastmill Sick Bay, was feverish, and kept on asking for me. Dr. James, with considerable bravery given his personality and circumstances, smuggled me in one evening to see the boy. He was obviously in pain, his face gaunt, the eyes big and shadowed, but he smiled to see me and undid his pyjama jacket carefully, slowly, lifting it aside to show me his chest. His brother, the one in the army who'd been home on leave, had paid for it. It was just possible to distinguish the outlines of a sailing ship through the crust of red and blue and green, the whole mess raised, heaving, cracking in furry scabs.

I can't remember what we said. I do remember the way he undid the jacket as though uncovering an icon and the tremendous heat his infected chest gave off.

This incident, now I come to think about it, would have made a suitable ending to the story. Touching. The suggestion of a kind of victory, however limited, over the forces of evil. David and Goliath. Readers like that sort of thing. But it would have been a sentimental lie.

Dennis was no hero. He was a bloody nuisance then and he's doubtless a bloody nuisance now. And the staff of that school weren't evil, though at one time, my mind clouded by the prating of A.S. Neil and such, I doubtless thought so. They were merely stupid. Their answer to the problem of Dennis was crude, but it was at least an answer. I just don't *know* any more. Time and experience seem to have stripped me of answers.

My life has been what most people would call "successful." I have a respected career. My opinions on this and that are occasionally sought. Sometimes I have been asked to address conventions. I love my wife. I love my children. I live a pleasant life in a pleasant house.

What, then, is the problem?

Fire at night seen through the forms of winter trees.

That is the problem.

You see, what I'm trying to get at, Dennis, is this. They told you all your life, the Wechsler-Bellevue merchants, the teachers, the guardians of culture, and, yes, me, I suppose, that you were wrong, stupid, headed for a bad end. But you had something, *knew* something they didn't. Something *I* didn't. Do you see now why it's so important for me to stress that I'm not romanticizing your life, Dennis, or the lives of the ignorant yobs and louts who were your friends? You can't even begin to grasp how appalling it is for me to attempt to say this. Say what? That my life, respectable, sober, industrious, and civilized, above all civilized, has at its core a desolating emptiness. That, quite simply, you in your stupid, feckless way have enjoyed life more than I have.

I've never escaped, you see, Dennis. I've never lived off hostile country.

Did you burn down houses in Penge? I don't know, can't remember if I invented that. But if you *did*, the blood gorging you with excitement, the smoke, the roar as the whole thing got a grip—I can hardly bring myself to say this, *must* say this—*if* you did, *Christ!* it must have been wonderful.

You don't understand, do you, what it means for me to make these confessions? To *have* to make these confessions, to face the death I feel inside myself?

Let me try to put this in a different way. Let me try to find words that perhaps you'll understand. Words! Understand! Good Christ, will it never end, this blathering!

Dennis. Dennis. Listen!

Dennis, I envy you your—

Christ, man! Out with it!

Dennis. Listen to me.

Concentrate.

Dennis, I wish *I* had a tattoo.

GENTLE AS FLOWERS MAKE THE STONES

Fists, teeth clenched, Jim Haine stood naked and shivering staring at the lighted rectangle. He must have slept through the first knocks, the calling. Even the buzzing of the doorbell had made them nervous; he'd had to wad it up with paper days before. The pounding and shouting continued. The male was beginning to dart through the trails between the *Aponogeton crispus* and the blades of the *Echinodorus martii*.

Above the pounding, words: "pass-key," "furniture," "bailiffs."

Lackey!

Lickspittle!

The female was losing colour rapidly. She'd shaken off the feeding fry and was diving and pancaking through the weed-trails.

Hour after hour he had watched the two fish cleaning one of the blades of a Sword plant, watched their ritual procession, watched the female dotting the pearly eggs in rows up the length of the leaf, the milt-shedding male following; slow, solemn, seeming to move without motion, like carved galleons or bright painted rocking-horses.

The first eggs had turned grey, broken down to flocculent slime; the second hatch, despite copper sulphate and the addition of peat extracts, had simply died.

"I know you're in there, Mr. Haine!"

A renewed burst of door-knob rattling.

He had watched the parents fanning the eggs; watched them stand guard. Nightly, during the hatch, he had watched the parents transport the jelly blobs to new hiding places, watched them spitting the blobs onto the underside of leaves to hang glued and wriggling. He had watched the fry become free-swimming, discover the flat sides of their parents, wriggle and feed there from the mucous secretions.

"Tomorrow . . . hands of our lawyers!"

The shouting and vibration stopped too late.

The frenzied Discus had turned on the fry, snapping, engulfing, beaking through their brood.

A sheet of paper slid beneath the door.

He didn't stay to watch the carnage; the flash of the turning fish, the litter floating across the surface of the tank, the tiny commas drifting towards the suction of the filter's mouth.

He went back into his bedroom and worked himself into the sleeping bag. Four more weeks and they would have lost their tadpole look, growing towards their maturity, becoming disc-shaped.

He studied the All-Island Realties notice. Nasty print. Two months rent: $72.50 per month; $145.00. And two more months before he could apply for the last third of his Arts Bursary. He reached for the largest butt and, staring into the flame of the match, considered his position. A change of abode was indicated. And preferably by evening.

Taking his night-pencil, his Granby Zoo pencil with animal-head pictures, he wrote on the back of the notice *God Rend You, All-Island Realties*. And then doodled. And then found himself writing out again from memory what he had completed the day before.

Into your hands, my father and my mother, I commend
My darling and delight, my little girl,
Lest she be frightened by the sudden dark
Or the terrible teeth of the dog who guards your world.

"Your world" was exactly right. No use in fucking about with "Hades" or "Tartarus."

Parvula ne nigras horrescat Erotion umbras
Oraque Tartarei prodigiosa canis.

"Sudden dark" wasn't bad, either.

There was a sense of rightness, too, in dividing the sentences of the original into stanzas.

The night had produced no advances on stanza two.

She would have been but six cold winters old if she had lived
Even those few days more;

That could stand. But

Inter tam veteres ludat lasciva patronos. . . . "Patronos," that was the bugger. "Protectors" was impossible; "guardians" too custodial. Something grave was needed, grave yet tender.

"veteres patronos"

His pencil worked loops and curlicues on the paper.

The muffled phone in the kitchen rang twice, stopped, rang again. Pulling on his jeans, he went to answer it.

"Jim? It's Jackie, man."

Jackie's voice dropped to a whisper.

"The Desert Express Is In."

"Good shit?" said Jim.

"Up a tree—you know? A real mindfuck, man."

"Far out," said Jim.

"Hey, and that Gold, man. What a taste! Two tokes and you're wasted!"

"Tonight, man," said Jim.

He hung up the phone and sighed.

"veteres patronos"

veteres patronos

His possessions, by design, fitted into two large cardboard cartons. Kettle and mug. Sleeping bag and inflatable mattress. Clothes. One picture. Writing materials. An alarm clock. The few books he had not sold.

He stirred the coffee and Coffeemate together and wandered into the front room. On the table there lay the medium felt pen, the fine, and the fountain pen. Beside them, the three pads of paper, white, yellow, and pale blue, the porcelain ashtray, the square of blotting paper, the Edwardian silver matchbox.

He sat at the table drinking the coffee. He tried to visualize the three stanzas of the completed poem on the page. He'd have to supply a title; and at the end, in brackets, "The poet commends the soul of a pet slave girl to his parents who are already in the lower world. Adapted from Martial. *Epigrams. Book V. 34.*" Less distracting than under the title.

"veteres patronos"

He stared at the aquarium; had only a half of the fry survived— a little half of all his pretty ones—growing to the size of a dime, a quarter, a silver dollar, he could have sold them through Réal to Ideal Import Aquariums for twelve to fifteen dollars each.

With the medium felt pen on white paper he wrote:

Sixty *Symphysodon discus* at a conservative $12.00 = $720.00
Minus $25.00 for the tank
$10.00 for the pump and filter
$30.00 for the breeding fish
$15.00 for weed, tubifex worm, whiteworm, brine shrimp, and *daphnia.*

An inevitable profit of $640.00.
Work was impossible.
He needed money; he needed a place to live.
He began packing his belongings into the two cartons. The $3,500 of his Canada Council grant eroded by child-support payments, eroded by the cling of old habits. He would have to abandon the aquarium and hope that Réal could get it out.
The last of the air from the mattress.
Pevensey!

Pevensey might be good for a $30.00 review. Maybe even $60.00 for a round-up. If he could be trapped. He rolled the mattress and sleeping bag brooding about the toadish Pevensey. Who had promised to review *The Distance Travelled* and lied.

Lack of space, old boy. Hands were tied.

In his Toad-of-Toad's-Hall tweeds and deerstalker.

In his moustache.

Who weekly reviewed *English Formal Gardens of the Eighteenth Century* or *The Rose Grower's Vade Mecum*, toadish Memoirs of endless toadish Generals.

Opening the freezer compartment of the fridge, he took out the perspex map-case which contained his completed poems and work sheets and wiped off the condensation; he kept them there in case of fire.

The kipper and the cardboard cup of Bar-B-Q Sauce he would leave to All-Island Realties as quit claim and compensation.

"Montreal *Herald*," said the girl. "Entertainments."

"Charles Pevensey, please."

"I'm sorry. He's not in this morning."

"Oh. That's strange. I'd understood he's been trying to contact me. Something about the length of my review."

"Oh," said the girl. "I see. Well, he might be in later. If you could call back at about eleven?"

Could one, he wondered, "beard" a toad?

Hefting his Air Canada bag, he stood looking around the bare white room. He'd shift the cartons after nightfall. The picture. The sleeping bag would protect it.

A potato-shape in black crayon. A single red eye near the top. Seven orange sprouts. He'd typed underneath:

"Daddy" by Anna Haine (age 2½)

The newsprint was yellowing, the expensive non-glare glass dusty; the top edge of the frame was furred. He wiped it clean with his forefinger.

Orange arms and legs of course, silly Jim.

He tried to recall the name of the girl who'd got it framed for him. A painter sort of girl. Black hair, he remembered.

Frances?

Sonia?

But it was gone.

The Montreal *Herald* building reared concrete and glass. As he walked along towards the main entrance, past the emporia of used office-furniture, the pawn shops, the slum side streets, he wondered, as he often wondered, why he always had a compulsion to lie about his occupation to the people who gave him lifts; why he claimed to be a professor at McGill, a male nurse, a pest-control officer, a journalist.

The escalator conveyed him to the potted palms of Third Floor Reception, the elevator to the Fourth. Below him on the first and second floors, the giant drums and rollers of the *Herald* presses. He smiled at the memory of a wrench-brandishing Charlie Chaplin swimming through the cogs. He turned down the corridor to Entertainments and pushing through the swing doors, walked up the aisle between the desks to Pevensey's corner. The desk was piled with review copies, a hundred more stacked in the window embrasure behind.

He stood irresolute for a few moments and then went into the pen and sat in Pevensey's chair. The clattering typewriters paid no attention. Opposite, on the other side of the room, he noticed another set of swing doors. Glass portholes. He glanced at the top copy-sheet in the folder; a review of *Heraldry and You*. He took three cigarettes from the open package on the desk.

A tall blonde girl was walking up the aisle, looked about twenty, shoulder bag, shades. Legs too thin. She went into the next pen and dropped her bag on the desk. A plaque on the desk said Youth Beat. Her typewriter cover was dotted with stick-on flowers and butterflies. He felt her staring at him.

"Excuse me, sir."

"Umm?"

"Are you looking for someone?"

"What an attractive pendant!" he said, staring at her breasts.

"Oh, thank you."

He turned back to the file of copy.

"Excuse me . . ."

He did his blank look.

"If you're waiting for Mr. Pevensey, I'm afraid . . ."

"Mr. Pevensey!" called Jim.

A tactical blunder.

Pevensey, what looked like a teapot in his hand, glanced, pushed back through the swing doors, disappeared. Jim hurried after him.

"Mr. Pevensey!" he shouted to the echo of the footsteps on the concrete stairs. He ran down and found himself in an empty corridor facing two doors.

"PEV-EN-SEY."

One door led to the cafeteria, the other to the library. The cafeteria was nearly empty; the library girl claimed not to know who Pevensey was. He walked back up the corridor, past the foot of the stairs, found a washroom. Locking himself into a cubicle, he took the Magic Marker from his Air Canada bag and wrote on the wall:

"Charles Pevensey has a PERSONAL subscription to *Reader's Digest*."

He lowered his trousers and sat.

He needed money.

He needed breakfast.

He needed a place to live.

A downtown breakfast would be more expensive than the Budapest where he usually ate; he liked the Budapest because George, the owner, had gold teeth and always said, "For you, gentlemans?" Today, he decided, would have to be a toast day.

Toast reminded him that it was Monday. He added a note to his list:

Cantor's Bakery 11:30 PM (if poss.).

The woman there sold him Friday's Kaiser rolls for two cents each. He also needed more tins of Brunswick sardines. Holding steady at twenty-nine cents a tin.

Moving upset him. And he was fond of the Victoria Manor Apartments. He would miss the conversations with Mrs. McGregor who gave him milk and who, on the day he'd moved in six months or so ago, had slipped a note under his door which read:

They are all FLQ in this building. Signed:
the Lady Next Door. (Scottish)

And Bernie who ran the FCI Detective Agency on the first floor. He'd miss the stairways which were always jammed with struggling furniture; the conversations with the basement owner of the Harold Quinn School of Music; the showcase outside the Starkman Ortho-pedic Shoe Company which was full of plaster casts of deformed feet.

The rest of the list read:

Call Réal.

Call McCready.

Night of the Jewish Ladies.

Staying with Myrna would be impossible; she'd want to screw all the time which was wasteful and irritating when he was nearing a possible form. Alan was still shacked up with the Bell Telephone girl.

Carol?

He remembered the last time he'd been forced to use her place. No. Not even for a few days could he live in the maelstrom of *her* emotional life. He remembered how, at her last gasp, she'd sobbed a stanza of Sylvia Plath. Nor, come to think of it, could he stomach her brown rice with bits in, wheat germ salad, and other organic filth. And he definitely wasn't inclined to endure lectures on the power of Sisterhood and the glories of multiple clitoral orgasm.

Remembering a glimpse of her naked in the bathroom, one foot on the rim of the tub, thigh, hip, the creases of her waist suffused in morning sunlight. Pure Bonnard stuff. Painter's work. He wondered if she still brushed her teeth with twigs, still washed her hair with honey.

He strained and grunted.

veteres patronos

He was being too literal. Again. He needed to get further from the text. To preserve. Intact. The main line of. Intent. But let. The.

The outer door banged shut; the bolt of the next cubicle slotted home. Checkered trousers rumpled over a pair of brown shoes.

Inter tam veteres ludat lasciva patronos
Et nomen blaeso garriat ore meum.

"Care!" said Jim.
The brown shoes cleared his throat.
Yes.
Expand it.

She would have been but six cold winters old if she had lived
Even those few days more; so let her walk
And run a child still in your elder care

"You beautiful, *inevitable* bastard!" said Jim.
"Are you okay?" said the brown shoes.
"What?"

———————

Breakfasted on toast and coffee (twenty-five cents) now 12:35 and his guts hollow. Used the counter phone. Professor McCready was teaching; would he care to leave a message? The white globes above the length of the counter reminded him of a night scene. A café. A woman singing. Degas? Renoir?

Just beyond, in that place between night and twilight, not to be pried at, not to be forced, the words were moving in his head.

He walked up towards Dorchester and the Queen Elizabeth Hotel weighing his chances in the lottery of grant renewal. His other two references were certain to be good. He'd sent McCready a Xerox of the central poems of *Marriage Suite* now nine days ago along with the Letter of Reference form. Sixteen days to the deadline.

He strolled into the foyer of the Queen Elizabeth and wandered around looking for the notice board. Conventions, Annual Meetings, Associations of. Sometimes, wearing shirt and tie, under buffet conditions, it was possible to lunch or dine with Travel Agents, Furniture Retailers, Pharmaceutical Sales.

In the hardcover Classic Book Store on St. Catherine Street, he checked the number of copies of *The Distance Travelled*, arranged them more advantageously. He was classified under "Canadiana" and surrounded by Esquimaux and whales.

He strolled back on the other side of the street to the paperback store and browsed through the literary magazines, off-set and mimeo, looking for work by his contemporaries. *Edifice, Now, Ssip*, another new thing from Vancouver called *Up Yours*.

He walked up to the Sheraton and consulted the notice board; looked in at Mansfield Book Mart; checked the Sonesta Hotel.

The same girl answered the phone again. Professor McCready had just left for the day; would he care to leave a message?

Ten cents.

He copied down McCready's home number from the directory.

Academe—Intercede for us

Standing closed in the phone booth, he stared out at the flow of cars along Sherbrooke.

Jury of Experts—Compassionately Adjudicate us

Significance of Past Contribution—Justify us

Selling the drugs for Jackie would probably bring him $40.00 or $50.00 but he resented the waste of time, the endless phone calls.

The Desert Express Is In.

Poor glazed bastard.

He wondered what peyote looked like; what one *did* with it? Smoked it? Made an infusion? Ate it? He went back towards Classics to find out. For all he cared, they could stuff it up their collective fundament. As he walked along, he constructed arguments:

Look, man. You've dropped acid. You've done chemicals. Okay. But this is pure, it's like ORGANIC.

Or, for the carriage trade,

It's like acid, but SMOOTH. It's the difference between a bottle of Brights and a bottle of wine.

In Classics he gleaned the necessary sales information.

You ate it.

Devotees of the cactus cult are said to be "following the Peyote Road"—he copied the expression into his notebook. The practice had spread from Mexico to the Kiowa, Comanche, and Apache Indians. Ingestion put one in touch with *mana*—the LIFE FORCE. Introspection resulted. Visions of God, Jesus, and those on the Other Side were vouchsafed.

The prospect of being forced to stay with Jackie was depressing. In the gloom of obligatory candles he would have to listen to the latest fragment of Jackie's novel—the action of which all took place in Jackie's head during a seven hour freak-out on top of Mount Royal and involved him in varieties of Cosmic Union with stars, planets, and a bi-sexual Cree Guide called Big Bear.

And he, in turn, would have to pay tribute by giving Jackie a copy of his latest verse. He'd already chopped *Howl* into tiny sections. He considered Gerard Manley Hopkins.

O the mind
         MIND
has mountains
         cliffs
         of
         fall
         SHEER
nomanfathomed.

It's like a lyric, man. They write themselves.
He resolved to call Carol.

For an hour or more, he stood watching the work on a construction site on Dorchester. He watched the tamping of the dynamite in the rock, watched the crane swing the coir nets and matting into place, waited for the dull *crump* and the heave of the matting and then the buckets grubbing out the boulders and the scree. He could feel the words edging closer. He watched until he no longer saw the yellow helmets, the clanking bulldozers, the trucks churning up the muddy slope, until his eyes grew unfocused.

The end of the afternoon was growing cold. The words hurried him across the approach of the Place du Canada where the wind was clacking the wire halyards against the aluminum flagpoles.

He found an empty table at the back of the Steerarama and sat warming his hands on the coffee cup. Shapes of figures passing beyond the net-curtained windows. Light on the chrome of the cash register. A sheen of light across the polished lino below the cash register, a green square, a red square, part of a green square before the carpet edge.

Et nomen blaeso garriat ore meum.

The horns were long, buffed and lacquered, the colours running from grey through beige to jet at the points. From the astrakhan middle where the horns were joined hung a card which read:

Our "Famous" Steerburger (6 oz. of Prime Beef)

As he tilted his head, the light ran the horns' curved length.

blaeso garriat demanded "lisping," "stammering."

The gloss had given him: "And lisp my name with stammering tongue."

Which made the child sound like a cross between a half-wit and Shirley Temple.

"lisping"

"prattle"

"babble"

He stared at the cinnamon Danish in the glass case on the counter. But the Night of the Jewish Ladies had promised refreshments.

Although a bending of the text, a real distortion of meaning even, and swaying on a tightrope over sentimentality, "baby talk" might.

Might.

If it was somehow balanced off.

He smoothed the paper place mat with the edge of his hand and sat staring at the drawing of the smiling waitress.

Bienvenue

He gave her spectacles, a moustache, gaps in her teeth. Suddenly he started to write.

> *She would have been but six cold winters old if she had lived*
> *Even those few days more; so let her walk*
> *And run a child still in your elder care*
> *And safely play, and tease you with my name in baby talk.*

Nodding at what he'd written, he stretched and leaned back. Everything depended now on the resolution of the final stanza. Blondin poised over Niagara had little on this. Lips working, he read the lines through again and again.

Precarious.

The *ands* repetition wasn't bad, wasn't *too* obtrusive in its suggestion of the child. But it was the tension in "tease"; it was only "tease" and its implications that were keeping him aloft.

He found that he was gazing at the cinnamon Danish; he wanted the cinnamon Danish very much. He could feel the pressure of the final stanza, the bulge and push of it in his head. The hunger had turned to hollow pain. Half an hour to his meeting Mrs. Wise on the mezzanine in her russet linen pant suit and carrying a copy of the Montreal *Herald*. A group of young wives, she'd said, meeting in each other's houses, quite informally, to discuss, to listen to speakers, to be stimulated, to broaden horizons.

Now you mustn't be modest, Mr. Haine. Quite a few of the girls saw your photograph and the piece about you in the Gazette.

He hoped they'd pay him the $25.00 after the reading and not at some polite interval; he hoped it was sandwiches and not cakes. Sandwiches with meat in.

Or egg.

Or cheese.

He felt an urge to delete the inverted commas on the *Our "Famous" Steerburger* sign with his Magic Marker.

He hoped that payment would be made in cash.

The last time had been cakes.

Seventeen members of the Canadian Authors' Association had gathered in a salon of the Laurentian Hotel. The president had asked everyone to stand one after another to announce their names. Most were hyphenated ladies.

Against their rising conversation, he had read from *The Distance Travelled*. During the last two poems a waiter had wheeled in a trolley of iced cakes and an urn of coffee.

The president, a large lady, had called the meeting to order.

When he'd finished reading, sudden silence ensued.

Answering the president's call for questions, a lady with aggressive orange hair had said:

"Am I right in assuming you've had your work published?"

"Ah, yes."

"And you didn't pay for it?"

"Pay for it?"

"To have it published."

"Oh. No."

"Well, my question is—who do you know?"

"Know?"

"In Toronto."

———

Alone in the cream and gold sitting room, he examined the mantelpiece with its tiny fluted columns, shelves, alcoves, its three inset oval mirrors. He examined the silver-framed bride and groom. He examined the Royal Doulton lady in her windblown crinolines, the knicknacks, the small copper frying-pan-looking thing that said *A Gift from Jerusalem*, the Royal reclining Doulton lady. Glancing round at the open door, he turned back and peered into the centre mirror to see if hairs were sticking out of his nose.

He sank for a few minutes into the gold plush settee.

The doorbell kept ringing; the litany continued.

Bernice! It's beautiful!

We only finished moving in three weeks ago.

The pair of brass lamps which flanked the settee were in the form of huge pineapples. He touched the prickly brass leaves. The lamp-shades were covered in plastic. On the long table at the far end of the room, a white tablecloth covered food; he stared at the stacked plates and cups and saucers, at the tablecloth's mysterious humps and hollows. He took a cigarette from the silver box. Which of the little things on the occasional tables, he wondered, were ashtrays? Each time the front door opened, the chandelier above him tinkled.

Oh, Bernice! And quarry-tile in the kitchen, too!

Would you like the tour?

And as the tramplings went upstairs, faintly:

master-bedroom . . .

cedar-lined . . .

A plump woman wandered in. He nodded and smiled at her. She hesitated in the doorway staring at him. The green Chinese lady gazed from her gilt frame. The plump woman went around the other end of the settee and stood fingering the drapes. He tried to remember the painter's name; Tetchi, Tretchisomething—a name that sounded vaguely like a disease.

"Are you the poet?" said the plump woman.

"Yes, that's right."

He smiled.

"We had a nudist last week," she said.

———————

Panty-hose. Stocking-top. The whites of their thighs.

Seated in the centre of the room on the footstool provided, he read to the assembled ladies. He read from his first Ryerson chapbook.

He read his Dylan orotundities:
In a once more summer time than this.
His Auden atrocities:
Love, now, like light.
He read for forty minutes, giving them Nature, Time, and Love.
The pièce de résistance proved to be lox.

With rye bread. And cream cheese. Salami. Half-sours. Parma ham. Lima bean salad with mint. Devilled eggs and sculptured radishes. The cheese-board afforded Limburger, Gouda, Cheddar, Danish Blue, Feta, and Gruyère.

Are poets different than other people?
Salami.
. . . or do you wait for inspiration?
Potato salad.
"No, of course not. It's my pleasure. For . . . ?"
"Bernice."
Jenny. Helen. Shirley. Joan. Ruby.
WITH BEST WISHES.
Nine Distance Travelled *at $6.00 (Author's Discount $2.00 = $18.00 Profit).*
"Well, I don't want to sound pompous, but I suppose you'd call it vision."
Radish.
"Pardon?"
". . . was wondering if Bernice had arranged a lift downtown for you? Because I'm leaving soon if you'd like a ride?"

"Over there," she said, as they crunched across the gravel. "What my dear husband calls 'the Kraut bucket'."

He wondered how old she was. Thirty-five. Expensively styled black hair. A year or two more maybe. Her strained skirt rode higher as they slammed the doors. He glanced at the nylon gleam of her thighs. She seemed unconcerned.

"Cigarette?" she said.

He leaned towards the flame. Her perfume was heavy in the car.

She blew out smoke in a long sigh.

"I liked your poems," she said.

"Thank you."

"I'm not just saying that. I thought they were really good."

"I really appreciate that."

"You're very polite—a very polite person, aren't you?"

She turned the key and roared the motor.

"What makes you say that?" he said.

She shrugged.

"Nothing."

As they turned out of the drive, she said, "How do you stand it?"

"Stand what?"

"Oh, for Christ's sake!" she said.

He stared at her profile.

"Why do you go then?" he said.

"Stand *what!*" she said.

"What the hell did you expect me to say?"

She shrugged and then crushed the cigarette into the ashtray.

"Are you married?"

"No," he said. "Why?"

She turned onto the access road to the Trans-Canada.

"Kids," she said. "My dear husband's dinners. Even Bernice Wise is a vacation."

She snapped on the radio.

They settled into the drive back from Pointe Claire. She drove with angry concentration. The nylon sheen of her thighs green in the glow from the radio dial. The winding and unwinding notes of a harpsichord, the intricate figurings, absolved him from conversation. Mesmeric the rise and fall of headlights, the steady bore of the engine, the weaving patterns of the lanes of traffic; mesmeric the play of light and shadow, the approach and fall of overpasses, the rush of concrete void. The heater was making him drowsy. The words were drifting. Her gloved hand moved on the gear-shift.

Trying to break free, the swell of words lifting and stirring like pan ice.

Mollia non rigidus caespes tegat ossa, nec illi,
Terra, gravis fueris: non fuit illa tibi.

The final movement of the poem, dear ladies, changing direction, *terra*, changing direction, *terra* in the vocative.

All, all, dear ladies, a question of balance.

"rigidus caespes"

"Sod" was ludicrous; he toyed with "rock," "turf," and "stones." He was being trapped into the literal again; the morning at the Montreal *Herald* was repeating itself.

"Charles Pevensey has a PERSONAL subscription to *Reader's Digest.*"

Pleasing.

There was something about the toadlike Pevensey that had been working on his mind all day. An echo of the name's sound. *Epitaph on Salomon Pavy.* Because it was an echo too, he knew, of Ben Jonson. *Epitaph on Elizabeth L.H.*

Pevensey. Pevensey.

Penshurst.

COUPLETS.

It needed couplets. *That* was the connection. The bastard needed couplets. He sat up and patted his pockets, finding a pencil stub in his shirt. His pad was in the Air Canada bag on the back seat. Removing the cigarettes from his package, wrapping them in the silver paper.

"Yes, please," she said.

"What? Oh, sorry."

"Will you light me one?"

As she took it from him, she said, "I'm sorry I was bitchy before."

"That's okay."

"Just one of those days," she said.

He spread the inner part of the packet on his knee and started to write, then scribbled over the words.

The car stopping and starting now. Neon signs. Salada Tea. Traffic lights. Uniroyal Tire.

They turned south onto Decarie heading downtown. Past the first of the restaurants.

"Mr. Haine?"

She glanced in the rear mirror and then smiled at him.

"If you want to write it down," she said.

"What?"

"It's 743-6981."

Gentle as flowers . . . he wrote.

"And if a man answers?"

She laughed.

Gentle as flowers make the stones

She pulled into the right-hand lane and took the exit to Queen Mary Road.

"You know something?" she said.

He grunted enquiry, crossing through a word he'd written.

"You've got a cruel mouth. I bet a lot of women have told you that."

"Me, cruel? I'm nice," he said.

"James Haine," she said. "Does anyone call you 'James'?"

"No. Nor Jimmy."

Dare he use "comfort"?

"Actually," she said, "my name isn't Rena. Well, it *is*, but my friends call me Midge."

"Midge?"

"Short for Midgicovsky—from school."

"That's a nice name," he said. "I like that."

"And you *have* got a cruel mouth."

"Oh, Grandmama!"

"What's that meant to mean?"

A girl's name—two syllables.

"You're making me sound like the Big Bad Wolf."

"*What?*"

"You know. All the better to bite you with sort of stuff."

She laughed.

"Well, you *have*," she said. "And anyway, you don't hear me screaming for help."

That comfort . . .

"Anyway, I like it," she said. "You're different."

He glanced at the Duc de Lorraine bakery as they turned onto Côte des Neiges. He used to buy warm croissants there in his richer days. Surprise her with coffee, cognac, croissants. After writing all night, walking up in the early morning with the dog before she was awake.

Two syllables.

She braked and changed lanes.

Gentle as flowers make the stones
That comfort Liza's tender bones.

Turning off Côte des Neiges, she took the road leading up to the Mountain.

"It's so beautiful up here at night," she said. "You don't mind, do you? I always come this way on the way home."

On the left the cemetery spreading up the slope for acres behind the black railings; mausoleums, statues, crosses, the dull glimmer of the endless rows of polished marble headstones.

Past Beaver Lake. On to the summit.

She parked the car at the Mount Royal Lookout, silence settling as they gazed over the lights of the city. A ghostly wedge from the revolving sweep of the searchlight on top of Place Ville Marie shone against the cloudbank to their left, shone, disappeared, shone.

"I never get tired of this view," she said.

He nodded.

She sighed.

"Jim?"

As he turned, she stretched across, her arms reaching out for him. She kissed his chin, the corner of his mouth, found his lips. Twisting towards her in the awkwardness of the seat, the gear-shift, he put his arms round her, one hand on a breast.

"Hold me," she whispered.

His back was hurting.

Her mouth was hot and open. Squirming, she reached up and unhooked her brassiere. After a few moments, she pushed her face into his neck.

"That's the sad thing about getting old," she said, her breath hot and moist on his flesh, "having your breasts fall."

"Not old," he mumbled.

She kissed him open-mouthed, then biting gently at his lower lip. She was breathing heavily.

"Get in the back," she whispered.

As they kissed again, her legs were stirring restlessly. His hand moved over nylon. She lifted herself, pulling up her skirt. She stretched out one leg and drew the other up, gasped as his fingers found her.

"We can't," she whispered. "We mustn't."

Her breathing was throaty.

"I'm off the pill and I haven't got anything with me."

His fingers were moving.

"You don't mind?"

She moved her bottom further off the edge of the seat; she was gripping his other arm and making noises.

The side of his face was sweaty against the shiny plastic upholstery.

She was arching, arching herself towards him.

Suddenly her body went rigid and she clamped his hand still. They lay quiet, the rate of her breathing slowing. Her eyes were closed; her face slack. He watched the sweep of the searchlight against the cloudbank.

Lie lightly, Earth . . .

No.

After a minute or so, she moved her legs, easing herself up.

"Mmmm," she sighed.

She pushed him towards the other side. Her hands undoing his belt buckle, she whispered, "Go on, lie back." She was pushing up his shirt. She lay with her cheek against his stomach and then he felt the heat of her mouth on him. Her hand moving too.

Her hair was stiff, lacquered.

He grunted and she moved her head; sperm pumped onto his stomach.

They lay in silence.

He could feel the sperm getting cold, running down his side, cold on his hip.

"There's some Kleenex in my purse," she said.

She wiped his thigh and stomach, and pulling down his shirt, snuggled up against him, kissing his mouth, his chin, his neck. He stroked her shoulders, back, running his hand down to her buttocks and up again. She pulled herself higher until her cheek was against his.

"Was it good for you, too?" she whispered.

"Mmm."

He felt a mounting excitement.

All, all, dear ladies, a question of balance.

And he'd found it.

His balancing pole, as it were, commas.

COMMAS

No risk of falling now; no staggering run up the incline of a sagging rope.

Earth COMMA *lie lightly on her* COMMA *who* COMMA *Living* COMMA *scarcely burdened you.*

Tears were welling in his half-shut eyes, the lights of the city lancing gold and silver along his wet lashes, the poem perfect.

Gentle as flowers make the stones
That comfort Liza's tender bones.
Earth, lie lightly on her, who,
Living, scarcely burdened you.

Feeling his hot tears on her cheek, she lifted her head to look at him.

"You're crying," she whispered. "Don't cry."
She brushed the backs of her fingers against his cheek.
"Jim?"
He stirred, shifting himself of some of her weight.
"Jim?"
She nestled against him.
"You know something?" she said. "You're very sweet."

THE YEARS IN EXILE

Although it is comfortable, I do not like this chair. I do not like its aluminum and plastic. The aluminum corrodes, leaving a roughness on the arms and legs like white rust or fungus. I liked the chairs stacked in the summer house when I was ten, deckchairs made of striped canvas and wood. But I am an old man; I am allowed to be crotchety.

By the side of my chair in the border are some blue and white petunias. They remind me, though the shade is different, of my youngest grandson's blue and white running shoes, Adidas I believe he calls them. They are one of this year's fads. He wears them to classes at the so-called college he attends. But I must not get excited.

It is one of her days. The voice of the vacuum cleaner is heard in the land. But I should not complain. I have my room, my personal things, the few books I still care to have about me. Before moving here, life was becoming difficult; the long hill up to the shopping centre for supplies I neither wished to cook nor eat, sheets, the silence broken only by the hum and shudder of the fridge.

Strange that this daughter of my first marriage, a child of whom I saw so little, should be the one who urged this home upon me. Or not so strange perhaps. I am old enough to know that we do not know what needs compel us.

The cartons were mentioned again this morning, those in my room and those in the basement. She calls them "clutter," and perhaps she is right. The papers are promised to Queen's University but I cannot bring myself to sort through years of manuscript and letters from dead friends. Much of the order of things I couldn't remember and it is a task which smacks too much of some finality.

I am supposed to be resting today, for this evening a man is coming to interview me for some literary journal or review. Or was it a thesis? I forget. They come quite often, young men with tape-recorders and notebooks. They talk of my novels and stories, ascribe influences I have never read, read criticism to me. I nod and comment if I understand them. I am not an intellectual; I am not even particularly intelligent. I am content to sit in my aluminum chair and stare at the weeping-willow tree in the next-door garden.

I have lived in Canada for sixty-one years covered now with honours yet in my reveries the last half century fades, the books, the marriages, the children, and the friends. I find myself dwelling more and more on my childhood years in England, the years when I was nine and ten. My mind is full of pictures.

My sleeplessness, the insistence of the pictures, are familiar signs. Were I younger, I would be making notes and outlines, drinking midnight coffee. But I will not write again. I am too old and tire too easily; I no longer have the strength to face the struggle with language, the loneliness, the certainty of failure.

I remember my own grandfather. I wonder if I seem to Mary and her children as remote as he appeared to me, talking to himself, conducting barely audible arguments in two voices, dozing, his crossed leg constantly jiggling, the dottle from his dead pipe falling down his cardigan front.

I remember the bone-handled clasp-knife, its blade a thin hook from years of sharpening. I can see his old hands slicing the rope of black twist into tiny discs, rubbing them, funnelling the prepared tobacco from the newspaper on his lap into his wooden box which stood on the mantelpiece. The mantelpiece had a velvet fringe along its edge with little velvet bobbles hanging down at two-inch intervals. I can see his old hands replacing the gauze mantle in the gas lamp, the white-yellow incandescence of the light.

Many might dismiss such meaningless particulars of memory.

I know that I am lost in silence hours on end, dwelling on another time now more real to me than this chair, more real than the sunshine filtering through the fawn and green of the willow tree.

Summerfield, Hengistbury Head, Christchurch, with their rivers, the Avon and the Stour, and always central in my dream and reverie, the spoiled mansion, Fortnell House. Were I younger, I would attempt to frame its insistence.

Fortnell House.

A short story could not encompass it; it has the weight and feel about it of a novella. But the time for such considerations is past.

I have not read much in late years; I lack the patience. But of the younger writers I have read Cary. Thinking of my rivers, my Headland and estuary, the bulk of my great grey Priory above the salt marsh, I looked again not a week since at a remembered passage in his novel *To Be a Pilgrim*. Old Wilcher speaking. It has stayed in my mind:

> The English summer weighs upon me with its richness. I know why Robert ran away from so much history to the new lands where the weather is as stupid as the trees, chance dropped, are meaningless. Where earth is only new dirt, and corn, food for animals two and four-footed. I must go, too, for life's sake. This place is so doused in memory that only to breathe makes me dream like an opium eater. Like one who has taken a narcotic, I have lived among fantastic loves and purposes. The shape of a field, the turn of a lane, have had the power to move me as if they were my children, and I had made them. I have wished immortal life for them, though they were even more transient appearances than human beings.

I, too, have thought myself a pilgrim.

In the summer, dilapidated farmhouses in the Eastern Townships; in the winter, Montreal's cold-water flats. My mother's letters to me when I was young, how they amused yet rankled: "living like a gypsy," "a man of your age," "not a stick of furniture to your name." My early books returned. All so many years ago.

A blue night-light burns on my bedside table. Mary put it there in case I have need of the pills and bottles which crowd the table-top, Milk of Magnesia, sedatives, digitalis, the inhaler, the glycerine capsules.

Yes, I have thought myself a pilgrim, the books my milestones. But these recent weeks, the images that haunt my nights and days . . .

I have seen the holy places though I never knew it. I have travelled on, not knowing all my life that the mecca of my pilgrimage had been reached so young, and that all after was the homeward journey.

Fortnell House.

The curve of the weed-grown drive, the rank laurels, the plaster-fallen crumbling portico. Lower windows blind and boarded.

I read once in a travel book of an African tribe, the Dogon, famed for their masks and ancestor figures. They live, if I remember aright, south of Timbuctu under the curve of the Niger. Their masks and carvings are a part of their burial rites; the carvings offer a fixed abode for spirits liberated by death. The figures are placed in caves and fissures where the termites soon attack the wood and the weather erodes.

I have seen such weathered figures in museums.

I stare at my wrist as it lies along the aluminum arm of the chair, the blue veins. The left side of the wrist might be the river Avon and its estuary, the right side the sea. And then my fist, the bulge of the Headland.

Away from the Southbourne beach, away from the sand, the bathers, and the beach games onto the five miles of crunching pebbles towards Hengistbury Head. Scavenging, I followed the line of sea-wrack, the tangles and heaps of seaware, kelp, and bladderwrack. In my knapsack I carried sandwiches, pillboxes for rare shells, and a hammer.

Sometimes among the tarred rope and driftwood branches, the broken crates, the cracked crab shells, and hollowed bodies of birds, were great baulks of timber covered with goose barnacles stinking in the sun. Scattered above and below the seaweed were the shells, limpet, mussel, periwinkle, whelk and cockle, painted top and piddock. Razor shells. The white shields of cuttlefish, whelks' egg cases like coarse sponge, mermaids' purses.

At low tide, the expanse of firm wet sand would shine in the sun, the silver smoothness broken only by the casts of lugworms.

The halfway point of my journey was marked by The Rocks. I always thought of them as a fossilized monster, the bulk of its body on the beach, its lower vertebrae and tail disappearing into the sea. The rocks in the sea were in a straight line, water between them, smaller and smaller, and almost invariably on the last black rock stood a cormorant.

I always liked the cormorant's solitary state. As I climbed up the rocks, it would usually void in a flash of white and fly off low over the water. My favourite birds were ravens; they nested on the Headland strutting on the turf near the dangerous cliff edge. Cormorant in Latin means "sea raven." I liked the sound of that; it might have been a name for Vikings.

I climbed among the rocks looking in the rock pools where small green crabs scuttled and squishy sea anemones closed their flowered mouths at a touch. I usually rested in the shadow of the rocks and used my hammer on the larger pebbles, often those with a yellowish area of discolouration; they broke more easily. I sometimes found inside the fossils of sea-urchins. I dug, too, at the cliff face dreaming of finding the imprint of some great fish.

Two or three miles past The Rocks I scrambled up where the cliff dipped to perhaps twenty feet before beginning its great rise to the Headland. At this point the Double Dykes met the cliff edge. The Dykes ran across the wrist of land to the estuary on the other side. They were Iron Age earthworks designed to cut the Headland off from attack by land, built presumably by the people whose barrows still rose above the turf and heather high up on the hill. They were perhaps twelve or fifteen feet high from their ditch, still a struggle up slippery turf to gain the other side.

They must have been much higher 2,000 years ago but were eroded now by time and rabbits; they formed a huge warren and the fresh sandy diggings were visible everywhere. The land beyond the Dykes was low on the estuary side and rose to 180 feet at the point of the Headland. On the estuary side there were woods and pools and marsh and then, as the land rose, short turf, bracken, and heather.

At the far end of the Dykes, the estuary end, stood the keeper's cottage. Mr. Taylor was of uncertain temper and had a collie with one eye, and ferrets, and an adder just over three feet long pickled in alcohol. On his good days he showed me the adder or gave me owl pellets; once he let me help with the ferrets.

Before going along the curve of the estuary into the woods, it was part of my ritual to climb the height of the land and sit beside the larger of the two burial mounds to eat my sandwiches. The Headland behind the Dykes had been a camp for many peoples. Before the legions arrived, some British king or chieftain had even established a mint here. Later, the Vikings, penetrating up the Avon and Stour, had used the Headland as a base camp. Although I knew that the larger barrow was of the Iron Age, or even earlier, I preferred to connect it with Hengist and Horsa, legendary leaders of the first Anglo-Saxon settlers in Britain. According to Bede, Hengist and his son Aesc landed and eventually reigned in far-away Kent. But for me, Hengistbury Head was Hengist's fort and I imagined inside the larger mound the war-leader's huge skeleton lying with his accoutrements. An axe and shield, a sword, spears, and his horned helmet. I knew that he was huge because I had read in the encyclopedia that Hengist was probably a personal name meaning "stallion." I gave alliterative names to his weapons.

"Bone-Biter" was one, I seem to remember.

I always poured a trickle of lemonade, wishing I had wine.

This was my Valley of the Kings.

Sitting by the burial mound I looked out over the estuary. It curved in at both sides where it met the sea, a narrow run of water between two spits of beach, the salmon run, and then white breakers beyond. On the far side of the estuary mouth was the village of Mudeford, eight or nine houses, one painted black. It was called, simply, The Black House, and in the eighteenth century had been a meeting place for smugglers. It had once been an inn, I believe, but now served teas to summer visitors.

I used to imagine moonless nights, a lugger standing off, the rowing boats grating up the shingle. The brandy, wine, and lace were taken by the winding paths across the saltings to Christchurch where it was rumoured they were hidden in a false tomb in the Priory graveyard.

Across the estuary sailed and tacked the white yachts like toys but at Mudeford the fishermen netted the salmon run or put out to sea with lobster pots. Although the run was less than fifty yards across there was no way of getting over and Mudeford could only be approached from the Christchurch side. I used to walk to Christchurch sometimes and then set out for Mudeford at low tide across the saltings, jumping from tussock to tussock, always getting plastered with mud. The knowledge of the paths was lost or they had eroded with the shifting tides. Sometimes I imagined myself a smuggler, sometimes a revenuer, but after I got the cutlass with its brass guard and Tower of London stamp near the hilt from Fortnell House I was always an excise man.

Behind Mr. Taylor's thatched cottage, on a triangular patch of land between the back of the house and a shed, there grew teazles. After the death of the purple flowers, the brown, spiky teazles stood tall and dry in the autumn. Every autumn I cut teazles for my mother. They stood in the Chinese dragon vase in the hall.

I often wondered if they were chance-sewn behind the house so thickly, or if for centuries the cottage people had grown them specially to card and comb the wool from sheep they grazed on the Headland.

I can still remember the maps I used to draw marking the cottage and the teazle patch, the burial mounds and Dykes, the wood, the estuary and salmon run, The Black House, dotted lines marking the smugglers' routes across the saltings, Christchurch Priory and the

river Avon in its tidal reaches to Wick Ferry, the nesting sites of
the ravens.

I can see those childish maps now as clearly as I see the petunias
by my chair or the willow in the next-door garden. I can remember
the names I gave to various areas: "The Heron-Sedge," "Badger's
Sett," "Lily-Pad Pond," "Honeysuckle Valley."

Dear God. I can smell the honeysuckle!

A pair of Monarchs chasing each other about the leaves of the apple
tree; the lawn is strewn with fresh windfalls. The sun is higher now.
The Monarchs will not find milkweed in this garden. Will you, my
beauties? No weeds here for you. Robert doesn't like weeds. Roots
them out. Weed-killer and trowel.

Were it my garden, I would sow it thick with milkweed so that
you would always grace me with your presence.

The windfalls surprise me; Robert will doubtless gather them this
evening. He has an oblong wooden basket of woven strips, cotton
gloves, a pair of secateurs. He does not know that such a basket is
called a "trug."

I hug the word to myself.

Earlier, Mary brought me lemonade. My bladder will not hold
liquid as it once did. I have to suffer the indignity of struggling from
this reclining chair like a wounded thing to go indoors to the lavatory.
She's still vacuuming, now upstairs. It is cool and dim in the bathroom. I urinate without control and when I have finished and zipped
up my trousers, I can feel a dribble of urine wetting my underpants.

I wonder if my room smells, if I smell? I often remarked it in old
people when I was younger. I can remember still the smell of my
grandmother. Thank God I will never know. I can, at least, still bathe
without assistance though she insists I do not lock the door. Some I
remember smelled medicinal, some of mothballs, some just a musti-
ness. I have not shaved today. I must remember to shave before
evening for the young man is coming to ask me questions.

The cushion for the small of my back.

The Monarchs have disappeared in search of ground less disciplined.

I have always disliked Wordsworth. Once, I must admit, I thought I disliked him for his bathos, his lugubrious tone. But now I know that it is because he could not do justice to the truth; no philosophical cast of mind can do justice to particularity.

I am uncomfortable with abstraction, his *or* mine.

I stood one morning in the fierce heat by the Lily-Pad Pond. Two frogs were croaking and then stopped. A dragonfly hovered and darted, blue sheen of its wings. Then I, too, heard it. The continuous slither of a snake moving through dead grass and sedge at the pond's edge. I knew, being by water, that it would be a grass snake. I stood rooted, staring at the yellow flags where the faint sound seemed to be coming from.

I had caught grass snakes and adders by the dozen, yet for unknown reasons felt upon me again that awful sense of intrusion, that feeling of holy terror. I stood waiting to see the snake curve into the water and swim sinuous through the lily pads, its head reared. But nothing happened. The snake did not move again. I stepped away backwards from the margin of the pond, placing my feet silently until I was at a distance to turn and walk downhill towards the wider sky and the open light of the estuary.

Again.

In the valley of the honeysuckle it was full noon; the bordering wood was dim. As I stepped into the wood's overgrown darkness, over a fallen tree and brushing aside some saplings, the air suddenly moved and above my head was a great shape. I never knew what it was. I was afraid to turn. I felt my hair ruffle in its wind.

A holiday in Dorset in my tenth year in the Purbeck Hills outside the haven of Poole. The cottage was called "Four Winds," I remember, and in the garden stood a sundial. I remember the collection of Marble Whites and variants I was netting. I went out every day with net and cyanide jar, happy to wander for hours along the cliff path and across fields.

The fields were separated by dry-stone walls and where stones had fallen I pulled them up from the gripping turf in search of slow worms. I carried the slow worms inside my shirt and kept them in a large box in the cottage garden.

One day I prised up a large stone by its corner. The earth beneath was black. A few white threads of roots. Three bright red ants. And there lay the largest slow worm I had ever seen. It was over twelve inches long, strangely dark on its back, almost black, and fat. It was as fat as two of my fingers together. It started to move. Its belly was fawn. I was filled with terror. It started to burrow into the grass roots surrounding the oblong of black earth, the length of its body slowly disappearing.

The sky was blue, the wind blowing over the grass from the sea. I knew I had seen the slow worm king. Filled with an enormous guilt, I ran from the place, my heart pounding, the killing-jar thumping against my back in the knapsack. I ran for three fields before the terror quieted and I remember then sitting on a pile of rocks emptying out the limp, closed Marble Whites from the cyanide jar; I remember the greenish veins of the underside of their wings as they lay scattered on the grasses.

Mary has brought me a tuna sandwich and a peeled apple cut into slices and has moved my chair back into the sun. She is still wearing a headscarf ready to attack another part of the house. As I eat the sandwich, I crave for all the things I am forbidden—cucumber, strong cheese, radishes, tomatoes in vinegar. Pork. Especially pork. I cannot abide this blandness. Like an old circus lion with worn down teeth.

Mounting the centre box, cuffing at the trainer.

Words on paper. Words on paper.

With my chair in this position I can see her through the kitchen window. The hair pulled back, framed in the scarf, the shape of her face seems to change; she has, surprisingly, my looks about her.

I always wanted to own a piece of land so that the children could grow up in the country or visit me in a place they could make their own. True, we lived in a variety of rural slums during the summers, but the children were always too young to begin to learn and appropriate things and place. It was only in the city I could hawk my largely unwanted talents. Hand to mouth for so many years as the books and dry times bore on, the struggle to make ends meet thwarted me. And by the time I could have afforded land, the time and the children were gone.

I have spent so many hours dreaming of that place. A stream running over rocks sweeping into deep, silent trout pools. Honeysuckle in the evenings. Near the house, clumps of brambles which in the late summer would be heavy with blackberries. A barn filled with hay for the children to run and jump in, sunlight filtering in through broken boards, swimming down in shafts of dust-motes.

I can hear their voices calling.

Would they, too, have made maps with magical names?

Once I felt bitter.

A memory of Mrs. Rosen fills my mind. She is sitting on a park bench holding a grey poodle on her lap and gazing across the baseball field.

I worked for Mr. Rosen for over five years. I taught English in the mornings in his private school trying to drill the rudiments into dense and wealthy heads and toiled over my typewriter in the afternoons and on into the early evening.

He is now long dead.

Rosen College Preparatory High School occupied five rooms on the floor above the Chateau Bar-B-Q Restaurant and Take-Out Service. There were three classrooms, the Library, the supplies locker, and the Office. The staff was all part-time and so in my five years I came to know only the morning shift—Geography, Mathematics, and Science. At recess, the four of us would huddle in the supplies locker and make coffee.

Mr. Kapoor was a reserved and melancholy hypochondriac from New Delhi who habitually wore black suits and shoes, a white shirt, and striped college tie. His only concession to summer was that he wore the gleaming shoes without socks. I remember his telling me one day that peahens became fertilized by raising their tail feathers during a rain storm; he held earnestly to this, telling me that it was indeed so because his grandmother had told him, she having seen it with her own eyes in Delhi. He taught Science in all grades.

Mr. Gingley was a retired accountant who taught Mathematics and wore a curiously pink hearing aid which was shaped like a fat human ear.

Mr. Helwig Syllm, the Geography teacher, was an ex-masseur.

Mrs. Rosen, who drew salaries as secretary, teacher, and School Nurse, would sometimes grip one by the arm in the hall and hiss: "Don't foment. My husband can fire anyone. *Anyone.*"

Exercising my dog one morning some three years or more after Mr. Rosen's death and some five years after I'd left the school, I saw his widow in the park. Bundled in an astrakhan coat against the weak spring sunshine, she was holding a grey poodle on her lap and gazing across the baseball field. Queenie, who was in heat, pulled towards her but I did not recognize her until I had passed and she did not notice me. I kept Queenie busy on the far side of the park and, throwing sticks for that ungainly dog, I suddenly felt loss, an absurd diminishment.

I wonder if this coming March I will be sitting across the desk from Mr. Vogel? When I first went to see him he was just a sprig but is now a portly middle-aged man. Even then, he made me feel a little like a truant youth before the principal. He shakes his head over the mysteries, his spectacles glint as he reproves me for lack of receipts. His fingers chatter over his adding machine.

His manner is dry; his inventions are fantastical.

"And now," he always says, "we come to Entertainment."

Flashing a glance of severe probity.

"A very *grey* area."

I do not want to be seen laughing aloud in the garden. I stifle the laughter and cough into my handkerchief.

Will Mr. Vogel and I invent my taxes this coming March?

Only the cartons of papers for Queen's await my attention; my other papers are in order. My will is drawn up, insurance policies in force, assigns of copyright assigned. I should not pretend any longer. I remember the papers in that outer room of Fortnell House, a scullery perhaps. I do not want my papers abandoned in that way, stored in the damp to rot. But if I do not put them in order perhaps they will be consigned to some air-conditioned but equal oblivion. Tomorrow, after the young man, I must start to sort them, the manuscripts, the journals, the letters from dead friends.

The doors had been nailed up.

That outer room in the rear of Fortnell House whose iron window bars we forced with a branch must have been a scullery or pantry. It was stone-flagged and whitewashed, green mould growing down the walls and on some of the damp papers. After the awful noise of screws being wrenched and wood splintering, we stood in the cold room listening.

Stacked in boxes were bundles of letters, newspapers, parchment deeds with red seals, account books, admiralty charts, and municipal records. The papers littered the floor, too, in sodden mounds where other boys had emptied boxes searching for more exciting things.

I stuffed my shirt.

I took bundles of parchment deeds, indentures, wills and leases, documents written in faded Latin.

THIS INDENTURE *made the second day of May in the seventeenth year of our Sovereign Lord George the Third by the Grace of God of Great Britain France and Ireland King Defender of the Faith and so forth and in: the Year of Our Lord . . .*

I remember, too, the half-leather ledger of the clerk of the Christchurch magistrate's court. The dates ran from 1863–65. The handwriting was a faded sepia copperplate, the name of the defendant in one column, the offence in a second, the fine in a third.

For bastardy, the commonest charge, the fine was five shillings.

The cover was, yes, mottled pink and white. The end papers were marbled. The leather spine was mildewed. The front lower corner was bruised, the cardboard raised and puffy with damp.

I can feel it in my hands.

The salmon fishers who netted the run between Mudeford and Hengistbury Head—the hours I have sat watching the two rowing boats laying the cork-bobbing net across the incoming tide. Mostly they came up empty, the net piling slack and easy. Perhaps twice a day the net would strain, a flash of roiling silver, and then the great fish hauled in over the side to be clubbed in the boat bottom.

The name for a bludgeon used to kill fish is a "priest." How I hug these words to myself, savouring them. "Priest" was not a local usage; I have seen it in print. It is not recorded in the *Shorter Oxford*.

One of Mr. Taylor's ferrets was brown, the other albino. I swung a stake with him one day on the Double Dykes despatching rabbits as they bolted into the nets pegged over their holes. The albino ferret eventually reappeared masked in blood. The ferrets frightened me; Mr. Taylor handled them with gauntlets. Some of the dead rabbits were wet underneath with trickles of thick, bright yellow urine which stood on the fur.

Over the two stone bridges and beyond Christchurch, along the New Forest road towards the Cat and Fiddle Inn, we cycled sometimes on our new Raleigh All-Steel bicycles to Summerfield. The Summerfield Estate stretched for miles over heath, farmland, and woods. We visited the roadside rookery where in late spring we gathered the shiny twelve-bore cartridge cases that the gamekeeper had scattered blasting into the nests from underneath. Beyond lay the heath where adders basked and kestrels circled the sky. We visited the hornets' nests in the trees in the dead wood and the pools where the palmated newts bred and we walked down the stream-bed to attach leeches to our legs. And always, past the cottages and the wheat fields and pasture, we headed down for the woods and coverts.

The gamekeeper was our invisible enemy; he was rumoured to have shot a boy in the behind. The raucous calls of pheasants held us in strained silence; rootling blackbirds froze us.

We trespassed into the heart of the wood where in a clearing we would stare at the gamekeeper's gibbet—a dead, grey tree hung with the corpses of rats, crows, owls, stoats and weasels, hawks and shapeless things. Some of the bodies would be fresh, others rotted to a slime. There in the still heat of the afternoon we stared. Over the bodies in a gauze of sound crawled the iridescent flies.

Children are, I think, drawn towards death and dying. I remember the ambivalence of a young girl of eight or nine to a litter of puppies at suck, the blind mouths and puddling forepaws at the swollen dugs —she, too, it seemed to me, sensed a relationship between herself and the bitch. I remember it vividly. The daughter of a friend. I seem to remember attempting a story once on that but as with so many of my stories, I could find no adequate structure.

———————————

The cutlass was about three feet long and slightly curved. The guard was brass and the Tower of London armoury mark was stamped on the blade near the hilt. The hilt was bound in blackened silver wire. I got the cutlass from one of the older boys—I forget his name—in exchange for six Christmas annuals and a William and Mary shilling. It was from him, too, that I learned the secret of Fortnell House.

I went there first on my own. The house was an eighteenth century mansion on the outskirts of Christchurch. It was invisible from the road; large padlocked gates marked the entrance to the drive. On the gate-pillars weathered heraldic beasts stood holding shields. The details of the quartering within the shields were little more than lumps and hollows. I think the beasts were griffins but time and the weather had so eroded the soft grey stone that the outlines of the carving were indistinct.

I climbed the iron spears of the railings and forced my way through the rank laurels onto the drive. The wood and the drive were overgrown and dark; the gravel had reverted to grass and weeds. The bottom windows of the house were blind and boarded; the front door was padlocked. Pink willowherb and weeds sprouted from the guttering. Some of the second storey windows were broken.

Around the back of the house were extensive grounds and a spinney, the lawns and terraces overgrown, the garden statuary tumbled. The windows were boarded and the doors nailed shut. I tried the doors with my shoulder. Inside, according to report, upstairs, room after room was filled with swords and spears and armour, guns, statues, strange machines, old tools, pictures, books—a treasury. The silence and the rank growth frightened me.

To one side of the house at the back, next to the coach house, stood three wooden sheds, their doors smashed open to the weather. Two were empty except for a rusted lawn-mower and an anchor but in the third I found a broken mahogany cabinet full of shallow drawers. It had contained a collection of mineral specimens, many of which were scattered about the floor. I filled my pockets with strange and glittering stones. In a corner of the shed were stacks of plates and dishes; many had been smashed. I found intact two large willow-pattern plates, meat chargers. The blue was soft and deep. I told my parents I had traded something for them.

Fortnell House had been built in the 1720s. The last Fortnell, Sir Charles, had left the house and his collections to the town of Christchurch as a museum. The town had accepted the gift but was disinclined or unable to raise the money to refurbish the building and install a curator.

Sir Charles had served for many years in India, the Middle East, and Africa. He was one of that vanished breed like Burton, Speke, and Layard—romantic amateurs who were gentlemen, scholars, linguists, and adventurers. Fortnell House became the repository of collections of minerals, fossils, books, weapons, tribal regalia, paintings, and carvings. On his retirement, Sir Charles had devoted his energies to Christchurch and the county, collecting local records, books, memorabilia, and the evidences of the prehistoric past.

It has become the fashion to decry such men as wealthy plunderers but we shall not see their like again. My youngest grandson, he of Adidas College, has called me fascist and them racist. I forbear to point out that his precious victims of oppression and colonialism despoiled their ancestral tombs for gold and used the monuments of their past for target practice. My heart does not bleed for the Egyptians; I do not weep for the Greeks.

It is, I suppose, natural to clash with those younger, natural this conservatism as one grows older; one has learned how easily things break.

What will the young man say to me this evening? And what can I say to him? It is difficult to talk to these young college men whose minds no longer move in pictures. Had he been here this morning I could, like some Zen sage, have pointed to the Monarchs about the apple leaves and preserved my silence.

Particular life. Particular life.

All else is tricks of the trade or inexpressible.

I have often wondered, I wonder still, what became of those willow-pattern plates I stole from Fortnell House. I brought them to Canada with me when I was a young man and they survived endless moves and hung on an endless variety of kitchen walls. They disappeared when June and I were divorced. She was quite capable of breaking them to spite me. Or, more likely, selling them. She had little aesthetic sense. She would have called them dust-gatherers or eyesores—some such thin-lipped epithet. So do they now hang on some Westmount wall or decorate an expensive restaurant?

I liked to be able to glance at them while I was eating; I used to like running my fingertips over that glaze. It comforted me. That deep lead glaze, the softness of the blue—one did not need to check pottery marks to know such richness was eighteenth century work.

I remember reading that Wedgwood used to tour the benches inspecting work. When he found an imperfect piece he smashed it with a hammer and wrote on the bench with chalk: *This will not do for Josiah Wedgwood.* I have always liked that story. We would have understood each other, Josiah and I.

As the years passed, I thought more often, and with greater bitterness, of those two large plates than I did of June. She is now the dimmest of memories. Strange that I cannot recall her features or her body; strange that she was Mary's mother. Alison, too, has receded now so far that I must concentrate to see her features, strain to hear her voice. She sends me Christmas cards from Florida.

Far clearer and more immediate is Patricia Hopkins. I see the scene like an enlarged detail from a great canvas. We are hidden in the laurel bushes in her garden; it is gloomy there though light hints on the glossy leaves. In the far distance the sunshine sparkles on the greenhouse. In the immediate background is a weed-grown tennis court along whose nearest edge the wire netting sags in a great belly. Patricia's knickers are round her knees. I am staring at the smooth cleft mound of her vagina. I am nine and she is eight.

Better remembered than the bodies of two wives.

I have always detested photographs. There was an article in Robert's *Time* magazine about that fellow Land and his Polaroid cameras. He called photography "the most basic form of creativity." So obscenely wrong.

But I must not get excited.

My third visit to Fortnell House was my last.

We got in through the bars of the scullery window and both lingered, turning over the sodden papers and documents that littered the floor, unwilling to go further into the dark house. Eventually we crept along a short passage into the kitchen.

One wall was taken up by a vast black range, another by two long sinks. In the middle of the room was a long wooden table. On the wall above the door that led out of the kitchen was a glass case of dials. Inside the dials were numbers and beneath the case hung two rows of jangly bells on coiled strips of metal—a device, we decided, for summoning servants to the different rooms.

A passage led from the kitchen through two doors to the hall. The hall was dark and echoey. On the walls hung the dim shapes of mounted heads and antlers. All the doors off the hall were closed. The staircase was uncarpeted. We started up it towards the first landing.

A few thin rays of light came through chinks in the boards that covered the landing window. A line of light ran up the handrail of the banisters. We spoke in whispers and walked on the outside edges of the stairs.

A board creaked; a shoe cap knocked hollow on a riser.

It was just as my hand was turning on the huge carved acorn of the newel post on the landing that a door opened below and a man came out. He was a black shape with the light of the room behind him, shelf after shelf of books. He called us down and demanded our names and addresses. He was cataloguing the library. He was sick of boys breaking in and was giving our names to the police. He fumbled the front door open and ordered us out.

Secure in our aliases, we walked away down the drive.

Now, in my dreams, I have returned.

Nightly I brave the weathered griffins, the rank laurels; nightly I climb those uncarpeted stairs; nightly my hand grasps the great carved acorn of the newel post. But my dream does not continue.

Perhaps one night I will not awaken in the blue dark to turn and stare at the blue night-light on the bedside table. Perhaps one night soon—I have that feeling—I will round the dark oak acorn and reach the rooms above.

The sun has long since passed over the house and I am sitting in the shade. Soon Robert will return from his office and change into his gardening clothes; he will gather the windfalls in his oblong wooden basket. Soon the garage will sound as my grandson, returning from his college, roars his motorbike into the narrow space; soon the kitchen will be full of noise. Then Mary will call me for dinner. I should go and shave. But I will sit a little longer in the sunshine. Here between the moored houseboats where I can watch the turn of the quicksilver dace. Here by the piles of the bridge where in the refracted sunlight swim the golden-barred and red-finned perch.

Following his divorce, frequent dinners with the Norths had become habit for Peter Thornton. Nancy fussed over him and stitched on lost buttons; Alan plied him with beer and had distracted him in the early months with ferocious games of chess. Now, two and a half years later, his family relationship was declared by their daughter, Amanda, to be that of Uncle the Best.

"I'm ready!" she yelled from upstairs.

"No, don't go up yet, Peter. Have some more coffee," said Nancy. "She still hasn't brushed her teeth."

"TEETH!" bellowed Alan.

"She's getting so bitchy and *cunning*," said Nancy. "She runs the tap, eats some toothpaste, smears it round the basin, but *now* the little swine's learned to wet the brush."

"They *all* seem to hate it, don't they?" said Peter. "Same thing with Jeremy."

"By the way," said Alan, "nothing new with the woman situation, is there?"

"No. Not particularly. Why?"

"Well, don't be too long up there. Might have something to interest you."

"What?"

"This wine," said Alan, emptying the bottle into his glass, "confirms one's prejudices against Hungarians."

"What might interest me?"

Alan shook his head and wagged a solemn finger.

"What are you being so mysterious for?" said Peter. "Oh, *no!* You haven't got someone coming over?"

He glanced at Nancy who shrugged.

"Our wife," said Alan, "privy though she is to our councils and most trusted to our ear . . ."

"READY!"

"Before you get *completely* pissed, dear husband," said Nancy, "you can help me with these dishes."

"Your merest whim, my petal," cried Alan, "is my command."

"Oh, Christ!" said Nancy.

As Peter went upstairs, Alan in the kitchen was demanding his apron with the rabbits on it; Nancy's voice; and then he heard the sounds of laughter.

"The woman situation."

Whom, he wondered, had Alan in mind for him?

The woman situation had started again for him some eight months or so after his wife had left him. The woman situation had started at the same time he'd stopped seeing Dr. Trevore, when he'd realized that he was boring himself; when he'd realized that his erstwhile wife, his son, and he had been reduced to characters in a soap opera which was broadcast every two weeks from Trevore's soundproofed studio.

And which character was he?

He was the man whom ladies helped in laundromats. He was the man who dined on frozen pies. Whose sink was full of dishes. He was the man in the raincoat who wept in late-night bars.

That office, and he in it, that psychiatrist's office with its scuffed medical magazines and pieces of varnished driftwood on the waiting room's occasional tables was the stuff of comic novels, skits, the weekly fodder of stand-up comedians.

In the centre of Trevore's desk sat a large, misshapen thing. The rim was squashed in four places indicating that it was probably an ashtray. On its side, Trevore's name was spelled out in spastic white slip. Peter had imagined it a grateful gift from the therapy ward of a loony bin.

It presided over their conversation.
How about exercise? Are you exercising?
No, not much.
How about squash?
I don't know how to play.
I play myself. Squash. I play on Mondays, Wednesdays, and Fridays.
In the evenings.

Following one such session he had gone home, opened the bathroom cabinet, regarded the pill bottles which had accumulated over the months. He had taken them all out and stood them on the tank above the toilet. He arranged them into four rows. In the first row he placed the Valium. In the second, the Stelazine. In the third, the Tofranil. In the fourth, the Mareline.

Uncapping the bottles, he tipped the tablets rank by rank into the toilet bowl. Red fell upon yellow, blue fell on red, tranquillizing, antidepressant psychotherapeutic agents fell, swirled, and sifted onto agents for the relief of anxiety, emotional disorders, and nausea.

The results had suggested to him the droppings of a Walt Disney rabbit.

Following this, he had twice attempted suicide.

In spite of Montreal's entrenched and burgeoning underworld, the only weapon he had been able to procure, and that in a junk shop, was an ancient .45. Bullets had proved impossible to obtain without a permit.

He shrank from the *mechanics* of a shotgun—bare feet and the cold, oily taste of gun metal filling his mouth and the absurd fear that in the second of death the kick of the barrels would smash his teeth.

His second attempt was with prescription sleeping pills, blue gelatine capsules. He had written to his mother and father, swallowed twenty-five, and lain wakefully on his bed clutching the plastic bracelet which had been secured round Jeremy's wrist at his birth. His stomach felt distended and after belching repeatedly the taste of the gelatine had made him vomit.

Subsequently, with a large weariness and a settled habit of sadness, he had become active in the world of those whose world was broken.

First it was the single women of his married friends' acquaintance, awkward dinners where he had learned the meaning of "intelligent," "interesting," "creative," and "kind." Later, he had encountered childless women, women married but embittered, divorced women with single maladjusted children who demanded to know if he was to be their new uncle. He had even met a twenty-eight-year-old virgin who one night confessed that she hated men because when they became excited their things came out of their bodies, red like dogs.

He had acquired an almost encyclopedic knowledge of Montreal's restaurants.

He had become an authority on films.

He had learned to avoid women who took pottery courses and had come to recognize as danger signs indoor plants, Alice in Wonderland posters, health food, stuffed toys, parents, menstrual cramps, and more than one cat.

Amanda was trying to whistle.

He whistled a few notes of the tune she was hissing.

"Come *on*," she called.

Her bed was littered with books; she had chosen *Paddington Bear* and *The Sleeping Beauty*. The Bear book was one he had recently given her. When he bought books for his son who now lived in distant Vancouver, he always bought Mandy duplicates. He mailed off a book and a letter weekly into the void from which few answers returned. Mandy snuggled against him as he read.

. . . mounted the Prince's white charger . . .

"What's a charger?"

"A big white horse."

. . . mounted the Prince's white charger and rode away to his kingdom in a far country.

"Look at all the flowers in the picture," she said.

"The end," said Peter, getting up and kissing her goodnight.

"Peter? How many flowers are there in the world?"

"THE END."

"More than people? More than cars? Not more than ANTS?"

"I don't know. Get to sleep."

"Will Nanny die?"

"Good night."

As he went along the landing, he heard her half-singing, "Nanny'll die and Grampy, Mummy and Daddy, Uncle Drew *and* the mailman and Mary and the Volkswagen *and* Nanny *and* Grampy . . ."

He stood silently in the bathroom for a few moments resting his hands on the edges of the washbasin, staring down. He saw, unbidden, like a succession of frozen movie frames, that other bathroom in a silent apartment where dirt and empty beer cans had accumulated until the lease expired.

In the cabinet, the daily reminder of the blue plastic diaper pin, the sticky bottle of Extract of Wild Strawberries, Gravol, the smiling tin of Johnson's Baby Powder.

The room that had been his son's he had not been able to enter. The frieze of animals sagging from its thumbtacks, a deflated elephant on the dusty carpet, scattered blocks.

He washed his face and then remembered to flush the toilet.

"No trouble?" said Nancy as he came into the living-room.

"She'll be off in a few minutes."

"A suggestion of cognac?" said Alan. "You'll have to use a tumbler because I broke the last snifter."

Peter sank into his usual armchair.

Nancy was lying on the couch staring into the fire.

Alan rolled the glass in his palms.

"Well?" said Peter.

"Well, what? Oh! Oh, yes."

Alan produced from the inner pocket of his jacket an envelope. He straightened a bent corner. He leaned forward and passed the envelope to Peter. He sat back. Peter opened the envelope and glanced at the contents.

"Funny," he said. "Witty. Exquisitely comical."

"I thought you'd react that way."

Peter tossed the letter over to Nancy.

"Oh, Alan!" she said. "That's not very funny."

"It wasn't intended to be," he said.

"'A Scientific Date with CompuMate,'" read Nancy.

"An unfortunate name, agreed," said Alan.

"Sounds like 'copulate'," said Nancy.

"'Consummate'." said Peter.

"Shut up!" said Alan. "Listen, I'm being serious. Okay? We've listened to you talking about the situation for hours on end so you can just sit there and hear me out. Now, I want to look at this rationally. The first fact is that you claim you want to get married again. God knows why, but that's *your* funeral. So what's stopping you? It isn't that you're not attractive to women because over the last couple of years there's been a veritable *parade* of the creatures . . ."

Peter sipped the cognac, martinis before dinner, wine with, conscious of becoming floatingly, pleasantly, drunk, watching the play of expression on Alan's face rather than paying attention to his words, feeling a great affection for him. It was soothing to be with friends in this room with a fire in the fireplace, in this room which was part of a house, part of a household; soothing to be, however briefly, in some sort of context.

". . . so it's not lack of opportunity. Montreal's *bulging* with women . . ."

A log in the fire slipped and sparks sailed up. When the fire had burned down and the talk had finished, he would have to go out into the snow. He thought of his apartment. In a closet in his apartment there still sat a carton not unpacked—a "barrel" the moving men had called it. For two years he had reached over it to take out his coat. He did not know what it contained.

". . . and just think of the bunch of . . . of Dulcineas you've brought round here," Alan was saying, "eating us out of house and home. And I expect they were the pick of the crop. Now what I'm getting at . . ."

Nancy's hand patted the carpet for the packet of cigarettes. Watching the oily curves of the cognac on the glass the word "meniscus" came into his mind but he knew it wasn't the right word. Bulky as the still-packed carton, sadness sat inside him.

"Well, *I* think the whole idea's *silly*," said Nancy, "Any woman who'd sign up for that'd be crazy."

"Why don't you *listen!*" exclaimed Alan with a drunken earnestness. "*Of course!* That's just what I've been saying. The women he's found on his *own* were mostly crazy. Right? What about that blonde one? Eh? You know."

"Marion," said Nancy.

"Right. All *that* nonsense. And that other woman with the adhesive tape over it. If you didn't know Peter, you wouldn't believe they were walking around, would you? *Of course* ninety per cent of these'd be mad as hatters, but what if there was *one* woman just like him. The same reasons, I mean. Why not? What's he got to lose?"

"Peter wouldn't like a woman who'd sign up for that sort of thing."

"How do you know?"

"Because I know Peter."

"And what do you mean 'that sort of thing'?"

"You know very well what I mean."

"Peter!" said Alan. "What do you think?"

"The other day," said Peter, sitting up, "I went into Dominion to get some apples and I was wandering around sort of glazed with the music and everything and I'd come to a halt in front of a shelf and I found myself staring at a box of toothpicks."

"Fascinating," said Alan.

"And do you know what it said on the box? It said: 'Stim-U-Dent: Inter-Dental Stimulators'."

"Do you want to give it a try or not?"

"I had a hamburger last week," said Peter, "that was served on a paper plate embossed with the word 'Chi-Net'. And I've sipped my milk through straws manufactured by the 'Golden Age Scientific Company'."

"Stop babbling," said Alan. "It's only fifteen dollars for a month's trial."

Peter laughed.

"Okay?" said Alan. "Or not?"

Peter shrugged.

"Good!" said Alan. " So we can fill in the form. I *love* forms. I'll just get something to rest it on."

He took a large book that was on the side table and near the couch.

"What the fuck's this!"

"It's that book club," said Nancy. "I keep forgetting to send the don't want cards back."

"Fish Cookery of Southeast Asia."

"They bury them until they rot," said Nancy.

"What?"

"Fish."

"Who?"

"Southeast Asians."

Alan stared at her.

"And you," he said, turning to Peter, "want to get married again."

Spreading out the form, he started to read.

Many of us have come to realize that we need the love and compan-
ionship of a compatible Mate with whom we can share our deepest
beliefs, our gravest sorrows, our wildest joys. CompuMate promotes
harmonious relationships between mature individuals and encourages
personal growth through deep and meaningful long-term, male–female
interaction. Any single or legally unattached person who is serious-
minded and of sound character and who meets the computer's acceptance
standards is eligible to become a CompuMember.

"Just who does that computer think it is?" said Nancy.

"Haughtyputer," said Peter.

"Now the first thing, then . . ." said Alan.

"Wait," said Peter. "How's all this nonsense supposed to work?"

"You answer all these questions and then it matches you with someone who's given the same kind of answers. And then you end up with a Computer Compatible."

"A 'Computer Compatible'?"

"Now don't start being awkward. Are you ready? Okay?"

Mark the Character Traits which are YOU: *Popular, Well-to-do, Artistic, Puritan, Sexually Experienced, Bohemian, Diplomatic, Free Spirit, Romantic, Shy, Well-Groomed, Sensual, Sporty, Sensitive, Smoker (non, moderate, heavy), Drinker (non, social, heavy).*

"So?" said Alan. "What would you like to be?"

"Artistic," said Nancy.

"Romantic, do you think?" said Alan.

"Of course," said Nancy. "And Sensitive. And Shy."

"Can't I be Sexually Experienced?"

"No," said Alan, "it might put her off."

He marked crosses in the appropriate boxes.

"And for smoking and drinking," he said, "I'm putting 'Moderate' and 'social'. Or we won't get any Compatibles at all."

Can Premarital Sex Be Justified?

"What choice do I have?"

Never. After Engagement. If in Love. Between Mature Individuals. Always.

"Do people still *get* engaged?" said Nancy.

"*I* was engaged," said Peter.

"Yes, but you're as old as we are."

"Not only was I officially engaged, I purchased an engagement ring complete with diamond."

"You're an antique," said Nancy. "Just like us."

Alan cleared his throat.

Which of the following interests would you like to share with your CompuMatch: Dancing, Athletics, Skiing, Water Sports, Spectator Sports . . .

"Hate *all* of them," said Peter.

. . . Politics, Photography, Music, Animals . . .

"Animals?"

. . . Animals, Fine Arts, Natural Sciences, Parties, Psychology and Sociology.

"I don't like any of them."

"Well you've got to."

"What do you mean, *animals*?"

"How the fuck should I know?" said Alan. "Take her to the zoo."

"It's not open in the winter."

"Oh, stop being difficult!" said Alan. "I'm putting you down for Music, Animals, and Fine Arts."

"And what's more," Peter said to Nancy, "the engagement was announced in the paper with, believe it or not, a photograph of the charming young couple. So how about that?"

"What are your age requirements?" said Alan.

"What?"

"How young and old are you prepared to go? There's a note here that says the wider the range the more choice the computer can provide."

"Remember her father, Nancy?" said Peter. "I even asked him for her hand in marriage."

"*Peter!* Come on! You're not paying attention."

"Sorry, sorry. What was it? How young, you said?"

There flashed through his mind a vision of an evening he had spent some eighteen months earlier. He had met her at a party. She was young and beautiful, her eyes dark and entrancing. At three-thirty in the morning he had escorted her back to her apartment on Sherbrooke West. Her apartment was furnished with plants, posters, and a pinball machine.

It was summer; she gave him a large glass of Kool-Aid. She went into her bedroom.

One of the posters was electric blue.

In the centre was a red circle.

Under the circle was the word NOW.

She reappeared in a long, white nightgown. Her bare feet were brown. Across the road from her apartment was the Montreal Association for the Blind. Yellow floodlights lit the front of the buildings. She insisted they go out into the night because she wanted to share with him something rare, something mysterious.

She flitted across to the island in the middle of the road, her legs dark through the white gown against the light of the approaching cars. She smiled and beckoned to him. On the lawn in front of the building she urged him to take off his shoes and socks to walk in the dew. His feet looked pale and silly in the dark grass. She took him by the hand and led him to one of the floodlights. Her hand was cool on his. She made him kneel and gaze into the glare of one of the yellow bars of light while she counted aloud to a hundred.

"See!" she cried, when they stood up. "Everything looks purple."

Peter drained the last drops of cognac.

"I'll put the maximum as your age," said Alan, "so how about twenty-five as minimum? That's ten years."

"Make it thirty."

"Why thirty?"

"The heart," said Peter, "has its reasons."

Alan crossed something out and turned the form over.

"How about race?" he said. "Of your CompuMatch, that is."

"Peter?" said Nancy.

White. Coloured. Oriental. Any.

"Apart from all *this*," she said, "do you know what sort of girl you really want? You know, if you could . . . Or is the whole idea just silly?"

"What *sort* of girl?" said Peter.

Protestant. Catholic. Jewish. Unaffiliated. Other.

He held up the empty glass looking through it at the fire.

"Yes," he said. "I know *just* the sort."

He tilted the glass creating changing shapes.

"I want a girl in gingham."

2

Peter sipped the coffee, watching the waitress, watching other diners, half listening to scraps of conversation near him, extending as long as was decent the minutes until he would have to pay the bill. He ate at Chez Jean-Guy two or three times a week. It was not exactly cheap but he liked the linen, wine, flowers on the table. The food was respectable. As he was a regular, they rarely hurried him and he often sat over coffee, sometimes cognac, glancing through trade journals and the catalogues.

Above the background sound of voices, cutlery, crockery, he heard a sharp click and *Jesus Christ!* from a man at the next table. He hadn't looked at the two men when they'd come in, as he'd been watching his waitress stretching to clear off a vacated table. Both men were in their forties and wearing expensively tailored versions of teenage clothing. One wore a necklace and medallion. On the near man a heavy gold bracelet.

"What a jeezely-looking thing!"

"Couldn't tell, eh?" said the necklace man. "Swear it was a Parker pen. I came through three international airports with that in my suit pocket."

Peter couldn't see what it was because of the flowers on their table.

"Where in hell did you *find* a thing like that?"

"This one?" said the necklace man. "Tokyo, this one. Never," he said, "never underestimate your Japanese."

"A very ingenious people," said the bracelet man.

"The Jews of the East," said the necklace man.

"Let bygones be bygones," said the bracelet man.

"Of course," said the necklace man, "in the travel business you're always on the move. Locating. Different countries all the time. The personal touch. And it's become—well, I suppose you'd have to call it a hobby of mine."

"Well," said the bracelet man, "it sure is different!"

There was another click.

"Refill all round?" said the bracelet man.

Beckoning to Peter's waitress, the necklace man said to the bracelet man, "Two more vodkatinis, are we?"

Peter felt a surge of irritation. They were ten years older than he was. Why couldn't they accept with dignity what faced them in the morning mirror? Slackening. Caries. The intimation of jowls.

He wondered what they thought about when locked alone in the burnished steel and strip-lighting of a jet plane's toilet.

"Yes," continued the necklace man, "every different place I go I buy their kind of switchblade. As I say, I suppose you'd call it a hobby."

The waitresses wore blue tunics with white blouses. Peter watched the changing blue planes across her thighs as she placed the martinis in front of them.

"But it's in the south," continued the necklace man, "the southern countries where I've found what I'd call my best pieces. The time before last in Mexico, for example, I bought a crucifix. Crown of thorns. Loincloth. Little nailheads in the hands and feet. Enamelled. Brown beard. But press his navel and you've got yourself five and a half inches."

The waitress smiled at Peter from her buffet and raised the coffee pot. Nodding, he smiled back.

He always tried to get a table at her station. The other girls were French-Canadian but she, he had discovered, was German. It was not the length of leg nor the strange severity of her haircut which attracted him but rather the way she spoke. There was something about her speech; it was nothing as definite as, say, a lisp; if it was an impediment at all it was so slight, so elusive, as to be indefinable. But he was not comfortable with the idea of "impediment"; it did not quite capture what he seemed to hear. That something, he had almost decided, must be the suggestion of a long-ago-lost accent. He found it charming.

He did not know her name.

Sometimes it was Eva. Sometimes Ilse.

She wore no rings.

The austere tunics reminded him of girls' gym-slips, stirred idle thoughts of Victorian pornography, the backs of hairbrushes, correction, discipline.

Miss Flaybum's Academy. Sexual pleasures he'd never been able to even vaguely understand.

Necklace and Bracelet had exhausted compact cars and the prime lending rate and were now fairly launched into the virtues of aluminum siding.

He watched her deft movements, her smile, the formal inclination of her head as she jotted down each order. The elusive something about her speech was, he decided, like a faint presence of perfume in an empty room.

He found himself wishing that he wasn't wishing that she wasn't German.

He embroidered upon the possible permutations of Alsace-Lorraine.

Recalled a poster he'd seen outside the Beaver for a movie called *Hitler's Hellcats*. A Nordic beauty aiming a sten-gun, her blouse severely strained. He had come to consider most psychological solemnities such as the gun–penis thing as dubious as Dr. Trevore and his lumpy ashtray. Yet the poster had stayed in his mind for months. And then, too, he remembered the security guard at Man and his World.

Last year with Jeremy. The mechanical delights of LaRonde, ice-creams, orange-crush. The rites of summer. And while Jeremy had been riding out his minutes on the merry-go-round, the paunchy guard *stroking* the revolver butt.

Peter cradled the globe of cognac.

Snapshots of Jeremy.

Half-frightened laughter into the sky as the chains of the swing groaned in the park. Magic markers. Counting his popsicle stick collection. Fear of spider webs. Tiny feet swinging under the kitchen table, the flannelette pyjamas, the pyjamas with elephants. Snapshots already fading, fading like the yellowed snapshots found in albums gathering dust in a thousand junk shops, the last unwanted effects of auctioned families.

Clinging to his refrigerator door were Jeremy's magnetic letters. He had saved them from that other apartment.

Reliques.

He used them to hold notes to himself, shopping lists, bills. Sometimes late at night, taking out another beer, he used the letters to compose messages.

Four of them presently held a sheet of paper from CompuMate which bore five names. The evening at Alan's had ended like so many evenings, vague memories the next day of snow, a taxi, swallowing down four aspirins with milk from the carton against the morning. He had been surprised and irritated with Alan when the list arrived.

He had ignored it for several days. The very idea was ludicrous. He knew himself to be incapable of phoning strange women.

Marjorie Kirkland
Stella Bluth
Nadja Chayefski
Elspeth McLeod
Anna Stevens

As the days had gone by he found the names wandering his mind. He wondered if Marjorie was once Margery; what nationality Bluth might be; if Nadja's hair was of raven lustre; if Elspeth were elfin and wandered lonely as a cloud, mist, rock, and heather.

But even more vividly he had imagined the conversations, the receiver glistening with sweat, silences, fingers clenched, armpits wet. That, most likely that, or fevered Woody Allen performances, fumbling blather ending with his accidentally garrotting himself with the telephone cord.

How, he had wondered, did one open? And, possibly worse, how did one close? And what could conceivably come between?

Marjorie Kirkland.

Marjorie Kirkland had been quite understanding. Marjorie it turned out, had been married for two years. She had reserved her asperity for CompuMate which, despite several registered letters, had not removed her name from the active list.

Stella Bluth.

Six generous cognacs followed by three Molson Export to prevent dehydration he had phoned Stella Bluth. After he had diffidently presented his credentials Stella Bluth had assumed command. It was best, she always found, for each to describe each other to the other and then, if they liked the sound of each other, he could call her again.

It's a good thing you can't see over the phone.
Why?
Because.

Because what?

Just because.

Silence.

Well, if you must know, my hair's all wet and I'm not completely dressed.

Stella Bluth was sobering; it took Peter only a few moments to form the impression that she was possibly unhinged. He would have liked to close the conversation at its start but was incapable of replacing the receiver.

She frankly held out little hope; she was a Cancer and he was an Aries and she was sure he knew what *that* meant.

Upon command, he described himself. He was thirty-five and six feet tall. He was divorced. He was of medium build. His hair was brownish. He worked as an appraiser for a firm of auctioneers. Appraiser meant he had to estimate the value of antiques and *objets d'art*. No, it wasn't a French company. He was interested in music and animals.

Are you sure you're not coloured?

Quite.

You sound *like you're coloured. Because I'm Catholic.*

Stella was twenty-seven years old. Why lie about it? It was nothing to be ashamed of. She wasn't married and she hadn't been. She wasn't fat and she wasn't thin. They said she had a good figure. Her hair was brunette. She was at Alcan and did seventy-three a minute. She wasn't in the pool; she usually worked personally for Mr. Edwards. Who was quite nice though she didn't want him to get the wrong impression and sometimes he took her to the Golden Hinde in the Queen Elizabeth where they gave you triple martinis. Did he know the Golden Hinde? But she was only a social drinker. That and if she went to a party. She liked hockey and animals.

In the silence, Peter had heard the magnified sound of his breathing.

And she was interested in the environment.

The advent of the two middle-aged ladies caused an eddy in the flow of restaurant movement as they were seated, the table pulled out, lifted back, chairs settled. They spoke loudly in American voices; one asked Ilse in English if she spoke English. They were a parody of affluent American middle-aged womanhood; white and rinsed hair tended, fingers bedizened with diamond rings. They were explaining to Ilse that they were on a Winter Tour; that the other girls were eating in the hotel; but they had read about Chez Jean-Guy in *Gourmet* magazine. And what did the menu mean?

Rejecting with increasing amazement kidney, cod, sausage blood and sausage garlic, quail and rabbit, they settled on poached salmon.

Peter signalled for his bill.

Three or four people were standing near the door waiting for a table.

Two full weeks had passed before curiosity and imaginings had nudged him into calling Nadja Chayefski. She had seemed abrupt and said she couldn't talk to him but had asked for his address.

A few days later in the mail he received an envelope from Sun Life. It contained a poem on Sun Life letterhead.

Hey You!

I love you—please, it's not "dirty"!
I love trees and grass and plants and anything that lives.
Do you believe me?

It's not an intended, on purpose thing,
it's just here, in me,
and I want you to know it.
Please, it's not "dirty."

Quite likely you won't need it
or want it.

But that's O.K.

I just wanted you to know.

"The flavour's very different from canned," said one of the American ladies.

Peter smiled as he scanned his bill.

One of the ladies clattered her fork on the plate.

"Your joints swell up," she said, looking at the back of her hand.

They were silent.

"One of the girls was taken sick last night," said the other, the one who had spoken first, the one who was wearing tinted spectacles.

Peter regarded her.

"Carrie told me. The Director had a doctor come," she went on. She paused.

"It was in the middle of the night."

They were silent again.

The other said suddenly, "It's all different since Herb's gone."

3

Peter had fortified himself for the encounter by drinking a severe vodka during his bath and another while dressing. He had then recleaned his teeth with Close-up: Super-Whitening Toothpaste and Mouthwash in One. Elspeth McLeod lived in a recent apartment building called the Michelangelo which boasted a commissionaire and live foliage in the foyer. On the fence surrounding the hole next door a large sign proclaimed the imminent construction of the El Greco.

The yellow light tacked its way up the indicator panel above which was a plaque that said Otis Elevator. He imagined Otis as the given name of the company's owner, a fat, cigar-smoking, Midwestern American; rotund Otis; Rotarian; orotund.

He realized that he was not entirely sober.

"Peter Thornton!" she said, opening wide the door.

His impression was of colour. Her hair was blonde, her dress white, but her face was tanned a stark and startling bronze. She ushered him into a white, Danish living-room, angles, glass tables, teak wall unit, striped grey couch.

"First things first," she said. "What can I get you to drink?"

"Well, whatever . . ."

"I've made some martinis if you'd . . ."

She went away. In the brighter light of the living-room the tan was even more unlikely. It looked as if she'd been enthusiastically made-up for some theatricals; the Chief's Daughter who falls in love with the Captured White Scout. Obviously, she'd been a little naughty on her CompuSheet. She was, he guessed, about forty. A year or two older possibly. Attractive in a carefully arranged kind of way. On the glass table in front of the couch lay a gigantic soapstone seal with a bulbous Eskimo trying to do something to it. He stared. Kitchen sounds, glasses, the slam of the fridge door. He wondered what he was doing here.

"Well," she said, raising her glass, "what's the new word that they're trying to make the Canadian word for 'Cheers!'?"

"Ookpic?" said Peter.

"Or 'Inuit' or something?" she said. "Is that how you say it?"

"Well," said Peter, "cheers!"

The martini stopped his breath and hit his empty stomach like a well-aimed brick.

"So," she said, nodding her head and smiling, "*you're* Peter Thornton."

He smiled.

With her every movement the massive silver charm-bracelet jingled.

"Your tan . . ."

"Florida. I've just come back. Three glorious weeks in the sun."

"So you missed the big storm," he said. "An eleven-inch fall, I think they said."

They made faces.

"Are you starving?"

"No, no, not at all."

"Because if you don't mind I'll start dinner now and it'll be ready in about an hour, if you'll excuse me."

The skirt was one of those skirts with lots of pleats in it. Fine legs. Her shoes were white too. He wondered if her legs under the brownness of the stockings were as intensely brown as her face and wrists.

He wandered over and looked at the things in the compartments of the wall unit. A stereo set. A photograph of a girl. A photograph of a boy. A few recent best sellers held upright by the polished halves of a geode—Yoga, Possession, Diet, Herbal Secrets, Yogurt. Some miniature bottles of liquor and a clustering of tiny animals in pink glass. The bowl caught his professional eye. Flower decoration, vigorous in the Kakiemon style. Opaque glaze. It felt right. He checked the hunting-horn mark. The Chantilly factory before 1750. He wondered what it was doing there, where it had come from, if she knew what it was. It contained a squashy peach.

He followed the sounds to the kitchen.

"Can I do anything to help?"

"Would you like another?" she said, setting down her glass. "This one's cook's privilege."

The kitchen gleamed. Appliances. The table was littered with chrome bar-implements; salt and pepper were contained in two large wooden blocks, each four inches square. He hefted one.

"Teak," she said, as she filled his glass.

"There's really nothing to do," she continued. "I bought a gorgeous cut of salmon."

As Peter watched, she enclosed the fish in two layers of aluminum foil, pinching and securing the seams. She then opened the dishwasher, placed the foil package on the upper rack, slammed and locked the door, and switched on.

Peter stared.

She looked up and caught something of his expression.

"I calculate by weight, you see," she said.

"By weight," repeated Peter.

"That'll need two full cycles," she said.

Peter nodded.

"Anything heavier," she said, "and I'd add two Rinse Holds."

"Ah," said Peter.

He carried the pitcher of martinis and a chrome ice-bucket thing and she brought the glasses, closing the kitchen door behind them to muffle the throb of the dishwasher. She put on some kind of Latin-Americany music and joined him on the grey striped couch.

"Well," she said, "you must tell me all about appraising. What does an antique appraiser do?"

"Well," said Peter, "furniture's the bread-and-butter side of . . ."

"That's a dip I make myself," she said, lifting a white limp leather handbag from the floor by the end of the couch and rummaging.

"But porcelain and silver," said Peter, "are my . . ."

"And I'm sorry about the chips—I was rushed and picked up those awful ones that taste of vinegar by mistake—but the dip's very good. It's very easy in a blender—sour cream and Danish Blue, chives, and a teaspoon of lemon juice."

She found cigarettes at the bottom of the bag.

"Delicious," said Peter. "Absolutely delicious."

And listened to himself crunching.

"Tell me," she said, snapping and snapping the mechanism of the slim gold lighter, "we didn't seem to talk about this, did we? Or did we? I was rather flustered—well, *you* know, and my memory's awful but did you say you *weren't* married? My memory! Sometimes I can't even seem . . ."

"No," said Peter, leaning across and lighting her cigarette with a match. "No, I'm not."

"You're lucky," she said.

He smiled and then sipped.

"Peter," she said, "you listen to me. You pay attention. You're a very lucky man."

"I don't know if I'd agree with that," he said with a smile.

She turned towards him.

"And just how," she said, "did an attractive man like you escape so long?"

"I'm divorced," he said.

"Aha!" she said.

"What about you?"

"I will be soon," she said. "Divorced. It's on the rolls for March."

He nodded.

"And it can't be soon enough," she said. "Let me tell you."

"It's a strange business," he said.

She filled her glass, holding the pitcher with both hands.

"Peter," she said. "Do you know what I'm going to do? I'm going to phone my friend."

"Your friend?"

"We girls have to stick together," she said. "Right? So I'll tell her *not* to come at nine. Because you're not *ugly* and you know what they say?"

"What?"

"Three's a crowd."

She got up and smoothed her dress, straightening pleats with her fingertips, running them down the pleats at her thigh.

"And I don't think you're likely to molest me," she said. She smiled down at him. "Are you?"

She started from the room.

"You have some more dip," she called back.

He was beginning to feel satisfactorily sloshed. He leaned back on the uncomfortable Danish couch and looked at his watch. He felt relaxed and the pitcher of martinis was still half full. He sucked his olive. He then initiated some exploratory dental work with the cocktail stick thing.

He had phoned Elspeth McLeod a week earlier on his return from dinner at Chez Jean-Guy. When he had entered his apartment, he had taken off his rubbers and put them on the sheet of newspaper inside the front door. The paper was scratchy with grit and sand; he had been meaning to change it for weeks.

He had tried to read but the conversation of the American ladies had echoed in his mind. Doors slammed. The TV in the next apartment was switched off. In the deepening silence, the refrigerator started and stopped.

Magnetic letters on the fridge door still held his CompuSheet. As he had stood over the toilet, he had seen into the empty room he maintained for Jeremy. Light from the bathroom glinted on the rims and spokes of the two-wheeler propped against the bedroom wall, last summer's birthday present. The bicycle had come in a large cardboard carton and he had skinned his knuckles working with an unaccustomed wrench to attach handlebars and pedals. Jeremy had been frightened of the bicycle and had hysterically resisted Peter's efforts, but had loved the carton, playing with it every day until it was forgotten overnight on the balcony and the rain rendered it limp and soggy.

Peter struggled to sit upright on the sloping couch. He dropped the olive into the crystal ashtray.

The toilet flushed and he heard water running.

The bicycle and the carton seemed as if they ought to be symbolic of something but of what, exactly, he was unable to grasp.

"Hello, again!" she said.

"I've been admiring your bowl," he said.

"Bowl? Oh. That belonged to my Drex. Well, he isn't but he *will* be. I've got a red ring around it."

"Pardon?"

"Oh, don't mind me," she said, "it's just my way, the way I am. It's what my girlfriend calls *hers*. She's a riot. My Drex did this, my Drex did that, she says. It stands for Dreadful Ex."

"What," said Peter, "have you got a red ring around?"

"March 17th," she said. "I was looking at it when I was on the phone. On the calendar," she added, in answer to his puzzled look. "Of course, I should have done it years ago. Everyone says so. So in a way I blame myself."

She fumbled at the lighter again.

She gestured encompassing the living-room.

"We used to live in the Town of Mount Royal. Do you know the Town? We lived in a very big house in the most expensive part, the most exclusive part. And we had three cars."

She eased off her shoes and let them fall on the carpet.

"Good old TMR!" she said.

She raised her glass.

"And what else," she said, "what else did we have?"

She started to tally.

"A large garden. And an Italian gardener who came twice a week. And a swimming pool. Fieldstone fireplaces. A woman came four times a week to clean and . . ."

"Sounds very pleasant," said Peter.

"Oh, yes. Very pleasant. Very, very pleasant. I can assure you it was certainly very pleasant."

She laughed.

"Boog," she said, "will not set foot in that house. I've just come back from Florida visiting him. Did I mention that?"

"Boog?"

"My son. He's working there now. In a hotel until he finds himself."

Peter looked at the white shoes, one of them standing, one lying on its side. He'd always felt absurdly moved by women's shoes. Such frail shells. Compared with men's shoes, like toys. Glass slippers. He'd never been quite sure, though, what he felt, sexually, about feet.

"Boog'll be up for the trial," she said. "It's physical and mental cruelty."

"Trial?"

"*Thing.*"

"I thought physical was supposed to be the hardest to prove?"

"Oh, I've got grounds," she said. "He's admitted it. I've got grounds all right. You just don't know."

"I hope it goes . . ."

"You just don't know," she said. "I could tell you all sorts of things."

Peter knew she would.

He recognized and remembered the condition. He remembered the need to tell friends and acquaintances, the compulsion to inform even strangers of his anguish. He remembered the long drunken nights in patient apartments, words said, actions described, the paralysing replay of words. He said. She said. Words becoming meaningless sounds which were the echo of the pain that would not go away.

He remembered standing in Dominion, the Muzak and bright light enveloping, standing in front of the freezer section, glass, chrome, gazing with unseeing eyes at the carcasses of butterball turkeys, tears running unheeded.

"He used to lock me in the bedroom," she said.

"Oh, yes!" she said in answer to Peter's raised eyebrow.

"He didn't even like me to leave the house. Always wanted to know where I was. There's nothing wrong with bridge, is there? Just a group of girls. It wasn't as if it was men. Because that isn't true. I mean, you understand these things. You've been married. I know he works very hard. You have to give him that. But he wouldn't for night after night and then sometimes when he did he couldn't, you know, couldn't manage. And then he used to shout at me and say it was my fault and beat me up. He used to hit me with a shoe-tree."

"Good God!" said Peter.

"And if I even spoke to another man at a party he'd beat me up when we got home. That's why Boog left. Boog hates him."

"Boog?"

"My son."

"Yes, I know. You said. But I mean *Boog*."

"In Florida," she said.

Peter stared down into the diminished ice cubes in his glass.

"There isn't any harm in discotheques, is there? I've always been a good girl. Nineteen years. Nineteen years and I've always been a good girl. But that's not what *he's* saying. And after I told him I was leaving, well, he wanted to do things."

She nodded.

"You mean . . . ?"

"*You* know," she said. "After I told him, after I'd seen the lawyer, he changed, couldn't get enough of me. Pestered me all the time wanting to do things in chairs and from behind and in the afternoon. I was a good wife to him. I bore him two children. I was always a good girl. He used to listen on the extension phone."

Peter shook his head.

"I shouldn't be telling you these things," she said.

Peter nibbled around the olive.

"He stopped going to the bathroom," she said.

"What?"

"Four or five months," she said, "he stopped going to the bathroom. Before, I mean. Before I left. That isn't normal, is it? You can't tell me that's the action of a normal person."

"What do you mean, 'He stopped going to the bathroom'?"

"Last Christmas," she said, "I bought him a winemaking kit— that was just part of his present—not *last*, Christmas *before* last— and there was a shiny thing in it like soda-water things, you know, the things that make soda-water, the bubbles, but it was for putting corks in bottles. He had a funnel from the office in the upstairs bathroom and another in the powder room—I did mention he was a doctor, didn't I?—the office's in the house, you see, and he did it in bottles and then he used the thing to put corks in."

"When I was a little boy," said Peter, "my mother used to make jam and she stuck on little labels with the name of what it was on it. They were white with a blue border. I remember that. Sticky on the back."

"Rows and rows and rows of bottles," she said. "It isn't very nice, is it? He kept them in the den."

"Perhaps," said Peter, "he was an oenophile."

"You're quite right," she said. "It's filthy. Nobody could call that normal."

She sighed and patted his arm.

"But the past's the past," she said. "Aren't I right?"

"Right," said Peter.

"So let's drink," she said, "to the future! To our futures!"

They drank.

He followed directions to the bathroom.

The dishwasher seemed to be mounting to some sort of climax.

It was nice in the bathroom. There were big mirrors and on the floor a furry carpet. And net curtains looped back on either side of the bath. And a coloured plastic box to put a box of Kleenex in. And a cut-glass jar of bath salts with a pink ribbon round the neck. He weighed himself. Trying not to make a noise, he eased back the mirrored cabinet doors and examined the pills, salves, tubes, pots, and potions. Here there were *two* jars of Vaseline; all women had jars of Vaseline; it was puzzling. He could think of only two bathroom uses for the stuff—to smear on infants or to facilitate the commission of unnatural acts. Neither seemed likely here, he hoped. Vaseline, he decided, was one of the mysteries of the female life.

He weighed himself again but it was difficult to see the wavering arrow. The toilet seat had a furry cover too and he suddenly wanted to know what it would feel like. He lowered his trousers and sat. It was nice.

He thought of the fallen white shoes, one standing, one lying on its side.

Sad he; sad she.

Children's feet, though, were a different matter. Children's feet were pink, diminutive, not deformed by shoes, veins, calluses, not hardened at the heels by yellowing skin.

Poor sad Peter Thornton he whispered to the furry floor *what are you doing in this sad lady's house?*

He would have liked to have stayed in the bathroom, read, gone to sleep on the carpet. Leaning forward was making him dizzy. He consulted his watch. Sitting on the furry seat was like what sitting on a St Bernard would be like. Which would rescue him and take him home and give him aspirins and milk. He stared at the tiled wall. Home, he thought, for no good reason, is the sailor home from sea, and the hunter home from the hill.

As he passed the kitchen door he saw Elspeth McLeod standing to one side of the open dishwasher throwing handfuls of green stuff into the billowing steam. The steam was making her hair wilt.

"What are you doing?" he said.

A strand of hair hung across her puzzled face.

"Parsley," she said.

"Parsley?"

"Forgot the garnish," she said.

She locked the dishwasher and started the cycle again.

"Did you know," said Peter, "there's a kind of wine called *Pisse Dru?*"

"You always forget something," she said.

She linked her arm with his and they went back into the living-room.

"I shouldn't really have told you the things I told you," she said, "but some faces you can tell about. I can see from your face that you've been through a lot of suffering. There are two kinds of people in this world—there are faces that have suffered and there are faces that haven't suffered."

She drew away from him and touched his brow, traced the corners of his mouth. Nodding, she snuggled closer again, drawing her legs up onto the couch. Her skirt was rucked. Peter looked at her thigh.

"Your face is nice," she said. "Very strong but very gentle. It's a masculine face."

He regretted the advent of panty-hose. A nasty garment; peculiarly asexual. Before, when he was younger, there had been brownness, sheen, then, shockingly, the stark contrast of white thigh. Always an incredibly intimate whiteness.

"You're a very cautious person, aren't you, Peter?"

"Am I?" he said.

He stared at the Eskimo carving. The larger they got the less artistic they became; great nasty lumpy thing.

"You don't have to be cautious with me," she said.

There was a silence.

The silence extended.

"Well," she said, "I've been telling you all about me. What about you?"

"There isn't much to tell. It all happened three years or more ago."

"But what happened?"

"She seemed to feel there was more in life or something. Or ought to be. And she met another man and . . . well, she just left."

"Does she love him?"

"She seems to, yes."

"And you were unhappy?"

He nodded.

"Yes."

He lighted another cigarette.

But she had said *what happened*?

It was a question he couldn't answer. Even after three long years he did not know what had happened. With the passage of time, it had all become, if anything, even more senseless. One day, it seemed to him now, he had been a father who brought home flowers and did the shopping on Saturdays, the next, the occupant of a dismantled apartment.

Of course it could not have happened in quite that way. There had been talk, a lot of talk. Words. "Growth," "Fulfilment," "Freedom," "Human something-or-other." He suspected now that for all the mornings he had awoken crying, he was merely victim of the clichés of *Cosmopolitan* and *Ms.*

And Jeremy?

What he felt, he did not know. He did not know.

"You're very quiet," she said. "Did I say something?"

"No, no. Sorry. Just thinking."

She sighed and squeezed his arm.

He stared at the Eskimo thing.

"How about another drink?" she said. "Do you think we should?"

They drank. She sighed again.

"You don't find me unattractive, do you? I'm not unattractive, am I?"

"You're *very* attractive."

"I'm not ugly or anything," she said. "I bore him two children."

"Certainly not," said Peter.

"I've got Hester," she said. "He needn't think he can kick me out without a penny."

"Certainly not," said Peter.

"There are some things," she said, "that people shouldn't say to other people. There are some things you just don't say."

"I think I'd agree with that," said Peter.

"My lawyer says it constitutes mental cruelty."

"What does?"

"When he'd done it—you know—*when* he did it, which wasn't very often *I* can tell you and it's not as if I'm unattractive, he'd stand up on the bed and shout at me—would you believe that? And I worried he'd wake the children because it isn't the sort of thing . . ."

"Shouting about what? What do you mean shouting?"

"Well, that's the point. That's mental cruelty."

"What is?"

"Because do you know what *I* had to say?"

"No."

"I had to say, 'You are, Robert.' Standing on the bed," she said, "shouting."

"You are what?"

"Not a thought for the children."

"You are what?" said Peter.

"What do you mean?" she said.

"What did he shout when you had to say you are?"

"You mean, what did he shout?" she said.

Drawing away from him, she straightened her back, turned.

"WHO'S YOUR MASTER?"

"Shsss!"

"WHO'S YOUR MASTER?"

"Shsss! They'll hear next door."

"Was I speaking loudly?"

"Just a bit."

"I'm sorry."

"It's just . . ."

"If I was speaking loudly," she said, "I'm sorry."

"That's terrible."

"I apologize," she said.

She peered into the empty cigarette packet and then dropped it on the glass table. She groped for the white handbag and rummaged again.

"Oh!" she said. "Look what I've found! I knew they were somewhere."

She opened a fat paper wallet of colour snaps.

"These were all taken in Florida," she said. "Did I mention that?"

Leaning heavily against him, giving his thigh a quick squeeze, she started to pass him the photographs one by one. Dutifully, one after another, he stared at beaches, palm trees, hotel façades, swimming pools, swim-suited groups, reclining people in reclining chairs.

That's me.

And with dismissive gestures, *You don't know these other people.*

That's the ocean.

He stared at two lounging young men who were grinning at him. They held tall drinks. They were tanned and muscled. One wore red trunks, the other white. There was a palm tree. The pool was blue. To the side of the picture stood a waiter in a white jacket.

"There's not an ounce of fat on their bodies," she said.

She tapped the photo with a beringed finger.

"They're famous," she said. "There's one—here it is—of me with them in a group. Here. You don't know these other people."

He stared at the captured smiles.

"They're very famous junior league hockey players," she said.

4

Sitting in the Happy Wanderer finishing his dinner and gazing at the travel posters of ruined castles, bare-knee bands, and Rhinemaids with steins, Peter realized that he had arrived at a decision.

Three weeks or more had passed since Elspeth McLeod. He had not been out much—a movie with Alan and Nancy North, a farewell

evening with one of the young assistants who was going to London
for a course at the V and A, bridge with Hugh and Noreen. He had
allowed the coming March sale to take up most of his time; afternoons and evenings spent examining the furniture and bric-à-brac
of lives, suggesting reserve prices, met always with incredulity that
cherished objects would fetch but a fraction of what had been paid
for them, bread-and-butter work usually left to the younger men.

Peter realized that the decision which had been growing in him
during these days and weeks was probably an inevitable one. It was,
he told himself, a decision towards which the course of his life had
inevitably and inexorably brought him. He examined the decision,
tried out forms of words in his head, declarations. Declarations which
began: *The die is cast . . . From now on . . . From this time forth . . .*

His quest, he had decided, was ludicrous. What had he to do with
Stella Bluth, Elspeth McLeod, and stretching fore and after, all that
sad sisterhood? His life was in need of rationalization and restructur-
ing. All, he told himself, was not lost. He was not exactly young—
middle age approached—but neither was he old; not handsome but
not unattractive. He had friends, a comfortable income, wide interests. He would embrace the single life, honourably discharge his
duties as a parent so far as that was possible, live to himself.

As a sign of this decision, he would make his apartment habit-
able, invest in it time and care. He would, after two years of camping
in it, *move into* his apartment. With growing excitement, he saw that
he would paint, polish, scour, and burnish, re-arrange the lighting,
buy new furniture. He would cook. He would buy supplies, utensils,
Copco enamel pots.

He finished his coffee.

His waitress was the large woman. He watched her making out
the bill. He was pleased he'd got her and not the small, Heidi-like
one. He pocketed his cigarettes and matches. The large woman's
handsome face had reminded him of some other face and the like-
ness had troubled him for months until he'd recognized it as the im-
passive gaze of the woman in Giorgione's *Tempesta*. The resemblance
was striking. She frowned as she figured the tax from the table on the

back of her pad. He imagined her as in the painting, naked, babe at breast. He left a large tip. Past the smelly, damp overcoats and striding towards his local A and P, he saw himself the painting's other character, that enigmatic youth against the violent sky.

In the foyer of the apartment building he checked his mailbox; it contained yet another letter from the Victorian Order of Nurses addressed to Mary Chan.

In his living-room, he took his purchases from the shopping bag and stood them one by one on the coffee table. Cling-Fast Dust Remover, Mr. Clean, J-Cloths, lemon-scented liquid furniture polish, Ajax, Windex.

He wondered where to start. He moved a sticky brandy snifter and picked up a sweater. He opened the closet to throw the sweater in and saw the carton still secured by glossy tape, the barrel. He hesitated and then with sudden resolution reached in to grasp its far corners. To unpack the carton was a kind of declaration, he decided, a laying of ghosts, a line ruled beneath the column. He wrestled the box out into the living-room and then sat on the couch to look at it. Someone had scrawled on the side "Bedroom."

He remembered the two moving men, white patches on the walls, echoes, the rooms becoming hollow. At nine in the morning they had been drinking beer. One, he remembered, called the other "Kangaroo."

He hunted for a clean knife in the kitchen and slit the glossy tape. Inside the carton:

three blankets
newspaper-wrapped things
a wooden train (Jeremy's)
bundles of catalogues from Sotheby's and Parke Bernet (his)
an electric appliance which made yogurt (hers)
a scarlet winter coat and her fur hat

He smoothed the fur and spoke her name in the silence. "Patricia." And immediately wondered why he had. He had never called her Patricia, always either Pat or a private name he would not now say.

Snowflakes drifting from the darkness into the light of the street lamp, glistening, settling, melting on the fur that framed her face. He tried to see her face within that frame but all he could recall was her face as it was in the few photographs he had kept.

The blankets, too. He touched the topmost blanket; it often must have covered them. He tried to remember her body, tried to remember making love, but she, his wife, Pat, dissolved, faded, assumed the postures of models in *Penthouse* and *Cavalier*.

He wondered why he felt so sad, her real face gone, her real body. The moving men remained more vivid, past drama more acute than present feelings. He wondered if perhaps he was deliberately inducing a sense of desolation. He tried the word "desolation" in his mind to see if he felt "desolated" but all the word conjured was the memory of a photograph of Ypres.

He felt, he decided, as if he'd suffered amputation. He was no longer whole. And the pain he felt, the sadness, was part real and perhaps part pain in a phantom limb. This formulation struck him as penetrating and clever and he sat on the couch staring at the carton. The carton was just a cardboard box full of things he once had used and now did not. He sat on the couch feeling sad and holding the wooden train.

The telephone in the bedroom shrilled. Rushing to answer it, he stumbled over a chair in the kitchen. The voice wanted George. The number was right? Then how come no George? Did George *use* to live there?

Peter sat on the edge of his bed and switched on the light which stood on the chest of drawers. The cat woman was on the next door balcony calling kitty—kitty. He could grow herbs in the summer on the balcony in a box—basil and oregano to flavour salads and egg dishes he would cook for friends. He could hang up strings of onions in the kitchen.

Kitty—kitty called the cat woman. *Kitty—kitty.*

He sat on the edge of the bed staring at the chest of drawers. In the chest of drawers, under his shirts, was the list from CompuMate. There remained Anna Stevens. Anna Stevens held for him no interest; the die was cast. But the sheet of paper was a presence. Taking out a daily shirt, he was aware that the list was there, grit and oyster, irritating. To throw the list away was to leave loose ends; to throw the list away was to leave unread, as it were, the final chapter. To throw the list away was, it might be argued, a refusal to test his position. To not phone her could be seen even as a weakness. To phone her was, in a way, part of cleaning up, unpacking, settling in.

He thought of a piece of Battersea enamel that had been through his hands the previous week, a seventeen-eightyish patch-box. The plaque had read:

Happy the Man who Void of Care and Strife
In Ease and Friendship lives the Social Life

Exactly so.
Who loves you the most in the world? called the cat woman.

He opened the drawer and took out the paper. It was rather late to phone but on the other hand he didn't much care what her reaction was. He wished to deal with the matter in a summary way. He felt about it, he decided, as he did when he stayed up late to finish a detective story. The action and the minor characters intrigued him but towards the end of the book exhaustion dragged him down and all that remained was the tedium of the explanation—a scene always contrived, the villain revealing all before pulling the trigger, the cast assembled in the library. Tedious, often silly, but essential before he could brush his teeth and go to bed.

He listened to the ringing, twice . . . three times . . . four.
"Oh . . . Miss Stevens, please."
"Speaking."
"I hope I'm not disturbing you calling at this hour?"
In the background Bach or Vivaldi.

"No."

"My name is Thornton. Peter Thornton. I was given your name by CompuMate."

"Oh, God!" she said.

He listened to the breathing silence for a few seconds.

"Hello?"

"I'm sorry," she said. "I didn't mean . . ."

"Is there something wrong?" he said.

"Look!" she said. "This is all a mistake. One of the men I work with filled out a form in my name and he's caused me a great deal of—"

"But that's exactly what happened to me!" said Peter. "A friend thought—"

"Then you know how distasteful—"

"But what a strange coincidence!" said Peter.

"Yes," she said. "It is."

"What do you mean? Don't you believe me?"

"Why shouldn't I?" she said.

"I'm sorry—just your tone."

There was silence.

"Mr. . . . Thornton, did you say? Let's agree that it *is* a strange coincidence and leave it at that. I really don't want to seem rude but it *is* late—"

"I wonder . . ." said Peter.

"What?"

"No. I'm sorry. I'm sorry to have troubled you."

He replaced the receiver. His hand was sweaty.

Later, lying in bed, drifting towards sleep, his thoughts wandered around the conversation. It was not the sort of ending he'd imagined. In the morning, first thing, he'd throw the list away. He had said, "I wonder . . ." and she had said, "What?" and then he'd said, "No." Had said, "No. I'm sorry." Vivaldi in the background. It was not what he'd imagined; not an ending he'd foreseen.

He wondered if somewhere in the city she too was lying in bed awake, wondering what he might have said when he said, "I wonder . . .", curious, less determined than she'd sounded, provoked perhaps by a coincidence so strange.

But mainly he thought about her voice. Ever since his adolescence he'd been oddly excited by women with a certain kind of voice and she had it. "Husky" did not describe it; that was the property of torchsingers and the like. "Deep" or "low" did not do it justice. For some reason he had come to associate the timbre with coolness, the coolness of moss, of ancient masonry, and over the years had imagined a scene which was somehow the equivalent of the voice.

At a cocktail party, he was introduced to a beautiful woman. They talked. He was holding her glass while she searched her purse for matches. Before taking the glass back, she placed her forefinger across the inside of his wrist for a second. Her finger was slim and cool. The touch was almost solemn yet shockingly erotic because proprietorial. A cool finger across the heat of his pulse, a sophisticated "yes."

And that was the sound of the voice.

During the next two days, Peter frequently caught himself thinking of the voice, the telephone conversation, that music, the strange coincidence of their situation. The coincidence was so strange that it might even be considered a sign or portent. While not at all superstitious or neurotic, Peter often made minor decisions, this restaurant or that, to go out, to stay in, by whether ten cars or more had passed while he counted fifty, by whether a bird flew across the portion of sky visible from his bedroom, by whether in ten dealt cards he drew an ace. On days when he forgot his nail-clippers on the night-table he felt oddly uncomfortable. This business of Anna Stevens deserved thought. He kept remembering something that Alan had said when he filled in the form—something about the possibility of there being one, the same sort of reasons, one like him.

Her existence in no way altered his earlier decision, of course, but he was forced to admit that he was intrigued. Although he entirely agreed with and approved of her attitude on the phone, her cool rejection had irritated him. An admittedly irrational part of him even felt hurt. On the other hand, had she not taken that position, had she accepted or welcomed his approach, he would probably have let her talk and, whatever might have been said, would have tended to consider the matter closed, brushed teeth and so to bed. Just like who was it—Groucho Marx?—whoever said that any club which would accept him as member was not the sort of club to which he wished to belong.

Silly.

He acknowledged his perversity.

She, of course, probably *did* consider the matter closed.

That was a problem.

The coincidence so tantalizing, the effect of her voice, her obvious intelligence and self-possession—she had deprived him of anything he could consider a fitting conclusion to this dismal adventure. This was not the way that stories ended. Before embracing his decision, he wanted to feel that his past—he sought an image—burning of boats, clearing a campsite before shouldering a pack and moving on, yes, that was it precisely. Litter buried, fireplace stones dispersed, the fire kicked out.

To phone her again was impossible; he was not a man who importuned strange women. The most sensible course of action was to write. This would obviate any embarrassment on either side and allow them both their dignity. He would include in the letter sufficient information about himself for her to make a reasoned response. If she chose not to reply, then he would accept that refusal as a considered refusal—the circumstances being completely different from an unexpected phone call. If she chose not to reply, he could accept that refusal as a fitting conclusion to what had been a silly business from the start.

If she *did* reply, if she did reply, then, simply, he would see what happened.

On his return from work on the third day, he sat down at the desk in his bedroom to construct the letter. He had determined on a light and civilized approach. The letter's stated intention was to apologize for his gauche intrusion upon her privacy. He presented himself as a victim of Alan's misplaced sense of humour who—but why had he co-operated, why phoned these dreadful women in the first place? *Pitfall*. Light-heartedly? Presumably he'd have phoned *them* in the same spirit he'd phoned *her*. *Pitfall*. He used up endless sheets of his office scratch-pad.

He wove all necessary information about himself into the fabric of his chronicle of misadventure. All references to his past, marital status, occupation, income, and interests were oblique and present only to make clear word and action. He did not request a meeting or any further contact—the fact of writing implied enough.

He wrote and rewrote, shading an emphasis here, burnishing a highlight, lengthening there, excising. Humour with a dash of pathos dealt with Stella Bluth and Nadia Chayefski. Elspeth McLeod he played as comedy degenerating into farce. He himself emerged as a slightly bruised idealist, rueful, the Philip Marlowe of the antique trade, a man unafraid to admit to loneliness, a man, who, in these untender times, was not ashamed to admit to the possibility of love.

Love, which, strip away our sterile sophistication, our bright brittleness, was perhaps . . . *etc. etc.*

Difficult, this part. Such rhetoric clashed with the letter's general tone. He struggled to bring it under control.

The letter was five pages long. Looking at his watch, he saw with surprise that he'd been working on it for more than three hours. He realized suddenly that he was hungry and exhausted. He felt light-headed, oddly disconnected from his bedroom with its familiar furniture, as if he'd been living for those hours in a different world where a part of him still lingered. He poured himself a large Scotch and read the letter through, smiling still at certain turns of phrase. The letter pleased him; it was a fine blend of humour, self-deprecation, and manly emotion. In a quiet way, it was moving.

He decided that he must eat before writing out a fair copy. He investigated the kitchen. He had bought supplies, tins, meat in the fridge, the *Penguin Book of French Provincial Cookery*. The haricot beans he had been soaking with the intention of using in a simplified version of cassoulet seemed to have gone funny. There was a grey scum on the water and they smelled. As he had further work to do on the letter and felt tired, he decided to eat, for the sake of convenience, at Chez Jean-Guy.

He took the Scotch and the letter into the living-room and sat down to read it again. It *was* moving. He sipped the Scotch. And what was more, he realized, it was *true*.

He mailed the letter the next morning and immediately began to brood about the anarchy of the Montreal postal situation. It was not unheard of for letters to take eight days to cross the city. Letters were sorted ten times, redirected, trundled to Ottawa and back, burned even by union goon squads. Burned, dropped down drains, stabbed through and through by separatist postmen.

His mail was usually delivered at about ten AM and on the third possible day for a reply he drove home at lunchtime to check his mailbox. It contained advertising matter from Simpsons and a Hydro bill.

The weekend intervened.

On Monday, however, the whiteness inside the mailslot was an envelope addressed in an unfamiliar hand.

The letter read:

Dear Mr. Thornton,

Thank you for your charming and humorous letter. There was no need to apologize. If apologies are needed, then I should apologize for being so abrupt. How were you to know that I'd been made the object of someone's spite? Strange as it may seem, passions in libraries *do* exist—it must be something to do with being so enclosed—I was about to say *cloistered!* Please don't feel guilty and excuse my curtness—I'm sure with *your* experiences, you'll understand it.

Yours sincerely,
Anna Stevens

Peter studied the letter.

The most important point, of course, was that she had written it at all. Any kind of reply was a clear indication of interest. That she had gone further and unnecessarily revealed the nature of her occupation . . . He wondered about the words "cloistered" and "passions"—words possibly full of obscure promise.

He imagined her voice saying those words.

On the phone she had said, "one of the men I work with" and the plural was interesting. In most public libraries, the staff was mainly women—one man, perhaps. But "men"? Possible in the main branch of a large city but Montreal had no large public English-language library. And the private or semi-private libraries—Fraser Hickson, Atwater, Westmount—were definitely female preserves. Could it be that, better and better, she worked in a university? And he wondered about "one of the men"—why he'd done that, filled in the form. A discontented underling? A rejected suitor, perhaps, spurred by bitterness.

The letter was written in ink not ballpoint—much in her favour. The paper was a heavy bond, pleasant to handle, the handwriting graceful and firm. The emphasis of "do" and "cloistered," and "your" and the excessive exclamation mark were possibly a little feminine but the letter was not hideous with green or purple ink and circles instead of dots over the i's—characteristics with which he had become familiar over the last three years, infallible indicators of mental or emotional unbalance.

What should be his response? To phone, even now, would be injudicious. Another letter was required, a letter simple and to the point. A letter which explained how he was haunted by how strangely they were yoked by coincidence, which proposed they meet entirely outside the sordid context of CompuMate, perhaps for dinner. Solitary dining uncheering and bad for the digestion. Something along those lines. He would gamble everything on one throw of the dice.

It was as he was labouring over the composition of this letter that the phone rang. He reached over from his desk.

"So what's new?" said Alan.

"Nothing much. You?"

"Just been invited to give a paper in England at a Shakespeare orgy. Expenses paid."

"Will Nancy let you go?"

"I'll have to try being nice to her for a bit," said Alan.

"I'll tell you what *did* happen," said Peter. "I've just met a most interesting new lady."

"What sort of lady?"

"A librarian lady. Very bright. Very good-looking. It all looks very promising."

"Large personalities, has she?" said Alan.

"Really, North!" said Peter. "Must you sully everything you touch?"

"Sully my ass," said Alan. "I'd rather have a pair of first-rate knockers than all those old Chinese pots and pans you moon over."

"You have a point, I suppose," said Peter.

"So have they," said Alan. "But listen. Enough of this Pat and Mike stuff. You want to come to dinner? Nancy's doing something disgusting from a new cookbook and I want you to eat some before I try it. Half an hour or so? Dress informal."

"I'll pick up some wine," said Peter.

"If you want," said Alan, "bring this librarian creature."

The next morning, after the alarm had gone off, dozing, Peter dreamed a most vivid dream which was part dream and part memory. It was the last day of his summer holiday at his uncle's farm. He was saying goodbye to the girl who lived at the next farm. He was thirteen and loved her achingly. Marjorie was twelve.

He was standing in the lane looking up at her where she sat on her pony. Their conversation was stilted. Suddenly he blurted out:

"Can I kiss you goodbye?"

A deep blush suffused her and she bent to pat the horse's neck.

After a silence she said:

"I'd like to but I can't."

They seemed held there then in the still sunshine, the shade of the hazel trees almost black, the buzz of insects in the roadside flowers. He stared at a place in the rein where the leather was cracked and blackened.

And then she said:

"You can have this to keep."

And she thrust at him her handkerchief, a large, man's handkerchief, white with a green and brown border. And later in the bedroom with the black oak beams where he always slept, he moved aside the basin and ewer and smoothed and folded the handkerchief on the washstand and put it in the brown plastic wallet his Auntie Anne had given him for a going-away present.

On his way to work, to his pots and pans as Alan called them, he drove down to the main post office and mailed the letter. He had thought of driving to a post office in Outremont where she lived and posting the letter there but realized that all mail probably went first to the main branch for sorting.

He did not doubt that she would reply.

He was working now on the catalogue, his desk covered with numbered file cards bearing descriptions of each item—dates, hallmarks, troy weights, factory marks, furniture labels, repairs noted, flaws and defects noted, provenance.

Pots and pans.

Thoughts of Anna Stevens possessed his mind.

A bedroom in Madrid full of sunlight, a red tile floor. Breakfast late, and then, in the afternoon, beer and *tapas* at a sidewalk café, she in a blue-and-white cotton frock, sunbrown legs. And at five in the afternoon, the black bulls in the bull ring, the yellow and magenta capes. And then through the warm and quickening streets strolling towards dinner at eleven.

He would take her to his favourite places, the farmlands of his childhood, Madrid, Angôulème, to the rows of dealers in Amsterdam in their ancient, leaning buildings, to the Hebrides, to his student rooms in the rue de Vaugirard.

Yes.

They would walk in the Jardin du Luxembourg eating lemon water-ice.

He thought again of Paco Camino, slim in a silver suit of lights, and counted the years in shock. He had seen the boy take his *alternativa*,

followed him in those sun-filled student days through San Sebast-
ian, Bilbao, Huesca, Pamplona, down through the orange groves to
Seville, watched him work the bulls with mad and terrifying grace.

So many years ago like yesterday. What had become of that nobil-
ity? Dead now, perhaps, or fat, or fighting bulls with shaved horns like
the rest.

Was he too old, Peter wondered, too old to start again?

File cards. Pots and pans.

The day bore on.

On the way home from work he bought the Montreal *Star*. His
mailbox contained a mangled *New Yorker* and a letter from an insurance company informing him that he had been chosen from thou-
sands to receive a prize. He poured himself a drink and sat in his
living-room. He got up and put on a record he'd bought in a Greek
store on Park Avenue, bouzouki music and a man singing, very sad-
sounding and Eastern, but after a couple of minutes he took the
record off.

The apartment, cleaned and now quite neat, was somehow oppressive. He stroked the intricate surface of the cloisonné vase that stood
on the bookcase. Pots and pans. He stood at the window looking out
and feeling restless. He wanted to be a part of the life out there but if
he went out he had nowhere he wanted to go. The glass of the window was cold. He went into his bedroom and called Alan but there
was no answer. Ray, too, was not back from work.

He sat looking through his address book. So many names crossed
out, friends of Pat's, acquaintances fallen by the wayside since his divorce. He stared at her familiar handwriting, numbers from their old
locality—grocers, beer, laundry, dry-cleaners, diaper-service.

He thought of Jeremy last summer and the summer before, of
those desert hours in the sandbox in the park, the suspicious stares
of the suburban mothers and their huddled conversations, the sun
crawling towards the hot tears of bedtime.

He saw himself in the living-room at night stupefied with exhaustion listening to the child's breathing, waiting for a sigh or a cry,
drinking Scotch too fast, too tired to eat.

He was unable to concentrate on the news in the *Star* and he found himself doing something that he never did, working his way through the classified section, through the columns of houses for sale. Outremont, lower Westmount, Montreal West.

He pictured them together, a family again. Anna and Jeremy, on picnics, at the seaside, in fields full of flowers.

After the third day of waiting, Anna's reply arrived. He had known that it would be there, had dawdled deliberately on the way home doing some unnecessary shopping. He did not open the letter in the elevator. In his apartment, he hung up his coat. He took a beer from the fridge and poured it into a pewter tankard he rarely used. He took the beer into the living-room and set it down on the table by his chair. He hunted for the brass letter-opener which he never used, a gift from someone once, its handle the three monkeys. He slit open the envelope and drew out the letter.

He read the note quickly, then read it through again. He could feel the smile stretching his face. He raised the tankard and said aloud, "Your health sir! Your very good health."

He felt so happy it was as if he'd breathed in as much as possible, then a bit more—he felt *full*. He blew a kiss to the drawing which hung near the door—gorgeous grainy charcoal, a backview of a nude brushing her hair.

"An army," he said sternly to her back, "marches on its stomach."

He took the dog-eared copy of *Where to Dine in Montreal* from the bookcase and started to thumb through it. He felt he could compile a better guide himself, one which named names, which exposed corruption in high places, which advised of the venerable patisserie, the Bisto sauces, the crêpes manufactured from Aunt Jemima at $6.50. It was mildly depressing to think of the procession of women he had squired to most of Montreal's many restaurants. He wished he could think of some other socially acceptable way of meeting her, of meeting Anna, something less *used*.

He needed a meal that would be lengthy with no pressure from waiters seeking to seat the starving hordes. He considered the St. Amable—tables too close together. Chez Bardet? Too oppressive, too much conscious good taste, everyone on his or her best behaviour. His own favourite going-out place was the Symposium but it was not a restaurant for intimate occasions—at nine o'clock it filled with rattletrap drummers, amplified bouzoukis, and men who danced intensely and alone.

He needed, then, an unhurried restaurant with a relaxed atmosphere, but not *too* festive, with tables decently separated, and, as he was dealing with unknown tastes, a cuisine not aggressively ethnic. The idea came to him of the Port and Starboard; if she didn't like seafood, the meat dishes were more than passable, salads good, wine list reasonable, the whole place nautically silly with portholes and pleasant and comfortable.

He felt that, even now, it would be safer to write again with day, place, and time but he knew that he could not stand more writing, more waiting, more hours, days, mailmen and letter-boxes.

The conversation was brief, the most convenient arrangement made, and even the part he'd been dreading was carried off with the minimum of awkwardness.

"This is rather ridiculous," he said, "like spy stories—but how will I recognize you?"

"I'll be the one," she said, "carrying a copy of *Pravda* and a saxophone and wearing a red coat."

He laughed deliberately and gratefully.

"Red coat it is," he said. "Until tomorrow, then."

Peter sat the next night, half an hour before the appointed time, in the Crow's Nest drinking a nasty drink called a Capstan. The Crow's Nest was a small bar just outside the main dining room of the Port and Starboard which gave a view of the staircase, the cashdesk, and the cloakroom. The tables in the Crow's Nest were made of barrels and the seats were fashioned from kegs. Special low prices were being offered on drinks called the Capstan, Bluenose, and Blow the Man Down.

Since his last visit, to his horror, the restaurant had fallen prey to a prodigal decorator. The overall effect was of an end-of-lease sale at the premises of an unsuccessful chandler. Every nook, recess, and area of wall had been jammed, plastered, and festooned with nets, buoys, bollards, binnacles, belaying-pins, barnacle-encrusted brass bells, anchors, cutlasses, hawsers, harpoons, lanterns, strings of bunting, and lengths of rusted chain.

Peter imagined the whole restaurant as a bad stage set for a musical. At the entrance to the Crow's Nest, facing the wide staircase, stood a ship's figurehead in the form of a mermaid. The sequence formed before his eyes—a muscular matelot in striped jersey and canvas bell-bottom pants dancing down the staircase, leaning forward from the waist, arms akimbo, to plant a chaste kiss upon the mermaid's carmine lips, and then whirling away into the restaurant proper to dance on tables for Annabelle, the Admiral's lovely daughter.

Peter felt nervous and looked frequently at his watch.

His drink was becoming nastier and *thicker* as he neared the maraschino cherry.

He felt constrained in his newly pressed suit and the white shirt he had bought that morning, dressed up, costumed. He fiddled with the knot of his tie. He fiddled with his silver cigarette lighter.

And then, on the stairs, a flash of red movement, legs, red coat, a girl standing on the bottom step looking about her.

He got up from the table and moved towards her. She was tall and had long black hair tied at the nape with a red wool ribbon like the ones that Nancy bought for Amanda. Her eyes were large and dark. She was beautiful.

She turned again and saw him coming towards her.

He raised his eyebrows.

She smiled.

"Anna?"

"Sorry I'm late," she said. "There's a blizzard starting out there—cars abandoned all over the road."

"I have a table through here," he said. "Thought you might like a drink while we're waiting."

"Lovely," she said.

"Shall I check your coat."

"No, thanks. I'm still freezing."

As she manoeuvred round the barrel and kegs to sit down, the hood of her coat caught on the fluke of an anchor and he had to disentangle her.

"I'm sorry," he said, gesturing at the walls. "It wasn't like this the last time I was here."

"I *like* silly places once in a while," she said. "What's that?"

"I've been wondering," said Peter. "I think it's a donkey-engine."

She undid the wooden pegs of her coat, slipped her arms out of it, and then settled it back over her shoulders. In the bar's half-gloom, pretending not to be watching, Peter saw that she was wearing a black turtle-neck sweater with some kind of large silver pendant over her breasts.

"Drinks!" said Peter. "What would you like? I'll wade through the lobster traps to the bar."

"Sherry, please. A *fino. Tio Pepe*, if they have it."

"This," said Peter, "is a Capstan, as advertised, and it is unbelievably vile and I'm going to get a Scotch to take the taste away."

When he came back from the bar, he raised his glass and said, "Well, Yo-ho-ho!"

"It does all crowd in on you a bit, doesn't it?" she said.

"I hope the food's still as good," said Peter. "If the decor's anything to go by we might be eating hardtack and tapping out the weevils."

"With lashings of putrid salt pork," she said.

"And dumplings sewn up in canvas," said Peter.

She sipped the sherry and smiled at him.

"I like dry sherry," she said, "but I don't like it as much as martinis but if I drink *them* before I eat I get tiddly and can't taste the food."

"Half-seas over, as it were," said Peter.

"Three sheets to the wind," she said.

"In irons on a lee shore," said Peter.

"You made that up," she said.

"I swear," said Peter, "by all that's nautical. I got it from a Hornblower book."

"What does it mean, then?"

"I don't know," he said, making a severe face, "but it's *not good*."

She giggled.

"You're silly," she said.

"Far from it," said Peter. "You behold one who is Captain of his Fate."

"Men who play," she said, "are more to be trusted than men who do not play."

"Is that one of your Laws?"

"The Third," she said. "And I don't feel so nervous now. Can I have a cigarette?"

"Me neither," said Peter.

They occupied themselves with cigarettes and his lighter and the ashtray.

"Can I ask you something I shouldn't?" said Peter.

"What?"

"Why did you come tonight?"

She shrugged.

"I don't know," she said. "It was against my better judgement but—well, I wasn't doing anything else. And your letter, I liked your letter. Curiosity. Who knows?"

"Meeting people is sort of sordid, isn't it?" said Peter. "I'm sorry."

She laughed.

"I didn't mean to be funny."

"I know you didn't," she said. "You just are."

They looked at each other smiling.

"When that wretched little man in the library sent in my name to that *thing*..."

"Why did he do that?"

"I think he thought it was funny," she said. "Men who work in libraries tend to be strange—not all of them, of course—but quite a few are eccentric or homosexual or just childish—I suppose like men who choose to teach elementary school or become nurses. The way things are, it's a strange occupation to choose. Shouldn't be, but it is. But you wouldn't *believe* some of the things I went through. Breathers and panters and abuse and men asking me how much I charged—"

"Good God!" said Peter.

"Someone kept sending religious tracts and one man kept sending me postcards—always the same one. On the writing side it always said I MEAN TO HAVE YOU and the picture-side was always a reproduction of a sort of scroll that had a chant or a prayer by Aleister Crowley on it."

She looked enquiry at him and he nodded.

"Always the same thing," she went on, "one of those 'Do What You Want Shall Be All Of The Law' Crowley things—gibberish, horrible—murder being good if you feel like doing it, you know? I was getting really frightened."

"I've always thought it was funny," said Peter, "that the Great Beast was cremated at Brighton. He should at least have disappeared in a clap of thunder and forked lightning."

"I didn't think *any* of this was very funny," she said.

"True," said Peter. "I was just thinking about Brighton."

"One man," she said, "even sent me a sheet of paper—foolscap— with some obscene doggerel at the bottom and with a drawing of his—his apparatus on the rest."

Peter laughed out loud.

"Really," she said. "And there was an asterisk by the, well, the *tip* of it and beside the asterisk it said 'Actual size'."

She joined in his laughter.

"Did he *need* foolscap?" said Peter.

"But what was funnier than *that*," she said, "if you stop to think about it, I mean, and sad too, it was a Gestetner stencil."

The maître d' appeared at the doorway of the Crow's Nest, menus cradled in his arm, and inclined his head in stately summons. They followed his measured pace and majestic bulk towards the dining-room. In the more brightly lighted foyer and corridor, Peter was violently aware of the swing of Anna's skirt, the trimness and tension of her body beside him.

The dining-room itself was less ravaged; the prints of Ships of the Line remained and the decorator had confined himself to blocks and tackle and a few flurries of swords. They quickly settled the details of the meal; Anna decided on crêpes stuffed with shrimp, clams, mussels, and oyster and baked in cream and cheese; Peter on a dish of herring and roe. Anna traded in an hors d'oeuvre for a dry martini and Peter ordered another scotch. Much ado was made with a wine cooler, napery, and the solemnities of label-inspection.

"I was meaning to ask you," said Peter. "Which library do you work in?"

"McGill," she said. "In the Rare Book and Special Collections."

"Aha!" said Peter. "I've had dealings with them. We once took some medieval manuscripts there we'd had in an estate sale—sort of contracts or leases—bits of parchment with wavy edges?"

He made scissors with his fingers.

"They're called foot of fine," she said, nodding.

"We wanted them dated," he said, "and not a soul in that place had even a clue."

"You aren't surprising me," she said.

"What's more than one of them? *Feet* of fine? Foot of *fines*?"

"Lovely," she said, putting her hand over his for a second. "You don't know how lovely it is to be talking to someone who you *know* won't say, 'What's the point of first editions when you can buy it in paperback?' Or, 'Is it fair to students to buy things they can't read?'"

"*They*," said Peter, "are always with us."

"I try," she said, "but I don't like *they*."

"Isn't it *nice*," he said, raising his Scotch in salute, "you with your squiggly old manuscripts and me with my old pots and pans, isn't it nice to have two *us's* together instead of an *us* and a *them*?"

"Yes," she said, "it really is nice."

A busboy arrived with wine glasses, a water pitcher, bread basket and butter dish and they drew apart as he busied himself.

"So tell me," said Peter, "what *are* the Special Collections?"

She laughed.

"The two main ones," she said, "are Winston Churchill and books and pamphlets relating to the Boy Scout movement."

"How depressingly Canadian," he said.

"And of course," she said, "even those were a bequest."

The cork was pulled, wine tasted, glasses filled.

Salads arrived.

"So it's not entirely fascinating?" said Peter.

"I often wish I'd stayed in London," she said.

"What were you doing?"

"Well, after university and library school here, I went there to King's College—I was taking the diploma course in palaeography."

"And then?"

"I *did* stay for a year but then I fled the country and here I am back with Winston Churchill and the Boy Scouts."

"Fled?"

She laughed.

"Yes, I really did flee—all very dramatic and intense. Possessions abandoned and dishes left on the table. It all seems very *young* and silly now."

"Don't be tantalizing."

"Oh, well, I was living with a very agonized Englishman who was trying to decide if he was or wasn't homosexual and one day I knew I just couldn't take it any more. I didn't know what to do. So I ran away. He was a Marxist, too, and that's a bad combination because they *talk* a lot."

She traced the rim of the wine glass with her fingertip.

"Perhaps it was the talking," she said, "more than any thing else."

Peter nodded.

"Bad talk," he said, "is not good."

"That's a profound remark," she said. "*You're* not a Marxist, are you?"

"No," said Peter, "nor homosexual."

"That's a relief," she said. "Most nice men are."

The waitress arrived. Dinner was served from casserole and plat-
ter onto plates, wine glasses were replenished. When the waitress
had withdrawn, Peter said,

"Okay. If we're asking intimate questions, let me ask you one."

She looked up.

"Have *you* got a cat?"

"A cat?"

"A cat."

"Can I take the Fifth?"

"Not allowed."

"Well," she said, "no. I hate them."

He nodded slowly, as if weighing her reply.

She made a mocking little-girl face at him.

"Did I pass?"

"We're not allowed to say," he said, preparing to dissect a herring.

She gestured at the seafood crêpes with her fork.

"*Delicious*, Peter. Like to try some?"

He shook his head.

"All that heaving brown cheese—it looks like a thing a friend of
mine makes—he calls it 'Disgusting Potatoes'. You'll like Alan."

As they ate, they chatted of other foods and restaurants, other
cities, until the talk turned, inevitably, to the drama of families. Anna's
mother was a martyr whose sufferings were inflicted on the entire
cast. She ironed underwear and saved paper bags. She rearranged
Anna's books in Anna's apartment according to colour. Anna's father
was a mining engineer who, unable to stand the provocation of ironed
underwear and paper bags, now lived in Edmonton. This desertion
was a matter of profound satisfaction to his estranged wife. The script
demanded from Anna guilt that she lived in her own apartment.

Peter related the saga of how his much-loved grandfather in an
inebriated state had introduced a horse into his grandmother's teetotal kitchen. This event with its conflicting values was, he explained,
the archetype of all relationships in his family. It explained, he said,
why his mother had a brooding fear of firearms, why his father had
built a second bathroom, and why his brother had gone to Australia.

Anna was smiling and stemming with Kleenex after Kleenex the explosive sneezes and sniffles which had overtaken her.

Plates were pushed away and cigarettes lighted.

Talk turned to Peter's job, the shop he had opened and which had folded, the general duplicity of the antique trade. Anna was fascinated by the fakes, the frauds, the piracy of buying and selling. He explained to her that contrary to appearances, provenance, or apparent age, *all* antiques were made in the closing years of the nineteenth century.

She kept making faces of apology for her fits of coughing and urged him to go on, to pay no attention.

He told her of the workshops and factories which turned out Luristan Bronze Age artifacts, Solingen sword blades, Delftware, and eighteenth-century English silver with genuine eighteenth-century hallmarks; of the intricacies of the aging process in the faking of early Quebec pine, how pieces were usually buried first for six to eight weeks in a manure pile; of the vast Chinese industry and the Chinese copies of European copies of Chinese originals.

Her coughing seemed to be getting more rasping and uncontrollable. He suggested ice cream in the hope it would soothe her throat. Her face was startlingly red and she kept mopping at her eyes. He suggested that they leave, that the night air might make her feel better, but she made a pantomime of refusal, of swallowing something followed by immense relief.

They sat waiting for the ice cream to arrive. It had become impossible to talk. She was restlessly plucking at the neck of her sweater, pulling it away from her throat. The coughing tore at her and between bouts her breathing was audible, harsh and wheezing.

"I've got an idea," said Peter. "I'll go and get some of those after-dinner mints from the bowl at the desk. The sweetness might do something for it."

He had to wait behind a noisy crowd of people arguing about whose privilege it was to pay the bill and then for an old man doddering over the choice of a cigar and then the bowl was found to be nearly empty and the girl insisted on refilling it from an enormous bag she had to fetch from a cupboard in the cloakroom. She then searched through drawers and cupboards for an envelope to put the mints in.

As he made his way back to the table, he saw standing there a waitress and the maître d'. They were looking down at Anna. As he came up to them, the maître d' said,

"It is too much to drink."

"She was doing that," said the waitress.

Anna was making movements with her hands as if unaware of what she was doing, rubbing the bunched sweater under and between her breasts. The red ribbon had come undone and her hair hung about her face. The chain of her pendant had snapped and it lay snaked on the table in front of her. There was something disturbing, almost frightening, about the movements of her hands; it was a movement that reminded him of the violence of a sleeping baby.

"Anna?"

Peter knelt beside her chair and lifted back her hair, smoothing it away from her face. Her eyes seemed to see him. Her skin looked coarse and grainy and sweat glistened under her eyes.

"Can you tell me what's wrong? Anna?"

He pried her fingers loose from the sweater and pulled it down to cover her. Her body was slippery with sweat.

"She would like to go to the ladies' room," said the maître d'.

Peter put his arm around her and prepared to lift her up but her head lolled.

"I don't think she can move," he said to the maître d'.

"She didn't say anything when I brought that order of ice cream," said the waitress. "She was just doing that."

They looked at her. Her breathing scraped at their silence.

"Well," said Peter, straightening up and turning to the maître d', "I don't think she can walk."

"It is wine," said the maître d'.

There was a crash of broken glass and cutlery falling as she collapsed across the table. Her shoulders were working and she was making noises. Vomit spread out around her face.

Her eyes were closed. Heads were turned; some people were standing up. Peter gathered her hair and lifted it from the path of the vomit. The hair was heavy and alive in his hands. Water dripped onto the floor. The maître d' started to pile the shards of glass at the corner of the table.

"Anna?" said Peter. "Can you sit up? If I help you?"

"Excuse me," said a voice behind them. "Thought I'd better pop over and take a look."

The dapper middle-aged man bent over her. His tie trailed in the spilled water.

"Are you a doctor?" said Peter.

"She has fainted," said the maître d'.

"Sneezing, coughing, and so forth," said the doctor. "How long's it been going on?"

"About half an hour," said Peter. "Maybe more. What is it? What's wrong?"

"Do you have oxygen?" said the doctor to the maître d'. "Canister sort of affair with a mask? Well, you should have."

"What's wrong with her?" said Peter.

"Shock," said the doctor. "Anaphylaxis."

"When I brought that ice cream . . ." said the waitress.

"I need a room," said the doctor, "and blankets."

"By the side of the cloakroom," said the maître d', "is the wine cellar."

"That sounds just the job," said the doctor. "And now phone for an ambulance—as fast as you like. You," he said to Peter, "take her other arm. Right? Better this way in case she vomits again."

As they lifted her, there was the sudden stench of diarrhea. Urine trickling down her leg.

"Never mind that," said the doctor. "They usually let it all go. Thank God for panty-hose, eh?"

In the long narrow room which served as a wine cellar they lowered her to the carpet. It was cold there and silent with the door closed. Her breath laboured on, harsh, rasping in the quietness. The sour smell of vomit and the sweeter stench of excrement hung on the chilly air. The doctor turned her head to one side. She was unconscious.

The doctor was breathing heavily from his exertion.

"Not getting any younger," he said.

"But what *is* this anaphylactic shock?"

"It's the devil of a thing," said the doctor, looking at his watch. "Like an extreme allergy reaction. Food can do it, insect bites."

There was a knock at the door and a waiter came in.

"The lady's shoe, sir."

"But I don't understand," said Peter. "She was all right. I was only away a few minutes . . ."

"Can be as short as two minutes," said the doctor.

"Is it . . . serious?"

"Well," said the doctor, scratching at his moustache with his thumbnail, "yes. I'm afraid it is."

"But I don't understand," said Peter.

"Results in a massive fluid imbalance, you see. The, ah, serum in the body engorges the tissue—can't breathe as a result of that. Throat closes. Lungs fill with liquid. That's what all the coughing and sputtering was in aid of. The whole thing—well, it's rather like drowning, you might say, but drowning from the inside."

There was another knock and the maître d' came in with two blankets.

"Any sign of that ambulance?"

The maître d' shrugged and shook his head.

"Phone again. Immediately. We haven't much time. And send us two brandies—none of your wretched bar stuff. You don't want two poisonings in one night. I don't like that fellow," said the doctor to the closing door. "He seated me in a draught."

He covered her with the blankets and knelt taking her pulse.

"No sense of humour these Italians," he said. "They hadn't got one in the war and they haven't developed one since."

Peter stared at her face.

"But what happens?" he said.

"Happens? Oh. Well, the heart beat becomes more rapid and eventually so fast that the heart isn't circulating at all. No crossover of blood between the, ah, whatnames. Everything demanding oxygen, you see, and the heart doing its best to push round what there is—works harder and harder with less and less—a losing game, you might say. And death results from cardiac arrest."

"Death?"

"No, *no*," said the doctor. "Clap on an oxygen mask—takes care of the breathing. And an injection of what you'd call adrenalin or cortisone steadies the heart—right as rain in no time."

He glanced at his watch and then felt the pulse in her neck.

"Boccaccio was a good chap," he said thoughtfully, "but I haven't a lot of time for them since."

The waiter entered with two snifters of brandy on a tray. He stared at Anna as they took the glasses. The doctor swirled the brandy, inhaled, swallowed. Peter drank from his gratefully. The smell of the room was beginning to make him feel queasy.

"Forbes," said the doctor.

"Pardon?"

"Forbes," he said. "I'm Forbes."

"Oh, I'm sorry. Peter Thornton."

"Wife?" said Forbes, gesturing with his glass.

"No. I've just met her."

Anna was stirring under the blankets.

"You just hang on, old girl," said Forbes.

"Do they have oxygen and adrenalin and things in the ambulance?"

"Standard equipment, old chap," said Forbes. "Not to worry. We can set her to rights down here."

Forbes checked her pulse again. Peter stared at Forbes' forefinger as it lay across the inside of Anna's wrist. The finger was bright yellow with nicotine. He tried to read the expression on the man's face. The face told him nothing.

They sat waiting. Peter began to count the wine bottles in the racks. The rasp of Anna's breath filled the silence. He counted all the bottles up to the first partition. There were one hundred and sixty-one bottles.

"They put me in one of their silly prisons, you know," said Forbes.

"Pardon?"

"The Italians. And a damned inefficient place it was."

They were silent.

"Come *on*," said Forbes suddenly.

"Is she all right?"

Forbes knelt by Anna's side again taking her pulse. He considered his watch.

"Is she?"

"Look!" said Forbes. "Scurry up there above-decks, would you, and investigate that bloody ambulance."

Peter hurried out past the mermaid with the carmine lips and up the wide staircase. He pushed open the heavy padded door and stared out into the blizzard. It was difficult to see much further than the width of the road. Side walk and kerb were obliterated, cars were white mounds. The wind nearly wrenched the heavy door from his grasp. From St. Catherine Street came the muffled sound of horns.

He stood shivering there trying to peer through the flying snow, straining for the sound of a siren.

As he opened the door to the wine cellar, he saw Forbes kneeling over Anna, the blankets thrown back, her sweater pulled up.

"Nothing?" said Forbes.

"You can't even see," said Peter. "Everywhere's blocked."

"Heart's moving into fibrillation," said Forbes, taking off his jacket. "We're going to have to get some oxygen in there."

"But there isn't any."

Forbes held out his wrists.

"Can you manage these damn cuff-links? Wife usually does it."

"What do you mean—oxygen?"

"Tracheotomy, old chap. Bit of a long shot, but . . ."

He pulled the blanket off again.

"Sweater?" he said.

They worked her limp arms out of it and pulled it over her head.

From his trouser pocket, Forbes produced a fat red knife.

"Swiss Army job," he said. "Ingenious thing. Use it in the garden. It's got a pair of scissors and a saw."

"But won't she bleed? I mean . . ."

"Can't make an omelette, old chap," said Forbes, rolling up his sleeves. "Simple enough. Not to worry."

Peter stared down at her. A small blue and white cotton tab stuck out from the edge of the left cup of her bra. It said: *St. Michael. Registered Trade Mark.*

"Get all that hair out of the way," said Forbes.

Then,

"Bloody HELL."

"What? What is it?"

Forbes crouched across her.

He remained like that for long moments.

Then, slowly, he raised himself up, sat back on his heels.

Then Peter, too, became aware of the difference, the change in the room. The room was silent. The sound had stopped.

Forbes took the tip of the blade between forefinger and thumb and eased the blade inwards to the half-closed position. He then pushed the back of the blade with the flat of his hand and the knife closed with a loud click.

Peter stared at her body. Just above her navel and to one side there was a faint brown birthmark. He stared across her at Forbes.

"But she was all right," said Peter. "I only went to the desk. I was only away a few minutes."

"I'm sorry," said Forbes. "Without oxygen, without drugs . . ."

He stood up and started to roll down his sleeves.

"It doesn't make sense," said Peter.

"It's all right," said Forbes. "Not your fault."

"But she was all right," said Peter.

"Look, old chap . . ."

"We were talking. She was all right."

"You need a drink," said Forbes. "Do you a world of good. I'll take care of details here. Phone and suchlike—have a word with Chummy out there. Then I'll join you. Right?"

Forbes led him to the door.

"Get yourself a drink. Doctor's orders."

Peter went out into the restaurant. It was noisy and warm. Her red coat was still draped over the back of her chair. The table had been cleaned and reset. The carpet was dark where the water had spilled. Someone had sprayed the area with a lemon-scented air-freshener. He sat down. He picked up a fork and sat staring at the flash of light on the tines.

A voice said something.

"Pardon?"

A waitress stood there with an order pad.

"Are you the party that was at this table before?"

He nodded.

"The other girl she's finished her shift. She's gone off now."

He stared at her.

She was middle-aged with frizzy, yellowed hair and glasses. She looked tired. Like the other waitresses, she was wearing baggy red pirate trousers and a blouse with puffed sleeves fastened at the breast with black thongs. Round her waist was a wide leather belt with a brass buckle. Stuck in the belt was a plastic flintlock pistol. She was wearing the sort of boots that are illustrated in children's stories, *Dick Whittington, The Brave Little Tailor, Puss-in-Boots.*

"Anything else?" he repeated.

"Yes," she said. "Something nice for dessert?"

P aul Denton's morning erection was thrusting the sheet into a comic tent. He regarded this sheeted protuberance with resigned pleasure. In one of those manuals which he somehow always found himself ashamedly scanning in bookstores, it had stated that REM sleep was accompanied by erections in males and by engorgement of the labia in females. He thought about that; he thought about engorged labia. He felt generally engorged most of the time but summers were more engorged than winters. He had thought when younger that sexual desire would diminish with age but now, his forty-sixth birthday approaching, he found it was getting worse.

The day's heat was already building.

He felt swept as if on tides of sap, febrile, almost deranged.

Visible in the corner of the window, a great, still spread of maple leaves. In front of the window, the hanging plant's soft tendrils were already brushing the Victorian balloon-back chair. At the back of the house, the small garden plot was teeming with a matto grosso of zucchini and cucumber, stiff hairy stems and open-mouthed flowers. The tomato plants were heavy with green clusters. The tight skin of the green tomatoes, their chaste shine, the hints of white and yellow beneath the green as though they were somehow lighted from within promising a warmth and swelling, made him think of firm, girlish breasts . . .

Beneath the sheet, he worked his ankle. The pain was quite severe. His laboured jogging along the canal would be impossible for a few days until the shin splints abated, which was probably just as well because it would spare him the torture of having to observe the bob of breasts, cotton shorts wedged in buttock clefts, nipples standing against sweaty T-shirts.

Though the word "bob" hardly summed the matter up. Some, simultaneously with the "bob," seemed to *shimmy*, a tremor of flesh which suggested, regardless of size, such confined amplitude, such richness, that it made him want to whimper.

He cranked his ankle harder to see if the pain would dispel, or at least control, the summer riot in his mind of breast, thigh, cleavage, pubic mounds etched by cotton shorts or wind-tautened skirts.

From three floors below rose the voices of Martha and Jennifer.

But what's so bad about goldfish?

Because white cords come out of them and it makes me sick and who has to flush them down the toilet?

What white cords? What are white cords? What . . .

The front door closed on the voices.

He regretted, daily, having been swayed by the mad enthusiasms of the renovator; he regretted, daily, the very idea of open-plan architecture. The restless night-turnings of his children, the blurts of sleeptalking, the coughs, the soft padding of bare feet on cushioned carpet, the rubber seal on the refrigerator door meeting rubber seal with a *plup*—from his bedroom eyrie in what had been the attic, he could have heard a mouse break wind.

It was open-plan design which he blamed, in part, for the impoverishment of his sex-life. Martha felt uncomfortable, unable to relax if the children were still awake or restless. They used the word "children" to refer to Alan and Jennifer who were eleven and eight. Peter at fifteen had passed beyond being thought a child by either of them and especially so by Paul.

It seemed to Paul that whenever he was gripped by sexual desire, which was very often, his desires were thwarted by Martha's worrying that the children would hear, would interrupt, that Peter, who was inevitably out, would come in, that the phone might ring, a phone that could not be taken off the hook because Peter, who was

out, might have been run over by a truck or fallen into the river or
been entrapped by white-slavers. Experience had taught him the
futility of attempting to counter these anxieties with reasoned argu-
ment; it was futile to point out that Peter had been crossing roads
unaided for ten years, that there were no open bodies of water
within miles of the movie theatre in which he was seated, that only
the most desperate of Arab potentates could lust after a boy with an
obnoxious mouth and purple hair.

Nor were the prospects any brighter if Peter *were* in, the family
door secured against the legions of burglars and perverts. If he *were*
in, he refused, flatly, to go to bed. This meant that lubricity in any
form was impossible because he was awake, probably listening, possibly *recording*, and almost certainly drinking the last of the milk
and eating the fruit for the children's lunches.

Outsitting him was not feasible strategy. Exhausted by her daily
labours at the Ministry of Energy, Mines, and Resources and then
further exhausted by cooking, homework consultations, and the
general wear and tear of motherhood, Martha was red-eyed with
fatigue by nine-thirty. Any sexual activity past that hour bordered
on necrophilia.

Mornings were an impossible alternative. The differences in their
circadian rhythms were such that Martha's eyes sprang open with the
dawn chorus while his were blear and his mood surly until eleven-
thirty, at which time Martha was beginning to droop.

Weekends were no better and were not exactly weekends. Saturday was his busiest day in the gallery and on Mondays, the traditional closing day for galleries, Martha was, of course, at work in the
Ministry of Energy, Mines, and Resources. This left Sundays. The
logistics of organizing the absence of all three children at the same
time and ensuring that absence for at least an hour were next to
impossible and if he attempted to hustle her upstairs for a rushed
sortie she complained that it didn't seem very "romantic," a charge
that left him stunned.

He had learned not to count his chickens even when Martha and
he, by some miracle, lay naked and entwined; open-plan coughing

would erupt, open-plan allergies would strike, so that nights which began with tumescent promise ended with the dispensing of Chlor-Tripolon and Benedryl.

When she or he returned from these errands of mercy—usually she because of his monstrous and adamantine visibility—she would always say:

I'm sorry, Paul. Do you mind if we don't tonight? It's just that, well, you know . . .

He did not, in fact, know *really* what it was that she presumed he knew because *he* would have been capable of enjoying intercourse had the house been under frontal assault by urban guerillas, but he always made polite noises before going into the bathroom and getting his mouth round the gritty-sweet neck of the Benedryl bottle in the hope that the side effects of two disgusting swallows would assist him towards unconsciousness.

Paul had endured these frustrations for years and as far as he could see they could only get worse, because when the other two were a little older they, too, like Peter, would stay up past nine-thirty and would wish to go out and come in.

In his more despondent moments, it seemed likely to Paul that he would not be able to make love to his wife again for ten more years—and that figure was based on the assumption that Jennifer would leave home at eighteen, which was probably being optimistic. At which time, and over his most violent objections, Peter, who would then be twenty-five, and who would have contracted a disastrous marriage, would doubtless be returning to off-load on them damned babies which would be subject every night to croup, grippe, projectile vomiting, and open-plan convulsions.

In ten more years he would be fifty-six.

In ten years after that, if he lived, sixty-six.

He thought about being old; about being him and being old; about being married and being old. He thought of a funny line from a forgotten thriller, an aging lecher who had said that intercourse in the twilight years was all too often like trying to force a piece of Turkish Delight into a piggy bank. Paul was perfectly prepared to accept that this might be so; what depressed him was the almost certain knowledge that he'd still ache to try.

Since his heart attack, or what he persisted in thinking of as his heart attack, he often found himself considering the form and shape of his life. He lived with a great restlessness and longing, as if the frustrations of his semi-celibacy had spread like a malignancy. He did not know what it was he longed for. His life, he felt, was like a man labouring to take a deep breath but being unable to fill out his lungs. Everything, he felt, seemed somehow to be slipping away, fading. He daydreamed constantly, daydreamed of robbing banks, of doing sweaty things with Bianca Jagger, of fighting heroically against BOSS to free Nelson Mandela from Robben Island . . . Kalashnikov rifles, the pungent reek of cordite . . .

This restlessness had expressed itself the night before in Montreal in his impulsive purchase at Pinney's Fine Art Auction of a stuffed grizzly bear. Driving back to Ottawa on Highway 17 with the grizzly's torso and snarling head sticking out of the window, he had felt pleased and superior to all the cars which lacked a bear.

Now, he did not wish to think about it.

He lay on his side of the bed listening to the throaty pigeons fluttering and treading behind the fretwork gingerbread which framed the dormer window and rose to one of the twin turrets which were the real reason for his having bought the house.

On the bedside table lay the packet of Nikoban gum.

"Effective as a Smoking Deterrent," he said into the silence of the bedroom, "since 1931."

The other turret rose above the curved end of the bathtub; during the night more granular insulation had sifted down. He had run out of renovation money eighteen months before. Only the ground floor was finished; the rest of the house looked as if it were in the early stages of demolition. The turret above the bathtub, the renovator had said, could be opened up and finished inside, painted white, lighted possibly, so that when one was lying in the tub it would be rather like looking up the inside of a "wizard's hat." Paul remembered his exact words; he remembered the turn of the renovator's wrist and fingers as he conjured this whimsy from the air. All that could be seen through the smashed hole in the ceiling was a dangling sheet of tin or zinc, pieces of two-by-four, and deepening blackness punctured by a point of light. Lying in the tub and gazing up always made Paul think not of the inside of a wizard's hat but of being trapped at the bottom of a caved-in mine shaft.

He bent to examine the wavering arrow. It returned obstinately to 168 lb.; this meant that despite not eating bread at lunch and despite passing up potatoes at dinner he had, in the face of the laws of nature, gained three pounds overnight.

He teased the four white hairs on his chest.

Treat this as a warning, Mr. Denton.

Staring unseeing into the mirror, he pictured himself jogging along the side of the canal, felt the flab over his kidneys jounce. His route unreeled in his mind like the Stations of the Cross: Patterson Avenue, past First, Second, Third, and Fourth Avenues, the stand of pine trees, then the Lansdowne Stadium stretch, and then, rounding the curve, the first sight of the Bank Street bridge. In the final stretch between the Bank Street bridge and the bridge at Bronson, the canal narrowed, the trees overhanging and the bushes crowding in to suggest a sombre tunnel. It was here that he always saw the carp, great silent shapes rising to the scummed surface to suck down floating weed, their lips thick and horny gaping into orange circles.

And then, rubbery legs, breath distressed, almost staggering, into the shadows of the Bronson bridge and out, out to the canal widening into the blue expanse of Dow's Lake sparkling, the open sky, the gentle slopes of the Arboretum on the far shore, white sails standing on the water.

Treat this as a warning, Mr. Denton.

He had known when the intense pains came that he was dying and so had done nothing. But Martha had detected it, something in his face or posture perhaps, and had badgered him until he'd admitted to some slight discomfort. It was she who had phoned their doctor and she who had secured him an emergency appointment. Constriction of the blood vessels and the muscles of the chest wall caused by tension was the diagnosis.

Overweight, under-exercised, a pack of cigarettes a day, tension . . . *treat this as a warning.*

"You would be wise to avoid," the pompous little fart had said, "life-situations which generate anxiety and stress."

Paul shook the can of shaving foam, tested the heat of the water in the basin.

He pulled flesh tight over the angle of his jaw.

How would *you* avoid, he would have liked to ask, how would *you* avoid being consumed with unsatisfied sexual desire? *Unsatisfiable* desire, given the combination of Martha's anxieties and the interior construction of the house. Answer me that, smug little physician. Go on! What do you suggest? Castration? Investing in a sound-proofed house? Trading in the present wife for something a touch more feral? Snuffing the kids?

And *how*, you scrawny little processor of Ontario Health Insurance Plan cards, how would *you* avoid just the faintest twinge of anxiety about a business that's barely paying the rent? A business, furthermore, of which the proprietor is ashamed.

Two aspirins and retire to bed?

Keep warm?

And while we're on the subject of tension, stress, anxiety, surges of adrenalin, and so on and so forth, here's a life-situation over which you might care to make a couple of magic passes with your little caduceus. What advice do you have to offer about the best way to avoid one's son?

Yes, son.

S-O-N.

He had noticed the blue-sprayed markings on neighbourhood walls weeks earlier. The script was cramped, busy, fussy squiggles and dots; he had thought it might represent slogans in a foreign language, possibly a very demotic Arabic or Farsi. Given the high concentration of Lebanese in his area, he had thought that these bright blue writings might possibly be charms against the Evil Eye. It had taken weeks of glancing before he'd suddenly recognized them as being in English.

Two of the more decipherable of these mysterious blue messages said:

Check out!

and

(something) *Zod!*

Coming home late one night from a local estate auction at the Ukrainian Hall, which had advertised "primitive African carvings" that had turned out to be two slick pieces of Makonde junk and a pair of salad servers from Nairobi, he had let himself into the silent house to find in the vestibule a can of blue spray-paint fizzling indelibly onto the newly installed quarry tile.

He had stood there long moments staring.

Paul no longer attempted to deny to himself or to Martha that the presence of his son snagged on his nerves and curdled the food in his stomach. He did not understand the boy; he no longer *wanted* to understand him. It was not unusual for Paul immediately after dinner to be stricken with nervous diarrhea.

Even *thinking* of Peter constricted Paul with rage, made his pulse pound in his neck, throb in the roof of his mouth. He knew that the words "burst with rage" were no cliché. During these rages, he always found the word "aneurism" swelling in his mind, pictured a section of artery in his neck or near his heart distending like a red balloon to the very palest of terrifying pinks.

Paul was enraged by his son's appearance, manners, attitudes, reflex hostility, hobbies, and habits. He was reduced to incoherent anger by the boy's having mutilated all his clothes by inserting zippers in legs and sleeves, zippers which were secured by bicycle padlocks, so that he looked like an emaciated scarecrow constructed by a sexual deviant, by his smelly old draped jackets which he purchased from what he called "vintage clothes stores," by his bleached hair which he coloured at weekends with purple food-dye, by his ruminant of a girlfriend whose mousy hair was bleached in two stripes intersecting at right angles so that she looked like a hot cross bun, by his wearing loathsome plastic shoes because he didn't want to be party to the death of an animal, by his advocacy of the execution of all "oppressors," which seemed to mean, roughly, everyone over twenty-five who could read, by his intense ignorance of everything that had happened prior to 1970, by his inexplicable and seemingly inexhaustible supply of ready cash, by his recent espousal of self-righteous vegetarianism, which was pure and total except for a dispensation in the case of pepperoni red-hots, by his abandoning in the fridge plastic containers of degenerating tofu, by his rotten music, by his membership in an alleged band called The Virgin Exterminators, by his loutish buddies, by the *names* of his loutish buddies, names which reminded Paul of science fiction about the primitive descendants of those who'd survived the final nuclear holocaust, names like Deet, Wiggo, Munchy, etc., by his diamanté nose-clip and trilby hat, which accessories, in combination with his dark zippered trousers and draped zippered jacket, gave him the appearance of an Hasidic pervert, by his endless readiness to chip in with his mindless two bits concerning: the Baha'i faith, conspiracies, environmental pollution, the injustice of wealth, fibre-rich food, the computer revolution, the oppressive nature of parental authority—*Jesus Christ! Oh, God, was there no end?*—by his festering bedroom, by his pissing on the toilet seat, by his coming into his, Paul's, bathroom and removing his, Paul's, box of Kleenex, by his pallor, his spots, his zits, his dirty long fingernails, his encyclopedic knowledge of carcinogens, his pretentious sipping of Earl Grey tea, his habit of strumming and chording during dinner on an imaginary guitar, of bursting into sudden ape-noises, of referring to him, Paul, as "an older person," by . . . *Dear Christ! How he hated that malignant cat with its obnoxiously pink arsehole!* Misguidedly saved but days ago from the SPCA without his, Paul's, permission. Not for *his* bloody son a kitten but a mangy, baleful presence which was missing one ear and had *things* in the other.

It would, inevitably, shed some of what hair it had left. The hair would, inevitably, stimulate a new range of allergies in Jennifer and

Alan. The allergy attacks would strike, inevitably, just as the stars stood in rare and fruitful conjunction leading, inevitably, to yet more nights of throttled rage and Benedryl.

Paul completed the series of faces indicative of amazed contempt, loathing, rage, and resignation, all of which were slightly invalidated by the blobs of shaving foam under his ears and on his Adam's apple, and washed off the razor under the hot tap. Only a friend, he thought with sudden honesty, could describe his pectoral muscles as "muscles." And even such minor movement as brushing his teeth set jiggling what once had been triceps.

Sunlight bathed the hanging plant and lay warm across his bare feet. His feet were sweaty on the cool tiles. The plant always received Martha's special attentions. It hung down in ropes of leaves shaped like miniature bunches of bananas. Peculiar-looking thing. He chomped with sudden savagery on the two pieces of Nikoban gum in the hope that this would release into his bloodstream increased surges of the active ingredient, lobeline sulphate, effective as a smoking deterrent since 1931.

He deliberately thought of breakfast as an antidote to thoughts of a Rothman's King Size. He could have one egg, medium, boiled, and one slice of toast, dry, with black coffee for a calorie count of (140) or a small bowl of Shredded Wheat with no sugar for (150) or a piece of melon, cantaloupe, medium, one half, for (60). And then, if at lunch he stuffed his face with alfalfa sprouts or handfuls of grass, he'd be able to splurge at dinner with a nice bit of tasteless chicken with the skin removed.

He could feel bad temper tighten and coil.

The bunches-of-bananas plant made him think with exasperation and affection of Martha and of the generally peculiar and incomprehensible nature of life. Martha would soon be picking off green tomatoes to make chutney, filling the house with the smell of vats of the evil stuff, onions, vinegar. She did it every year. No one ever ate the chutney. Not even Martha. In their various moves, the vintages of preceding years had accompanied them. The basement was full of the stuff. She put little labels on the jars. It seemed to be some blind, seasonal activity like spring-stirred badgers lugging out the old bedding or bower-birds dashing about in the undergrowth collecting shiny stones, though the chutney-making had, so far as he could see, absolutely no sexual motivation overt or otherwise. It only made her more tired than usual.

Over the shower rail hung a damp and dwarfish pair of panty-hose.

The edge of the wash-basin and the counter-top were freckled, as they were every day, with some dark orange powder she brushed on her face. He wiped it off with a Kleenex as he did every day. When he put on his bathrobe after his shower, her plastic shower-cap, always lodged on top of his bathrobe on the back of the door, would plop onto the floor.

He stood staring at the array of her bottles, unguents and lotions, creams. With its scarlet cap, there stood the bottle, the red label: *Dissolvant de polis d'ongles.*

Norma, the girl he'd come to think of as Polly Ongle, would soon be in the gallery, would soon be busying herself shining up bits of Ethiopian silver, necklaces, pendants, Coptic crosses hammered from Maria Theresa *thalers*. He could picture her working over the glass top of the display case, the curtain of black hair, the incredibly slim waist cinched by the wide, antique Turcoman belt studded with cornelians, her long fingers sorting and stringing old trade beads and copal amber, following the designs in colour photos in *African Arts* magazine.

Since Christmas Eve, he had tried to stop himself thinking about her hands, those slender fingers.

He sighed as he settled himself on the toilet seat.

He enjoyed the emptiness of the house in the mornings, Martha off to work, the deepening silence left behind by the children after the fights about who'd taken this, touched that, *his* lunch had grapes, well *yours* had an orange, the penetrating *shushings* rising to shouts of *Be quiet! Daddy's sleeping!*

This morning hour seemed the only period of complete peace in the entire day.

He reached round behind him for his copy of *The Penguin Book of Modern Quotations*. He placed the box of Kleenex at his feet. Recently, bowel movements had been accompanied by a stream of clear liquid running from his nose. He had thought at first that this was probably the symptom of some terminal disease but as nothing had happened further and he felt relatively healthy he had accepted it as possibly being natural. Though it had never happened to him before and he'd never heard of it happening to anyone else. But, on the other hand, it wasn't the kind of thing likely to crop up in normal conversation.

The bear was worrying him.

He was pleased that he'd had the sense to stow it away in the gallery stockroom before coming home. He could not have stood a morning conversation with Martha about stuffed bears, the questions leading to denunciations and accusations of fecklessness and immaturity, the whole entirely justified harangue shrilling off into the price of sneakers, orthodontistry, day camps, the mounting fines at the Ottawa Public Library because he was so bloody lazy, the price of meat.

"Ha!" he said aloud.

His eye had fallen on an apposite quotation from Frances Cornford concerning Rupert Brooke:

Magnificently unprepared / for the long littleness of life.

He wondered what would have happened to Rupert Brooke if he'd lived long enough to have had a slight paunch, stuff running out of his nose every time he had a crap, and a kid with purple hair. No one was prepared for that. Who could imagine it?

Who in *hell* could he sell a very large bear to?

He wondered what Polly had thought when she'd opened the stockroom and seen six feet three of reared grizzly.

He thought about the Turcoman belt studded with cornelians; he thought about the belt clasping her waist; he tried to stop himself thinking about navels. Shirts or blouses knotted above the waist exposing midriffs, in strong sunshine a down of fine hair glinting . . .

He had given her the belt for Christmas. He had not told Martha
that he had given it to her. He felt vaguely guilty about having given
it to her. He felt uncomfortable both about the gift and about keeping it from Martha.

On Christmas Eve, after the flurry of last small sales, he had taken
Polly for a Christmas drink. Nothing had happened. They were sitting in a booth at the back of the dimly lit bar. On the wall just above
the table was a lamp with a yellowed shade. It cast an almost amber
light. She'd been drinking Pernod. She didn't usually speak much;
she'd been saying something about the ambassador from Togo who'd
been in that morning and who'd been offensively imperious, as he
always was.

Her hands were within the pool of amber light. He'd been tranced
by the light glinting on the clear nail-polish, hinting as she gestured.
That was all. Light, glancing. That was all that had happened.

Paul stiffened and stared at the back of the closed bathroom door.

From below, a door knob, footsteps.

He gripped the book.

A stream of urine drilling into the toilet bowl.

PETER!

Must have persuaded Martha he was sick.

Probably had an exam.

Or gym.

A loud, moist fart.

Orangutan noises.

Bam BAM ba-ba Bam

Bam BAM ba-ba Bam

Burn DOWN the fuck'n town.

A drawer opening, slamming.

"Dad-ee?"

Creakings up the stairs.

"Oh, Dad-deee!"

Probably peering through the open-plan banisters like something from a zoo.

Only feet away.

Outburst of ape-gibbering.

Pyjama bottoms wrinkled round his ankles, breathing carefully through his open mouth, silently, Paul sat tense on the toilet.

Paul followed what Dr. Leeson called his "auxiliary" into what Dr. Leeson called, always, "the inner sanctum."

"How!" said Dr. Leeson, raising a palm.

Paul smiled.

Dr. Leeson had started greeting Paul in this way some four years earlier after he'd chanced to see in the Ottawa *Citizen* a review of an exhibition of Indian *pechwais* in Paul's gallery. Despite references in the review to India and to Krishna, Ganesh, and Shiva, Dr. Leeson had somehow understood the show to concern Indians from North America. Paul thought the greeting was probably a fair sample of dental humour.

"No more gum trouble? Bleeding?"

Paul shook his head.

"No more looseness in the front here?"

"No, just fine."

"That looseness," said Dr. Leeson, "that can be a sign of adult diabetes but periodontal infection's the—that's it, your head here towards me . . . *hmm hmmmm—hmm hmmmm . . .*"

Warm peppermint breath.

"*. . . and broke it apart, Suzanne, Oh my Suzanne!*"

Paul, his eyes pulled open wide, stared over the back of Dr. Leeson's immense hand at the setting sun, an orb in yellow majesty against a wild red deepening to a foreground black. Printed on the blackness of the poster in white were the words:

The goal for my practice is simply to help my patients retain their teeth all of their lives if possible—in maximum comfort, function, health, and aesthetics—and to accomplish this appropriately.

Dr. Leeson settled the small rubber nose mask and pulled the tubes high up onto Paul's cheeks. Paul breathed in the thick, slightly sweet gas waiting for the tingling in his hands and feet to start. The mask quickly became slimy, a rubbery smell mixing with the smell of the gas. His mouth was dry. He closed his eyes.

". . . up to the lake?" said the auxiliary.

Sounds of instruments on the plastic tray.

"How you doing?"

Paul grunted.

In the coloured darkness, his mind raced. He made a mental note to speak to the kids about picking at the plaster on the second floor. And about not leaving their skateboards in the hall. After this, the bank. Capital Plastics, another phone call that had to be made.

"Relax," said Dr. Leeson, "we're doing good."

As always when the noise started, he felt panicky, felt he must be insane to trust a man younger than himself who wore plaid trousers, felt he *must* check the man's credentials, actually *read* those framed certificates. He felt that no really responsible doctor would wear cowboy boots to work; there was something about the man, something about his large red face and blond eyelashes, which suggested the Ontario Beef Marketing Board; this Leeson, he realized, in whose hands he was, frequented road-houses and rode mechanical bulls.

The steel was in his mouth.

They were talking at a dark remove from him; he had a sudden conviction their relationship was more than dental.

He concentrated on picturing the silent kitchen where for breakfast he'd eaten half a cantaloupe; he conjured up the Boston fern in its earthenware pot, the sleek chrome-and-black-plastic design of the Italian espresso machine Martha had bought him for Christmas, the dark aroma of the coffee beans in the waxed-paper Van Houte bag, cluttering the fridge door the invitations to birthday parties, the shopping lists, medical appointment cards, crayonings of intergalactic battle, all held by Happy Face magnets.

Until he'd heard Peter slamming out of the house, Paul had remained hidden in the bathroom.

On the kitchen counter beside a glass that had contained orange juice, Peter had left a library book. The book was in French. Judging from his report cards and the comments of Mrs. Addison on the last Parent-Teachers Evening, he'd be entirely incapable of reading it. The book was entitled *C'est Bon La Sexualité* and contained diagrams of wombs.

Sitting there in the whiteness of the kitchen, the sunshine, the silence, Paul had been moved by a surge of pity and compassion.

He was swallowing water; could feel wetness on his cheek.

He tried to think, deliberately, of what was to be done that day.

Letters to go out, bulk mailing, for the exhibition of Shona stone carving. The photo-copy place. Capital Plastics to price lucite bases for the Mossi flutes. Rosenfeld in Washington to deal with over the crate of pre-Columbian pots; Customs. A new rubber ring-thing— what *was* the word?—rubber *belt* for the carpet part of the vacuum-cleaner.

The carpet in the gallery was coir matting, suitably simple and primitive, hard on the vacuum-cleaner's wheels and brushes.

The word "coir" made him think of "copra," "coitus," "copulation." Nearly everything did.

The current exhibition at the Uhuru Gallery of Primitive Arts was a collection, on consignment, of modern Makonde carvings, every single one of which he loathed. Preceding them had been exhibitions of contemporary "temple" carvings from India, shadow-puppets from Indonesia, *papier-mâché* anthropomorphic frogs from Suriname, garish clay airplanes from Mexico, and drawings from the remote highlands of New Guinea executed in Magic Marker.

Soon it would be twenty years since his life had taken the turn which had led him to where he was now. Okoro Training College. Port Harcourt. Sometimes when he looked through the old snap-shots in the chocolate box he felt he was looking at preposterous strangers: Martha with long black hair tied back with a ribbon; he wearing ridiculous British khaki shorts and knee socks; Martha

standing with Joseph, the houseboy, in his shabby gown, long splayed
toes; Mr. Oko Enwo in his academic gown; he and Joseph posing on
either side of a dead snake slung over the compound clothesline.

Strangers.

Sun-bleached strangers.

At first, the gallery had done well; he had sold, cheaply, many of
the good carvings he'd collected in Nigeria. But then what small
supply there was dried up. The young men were drifting from the
ceremonies of the dance to the beer-hall bands and city discos. The
world he'd been privileged to glimpse on holiday expeditions to
those Igbo villages upcountry all those years ago had been even then
a world close to extinction, a world about to be swept away on a tide
of plastic sandals, cheap stainless steel watches from Russia, Polaroid
cameras, calculators.

The Uhuru Gallery, which had opened with passion and vision,
had become little more than an emporium of Third World tourist
junk. The only genuine carving on his walls was a stern Bambara
mask whose austerity was a daily rebuke.

He dreamed sometimes still of the journeys upcountry jammed
in the back of the rackety Bedford lorries which served as buses,
journeys of dust and shimmering heat which ended in the packed
excitement of the village commons surrounded by the mud walls
and thatch of the compounds.

Often he had been offered a seat of honour among the elders
in the shade, while Martha had been packed in with the women and
the glistening children, the sun splintering through the leaves and
fronds of the trees beyond the compounds.

And then the tranced hours of the festival, glasses of palm wine
cloudy green, the sun beating down and the air pulsing with the
rhythms of the four drummers, quivering with the notes of the
gongs and the village xylophone, shush-shuffle of seed-rattles. Muzzle-
loaders exploding into the blue signalled the approach of the procession from the Men's House of the cloth and raffia-clad masks—*beke,
igri, mma ji, mkpe, umurumu*—individual dancers breaking from
the chorus to raise the red dust until their feet were lost in the haze.

Then the slow unfolding of the story-songs, the high call and response of the two leaders, the great wave of sound from behind the painted masks. And between the stories, the masked dancers burrowing into the crowd to demand "dashes," the lines of *akparakpa* dancers in parody of female dancing, each man wearing thick rolls of women's plastic waist beads, buttocks stuck out, greeted by the women with shrieks of *aiy aiy aiy aiy aiy*. Until there seemed no end, the drums sounding inside one's head, the notes of the xylophone vibrating, gong and slit-drum, dust, sun, the praise-sayers, the singing.

"Mr. Denton?"

"Umm?"

The chair rising to an upright position.

"Mr. Denton! You're all finished now. I'm going to leave you just on the oxygen for a couple of minutes, okay? Like we usually do? Okay?"

He opened his eyes.

Yellow. Red. Black patterned with white marks.

"Fine. Sorry. Yes, sure."

He lay staring at the poster of the setting sun against the wild red sky.

———

The fragrance from a tangle of wild roses in front of a house on Gilmour Street lay heavily on the humid air. Paul stopped to breathe it in; it was almost indecent. His teeth felt foreign. Exploring them with his tongue, he turned onto Elgin Street. After the darkness of the gas, after the strange shapes of chairs, carpets, counters, the buttons in the elevator, had once again assumed their form and function and steadied into place, he always felt almost resurrected when he walked out into the world.

Sunlight glittering on spokes and rims. Back straight, fingertips of one hand on top of the handlebars, a girl on a ten-speed bike coasting in towards the red light. White top, blue linen skirt, she jutted like a ship's figurehead. Just before she drew level, she swooped to apply her brakes. Staring into an abyss of pristine cleavage, Paul stumbled over an Airedale terrier and babbling apologies shot through the doorway into Mike's Milk.

After prolonged dental torture, nerves stretched to breaking-point, *one* cigarette, he reasoned, was understandable and forgivable; he was not really letting himself down; he would probably throw away the rest of the package. Or perhaps ration them judiciously, using them in conjunction with the Nikoban gum to effect a more *rational* withdrawal; it was, he thought, an unrealistic and possibly injurious strain on the system to diet, jog, and stop smoking all at the same time.

With some five minutes in hand before the bank opened, he strolled down Elgin Street. The cigarette tasted so wonderful that he felt he ought to be smoking it through a long onyx holder. His trousers seemed definitely looser at the waist. He crossed against red lights.

Standing in the line-up idly watching the top halves of tellers, he thought about the girl with the huge hoop earrings, wisps of hair escaping from her collapsing bun, the absent eyes. Unless she was in the vault, she wasn't on duty. Oddly *Victorian*-looking girl. As one might imagine the daughter of an impoverished rural vicar in an old novel. He suspected she was profoundly crazy and was attracted by the idea of whatever mayhem or enforced redistribution of wealth she might be capable of. Once when he hadn't seen her in the bank for some weeks, he'd asked her if she'd been sick.

Oh, no, she'd said, *I'm a floater.*

He still wondered what she'd meant and why he kept on thinking about it.

Despite the air-conditioning, the cheques were wilting in his hand. Beside him, a rack containing deposit slips, brochures about Registered Retirement Savings Plans, copies of that month's Royal Bank Letter entitled: *Regarder la mort en face.* The next shuffle forward brought him round the curve of the furry blue rope and closer to the counter; he stood watching the outline of panties beneath the slacks of the teller who was waiting at the central cage for cash.

He walked on up Elgin past the National Gallery and the National Arts Centre. Before crossing towards the Château Laurier, he paused to glance in the window of the Snow Goose at the latest display of native Canadian arts, alleged Haida masks, horrible great green lumps of Eskimo soapstone. Not, he thought, with sudden heaviness of spirit, that he could afford to feel superior; they were no worse than Indonesian frogs with hats on. He decided to phone the Snow Goose later to see if they'd like a nice grizzly bear; just the thing to pull in tourists and their kids. Stick it out on the sidewalk opposite the London double-decker tour bus.

He had promised Jennifer and Alan to bring home those plastic things from the bank for saving a dollar's worth of pennies and had forgotten; he had promised Jennifer bubblegum with Star Wars cards inside. If he could have raised ten thousand dollars, he'd have bid the night before in Montreal on all the Sepik River lots, bid against Mendelson, and against Lang, Klein, too. What a delight it would have been to have mounted a genuine exhibition, authentic tribal art, masks and boards made long before the luxury boats started pulling into the river bank villages to disgorge the corruption of tourists. But the whole game was climbing beyond his reach. He thought of the dinner he'd had on rue St. Denis before the auction, a street completely changed since his day. And walking along Sussex Drive towards the Uhuru, he found himself thinking for some reason or other of a rented room in a house on rue Jeanne Mance.

Strange that after all those years he could still see the room so clearly after he'd been in it only once; strange, too, that he had only the vaguest memory of the girl. He could see the frayed central hole in the threadbare carpet, the paperbacks on the mantelpiece between two white-painted bricks, empty Chianti bottles strung above, the mobile, tarot cards, Braque poster of white dove, vast glass carboy containing moulting bulrushes, the brass incense-burner in the shape of a Chinese lion . . .

He remembered how intensely excited he'd been returning with her to her room after an afternoon drinking Québerac—*that* was what he remembered so clearly. The intensity of it. It wasn't simply sexual anticipation but something more complicated, more difficult to think about, mysterious. A room—bed, hotplate, wash-basin—was so much more private than a house. Being in a stranger's room, a room that contained the bed in which she slept, a room which was furnished with the things that were hers, entering into that privacy was somehow at that moment more intimate, more exciting than nakedness. There had been a pink facecloth, he remembered, draped over the edge of the basin.

It was the revealing, the unfolding, the unfurling, the opening up of what had been closed that excited him, the sense that this intimacy—difficult to put this into words, difficult to think of the feeling—the sense that this intimacy could draw him into a new . . . well, *current* suggested the sort of thing, a current that would carry him out from the mundane shores, sweep him into the violent invigoration of white water.

So far as he could remember, the intimacy had dissipated in suddenly awkward talk. Of what, he wondered?

Some comically pretentious nonsense.

The wisdom of the Upanishads, perhaps.

In those now distant undergraduate days at Sir George Williams University, he'd spent much of his time with the arty crowd in the various cafés on Stanley Street, the Riviera, Carmen's, The Pam-Pam, The Seven Steps, Marvin's Kitchen. Sitting for hours over a single cup of coffee, he'd yearned after the arty girls, the girls who sat with guys who'd published poems. Arty girls then had all looked much the same. Hair very long and straight with bangs, faces mask-like with makeup, eyes rimmed with black. Black turtlenecks, black skirts, black mesh stockings. The way they all looked, it all had something to do with Paris, Sartre, existentialism, and a movie starring Juliette Greco. He wondered if Sartre was still alive and hoped not.

And the artiest ones of all, he remembered, wore green nail polish and white lipstick. How had he forgotten that? That lipstick. And ballet slippers. And handmade silver earrings. And carried huge handmade leather bags. And they'd all looked anorexic and temptingly *unwholesome*, as though they'd lend themselves, impassively, to amazing sexual practices. Not that Polly Ongle was at all like those girls. But there was something of all that about her. Something of that sort of stance. She was, he suspected the same *sort* of girl.

———————

"*Tabarouette*!" said the waitress, depositing on their table a bowl of potato chips. "Me, I'm scared of lightning!"

Turning the glass vase-thing upside down, she lighted the candle inside.

"Cider?" she repeated.

"No?" said Paul.

"Oh, well," said Norma, "I'll have what-do-you-call-it that goes cloudy."

"Pernod," said Paul. "And a Scotch, please."

"Ice?"

"They feel squishy," said Norma, stretching out her leg.

"Umm?"

"My sandals."

He looked down at her foot.

It was the Happy Hour in the bar on the main floor of the Château Laurier. People drifting in were pantomiming distress and amazement as they eased out of sodden raincoats or used the edge of their hands to wipe rain from eyebrows and foreheads. Men were seating themselves gingerly and loosening from their knees the cling of damp cloth; women were being casually dangerous with umbrellas. Necks were being mopped with handkerchiefs; spectacles were being polished with bar napkins.

"Well," said Paul, raising his glass, "home and dry. Cheers! Thank God for that old umbrella of yours."

She smiled and made a small gesture with her glass.

"What's this obsession you seem to have with cider?" said Paul.

"It's not an obsession. It's just that it doesn't have chemicals in it, that's all. It's just straight juice."

"Well, not *quite* straight," said Paul.

She shrugged.

"But I don't use alcohol much at all usually."

"Not like this stuff," said Paul, tapping his glass. "It's supposed to be full of some sort of stuff—estrogen?—no, a word something like that. *Esters*, is it? Some sort of *oils*. Begins with 'e', I think. Anyway, supposed to be *very* bad for you."

"You shouldn't do things that are bad for you."

"Well, that sounds a bit boring," said Paul, smiling. "Now and again, things that are bad for you are fun."

Norma stirred her ice-cubes with the plastic paddle.

"No?" said Paul.

"Maybe," she said.

Small talk, chat, flirtation, all were uphill work with Polly. Silence didn't seem to bother her one bit. She was usually rather taciturn and—not grumpy exactly—but perhaps "contained" was the word. Or "detached." She gave the impression of being always an observer. She reminded him uncomfortably at times of Jennifer. Once when Jennifer had been four or five, he'd taken her to a zoo where she'd considered the llama over which he was enthusing and had said,

"What's it for?"

He was painfully aware that he seemed unable to strike the right tone, that his chatter sounded less flirtatious than avuncular. The whole situation made him feel like an actor in a hopeless play, plot implausible, dialogue stilted.

He glanced again at the dangling sandal. They were rather elegant. They were what he thought were called buffalo-thongs, just a sort of leather ring which held the sandal on the foot by fitting round the big toe. Her toes were long and distinctly spaced, not cramped together, the little toes not at all deformed by shoes. He wondered how that was possible. They were almost like fingers. He felt an urge to trace their length with his fingertip.

"Pardon?"

"I said, 'Do you know where the washroom is?'"

He watched her threading her way through the tables. The black harem pants were loose and baggy but in places, as she moved, very much *not* loose and baggy. All through the hot, close afternoon he'd been disturbingly aware of them. Her slimness, the tautness of her body, her carriage, she moved like a dancer; the silk scarf knotted round her waist as a belt added to the suggestion. In the patches of spotlighting, the white cotton top glowed blue and purple.

It was irritating him that he couldn't remember the name of the carcinogens that, according to Peter, Scotch was supposed to contain. He had, God knew, heard it often enough. And Polly's saying that she didn't "use alcohol much" also reminded him of Peter; it was an expression always used by Peter in some such formula as, "Older people use alcohol but young people prefer soft drugs"; the expression irritated him on a variety of fronts.

At the next table, the two ghastly government women were still trading acronyms. The older, dykey woman's voice was husky. In front of her was a large round tin of tobacco and a packet of Zig-Zag cigarette papers. Her lipstick was thickly applied and shiny; when her face was in the light from the candle, he could see a faint smear of lipstick on her front teeth. Her bechained spectacles hung down the front of her beige linen suit. She kept relighting the cigarettes with a flaring Zippo lighter. As she talked, she was scattering ashes. Paul thought that in some way he didn't understand she was being cruel; there was something in the conversation of cat and mouse. The younger, softer-looking woman had fluffy hair and was wearing a blazer; the brass buttons glinted.

Oh, I do so agree! said the older, rapacious one. *David's a heaven guy. Just a heaven guy! But there's the problem of Beth, baby girl.*

But Beth's just not a mainstream person.

Well, yes, darling, agreed—and therewith you win the coconut.

Paul signalled to the waitress for another round.

What Beth needs, baby girl, is a vote of confidence from life.

But I thought there was consensus . . .

Darling, said the other, sticking out the tip of her tongue and picking off a shred of tobacco and then leaning forward and placing her hands over the younger woman's hand, *let's approach what one might call the nub.*

He saw Polly coming back through the tables and stood up.

"Look, I'll just be a minute," he said. "Got to go myself."

Once out of the bar, he wandered into the hotel lobby in search of a public phone. He was directed past a florist's and a showcase exhibiting portraits by Karsh. He found that he'd travelled more or less in a circle and had ended up at the rear entrance to the bar. The phones were between the two washrooms. As he was looking for a quarter, a woman in an elaborate bridal outfit came out of the washroom. Two other brides followed her. Pinned on the bosoms of the brides were buttons the size of saucers which said: Happy Occasions Inc.

"Honey?" an American man was saying. "Yeah. I'm in Ottawa. It's the capital of Canada. We're coming into Kennedy tomorrow in the morning."

Paul listened to the ringing.

"Martha? Everything okay?

"I'm in the Château Laurier having a drink.

"No, just a bit damp. I managed to get in here before it really got started. And you? Did you get a cab?

"What? Can't hear you. It's all crackly and your voice keeps fading.

"Well, that's what I'm phoning for. I'm not sure exactly when. I've arranged to meet a guy here to look at some photographs of carvings he wants to sell. If he ever shows up in all this. So I don't really know.

"No, no. You go ahead. Eat with the kids and if I get back I'll get a sandwich or something. And if I'm going to be late, I'll probably get something out somewhere. Okay? So don't worry about it.

"No. There's no reason why I should be. But if I am, don't wait up for me. But I won't be.

"Don't forget tomorrow's *what*?

"*Garbage* day! Thought you said 'Harbour'. Yes, I'll put it out when I get back.

"The meat tray in the fridge—I got that bit.

"Salami. Good.

"What do you mean?

"How *can* I be careful? Please, for God's sake, don't start one of these. If lightning is going to strike me, Martha, what can I do to prevent it?

"Yes, okay. I promise not to go near metal street-lights.

"No. I'm not just saying it.

"Love you, too. 'Bye.

"What?

"Alan lost his *what*?

"I'll speak to him tomorrow.

"'Bye.

"Yes.

"'Bye."

He wandered back into the hotel lobby and pushed out through the revolving doors. The wind was chilly. He stood under the noisy canvas awning. The rain was still lashing down with a violence that reminded him of the rains in Africa; it was as if the asphalt of Wellington Street had quickened into a broad river. He stood watching the rain pock the surface of the sheets and rills of water flooding down towards Rideau Street.

Just off the main lobby near the entrance to the bar were the windows of an art gallery. He stood there. It had recently changed hands. The stock, however, looked much the same. He stood staring at all the landscapes, the still-lifes, the flowers in vases, the paintings of decrepit barns and split-rail fences, the paintings involving horses, maple syrup, logs.

He could have told her he was sitting out the storm with Norma without bothering her in the slightest. There was no reason not to have told her. Amazingly, she seemed to think of Norma as a pleasant enough girl who was useful in the gallery; she'd once said that Norma would look so much more presentable if only she'd do something about her hair.

He stared at a large, gilt-framed picture which was exhibited on an easel; lumpy purple mountains, the central lake, the maple trees.

It could as easily have been the other view: lumpy mountains, central lake, foreground rock, jack pines. It was all the same, the same sort of thing as Eskimo carvings and frogs from Suriname with hats on.

After the Makonde, the Shona stone.

As he walked through the archway and into the bar, he saw that the two government women had left, and felt an odd sense of relief.

"It's still absolutely pouring out there," he said, sitting down and hitching the chair closer. "And the sky's still black with it. Hasn't that waitress come yet?"

"Paul?"

"What?"

"You know, Paul," she said, leaning forward to rest her arms on the table, "I've been thinking."

"What about?"

"You really *ought* to take better care of yourself."

"Pardon?"

"Well, you can't just ignore it."

"Ignore what?"

"The trouble you had with your . . . your chest. Those pains."

"You're losing me. How did we get onto *this*?"

"What we were saying before. About cider. About drinking things that can damage your body."

"Oh! I see. Well, what are you trying to suggest? That I drink too much?"

"No, of course not. But . . ."

"Sound," said Paul, opening his jacket and tapping himself over the heart, "as a bell. Lively as a two-year-old. Chirpy as a cricket. Fit as the proverbial fiddle."

"Don't *joke* about it!"

He stared at her across the table, at her eyes, the long eyelashes somehow accentuated by the glow from the candle below. The candlelight was picking up auburn tints in the sweep of her black hair.

"What's all this great seriousness in aid of, Norma?"

"You don't have to treat me as if I'm a child!"

"I wasn't aware that I was. I don't. But what I mean is, what brought all this on? I mean, so suddenly?"

"No reason."

"Well, what are you so annoyed about?"

She shrugged.

"Norma?"

She concentrated on stirring about the remains of her ice cubes.

"Hello?"

"It shouldn't take a genius," she said, "to work it out."

The waitress placed the Pernod and the Scotch on the brown napkins, glanced through the checks on her tray, propped their check between the bowl of chips and a triangular cardboard sign advertising a specialty of the house, a drink involving rye whisky, Piña Colada Mix, orange juice, egg whites, and a maraschino cherry.

It was called Sunset Flamenco.

He couldn't think of anything to say.

Norma was sitting back in her chair, head bent, plying the plastic paddle. He stared at the white line of the part in her hair.

He felt—he wasn't sure *what* he felt. It was many, many years since he'd played verbal footsie with girls in bars. If she'd meant what he *thought* she'd meant, the situation seemed to be opening up to possibilities he'd tried to stop himself thinking about for months. But it was entirely possible that she hadn't meant to imply what he thought she'd meant to imply, that the inferences he'd drawn were influenced by desire, by watching all afternoon the folds and furrows of the matte black material of those harem pants . . . but it certainly *felt* as if the inference he'd drawn was what had been intended.

He drained his glass of Scotch.

"Ah . . . ," he said, "you know what I think would be a good idea? If it's all right with you, I mean. If you haven't got anything planned. Norma?"

"What?"

"Well, as it's still pouring, if we had dinner here together. What do you think?"

"No, I haven't got anything planned."

"So would you like to?"

"Why not?" she said. "Sure."

"Good!" he said. "I'd like that."

He glanced at his watch.

"It's a bit early yet," he said, "so if you think our bodies could stand the strain, we'll sit for a bit over another drink. Okay?"

She nodded.

He wished he hadn't used the word "bodies."

He lighted a cigarette.

"I thought you'd quit," she said.

He blew out a long, deep jet of smoke.

"I am in the process of quitting."

"Is it—" she said.

"I think—" he said. "Sorry. What were you . . ."

"No," she said.

"I was just going to say that I think there's supposed to be a band."

"Where?"

"In the restaurant."

"What sort of band?"

"I don't know. A dance band, I suppose. It's supposed to be quite good. The restaurant, I mean."

"Do you like dancing?" she said.

"Not much, I'm afraid. Do you?"

"It depends."

"You *look* like a dancer."

"What do you mean?"

"A professional dancer."

She smiled.

"What's funny?"

"I was thinking about you dancing."

"So what's funny about that?"

"I couldn't imagine it."

"Why not?"

She shrugged.

"Well, in the gallery you always seem so . . . oh, I don't know."

"Seem so what?"

"Well . . . *dignified.*"

"What do you mean, exactly, by 'dignified'?"

"I mean . . . I couldn't imagine you dancing."

"Let me tell you," he said, "that in the days of my youth . . ."

"You're not old," she said.

"Well, of course I'm not *old* but . . ."

"You're *not,*" she said. "You shouldn't say that."

She was staring at him with uncomfortable intensity.

He decided it would be a very good idea to go to the washroom again.

It was empty and echoey in the washroom and smelled of the cakes of cloying air-freshener stuff in the urinals, a smell that he was rather ashamed of not disliking. He examined himself in the mirrors and combed his hair. All he'd had for lunch had been a container of yogurt. He was beginning to feel the effects of the Scotch.

He thought of Polly's eyelashes.

Like Bambi.

What else *could* she have meant?

To the blank tile wall facing him, he said in a deliberately boomy voice,

"Bum like a plum."

In the farthest cubicle, someone stirred, shoes grating on tiled floor.

Paul coughed.

———————

Facing them just inside the entrance of the Canadian Grill as they waited for the maître d' stood a sort of Islamic tent.

It was octagonal. It was large enough to have slept two. But higher. It rose to an ornate finial. Or rather, it was *tent-like.* Gauzy, chiffony stuff was stretched over the eight ribs. The shape suggested something of the dome of a mosque or a Mogul helmet. On a platform inside stood a huge basket of artificial flowers.

Paul stared at this amazing thing wondering who could have imagined such a folly in a Canadian National Railways Hotel in a room whose decor seemed otherwise baronial.

Or it might have been intended to suggest a miniature band-stand.

Or a gazebo.

"I don't think I'm dressed for this," whispered Norma.

"Nonsense," he said. "You look beautiful."

He smiled at her.

"As a matter of fact," he said, "you *always* look beautiful."

He followed her down the acres of tartan carpet, the khaki army-surplus bag bumping on her hip. Sticking out of it towards him was the shiny black handle of a hairbrush. The maître d' was a short, gorilla-shaped man in a bulging tuxedo. He kept hitching at his white gloves. His face was battered and as he walked he moved his head and shoulders as if shadow-boxing.

At a table at the edge of the dance floor, the maître d' heaved out Norma's chair with his left hand and, raising his right, with his gloved fingers fumbled a silent snap. They sat and were overwhelmed by waiters. Waiters seemed to outnumber customers. The waiters wore tuxedos but the servers and their servitors wore brown outfits with orange lapels; the width of the lapels seemed to indicate gradations of rank. Narrow lapels poured glasses of water. Wide lapels placed baskets of bread. Tuxedos inquired if they desired an apéritif.

"Scotch," said Paul.

"What a weird man!" said Norma.

"Which?"

"That head waiter."

"He's a retired boxer," said Paul.

"How do you know?"

"Undefeated CN/CP Bantam Champion."

"Really?"

"They use him for thumping temperamental chefs."

"Oh, he isn't!"

"Customer complaints a specialty."

"I've never been in a place like this," said Norma.

It was as if the decorator had attempted to marry vague notions of a baronial Great Hall with the effects of an old movie theatre. Diners formed islands in the room's vast emptiness.

"Wine?" said Paul to the waiter. "Oh, I would think so but we haven't decided yet what we want to eat."

They opened the padded leatherette menus.

"*L'omble de l'Arctique,*" said Paul.

"Oh, look!" said Norma. "Behind you, look!"

"What *is* an Arctic omble?"

"Paul, look!"

Waiters were converging.

A party of nine all of whom seemed to have ordered roast beef.

Narrow lapels were hurrying in bearing aloft silver-coloured covered dishes; servers were pushing up to the table wheeled heating grills; servitors were lighting the gas. Wide lapels were taking the dishes from the narrow lapels and were handing them to the tuxedos, who plucked off the domed lids and slid the dishes onto the flames, poking artistically at the contents with spoon and fork until the gravy was boiling briskly.

An atmosphere of muted hysteria gripped the drama. There was much tense French-Canadian cursing. Chafing-dish lids were left with an edge in the flames so that narrow lapels burned their fingers removing them; a Yorkshire pudding fell on the floor; lapel bumped into lapel; dishes forgotten on the flames sent up fatty smoke as the gravy burned onto them.

"Tell him!" said Norma.

"Monsieur?"

"Your napkin thing," said Paul, pointing. "On your arm. Appears to be on fire."

Norma was hidden behind her menu giggling.

"Value for money, eh?" he said.

He was beginning to feel merrily sloshed.

The smouldering napkin was rushed from the room in a covered dish.

The acrid smell lingered.

One of the waiters was touring the table with a gravy boat; his progress was sacerdotal. Each time he stooped to dispense horserad-ish, his abbreviated jacket rose, revealing under his rucked shirt the elasticized top of his underwear.

"You know what it's all like?" said Paul. "It's like a Fernandel movie or Jacques Tati. That film he made about a restaurant. What *was* that called? The one that came before *Traffic*?"

"Are they French?"

"The reason *is*," said Paul, "the reason it's all a bit off-centre, is because it's a railway hotel. All these Bowery Boys aren't *real* waiters. They're all guys off *trains*—the guys that put the hot-dogs in the microwave ovens at the take-out counter place. The guys that are grumpy about serving you once you've passed Kingston because it takes them two hundred miles with their lips moving to fill in the sheets about how many sandwiches they've sold. Which are full of ice crystals anyway. And after years of loyal service on the Montreal–Toronto run, they're all rewarded with a job here on land. Which is why there's so many of them. And look! Here he is. He's coming again."

They watched the bobbing and weaving of the maître d' as he led a couple to a nearby table.

"The Caboose Kid," said Paul.

"What?"

"That's the name he used to fight under. No. That's not quite right, is it? *Kid Caboose*! That's it. That's better."

"Honestly!" said Norma. "You're so *silly*."

Head on one side, she was considering him.

"You really get into it, don't you?"

"What do I 'get into'?"

"All this stuff you make up."

He shrugged and smiled at her.

"Do I?"

He was beginning to find it difficult to keep his mind on what his lips were saying. For some moments, he'd been aware of her leg touching his beneath the table; this contact was generating a most marvellous warmth. The play of the matte black material filled his mind, furling, fitting plump, furrowed. Through his lower body and down his thighs seeped a different kind of warmth, luxurious, languorous, as if he were bleeding heavily from the hot centre of a painless wound.

He knew that he ought to be saying something.

He glanced across at her.

"Oh! Are those new?"

"What?"

"Those earrings. Hadn't noticed them."

With the back of her hand, she lifted and steered away the weight of her hair. This movement and the cocking of her head tensed the tendon down the side of her neck and raised her left breast towards him.

What he had intended as an *mmmm!* of appreciation broke from him as something closer to a groan.

"It's lovely," he said.

"Vous avez choisi?"

Startled, Paul glanced up.

"Pardon? Oh, I don't know. Ah, Norma?"

"Oh," she said, and opened the menu again.

"Oh, I don't know. I'd like a steak, I think."

"L'entrecôte, madame?"

"I guess so."

"Monsieur?"

"*L'omble de l'Arctique à l'infusion d'anis,*" said Paul. "What *is* it?"

"L'omble de l'Arctique," said the waiter, "it is a fish."

"What kind of fish?"

"That's a pink fish."

"Pink," repeated Paul.

"Inside the fish," said the waiter, gesturing with pad and ball-point, "is pink."

An arm removed the ashtray and replaced it with a clean one; cutlery was set; the *sommelier* performed upon foil and cork. Paul duly tasted the grotesquely overpriced Mouton Cadet, remembering when it had been available for the present price of a pack of cigarettes and not much of a bargain even then.

She raised her glass and touched it to his.

Bambi.

Light danced off the polished tops of the salt and pepper shakers, flashed off cutlery. He watched the wink of light inside his glass, the play of pinks cast on the tablecloth. He was aware of light and shadow above him. He was, he realized, more inebriated than he'd thought. He tried the word "inebriated" inside his head. It seemed to work perfectly.

The brown sleeve placed under him a shrimp cocktail.

He stared down into it.

"Et pour madame, les hors d'oeuvres variés."

The shrimps were minuscule, greyish and frayed. He speared one. It was limp and didn't taste of anything at all. He would have sworn under oath that the sauce was a combination of ketchup and Miracle Whip.

"It's not good?" said Norma.

"Try it," said Paul. "Here. I'll put some on your plate."

"No," she said. "Just give me some on your fork."

Holding the fork poised, she said,

"Paul?"

"What?"

"You didn't really think I'd mind, did you?"

"Mind what?"

"Using your fork," she said. "I don't."

He watched her lips close over the tines.

From behind the stage curtains with their flounced valance, a tuning "A" sounded three times on a piano. It was approximated by a guitar.

She wrinkled her nose.

"It's not special, is it?" she said, handing back the fork.

Three ascending trumpet notes sounded.

The last one cracked.

The curtains drew back to reveal the resident band. They all wore baby-blue blazers and blue shirts with blue ruffles. They looked dispirited. The trumpet player spoke too close to the microphone so that the only words Paul caught were what sounded like "block and tackle" and "for your dining pleasure" and then they launched into "The Tennessee Waltz."

After they'd worked it through, there was scattered applause.

"Oh, groan," said Norma. "Groan. Groan."

"This place," said Paul, "is beginning to make me feel about ready for my pension."

"You know what we ought to do?"

"What?"

"Well, if you feel like it, I mean."

"Like what?"

She paused.

"I think," she said, "that you're beginning to get spliffed."

"Spliffed? Oh! Certainly not," he said. "Here, in an amazing exhibition of total clarity, is precisely what you said. You said that you'd like to do something if I felt like it but you didn't say what. You see?"

"Go somewhere where there's some non-plastic music."

"Where's that?"

"I know somewhere. Would you like to?"

"A magical mystery tour?"

Accented with rattles, wood-blocks, and a cow-bell, the band started hacking at something vaguely Latin-American.

"Well," said Paul, "nothing could be much worse than this."

"Oh, look!" she said. "I think this is us."

A wheeled grill was advancing on their table; domed dishes held on high were heading in their direction; servitors were congregating.

The mummery commenced.

When bits of this and clumps of that had been arranged and rearranged, the plates were set before them.

"Et, voilà!" said the waiter.

Beside the chunk of fish was a plump greyish thing whose outer layers were almost translucent; these translucent leaves were heavily veined; they looked like veined membranes, like folded wings; whatever it was resembled the cooked torso of a giant insect.

They studied it.

"Could it be one of those things you get in salads?"

"Oh!" said Paul. "An endive? I suppose it *could* be. Braised?"

It reminded him of the nightmare things he'd batted down with a tennis racquet in their bedroom in Port Harcourt. He pressed it with his fork and yellow liquid issued.

He pushed the plate away.

He summoned a waiter.

He studied the brandy's oily curve on the side of the glass. Changing with the angle of the glass, the brandy's colours reminded him of stain and varnish, of the small chest of drawers he'd promised to strip and refinish. He tipped and tilted the glass; oak, amber, the colours in the centre exactly the colours of the patina on rubbed and handled carvings.

After the Makonde carvings, the Shona stone.

And after the Shona stone, Rosenfeld's pre-Columbian pots, and after Rosenfeld's pots . . . he looked down a dreary vista of crafts elevated to the status of art wondering if the honest thing wouldn't be a return to teaching.

He thought of the years after his return from Nigeria, years no longer cushioned by a salary from CIDA and a government house, the years he'd spent languishing at Lisgar Collegiate. What with the compelling arguments of Martha, the baby, the mortgage payments, he'd tried to persuade himself that he cared about teaching and the minutiae of school life, but the future had yawned before him, mountains of exercise-books in which until the age of sixty-five he'd be distinguishing with a red pencil between "their" and "there."

Uhuru!

He grunted.

And after Rosenfeld's pots . . .

He was startled by the applause.

A girl had come out onto the stage. She was blonde and pretty. She was wearing a long green dress, the sort of dress that Paul thought of as a "party dress." Her voice was small but sweet.

He found that he was humming along audibly with the melody of "These Foolish Things." And then began to find his phrasing diverging from hers. He was so used to Ella Fitzgerald's version of the song that he was anticipating adornment and shading which this girl could never reach. Pretty but somehow asexual, she was a crunchy-granola girl, an advertisement girl, impossibly wholesome, a tooth-paste girl, under her party dress and white immaculate undies as waxen and undifferentiated as a doll.

He breathed in the brandy's rising bouquet. Opening the pack of Rothman's King Size, his fingers fumbled to discover that there were only two left. He somehow had smoked twenty-three cigarettes since ten o'clock in the morning.

The girl was singing "Ev'ry Time We Say Goodbye."

When, he wondered, could he have smoked them?

Tried to recall; tried to count.

He was moved and moving with the melody, could feel his head swaying.

He closed his eyes.

. . . how strange the change
from major to minor
ev'ry time we say goodbye.

Behind the girl's voice, he seemed to hear Ella's voice, dark and brooding.

He'd always liked the song, thought it the best of Cole Porter's, the least offensively clever, one of the few where intelligence and emotion seemed to marry.

He gazed into the snifter, amber light fragmenting, sipped.
The song was drawing to its close.

. . . from major to minor
ev'ry time we say goodbye.

He thought about that. Admired the subtlety, the poetry, admired the line's *movement*. Was "elegance" the word he was looking
for? Partly. It was partly that. But it was also *true*. Things *did* move
from major to minor. Though in *his* case it was more minor to major,
more a question of hello—the long day in the Uhuru and then the
anticipation on the homeward journey, *the seeing her*. But major to
minor, minor to major—that didn't, so far as he could see, change
the *point*. Change the point of what the song *said*.

He suddenly found himself groping.

What?

Said?

Said what?

He considered the possibility of his being drunk. His thoughts
seemed to be moving slowly, thickly, as if viscous, somehow like the
brandy in the glass. Which added up to roughly (200) calories. He
patted his pockets, listening for the rattle of the Nikoban gum.
He attempted the painful mental arithmetic of computing the
number of calories he'd drunk; it was hard; large numbers were
involved; it seemed to total somewhere in the region of (2,000).

Not taking into account two bowls of potato chips.

And shrimps slathered in mayonnaise.

The girl was singing "Misty."

He closed his eyes again.

I get misty,

she sang,

just holding your hand . . .

Suddenly, he felt like crying.

It was true.

Yes, it *was* true.

Even after all these years, he *did*, he *did* get misty. Not that there weren't other parts of her he'd like to hold, and much more frequently. But sometimes still—after dinner, say, when the kids were in bed, and they strolled up in the twilight towards the yellow bloom of the corner-store window for an ice cream or an Oh Henry bar, along the sidewalks black where the sprinklers were arcing, under the deepening green mounds of the maples, past the squall and chirping of sparrows roosting behind the Virginia creeper on the side of St. Andrew's Church—sometimes still he'd hold her hand shy and happy as a boy.

He shifted his chair further from the table, crossed his legs. Banged his knee.

Straightened the rucked tablecloth.

The girl was singing.

the way you sip your . . . the memory of all that . . .

Nothing *could* take away from him the things they'd shared, the way they'd become. The way she worried he'd be struck by lightning via metal street-lights, the way she unpacked grocery boxes on the front porch to prevent the entry of mythical cockroaches, the way she poked with a broom handle because of miners' lung disease, parrots, psi-something, whatever it was called, poking with a broom handle attempting to dislodge nesting pigeons from the upper windows' gingerbread—the list was endless, part of life's fabric, a ballad without end. And this morning? What had been this morning's contribution? Goldfish!

White strings.

In which case, that being so, which it unarguably *was*, what, just *what* was he doing in this ridiculous restaurant with this—*ordinary*. With this very *ordinary* girl? What was he doing with a girl who was nearly young enough to be his daughter? *Was* young enough to be his daughter. With a girl who was only—he calculated—was only— good God!—*five years older than Peter*!

What was he doing with a girl whose silences were abrasive, whose conversation was boring? Who spoke of "getting into" things? What was he doing with a girl who'd never heard of Jacques Tati? With a girl in whose hands he'd once seen an historical romance, tartan and claymores, entitled *The Master of Stong*? What was he doing with a girl who transported her toiletries in an army-surplus bag?

He stared at it where it hung from the back of her chair.

The writing in gilt on the hairbrush handle glinted.

Pinned to the front of the bag was a black and white button that said:

GRAVITY SUCKS

Behind her head, the movement of figures on the dance floor.

The brightly lighted stage.

Knife and fork.

She looked up and smiled.

With sudden and startling clarity, the realization came to him that she wasn't her at all. *She simply wasn't her.* Polly, he realized, was Polly but Norma wasn't.

But Polly . . .

What of Polly? What was she?

He sat thinking about that.

————

The waitress was mouthing something. Leaning forward and peering up at her face from about eighteen inches away, he watched her lips moving.

He pointed at his ear and shrugged.

He traced on the low tabletop a figure 5 and a zero. Her lips seemed to shape: 50?

She disappeared into the gloom.

The noise was hurting his eyes.

Beside him on the banquette sat a pair of lovelies whose hair was shaved off to a line an inch or so above the ears; above that, it was cut the same length all the way round so that it sat on their heads like caps. They reminded him of the mushrooms in *Fantasia*. Of collaborators. Of a boy called Gregory who'd had ringworm. Light glanced

off the skulls, off the shiny, pallid skin. The girl was drenched in
obnoxiously cheap perfume which was beginning to make him feel
nauseated. Under the shiny skin, a vein crawled. Her escort was
naked to the waist save for red-and-white suspenders.

From behind the amplified drummer, lights like lightning flick-
flickered flick-flickered. He began to fear induced epilepsy. On the
dance floor in front of the stage, shapes heaved and cavorted in the
stuttering light. Some were running-on-the-spot. Some seemed to
be miming log-rolling. Others were leaping erratically as though to
avoid bowling balls being launched at their ankles.

One of the guitarists was wearing ear-mufflers of the kind worn
by ground crews at airports.

The Iron Guard looked much like all the other sneering degener-
ates who adorned the record albums littering Peter's room—sexually
ambivalent, grubby, *used*.

The banquette itself was vibrating. The amplified white-plastic
violin which had started up was making his teeth ache. Its sound
was demented. He could feel vibration deep inside his body; his
very organs were being shaken loose.

Norma had described The Iron Guard as being "mainstream"; he
could not imagine the sound of something she'd consider avant-
garde. The word "mainstream" made him think of "midstream," of the
tests he'd undergone after his heart-thing, of his kidneys vibrating.

The waitress plonked down two bottles of Labatt's Fifty Ale and
two wet glasses, took his proffered ten-dollar bill, and disappeared
into the fug. He felt Norma's breath on the side of his face as she
shouted something. He smiled back then stopped because smiling
seemed to intensify the pain in his teeth.

Now and again, he caught a few words bellowed by the lead
degenerate . . .

MIS-ER-*RY*

AS YOU ALL CAN *SEE* . . .

A large pink bubble was swelling from the mushroom girl's blank
face. She and her mushroom consort looked, he thought, as if they'd
been used for medical experiments.

He wondered if they found each other sexually attractive; he wondered if they would breed.

He was feeling very tired and very old.

He wished, more than anything, that he was at home in the silent kitchen with a peanut butter sandwich, a glass of milk, three aspirins, and a new issue of *African Arts*, the only sound the occasional scrabble of the basement mouse.

Outside the Château Laurier, and before the taxi, he had not been able to think of any kind and plausible way of excusing himself but now, oppressed by guilt and toothache, he decided that he would leave—the advancing hour—as soon as the beer was finished and the band had executed another number. If this monstrous and outrageous noise was indeed divided into "numbers."

It seemed more than possible that it just went on.

Despite his severe pangs of guilt, despite his realization that Polly wasn't Norma, or, more clearly, that Norma wasn't Polly, and despite his welling love for Martha, it was, at the same time, undeniably flattering that Norma felt attracted to a man with drooping pectorals and four white hairs on his chest. But flattering as it *was*, he almost winced as he thought of the way the evening *could* have turned out. He dwelt for a few moments on the compounding horror of an embroilment with a child-woman and employee. He blessed his blind and stupid luck that had preserved him from laying hot hands on her essentials.

Surveying his behaviour over the course of the evening, he could not recall having responded in any way, verbally or physically, that had in any sense committed him. His responses had, he believed, been sufficiently ambiguous. It was she, amazingly enough, who had made all the running. He had not really stepped over the line. Legs under tables could, he decided, be looked on merely as friendly contiguity. Bridges intact, retreat was possible.

Caught in an extraordinary storm, a pleasant evening with a charming young employee of whom he was fond. A few comments tomorrow about how pleasant it had been, up past his bedtime, a matter of taste, of course, but this sweating hellhole perhaps better suited to the younger generation . . .

Harrumph!

Major Hoople.

That was the stance.

Avuncular.

The harem pants stretched over her long thighs, she was leaning back on the banquette with her feet up on the ledge beneath the table. He looked at her pale toes.

She *was* attractive, of course, impossible to deny, but he saw that it was the attractiveness of a kitten or a puppy, the charm of a filly in a summer field. A matter of sentiment and aesthetics. He appreciated her, he decided, much in the way that he appreciated a painting or a carving.

No.

That had some truth in it but it was not *strictly* true.

He thought of the glycerine-drenched inner parts of ladies which greeted him in the corner-store every time he went to buy a quart of milk.

Fantasy.

That seemed the essential point to hold onto.

Surreptitiously, he tried to lick off the back of his hand the blue heart and arrow the doorkeeper had stamped him with.

A change in the noise was taking place. To the continuous-car-crash effect was being added a noise which sounded like the whingeing of giant metal mosquitoes. The mushroom girl was gawping, a bubblegum bubble deflated on her lower lip. And then the white-plastic violin capered into high gear and the lead degenerate, bent double for some reason, started moaning and bellowing again and Paul realized that the whole thing was still the

MIS-ER-*RY*

AS YOU ALL CAN *SEE*...

recitative *still* going on but possibly, he dared to hope, ending.

There was a long-drawn-out crescendo of appalling noises— noises of things under dreadful tension snapping and shearing, of tortured metal screeching, of things being smashed flat, crushed, ripped apart, ricocheting—and then, suddenly, silence.

The crowd's applause, wild whistles, and rebel yells sounded by comparison soft and muted as the shush of waves on distant shore.

He could scarcely believe it had stopped.

He extended his wrist and watch towards Norma and tapped the watch-face.

He mouthed: Let's go.

"What?"

"Sorry."

"Go?" she said.

"It's late. I need my beauty sleep."

"But we've only just got here."

He stood up.

He wanted to be on the other side of the padded doors before The Iron Guard grated again into gear. Sound was coming to him oddly as it sometimes did during the descent into an airport; the inside of his head felt as though it had been somehow *scoured*.

The set of Norma's body suggested disgruntlement.

They threaded their way through the hairstyles and vintage clothing and he heaved open one side of the heavy doors. It was immediately easier to breathe. The tiny foyer was ill-lighted and tiled white like a public washroom. The concrete stairs rose steeply to the door that led out onto the sidewalk.

He was still trying to think of something to say which would be suitably old-dufferish, avuncular, and affable and which would set the tone for their parting, and, more to the point, for their meeting again in the morning, when the street door above them banged back against the wall and the narrow doorway was jammed by three struggling figures in black. The two outer figures were manoeuvring a central, drooping figure.

As Paul and Norma stared up at these noisy shapes looming over them, the nearest stumbled on the first step. He let go of the central figure to save himself. The central figure slumped to one side pulling the other supporting figure off balance and then, as if in slow motion, fell forward. A yell was echoing. Rubbery, more or less on his feet, gaining momentum, his body hit the handrail, caromed off to hit the wall, bounced off the wall turning somehow so that he was tumbling backwards, windmill arms, hit the rail again. Reflex pushed Paul forward and the figure landed against his chest and arm. He staggered back under the impact.

"Fuckin*ankle*!" screamed a voice on the stairs.

Paul was staring down at the face of his son.

"Peter!

"Peter! Are you hurt? *Peter*!"

His face was white and his eyes were closed.

"Who is it?" said Norma.

"Come on! Peter!"

Someone belched.

"What happened to him?"

"Oh, good evening, Mr. Denton."

It was the one in his twenties who wore things suspiciously like blouses.

"What *happened* to him?"

"Do you mean," said Norma, "it's *your* Peter?"

Paul lowered the body to the tiled floor and knelt beside him. He quickly checked arms and legs. Felt round the back of his head. Nothing was obviously broken.

"For Christ's sake, what *happened* to him?"

"Is it?" said Norma. "Peter?"

"Well, I lost my balance, Mr. Denton, and he . . ."

"I *know* you lost your balance, you fucking dimwit. I want to know what happened to him *before*."

Peter groaned and opened his eyes.

His head rolled.

He seemed to be staring at Norma.

"Peter? Hey, Peter!"

He was trying to say something.

Bent over him, trying to peer at his pupils in the uncertain light, Paul could scarcely believe the obvious: it was not concussion; it was not hypoglycemia; it was not cerebral edema; it was booze. The boy reeked of booze. He felt suddenly weak and shaky; he could still hear the terrifying sound the boy's head would have made as it hit the tiled floor.

He stared up at—Deet, was it? Wiggo? Or was this the one that sounded like something from *Sesame Street*?

He was regarding Paul and Peter owlishly.

As Paul stared at him, he wrinkled his upper lip and nose and sniffed moistly. He wiped his nose on his sleeve.

Paul shook his head slowly.

"Jesus Christ!" he said. "*Je-sus Christ!*"

"Paul?" said Norma. "Is he okay?"

Paul got slowly to his feet.

With both hands, he smoothed back his hair.

He lowered his head and massaged the muscles in his neck.

"Norma," he said, looking up, "I'm sorry, but I'm going to have to ask you to excuse me. I think it'd be better if you left me to deal with this."

"Oh," she said. "You mean . . ."

"I'd like to talk privately to these . . ."

He gestured at Wiggo and at the other character who was sitting on the steps.

"Well," she said. "Umm . . . okay."

"I'll talk to you in the morning."

She hitched up the strap of the army-surplus bag.

"I'm sorry," said Paul.

"Well," she said, "thank you for dinner."

Paul nodded.

Her sandals slapped up the echoing stairs.

At the top of the stairs, she looked down and said,

"Well, goodnight, Paul."

The push-bar door clanged shut behind her.

"*Now,*" said Paul. "Let's start again. Wiggo, isn't it?"

"It's Munchy, Mr. Denton."

The one who worked in the Speculative Fiction bookstore, the one Peter had said was into Tolstoy.

"Munchy, then. Listen carefully, Munchy. I am going to ask you a question. Where has Peter been and what happened to him?"

"We were in my apartment, Mr. Denton."

"*And?*"

"Listening to tapes."

"You were in your apartment and you were listening to tapes— I haven't got all night, Munchy."

He could feel the pounding of his heart, the dryness in his mouth. It would have been a release and a pleasure to have thumped this pair until stretchers were necessary. He felt pressure at his temples and behind his eyes, thought of tubes contracting, pictured pink things swelling. He took a deep breath and held it.

Munchy was groping about in his pockets.

"Pay attention! I'm *talking* to you!"

"I'm sorry, Mr. Denton. Have you got a Kleenex?"

Peter was stirring on the floor, groaning. Paul glanced down at him. Then stared. He was drawing his knees up to his body. His exhalations were becoming harsh and noisy. Red-tinged saliva was drooling and spindling from the corner of his mouth. It was beginning to pool and glisten on the white tiles.

Quickly, Paul knelt beside him.

"Did he fall before? Was he hit or something? A car?"

Munchy shook his head.

"Did he hurt himself *before* he fell downstairs?"

Munchy shook his head.

"*Answer me!*" shouted Paul. "Can't you see he's bleeding? What kind of friends *are* you? He's bleeding and he's bleeding *internally. What happened to him?*"

They stared at him.

"He didn't," said Munchy.

"Jesus Christ!" said Paul. "Go! Just go! Go and phone for an ambulance."

"*No, no, no,*" said the other creature, shaking his head emphatically.

"What do you mean, *no?*"

Pointing at Peter, he said,

"Issribena."

Paul stared at him. The hair was bleached to a hideous chemical yellow and he was wearing a combination false-nose-and-spectacles. His T-shirt was imprinted with the word: Snout.

"It *is*, Mr. Denton," said Munchy. "That's what it is."

"Is *what?*"

"*Issribena!*" said the one on the steps.

"What," said Paul, "is *it?*"

"Ribena," said Munchy.

Paul wondered if The Iron Guard had done something permanent to his head.

He said:

"Say that again."

"Ribena?" said Munchy.

"Yes. What do you mean, 'Ribena'?"

"It's black-currant juice."

"Ribenasafruit," added the creature with the chemical hair.

Paul knelt again and smeared his finger through the slimy, red-tinged spittle. He smelled it. It immediately made him feel queasy.

He got slowly to his feet.

The Iron Guard sounded through the padded doors like the throb of industrial machinery.

Brushing the dust off his pants, he said,

"Ribena, eh?"

"It isn't bleeding, Mr. Denton."

"No," said Paul. "And Ribena did this to him, did it, Munchy?"

Munchy shook his head.

"It didn't?"

"Grover put rum in it."

Paul nodded slowly.

"*That* is Grover?"

There didn't seem much point in trying to talk to Grover. He was engrossed in trailing his fingertips backwards and forwards along the concrete step.

"But *you* didn't drink much of it."

"Well, I don't use it, Mr. Denton. I'm not really into alcohol."

Paul closed his eyes.

He breathed, consciously.

After a few moments, he said,

"Do you know how old Peter is?"

Munchy nodded.

"Speak to me, Munchy."

"Pardon?"

"Tell me. In words."

"Peter?"

Paul nodded.

"Fifteen?"

Paul nodded.

"Well?" he said. "Do you have anything to say?"

Grover was making automobile noises.

Munchy snuffled.

Paul stared at Munchy.

Staring at Munchy, at his eczema, at his safari shirt over which he wore a broad belt in the manner of Russian peasants, at his tux pants and what looked like army boots, the words "diminished responsibility" came into Paul's mind. Munchy was the sort of character who'd be sentenced to months of community service for drug possession and who'd genuinely find emptying bedpans a deeply meaningful learning experience; interrogating him was like wantonly tormenting the Easter Bunny.

Munchy wiped his nose on his sleeve again.

Paul looked down at Peter and sighed.

He felt immensely weary.

Above the door that led out onto the sidewalk the EXIT sign flushed the white tiles red.

"It's the pollen," said Munchy.

"What?"

"In the season, I always suffer with it."

He pointed at the tip of his nose with his forefinger.

"Or sometimes," he added, "just with environmental dust."

"Munchy," said Paul, "SHUT. UP. Do you understand?"

Munchy nodded.

"Right. Good. Now get hold of his other arm."

Munchy pushed his glasses higher on the bridge of his nose and stooped.

"And Munchy?"

The glasses flashed.

"Don't speak to me!"

Munchy nodded.

"Just don't speak to me!"

––––––––––

It was drizzling, a thin mist of rain. There were few people on the streets. Paul had hoped that the torrential storm would have cooled and rinsed the air but it was still close and muggy. Peter's head hung. His legs wambled from sidewalk to gutter; his legs buckled; his legs strayed. Most of the passing couples averted their eyes. Supporting him was like wrestling with an unstrung puppet.

Back wet with sweat, Paul propped him against a hydro pole. It was not when he was moving but when he stopped that he felt the pounding of his heart, that his hot clothes clung, that the sweat seemed to start from every pore. The boy felt so thin, his chest like the carcass of a chicken; it amazed Paul that such frailty could weigh so much.

Leaning against Peter to jam him against the pole, Paul stared across the road unseeing, his clumsy tongue touching the dry corrugations of his palate. The muscles in his shoulders ached. Pain stitched his side. He did not seem able to breathe deeply enough.

A lot of girls in a passing car yelled cheerful obscenities.

His eyes followed the ruby shimmer of their rear lights in the road's wet surface.

Stapled to the hydro pole above Peter's head was a small poster advertising a rock group. The band's name seemed to be:

BUGS HARVEY OSWALD

He changed his grip on the boy's wrist and stooped again to take the weight.

Lurching on, he began to set himself goals: as far as the gilt sign proclaiming Larsson Associates: Consultants in Building Design and Research; as far as the light washing the sidewalk outside the windows of the Colonnade Pizzeria; as far as the traffic lights; as far as the next hydro pole.

And the next.

When he reached Elgin Street, he stood propping Peter at the curb waiting for the traffic lights to change. Further up the street, someone in a white apron was carrying in the buckets of cut flowers from outside Boushey's Fruit Market; knots of people were saying noisy good-nights outside Al's Steak House; a couple with ice-cream cones wandered past; he realized that although it felt much later it must just be approaching midnight. He stood staring across Elgin into Minto Park, into its deepening shadows beyond the reach of the street-lights.

It was quiet in the deserted park; the surrounding maple trees seemed to soak up the noise of the traffic. The wet green benches glistened. The houses along the sides of the square looked onto the park with blank windows. Paul felt somehow secluded, embowered, as though he were in an invisible, airy, green marquee. Just before the shadowed centre of the park with its circular flower-bed, the path widened and there stood the large bronze bust. The bust sat on top of a tall concrete slab which served as a pedestal. Before lowering Peter to a sitting position on its plinth, Paul glanced up at the massive head, the epaulettes, the frogging on the military jacket. Against the bank of moonlit cloud behind, the head stared black and dramatic.

Peter sat slumped with his back against the slab.

Paul rearranged the boy's limbs.

The drizzle had stopped; the sky was breaking up. He began to hear the short screech of nighthawks.

He worked his shoulders about and stretched. His legs felt trembly. He thought of quenching his thirst with a quart of Boushey's fresh-squeezed orange juice but imagined Peter's body being discovered in his absence by a dog-walker, imagined sitting in the back of the summoned police car giving chapter and embarrassing verse.

The cuffs of his shirt were sticking to his wrists.

Beyond the central flower-bed was a drinking-fountain.

Two of the four lamps had burned out, their white globes dull and ghostly.

Zinnias. Zinnias and taller pink flowers whose name he didn't know.

His footsteps echoed.

He drank deeply at the fountain and splashed water on his face.

He walked back slowly to the bust. Around at the front of it Peter was invisible but audible, groaning exhalations. Paul bent forward and peered at the bronze plaque bolted into the back of the pedestal.

April 19, 1973

The Embassy of Argentina presents this bronze to the City
of Ottawa as a symbol of Canadian-Argentine Friendship
Mayor of Ottawa
Pierre Benoit
Ambassador of Argentina
Pablo Gonzalez Bergez

Paul walked around the plinth. Peter had not moved. He leaned close to the pedestal to read the plaque above the boy's head. It was darker on this side, the bulk of the bust and pedestal blocking most of the light from the two lamps, and he had to angle his head to make out the words.

GENERAL JOSÉ DE SAN MARTIN

Hero of the South-American Independence
Born in Argentina on Feb. 25, 1778

Died in France on Aug. 17, 1850
He ensured Argentine Independence, crossed the
Andes and liberated Chile and Peru

Sirens.

Sirens on Elgin Street.

Ambulance.

Silence sifting down again.

Crunching up two tablets of Nikoban gum, Paul stood looking down at Peter. The drizzle had wet his hair and purple food-dye had coloured his forehead and run in streaks down his face. Pallor and purple, he looked as if he'd been exhumed.

Paul sat down beside him on the plinth.

"Peter?

"How are you feeling now? Feel a bit better?

"Peter! Listen! Are you listening? I'll tell you what we're going to do. We'll stay and rest here for a while and let you get sobered up a bit. If your mother saw you like this neither of us'd ever hear the end of it. Come on, now! Sit up! You'll feel a bit better soon.

"Okay? Peter?"

Peter mumbled.

"What? What was that? *You're* tired! And what? You don't feel very well. No. I can imagine. You're a lucky boy, you know. Do you realize that? It was an amazing coincidence I happened to be in that place tonight. It was the first time I'd ever been there and I can assure you that it was also the last. That *violin*! Christ! It was like root-canal work. If that's the kind of place you hang out in, it's a wonder to me you aren't stone deaf. But you're lucky, Peter. It could have turned out differently. You could have hurt yourself badly on those stairs. You might have been in the hospital right now with your skull smashed. You think about that."

"*ohhhhhhhh,*" said Peter.

"Yes," said Paul, "you think about it."

He cleared his throat.

"Norma and I—you saw Norma, didn't you? Norma who works

for me? You met her once, I think. It was pure chance that I—that we—were there. As I said before. We'd been having dinner after work with a guy who's got some masks for sale and after dinner he wanted to go on and listen to some music—you know, visiting fire-man sort of stuff—tedious really—and Norma'd heard of that place so that's where we ended up."

Paul again glanced at Peter.

"Fellow from Edmonton."

Peter seemed to be studying his kneecap.

"And it was your good luck we did. End up there.

"Even if you hadn't hurt yourself on the stairs, the police would have picked you up. Imagine that? And Munchy and that other creep wouldn't have been much use to you either. Christ! What a pair! One pissed and the other congenital. You ought to have a think about those beauties, Peter. *Real* friends wouldn't have let you get like this. But can you imagine it? You know how she gets. Your mother down at the police station? In the middle of the night? In full flow?

"Anyway, you're safe. That's the main thing. I don't intend to go harping on about this. I just want you to think about it. That's all. Think about what *might* have happened. Okay?"

"*ohhhhhhhh,*" said Peter.

"Yes," said Paul, "well, that's what happens when you drink Ribena."

He leaned back against the pedestal listening to the screech of the invisible nighthawks. The cries grew louder and then dimin-ished, fading, grew harsher again as the birds swept and quartered the sky above.

"It's strange, really," he said. "I was just thinking about it. About that club and that abominable bloody music. Know what I was thinking about? It hadn't really occurred to me before. And perhaps it should have. But when *I* was your age I used to drive *my* parents mad with the stuff *I* listened to. Of course, with me it was jazz records. To hear my mother on the subject—well, you know what your grandmother's like—you'd have thought it was Sodom and

Gomorrah and the papacy rolled into one. And it didn't help, of course, that most of them were black.

"Oh, I've had some memorable fights with her in my time. She was sort of a female Archie Bunker, your grandmother. Backbone of the Ladies' Orange Benevolent Association. A merciless church-goer. She refused to listen to the radio on Sundays till she was about sixty-five. Yes, in the days I'm talking about your grandmother was a woman of truly *vile* rectitude.

"I remember one time up at the cottage—one summer—I hated it up there when I was about your age. Every day—every single day—she used to bake bread on that old wood stove. Can you imagine? In that heat? It was all just part of her summer campaign to make life unbearable and martyr herself. And piss my father off. But when I was about your age, that summer . . .

"I'd only got a few records. I can see them now. 78s, of course. And an old wind-up gramophone. Benny Goodman and Artie Shaw and Ellington and Count Basie. Buddy de Franco.

"I used to sit out there on the porch—it wasn't screened in those days—I used to sit out there playing them over and over again. 'Take the A Train' and 'Flying Home'. And she could have *killed* me. When *she* listened to music—and she didn't really *like* music—she used to listen to a dreadful unaccompanied woman called Kathleen Ferrier singing some damn thing called 'Blow the Wind Southerly'. A very horrible experience, my boy. And if it wasn't that, it was the other side. 'We'll Lay the Keel Row'. Which was, if possible, worse. You don't know what suffering *is*.

"But the stuff *I* played was like waving a red flag. Getting up late and not eating a proper breakfast and then refusing to swim and just sitting, sitting listening to that . . . to that . . . And off she'd go about vulgarity and nigger minstrels and why couldn't I listen to something decent like John McCormack and then *I'd* say that Benny Goodman was not only white but a respected classical musician and then it'd get worse and her face red with rage and it'd swell into all decency fled from modern life and girls flaunting themselves shamelessly and listening to that concatenation of black booby-faces . . . well, you can imagine what it was like. You know how easy it is to get her started. Though she's mellow now compared with the way she used to be. All that business over Jennifer's shorts last year. About their indecency? Remember that?

"Anyway. What I'm getting at is that maybe when you get a bit older you forget—I don't mean *you*—you, Peter—I mean *one*. One forgets what one was like oneself. *That's* what I'm trying to say. Understand? And I'm trying to say that I don't want to be towards you the way your grandmother was to me.

"What?"

"*nerrrrrrrr,*" said Peter again.

"No? No you don't want me to be?"

"*nrrrrrrrr,*" said Peter.

"Now," said Paul, "I'm not saying I could ever *like* the music you like because, in all honesty, I couldn't. And I don't want to lie to you. But certainly I ought to be able to tolerate it. Because I don't want something like taste in music to come between us. There'd be something . . . well . . . so *petty* about that, wouldn't there?"

Peter said nothing.

His head was back against the pedestal and he seemed to be staring up into a maple tree. Paul got to his feet and stood looking down at him.

"Wouldn't there, Peter? Be something petty about that? And that's something that, well . . . you know, as we *are* talking, it's something we ought to talk about. I know it isn't *just* the music. It's everything the music *stands for*. I realize that. And whatever you might *think*, I *do* understand, Peter, because that's what jazz used to stand for. For me, I mean. When I was fighting with *my* father and mother. It meant the same kind of thing that punk or new wave or whatever you call it means now. But I'll tell you what I resent. What I resent is this being cast in the role of *automatic* enemy. *I'm* not Society. *I'm* not The Middle Class. I'm *me*. A person. Just like you're a person.

"And *I've* got feelings, too.

"Okay?"

Paul stood looking down at Peter's bowed head.

"Look!" he said, beginning to pace. "We've been having a pretty hard time lately, haven't we? Always arguing and squabbling about one thing or another. Getting on each other's nerves. And it's been making me very unhappy, Peter. But you know, for my part, I only criticize you because I want you to grow up decently and become a kind and considerate person. I don't *enjoy* fighting with you. Believe me. But think of it this way. If I *didn't* care about you and love you— care about what you're going to become—and care very deeply— I wouldn't bother with you, would I? It'd be much easier just to ignore you, let you go to hell in a handcart. It'd be a lot easier for me just to shrug my shoulders, wouldn't it?

"But I don't do that, Peter.

"And I think, really, that you *know* why I don't.

"Don't you?"

Paul sat down on the plinth again and turned to face Peter. Peter had not moved. Paul looked at him and then looked down at his shoes. A breath of wind shuddered the leaves in the maple trees and drops of rain-water pattered down on the concrete path.

"I don't know, old son. It's a funny business—the way things work out—and I don't make much claim to understand it. I suppose we all just blunder along doing the best we can, just hoping for the best but . . . *this* thing—you and me, I mean—it's all so *ridiculous*.

"Peter?"

Paul put his hand on Peter's arm and then shook him gently.

"What? Yes, *I know* you're tired. What? Yes, soon. We'll go home soon. But listen! Let's get this thing thrashed out. I was saying how ridiculous it was, this constant squabbling about things. I mean, it wasn't so long ago that you went everywhere with me. I couldn't even go to the store for a packet of cigarettes without you tagging along. And remember how we used to go fishing every weekend? Just you and me? Remember that? All those sunfish you used to catch? Remember that day a racoon ran off with our package of hot-dogs? And those water snakes you used to catch? Revolting damned things! I used to be quite scared of them. You didn't know that, did you? You thought I was just pretending. And remember that day you made me hold one and it vented all that stuff on my hands and shirt? And how it stank? You thought that was *very* funny.

"Remember, Petey?

"So what I'm getting at is that although we've been getting on each other's nerves a bit lately, you can't just wipe out the past. You can't just ignore . . . well, what it amounts to, most of your life. I guess we're just stuck with it, aren't we? Wretched thing that I am, I'm your father. And you're my *son*, Petey. So I guess . . ."

"*nrrrnnnnnnnn.*"

"What?"

Peter leaned forward and, without apparent effort, gushed vomit.

Paul jumped up and out of range.

Peter sat staring ahead, his mouth slightly open.

Threads of drool glistened from his lips.

"Peter?"

Paul passed his hand in front of the boy's face. He did not blink; he did not stir.

"*Peter!*"

Paul stared down at him, astounded.

"You ungrateful little *shit*! You're the next best thing to unconscious, aren't you? You selfish little turd! You haven't heard a single goddamned word I've been saying to you, have you? I've been wasting all these pearls of wisdom on the desert air, haven't I? Hello? Hello? Anyone in there? *Peter*! YOUR FATHER IS TALKING TO YOU.

"Nothing, eh?

"The motor's run down, has it?

"Ah, well . . .

"I suppose it makes a change, though. Your not answering back. I ought to be grateful, really. You've got a mouth on you like a barrack-room lawyer. Always arguing the toss, aren't you? Black, white. Day, night. Left is right and vice versa. I ought to be grateful for brief mercies. I've daydreamed sometimes of having myself surgically deafened.

"You're always bleating about social justice and revolution—and look at you! Purple hair and vintage puke-slobbered clothing. Let

me tell you, my little chickadee, that any self-respecting revolution-
ary would shoot you *on sight*. Thus displaying both acumen *and*
taste.

"Some revolution you'd run. You and Munchy and Bunchy and
Drippy and Droopy. What would you do after you'd liberated Baskin-
Robbins?

"That's a nice touch. Doing your face purple as well. Suits you.

"Neat but not gaudy.

"And to revert for a moment to the subject of music. You, my
dear boy, and your fellow-members of The Virgin Exterminators,
are about as much musicians as is my left bojangle. You'd be hard
put to find middle C under a searchlight. Musically speaking, blood
of my blood and bone of my bone, you couldn't distinguish shit
from shinola.

"Hello?

"Yoo-hoo!

"Anyone at home?

"*You're an offensive little heap*! What are you? 'I'm an offensive little heap, Daddy.' Yes, you are! And you're also idle, soft, and spoiled.
And in addition to that, you've spewed on my shoe.

"What do you imagine's going to happen to you? Who the hell's
going to hire you when you leave school? For what? What can you
do? You can't even cut the lawn without leaving tufts all over the
place. And dare I ask you to trim the edges with a pair of shears? You
were outraged, weren't you? 'By *hand*!' you said. How do you think
I do it? By foot? Wanted me to buy one of those ludicrous buzzing
machines to save your poor back from stooping. And when you've
chopped it to pieces so that it looks as if you've gone at it with a
knife and fork, you have the nerve to demand two bucks. It's all so
easy, isn't it?

"Just shake the old money tree.

"Well, life isn't like that, my little cherub. Life isn't a matter of
rolling out of your smelly bed at eleven in the morning and lounging around sipping Earl Grey tea and eating nine muffins rich in
fibre. Life, my little nestling, is tough bananas.

"And what are you doing to prepare yourself for its rigours? Studying hard? Mastering your times-tables? Practising the old parlez-vous? Getting a grip on human history? History! Dear God! Stone hand-axes, the Magna Carta, the Pilgrim Fathers—it's all the same sort of thing, isn't it? Events that took place in that dim and inconceivable period before the Rolling Stones. The glories of civilization—it's all B.S., isn't it?

"Before Stones.

"And math? You don't even know your tables. Oh, I'll admit you're very handy with the calculator on that fancy watch of yours but I'm afraid *you'd* have to admit that you'd be up the well-known creek if the battery gave out.

"In sum, then, you're close to failing in damn near every subject. And why is that? What was the reason you advanced? Something about school being 'a repressive environment'. I'm not misquoting you, I hope. And what was it you received a commendation in? A discipline I hadn't encountered before. 'Chemical Awareness', I believe it was called.

"In which you have now moved on, I see, to practical studies.

"Pissed out of your mind at fifteen.

"What mind you have.

"And speaking of pissed, and I apologize for bringing this up, as it were, when you're a little under the weather, but I'd be gratified if you could remember in future to raise the toilet seat before relieving yourself.

"I mention this because I am tired of living knee-deep in balled Kleenex, soiled underwear, crusted piss, and rotting tofu.

"I am, as a matter of fact, tired of a hell of a lot of things.

"Oh!

"Yes.

"I also wish you'd shave your upper lip every couple of weeks now you're nearing man's estate. You look like a spinster with hormonal imbalance.

"And another matter of petty detail.

"That cat.

"I don't like it.

"That cat is going back to the SPCA *forthwith*. To be humanely electrocuted to death IN A WET STEEL BOX."

Stooping and grabbing up a rotten branch which had fallen in the storm, Paul beat it against the trunk of the nearest maple until it shattered into fragments. He threw the pieces, one by one, as far as he could out onto the grass. He threw them with all the power and violence he could command. He threw them until his elbow joint began to hurt.

He turned and walked back towards the pedestal. The pool of vomit between Peter's feet glistened. He sat on a nearby bench and spread his arms along the back.

He crossed his legs.

He breathed in deeply and then sighed profoundly.

He stared up at the great bronze bust of San Martin.

"*Well?*" he demanded of the moonlight touching the high military collar, the frogging, the starburst of a military decoration or royal Order.

"What do you say, José? How was it with you? What do *you* have to offer? You wear your seventy-two years easily, I'll say that for you. You have that calm and peaceful look about you of the man who gets laid frequently. I'd lay odds *you* didn't live in an open-plan house.

"It's about all I *can* lay.

"Odds.

"And what about *Mrs.* José de San Martin? Doubtless a beauty, you salty dog. Veins surging with hot southern blood? Bit of a handful? I don't suppose *she* had to go out to work. Wasn't too tired at night? Wasn't worrying that the children might hear? That the tomato chutney in the basement might explode?

"Lucky man, José.

"And the kids? I expect they were tucked up in their nursery half a mile away in the East Wing?

"And *not* by you.

"Very sensible, too.

"And she adored you?

"Well mine adores me but she's got a lot on her mind. Is the gas turned off? Did she or didn't she put Tooth Fairy money under Jennifer's pillow? Will chutney attract rats? It takes the bloom off it, José.

"But I've always been faithful to her. Up till tonight, that is.

"What happened? That's a good question, José. I wish I knew. There's this girl, you see. Polly Ongle. And . . . well, I *wasn't* unfaithful. Though I could have been. Or maybe *not*. No. There's a thought. Maybe not. And anyway, this one turned out to be Norma. To tell the truth, I'm a bit confused about it, José. You see, I'm beginning to suspect it was all about something else.

"Can I put it more clearly? I'm not surprised you ask.

"No.

"But you. These campaigns of yours. When you were away from her. I expect you rogered your way across the continent. I don't suppose you went short of a bit of enchilada, did you? Oh, don't misunderstand me! I'm not being censorious. If anything, I'm envious, José. It's just that it isn't so simple now. A lot of other things have been liberated since Chile and Peru.

"I wish I'd flourished then.

"It seems more vivid, somehow. Somehow simpler.

"Jingling home after you'd given the hidalgos a severe thumping about in the course of liberating this or that, clattering into the forecourt of the ancestral home, tossing the reins to one of the adoring family retainers, striding through the hall in boots and spurs,

"'Coo-ee, *mi adoracion*! I have returned! It is I.'

"And then off with the epaulettes, down with the breeches, and into the saddle.

"*Whereas*, José, when *I* return—granted not from a two-year campaign but from a two-day business trip—there's no question of skirts up and knickers joyfully down. I have to suffer a lengthy interrogation about expenditures on my Visa card.

"Following which she promptly collapses.

"Why, you ask?

"Because, José, for two nights she has not slept. She has not slept because she has lain awake, José, worrying (a) that I might have been killed in any of an astounding variety of ways and (b) that the burglars and perverts who surround my house would take advantage of my absence and kill *her*.

"After first buggering, of course, all the children.

"Talking of which, how did yours turn out?

"Children, I mean.

"A comfort to you in your old age? A source of pride? Or did they cause you grief? Blackballed from clubs? Welshed on debts of honour? Or did they rally round bringing Dad his cigar and nightly posset?

"Tell me, José, what would *you* have done with *this*? Head under a pump and a stick across his back, eh? It's an attractive thought. Very attractive. But he'd have me up in front of the Children's Aid soon as look at me. Probably argue his own case, too. With *his* mouth, he wouldn't *need* a lawyer. And I'd end up being forced to increase his allowance and buy him a colour TV.

"The army? Well, these days I'm afraid they don't take all comers. They tend to ask questions. Such as what's five multiplied by twelve. And I don't suppose they'd let him use his watch.

"I don't know, José. This one's bad enough. But I've got two more coming to the boil. What are *they* going to dream up to break my heart? Need I ask? I *know*. In the middle of the night, I *know*. My little daughter will get herself tattooed and fuck with unwashed, psychotic bikers. My other son will blossom suddenly queer as a three-dollar bill. What does one do? What does one *do*?

"You lived a long time, José."

Close ranks and face the front.

"Well, there's a gem from the military mind. *Very* comforting. But forgive me. I'm being rude. I'm forgetting. You *do* know more about fortitude than I do. I'd forgotten that. Was it a daily bitterness? All your titles resigned, your honours returned. Thirty-odd years, wasn't it? In France? Thirty-some years in voluntary exile. And all in support of a monarchy nobody wanted.

"I don't know, José.

"But on the other hand, it couldn't have turned out worse than generals in sunglasses.

"Was it worth it, José? Looking at it now? I've never been there. Argentina. Used to read about it when I was a kid. Gauchos deadly with knife and bola. That sort of thing. But if the rest of the world is anything to go by, the gauchos are probably wired to Sony Walk-mans and the pampas is littered with Radio Shacks.

"Still, you did it when the doing of it was fun. Horses. Gorgeous uniforms and women swooning. South American heart-breakers all looking like Bianca Jagger with flowers in their teeth.

"'Was it worth it?'

"What a stupid question!

"Of *course* it was worth it.

"Before. After. All those years in bitter exile.

"Of *course* it was worth it. Leather, harness, steel, pennons snap-ping in the wind. For those eight years you were larger than life. Coming down out of the mountains, your columns trailing you, the guns bouncing on their limbers—you were living in a dream. Oh, don't think I don't understand!

"I envy you, José.

"You breathed an air I've never breathed.

"I envy you that, José.

"God! I envy you that.

"'*Was it worth it*.'

"Look at us!

"Here's me down here with puke on my shoes—ever tried to get it off suede?—and there's you up there growing greener every year.

"Ah, well . . .

"What can you do?

"As my father-in-law, the philosopher says,

"'What can you do?'

"What can you do, José?

"What can you do, flesh of my flesh?

"No contributions from you?

"No ready answers?

"Good.

"That's a relief.

"Come on, then. Heave! Up you come! Don't *step* in it! Beddy-bye time for you. Come on! That's it. We're going walkies. *Hasta la vista, José.* Come on, Peter. Say goodnight to the General. That's it. Christ, you smell revolting! Get your feet out of the zinnias, there's a good boy. *This* way! This way. Come on! Five more blocks. Walk *straight*! Come on, Petey. You can do it. Five more blocks and then you can sleep. Good! That's it. Good boy. Good boy, Petey.

"Left, right.

"Left, right.

"Not so *much* left.

"Right.

"Steady the Buffs! Steady! Correct that tendency to droop. And get your leg out of that juniper bush. What do you think this is, you 'orrible little man? A nature ramble? Now, then. Close ranks and face the front. *That's* the front—where the street-light is. And on the word of command, it's forward march for us.

"Ready?

"*Forwaaard—*

wait for it!

wait for it!

MARCH."

THE NIPPLES OF VENUS

Rome stank of exhaust fumes and below our hotel room on the Via Sistina motor bikes and scooters snarled and ripped past late into the night rattling the window and the plywood wardrobe. The bathroom, a boxed-in corner, was the size of two upright coffins. It was impossible to sit on the toilet without jamming your knees against the wash-basin. In the chest of drawers, Helen discovered crackers, crumbs, and Pan Am cheese.

I'd reserved the room by phone from Florence, choosing the hotel from a guidebook from a list headed: Moderate. We would only have to put up with it for Saturday and Sunday and would then fly home on Monday. After nearly three weeks spent mainly in Florence and Venice, I had no real interest in looking at things Roman. I felt . . . not tired, exactly. Couldn't take in any more. I'd had enough. "Surfeited" was the word, perhaps. I was sick of cameras and photographs and tourists and tourism and disliking myself for being part of the problem. I felt burdened by history, ashamed of my ignorance, numbed by the succession of *ponte, porta, piazza,* and *palazzo.* I was beginning to feel like . . . who was it? Twain, I think, Mark Twain, who when asked what he'd thought of Rome said to his wife:

Was that the place we saw the yellow dog?

Helen was bulged and bloated and the elastic of her underpants and panty-hose had left red weals and ribbing on the flesh of her stomach. She'd been constipated for nearly two weeks. I'd told her to stop eating pasta, to relax, to stop worrying about whether the children would leave the iron switched on, about aviation disasters, devaluation of the lira, cancer of the colon, but at night I heard her sighing, grinding her teeth, restless under the sheets, gnawing on the bones of her worries.

That waiter in—where was it? Milan? No. Definitely not in Milan. Bologna?—a waiter who'd worked for some years in Soho in the family restaurant—he'd told us that the tortellini, the tiny stuffed shells of pasta in our soup, were commonly called "the nipples of Venus."

Fettuccine, tuffolini, capelletti, manicotti, gnocchi . . .

Mia moglie è malata.

Dov'è una farmacia?

Aspirina?

Bicarbonato di soda?

. . . polenta, rigatoni, tortellini . . .

Praaaaaaaaaap . . .

Scooters on the Via Sistina.

Praaaaaaaaaap . . .

Helen passing gas.

———————

The Spanish Steps were just at the top of the street anyway and at the very least, Helen said, we had to see the Trevi Fountain and St. Peter's and the Pantheon.

They all looked much as they looked in photographs. Not as attractive, really. The Spanish Steps were littered with American college students. The sweep of St. Peter's Square was ruined even at that early hour by parked coaches from Luton, Belgrade, Brussels, and Brighton. Knowing that St. Peter's itself would be hung with acres of martyrdom and suchlike, I refused to set foot in it. The Trevi Fountain was rimmed with people taking its photograph and was magnificent but disappointing.

Places of historical interest often make me feel as if I'm eight again and the sermon will never end. I enjoyed the *doors* of the Pantheon—I always seem drawn to bronze—but the hushed interior struck me as lugubrious. Helen, on the other hand, is an inveterate reader of every notice, explication, plaque, and advisement.

Straightening up and taking off her reading glasses, she says, "This is the tomb of Raphael."

"How about a coffee?"

"Born 1483."

"Espresso. You like that. In the square."

"Died in 1520."

"Nice coffee."

And then it was back to the Spanish Steps because she wanted to go jostling up and down the Via Condotti looking in the windows— Ferragamo, Gabrielli, Bulgari, Valentino, Gucci. And then in search of even more pairs of shoes, purses, scarves, gloves, and sweaters, it was down to the stores and boutiques on the Via del Tritone.

For lunch I ate *funghi arrosto alla Romana*. Helen ordered *risotto alla parmigiana* and had to go back to the hotel. She said she'd just lie there for a bit and if the pains went away she'd have a little nap. She asked me if I thought it was cancer, so I said that people with cancer *lost* weight and that it was *risotto, manifestly* risotto, *risotto first and last*.

"There's no need to shout at me."

"I am *not* shouting. I am speaking emphatically."

"You don't mind?" she said. "Really?"

"I'll go for a stroll around," I said.

"You won't feel I'm deserting you?"

"Just rest."

I strolled up the Via Sistina and stood looking down the sweep of the Spanish Steps. Then sauntered on. Some seventy-five yards to the right of the Steps, seventy-five yards or so past the Trinità dei Monti along the stretch of gravel road which leads into the grounds of the Villa Borghese, tucked away behind a thick hedge and shaded

by trees, was an outdoor café hidden in a narrow garden. The garden
was just a strip between the road and the edge of the steep hill which
fell away down towards the Via Condotti or whatever was beneath.
The Piazza di Spagna, perhaps. Houses must have been built almost
flush with the face of the hill because through the screening pampas
grass I could glimpse below the leaning rusty fence at the garden's
edge the warm ripple of terra cotta roof tiles.

The garden was paved with stone flagstones. Shrubs and flowers
grew in low-walled beds and urns. In the centre of the garden was a
small rectangular pond with reeds growing in it, the flash of fish red
and gold. The tall hedge which hid the garden from the road was
dark, evergreen, yew trees.

It was quiet there, the traffic noises muted to a murmur. Round
white metal tables shaded by gay umbrellas, white folding chairs.
Two old waiters were bringing food and drinks from the hut at the
garden's entrance. There were only three couples and a family at
the tables. The yew hedge was straggly and needed cutting back. The
shrubs and flowers in the stone-walled beds were gone a little to seed,
unweeded.

I sat at the only table without an umbrella, a table set into a corner formed by the hedge and a low stone wall. The wall screened the
inner garden a little from the openness of the entrance and from the
shingled hut-like place the food came from. All along the top of the
wall stood pots of geraniums and jutting out from the wall near my
corner table was the basin of a fountain. The basin was in the form
of a scallop shell. The stone shell looked much older than the wall. It
looked as if it had come down in the world, ending up here in this
garden café after gracing for two hundred years or more some ducal
garden or palazzo courtyard. The stone was softer than the stone
of the wall, grainy, the sharpness of its cuts and flutes blurred and
weathered.

I sat enjoying the warmth of the sun. The Becks beer bottle and
my glass were beaded with condensation. Sparrows were hopping
between tables pecking crumbs. Water was trickling down the wall
and falling into the stone scallop shell from a narrow copper pipe

which led away down behind the wall and towards the hut at the garden's entrance. Where the pipe crossed the central path feet had squashed it almost flat. The small sound of the water was starting to take over my mind. The glint and sparkle of the sunlight on the water, the tinkling sound of it, the changes in the sound of it as it rose and deepened around the domed bronze grate before draining—it all held me in deepening relaxation.

Somewhere just below me were famous guidebook attractions— the Barcaccia Fountain, the Antico Caffe Greco, the rooms where John Keats died now preserved as a museum and containing memorabilia of Byron and Shelley—but all I wanted of Rome was to sit on in the sunshine drinking cold beer and listening to the loveliness of water running, the trill and spirtle, the rill and trickle of it.

Watching the sparrow, the small cockings of its head, watching the little boy in the white shirt and red bow-tie balancing face-down over his father's thigh, I was aware suddenly at the corner of my eye of flickering movement. I turned my head and there, reared up on its front legs on the rim of the stone scallop shell, was a lizard. It stood motionless. I turned more towards it. Its back was a matte black but its throat and neck and sides were touched with a green so brilliant it looked almost metallic, as if it had been dusted with metallic powder.

Set on the stone surround of the scallop shell were two pots of geraniums and from the shadow of these now appeared another lizard, smaller than the first, not as dark in colouring, dun rather than black and with not a trace of the shimmering peacock green— compared with the male a scrawny creature drab and dowdy.

This lizard waddled down into the curve of the stone basin where she stopped and raised her head as if watching or listening. Or was she perhaps scenting what was on the air? I'd read somewhere that snakes "smelled" with their tongues. Were lizards, I wondered, like snakes in that? Would they go into water? Was she going to drink?

I was startled by loud rustlings in the hedge near my chair. A bird? A bird rootling about in dead leaves. But it wasn't that kind of noise quite. Not as loud. And, I realized, it was more continuous than the noise a bird would have made—rustling, twig-snipping, pushing, scuffling. The noise was travelling along *inside* the hedge. Slowly, cautiously, not wanting to frighten away the lizards on the stone scallop shell, I bent and parted branches, peering.

And then the noise stopped.

As I sat up, I saw that the stone bowl was empty, the brown lizard disappeared behind the geranium pots again. The green lizard was still motionless where he'd been before. Every few seconds his neck pulsed. Suddenly I saw on the wall level with my knee a lizard climbing. Every two or three inches it stopped, clinging, seeming to listen. It too was green but it had no tail. Where its tail should have been was a glossy rounded stump.

Lacking the tail's long grace, the lizard looked unbalanced, clumsy. About half the tail was gone. It was broken off just below that place where the body tapered. The stump was a scaleless wound, shiny, slightly bulbous, in colour a very dark red mixed with black. The end of the stump bulged out like a blob of smoke-swirled sealing-wax.

Just as its head was sticking up over the edge of the stone shell, the other lizard ran at it. The mutilated lizard turned and flashed halfway down the wall but then stopped, head-down, clinging. The pursuing lizard stopped too and cocked its head at an angle as if hearing something commanding to its right.

Seconds later, the stubby lizard skittered down the rest of the wall, but then stopped again on the flagstones. The pursuing lizard pursued but himself stopped poised above the wall's last course of stones. It was like watching the flurry of a silent movie with the action frozen every few seconds. And then the damaged lizard was negotiating in dreamy slow motion dead twigs and blown leaves on his way back into the hedge. He *clambered* over them as if they were thick boughs, back legs cocked up at funny angles like a cartoon animal, crawling, ludicrous. His pursuer faced in the opposite direction intently, fiercely.

Peculiar little creatures.

I signalled to the waiter for another beer.

I sat on in the sunshine, drifting, smelling the smell on my fingers of crushed geranium leaves, listening to the sounds the water made.

And then the noises in the hedge started again.

And again the lizard with the stump was climbing the wall.

And again the lizard on the top was rushing at it, driving it down.

By the time I was finishing my third beer, the attacks and retreats were almost continuous. The stubby lizard always climbed the wall at exactly the same place. The defending lizard always returned to the exact spot on the stone surround of the scallop shell where the attacking lizard would appear. The stop-frame chases flowed and halted down the wall, across the flagstones, halted, round an urn, into the hedge.

But with each sortie the damaged lizard was being driven further and further away. Finally, the pursuing lizard hauled his length into the hedge and I listened to their blundering progress over the litter of twigs and rusty needles in the hedge-bottom, the rustlings and cracklings, the scrabblings travelling further and further away from my chair until there was silence.

The sun had moved around the crown of the tree and was now full on me. I could feel the sweat starting on my chest, in the hollow of my throat, the damp prickle of sweat in my groin. I glanced at my watch to see how long she'd been sleeping. I thought of strolling back to the hotel and having a shower, but the thought of showering in the boxed-in bathroom inside the glass device with its folding glass doors like a compressed telephone booth—the thought of touching with every movement cold, soap-slimy glass . . .

I lifted the empty Becks bottle and nodded at the waiter as he passed.

A dragon-fly hovered over the pond, its wings at certain angles a blue iridescence.

I wondered about my chances of finding a Roman restaurant or trattoria serving *Abbracchio alla Romana*, a dish I'd read about with interest. And while I was thinking about restaurants and roast lamb flavoured with rosemary and anchovies and about poor Helen's *risotto* and about how long I'd been sitting in the garden and Helen worrying there in that plywood room heavy with exhaust fumes . . .

you might have been killed . . . you know I only nap for an hour . . .
I got so scared . . .

. . . while I was thinking about this and these and listening to the water's trickle and looking at the white, heavy plumes of the pampas grass, there on top of the wall, my eye caught by the movement, was the lizard with the stump.

I studied the face of the wall, scanned the bottom of the hedge, looked as far around the base of the urn as I could see without moving, but there was no sign of the other lizard, no sound of pursuit.

He stood motionless on top of the wall just above the scallop shell where the scrawny brown female still basked. The stump looked as if blood and flesh had oozed from the wound and then hardened into this glossy, bulging scab.

The coast's clear, Charlie!

Come on!

Come on!

He was clinging head-down to the wall inches above the stone shell.

The female had raised her head.

Now he seemed to be studying a pale wedge of crumbling mortar.

Come on!

And then he waddled down onto the stone surround and seized the female lizard firmly about the middle in his jaws. They lay at right angles to each other as if catatonic. The female's front right leg dangled in the air.

Come on, you gimpy retard! Let go! You're biting the wrong one. It's
the GREEN ones we bite. The brown ones are the ones we . . .

The waiter's voice startled me.

I smiled, shook my head, picked up the four cash-register slips, leaned over to one side to get at my wallet in my back pocket. When he'd gone and I turned back to the stone scallop shell, the female had already vanished and the end of the stump, somewhere between the colour of a ripening blackberry and a blood blister, was just disappearing into the shadows behind one of the pots of geraniums.

I got up slowly and quietly. I was careful not to scrape my chair on the flagstones. I set it down silently. I looked down to make sure my shoe wasn't going to knock against one of the table's tubular legs. One by one, I placed the coins on the saucer.

———————

No, I told Helen on Sunday morning, not the Forum, not the Colosseum, not the Capitoline, the Palatine, or the Quirinal. I wanted to be lazy. I wanted to be taken somewhere. But not to monuments. Trees and fields. But not *walking*. I didn't want to *do* anything. I wanted to see farmhouses and outbuildings. What I wanted—yes, that was it exactly—a coach tour! I wanted to gaze out of the window at red and orange roof tiles, at ochre walls, poppies growing wild on the roadsides, vines.

At 10 AM we were waiting in a small office in a side street for the arrival of the coach. The brochure in the hotel lobby had described the outing as Extended Alban Hills Tours—Castelli Romani. Our coach was apparently now touring some of the larger hotels picking up other passengers. The whole operation seemed a bit makeshift and fly-by-night. The two young men running it seemed to do nothing but shout denials on the phone and hustle out into the street screaming at drivers as coach after coach checked in at the office before setting out to tour whatever they were advertised as touring. Commands and queries were hysterical. Tickets were counted and recounted. And then recounted. Coaches were finally dispatched with operatic gesture as if they were full of troops going up to some heroic Front.

As each coach pulled up, we looked inquiry at one or other of the young men. "This is not yours," said their hands. "Patience." "Do not fear. When your conveyance arrives, we will inform you," said their gestures.

We were both startled by the entry of a large, stout man with a shaved head who barged into the tiny office saying something that sounded challenging or jeering. His voice was harsh. He limped, throwing out one leg stiffly. Helen sat up in the plastic chair and drew her legs in. Something about his appearance suggested that he'd survived a bad car-crash. He leaned on an aluminum stick which ended in a large rubber bulb. He was wearing rimless blue-tinted glasses. His lip was permanently drawn up a little at one side. There was a lot of visible metal in his teeth. He stumped about in the confined space shouting and growling.

The young man with the mauve leather shoes shouted "no" a lot and "never" and slapped the counter with a plastic ruler. The other young man picked up a glossy brochure and, gazing fixedly at the ceiling, twisted it as if wringing a neck. The shaven-headed man pushed a pile of pamphlets off the counter with the rubber tip of his aluminum stick.

A coach pulled up and a young woman in a yellow dress got down from it and clattered on heels into the office. They all shouted at her. She spat—*teh*—and made a coarse gesture.

The young man with the mauve leather shoes went outside to shout up at the coach driver. Through the window, we watched him counting, pulling each finger down in turn.

. . . five, six, *seven*.

Further heart-rending pantomime followed.

Still in full flow, he burst back into the office brandishing the tickets in an accusatory way. Peering and pouting into the mirror of a compact, the girl in the yellow dress continued applying lipstick. They all shouted questions at her, possibly rhetorical. The horrible shaven-headed man shook the handle of his aluminum cane in her face.

She spat again—*teh*.

The bus driver sounded his horn.

The other young man spoke beseechingly to the potted azalea.

"Is that," said Helen, "the Castelli Romani coach? Or isn't it the Castelli Romani coach?"

There was silence as everyone stared at her.

"It *is*, dear madam, it *is*," said the horribly bald man.

"Good," said Helen.

And I followed her out.

We nodded to the other seven passengers as we climbed aboard and seated ourselves behind them near the front of the coach. They sounded American. There were two middle-aged couples, a middle-aged man on his own, rather melancholy-looking, and a middle-aged man with an old woman.

"Here he comes goosewalking," said Helen.

"*Stepping*," I said.

The shaven-headed man, leg lifting up and then swinging to the side, was stumping across the road leaning on the aluminum cane. His jacket was a flapping black-and-white plaid.

"Oh, *no!*" I said. "You don't think *he's* . . ."

"I told you," said Helen. "I told you this was going to be awful."

The shaven-headed man climbed up into the bus, hooked his aluminum cane over the handrail above the steps, and unclipped the microphone. Holding it in front of his mouth, he surveyed us.

"Today," he said with strange, metallic sibilance, "today you are my children."

Helen nudged.

"Today I am taking you into the Alban Hills. I will show you many wonders. I will show you extinct volcanoes. I will show you the lake of the famous Caligula. I will show you the headquarters of the German Army in World War II. Together we will visit Castel Gandolfo, Albano, Genzano, Frascati, and Rocca di Papa. We will leave ancient Rome by going past the Colosseum and out onto the Via Appia Antica completed by Appius Claudius in 312 before Christ."

He nodded slowly.

"Oh yes, my children."

Still nodding.

"*Before Christ.*"

He looked from face to face.

"You will know this famous road as the Appian Way and you will have seen it in the movie *Spartacus* with the star Kirk Douglas."

"Oh, God!" said Helen.

"Well, my children," he said, tapping the bus driver on the shoulder, "are you ready? But you are curious about me. Who *is* this man, you are saying."

He inclined his shaved head in a bow.

"*Who* am I?"

He chuckled into the microphone.

"They call me Kojak."

Cypresses standing guard along the Appian Way over sepulchres and sarcophagi, umbrella pines shading fragments of statuary. Tombs B.C. Tombs A.D. Statuary contemporaneous with Julius Caesar, of whom we would have read in the play of that name by William Shakespeare. It was impossible to ignore or block out his voice, and after a few minutes we'd come to dread the clicking on of the microphone and the harsh, metallic commentary.

You will pay attention to your left and you will see . . .

A sarcophagus.

You will pay attention opposite and you will see . . .

"Opposite what?"

"He means straight ahead."

"Oh."

. . . to your right and in one minute you will see a famous school for women drivers . . .

Into view hove a scrap-metal dealer's yard mountainous with wrecked cars.

You will pay attention . . .

But despite the irritation of the rasping voice, I found the expedition soothing and the motion of the coach restful. The landscape as it passed was pleasing. Fields. Hedges. Garden plots. The warmth of terra cotta tiles. Hills. White clouds in a sky of blue.

The Pope's summer residence at Castel Gandolfo was a glimpse through open ornate gates up a drive to a house, then the high encircling stone wall around the park.

Beech trees.

In the narrow, steep streets of the small town, the coach's length negotiated the sharp turns, eased around corners, trundled past the elaborate façade of the church and through the piazza with its fountain by Bernini.

The famous Peach Festival took place in June.

At Lake Albano we were to stop for half an hour.

No less, my children, and no more.

The coach pulled into the restaurant parking lot and backed into line with more than a dozen others. The restaurant, a cafeteria sort of place, was built on the very edge of the lake. It was jammed with tourists. Washrooms were at the bottom of a central staircase and children ran up and down the stairs, shouting. There was a faint smell of disinfectant. Lost children cried.

In the plastic display cases were sandwiches with dubious fillings, tired-looking panini, and slices of soggy pizza that were being reheated in microwave ovens until greasy.

The man from our coach who was travelling with the old woman sat staring out of the plate-glass window which overlooked the lake. The old woman was spooning in with trembling speed what looked like a huge English trifle, mounds of whipped cream, maraschino cherries, custard, cake.

Helen and I bought an ice cream we didn't really want. We stood on the wooden dock beside the restaurant and looked at the lake which was unnaturally blue. There was a strong breeze. White sails were swooping over the water. I felt cold and wished we could get back in the coach.

"So this was a volcano," said Helen.

"I guess so."

"The top blew off and then it filled up with water."

"I suppose that's it."

The man from our coach who was on his own, the melancholy-looking man, wandered onto the other side of the dock. He stood holding an ice-cream cone and looking across the lake. He looked a bit like Stan Laurel. We nodded to him. He nodded to us and made a sort of gesture at the lake with his ice cream as if to convey approval.

We smiled and nodded.

The engine of the coach was throbbing as we sat waiting for the man and the old woman to shuffle across the parking lot. The stiff breeze suddenly blew the man's hair down, revealing him as bald. From one side of his head hung a long hank which had been trained up and over his bald pate. He looked naked and bizarre as he stood there, the length of hair hanging from the side of his head and fluttering below his shoulder. It looked as if he'd been scalped. The attached hair looked like a dead thing, like a pelt.

Seemingly unembarrassed, he lifted the hair back, settling it as if it were a beret, patting it into place. The old woman stood perhaps two feet from the side of the coach smiling at it with a little smile.

And so, my children, we head now for Genzano and for Frascati, the Queen of the Castelli . . .

We did not stop in Genzano which also had Baroque fountains possibly by Bernini in the piazzas and a palazzo of some sort. Down below the town was the Lake of Nemi from which two of Caligula's warships had been recovered only to be burned by the retreating Adolf Hitler.

The famous Feast of Flowers took place in May.

"Why do I know the name Frascati?" said Helen.

"Because of the wine?"

"Have I had it?"

I shrugged.

"I had some *years* ago," I said. "Must be thirty years ago now—at a wedding. We drank it with strawberries."

"Whose wedding?"

"And I don't think I've had it since. Um? Oh . . . a friend from college. I haven't heard from him—Tony Cranbrook . . . oh, it's been *years*."

"There," said Helen, "what kind of tree is that?"

I shook my head.

Frascati.

The wine was dry and golden.

Gold in candlelight.

The marriage of Tony Cranbrook had been celebrated in the village church, frayed purple hassocks, that special Anglican smell of damp and dust and stone, marble memorials let into the wall:

. . . departed this life June 11th 1795 in the sure and certain hope of the resurrection and of the life everlasting . . .

Afterwards, the younger people had strolled back through deep lanes to the family house for the reception. I'd walked with a girl called Susan who turned out to be the sister of one of the bridesmaids. She'd picked a buttercup and lodged it behind her ear. She'd said:

Do you know what this means in Tahiti?

Late in the evening they'd been wandering about the house calling to us to come and eat strawberries, calling out that I had to make another speech.

Jack?

We know you're there!

Susan?

Jack and Su-san!

The larger drawing-room was warm and quick with candlelight. In the centre of the dark polished refectory table stood a gleaming silver épergne piled with tiny wild strawberries. By the side of it stood octagonal silver sugar casters. The candelabra on the table glossed the wood's dark grain. Reflected in the épergne's curves and facets, points of flame quivered.

You will pay attention to your right . . .

Traffic was thickening.

Fisher!

The bus was slowing.

Susan Fisher!

. . . above the piazza. The Villa is still owned by the Aldobrandini family. You will notice the central avenue of box trees. The park is noted for its grottos and Baroque fountains.

"Doubtless by Bernini," I said.

"Is that a *palm* tree?" said Helen.

The Villa is open to tourists only in the morning and upon applica-
tion to the officials of the Frascati Tourist Office. If you will consult your
watches, you will see that it is now afternoon so we will proceed imme-
diately to the largest of the Frascati wine cellars.

The aluminum cane with its rubber bulb thumping down, the leg swinging up and to the side, Kojak led the straggling procession towards a large grey stone building at the bottom end of the sloping piazza. A steep flight of steps led down to a terrace and the main entrance. Kojak, teeth bared with the exertion, started to stump and crab his way down.

"Oh, look at the poor old thing, Jack," said Helen. "He'll never manage her on his own down here."

I went back across the road to where they were still waiting to cross and put my arm under the old woman's. She seemed almost weightless.

"I appreciate this," he said, nodding vigorously on the other side of her. "Nelson Morrison. We're from Trenton, New Jersey."

"Not at all," I said. "Not at all. It's a pleasure."

The old woman did not look at either of us.

"That's the way," I said. "That's it."

"She's not a big talker. She doesn't speak very often, do you, Mother?"

Step by step we edged her down.

"But she enjoys it, don't you, Mother? You can tell she enjoys it. She likes to go out. We went on a boat, didn't we, Mother?"

"Nearly there," I said.

"Do you remember the boat in Venice, Mother? Do you? I think it's a naughty day today, isn't it? You're only hearing what you want to hear."

"One more," I said.

"But she did enjoy it. Every year you'll find us somewhere, won't he, Mother?"

Inside, the others were sitting at a refectory table in a vaulted cellar. It was lit by bare bulbs. It was cool, almost cold, after coming in out of the sunshine. In places, the brickwork glistened with moisture. Kojak, a cigarette held up between thumb and forefinger, was holding forth.

The cellars apparently extended under the building for more than a mile of natural caves and caverns. In the tunnels and corridors were more than a million bottles of wine. Today, however, there was nothing to see as the wine-making did not take place until September. But famous and authentic food was available at the café and counter just a bit further down the tunnel and bottles of the finest Frascati were advantageously for sale. If we desired to buy wine, it would be his pleasure to negotiate for us.

He paused.

He surveyed us through the blue-tinted spectacles.

Slowly, he shook his head.

The five bottles of wine on the table were provided free of charge for us to drink on its own or as an accompaniment to food we might purchase. While he was talking, a girl with a sacking apron round her waist and with broken-backed men's shoes on her feet scuffed in with a tray of tumblers. Kojak started pouring the wine. It looked as if it had been drawn from a barrel minutes before. It was greenish and cloudy. It was thin and vile and tasted like tin. I decided to drink it quickly.

I didn't actually see it happen because I was leaning over saying something to Helen. I heard the melancholy man, the man who was travelling alone, say, "No thank you. I don't drink."

Glass chinking against glass.

"*No thank you.*"

A chair scraping.

And there was Kojak mopping at his trouser leg with a handkerchief and grinding out what sounded like imprecations which were getting louder and louder. The melancholy man had somehow moved his glass away while Kojak was pouring or had tried to cover it or pushed away the neck of the bottle. Raised fist quivering, Kojak was addressing the vaulted roof.

Grabbing a bottle-neck in his meaty hand, he upended the bottle over the little man's glass, wine glugging and splashing onto the table.

"Doesn't drink!" snarled Kojak.

He slammed the bottle down on the table.

"Doesn't drink!"

He flicked drops of wine onto the table off the back of his splashed hand.

"*Mama mia! Doesn't drink!*"

Grinding and growling he stumped off towards the café.

He left behind him a silence.

Into the silence, one of the women said,

"Perhaps it's a custom you're supposed to drink it? If you don't it's insulting?"

"Now wait a minute," said her husband.

"Like covering your head?" she added.

"Maybe I'm out of line," said the other man, "but in my book that was inappropriate behaviour."

"I never did much like the taste of alcohol," said the melancholy man.

His accent was British and glumly northern.

"They seem to sup it with everything here," he said, shaking his head in gloomy disapproval.

"Where are you folks from?" said the man in the turquoise shirt.

"Canada," said Helen.

"You hear that, June? Ottawa? Did we visit Ottawa, June?"

"Maybe," said June, "being that he's European and . . ."

"It's nothing to do with being European," said Helen. "It's to do with being rude and a bully. And he's not getting a tip from *us*."

"Yeah," said June's husband, "and what's with all these jokes about women drivers? I'll tell you something, okay? *My wife drives better than I drive.* Okay?"

He looked around the table.

"Okay?"

"I've seen them," said the melancholy man, "in those little places where they eat their breakfasts standing up, I've seen them in there first thing in the morning—imagine—taking raw spirits."

The old woman sat hunched within a tweed coat, little eyes watching. She made me think of a fledgling that had fallen from the nest. Her tumbler was empty. She was looking at me. Then she seemed to be looking at the nearest bottle. I raised my eyebrows. Her eyes seemed to grow wider. I poured her more and her hand crept out to secure the glass.

"*Jack*!" whispered Helen.

"What the hell difference does it make?"

I poured more of the stuff for myself.

June and Chuck were from North Dakota. Norm and Joanne were from California. Chuck was in construction. Norm was on a disability pension and sold patio furniture. Joanne was a nurse. George Robinson was from Bradford and did something to do with textile machinery. Nelson and his mother travelled every summer and last summer had visited Yugoslavia but had suffered from the food.

I explained to June that it was quite possible that I sounded very like the guy on a PBS series because the series had been made by the BBC and I had been born in the UK but was now Canadian. She told me my accent was cute. I told her I thought her accent cute too. We toasted each other's accents. Helen began giving me looks.

June had bought a purse in Rome. Joanne had bought a purse in Florence. Florence was noted for purses. June and Chuck were going to Florence after Rome. Helen had bought a purse in Florence—the best area of Florence for purses being on the far side of the Ponte Vecchio. In Venice there were far fewer stores selling purses. Shoes, on the other hand, shoe stores were everywhere. Norm said he'd observed more shoe stores in Italy than in any other country in the world.

Nelson disliked olive oil.

George could not abide eggplants. Doris, George's wife who had died of cancer the year before, had never fancied tomatoes.

Nelson was flushed and becoming loquacious.

Chuck said he'd had better pizza in Grand Forks, North Dakota, where at least they put cheese on it and it wasn't runny.

George said the look of eggplants made him think of native women.

Joanne said a little pasta went a long way.

Milan?

After Venice, Norm and Joanne were booked into Milan. What was Milan like? Had anyone been there?

"Don't speak to me about Milan!" said Helen.

"Not a favourite subject with us," I said.

"We got mugged there," said Helen, "and they stole a gold bracelet I'd had since I was twenty-one."

"'They'," I said, "being three girls."

"We were walking along on the sidewalk just outside that monstrous railway station . . ."

"Three *girls*, for Christ's sake!"

"They came running up to us," said Helen.

"Two of them not more than thirteen years old," I said, "and the other about eighteen or nineteen."

"One of them had a newspaper sort of folded to show columns of figures and another had a bundle of tickets of some sort and they were waving these in our faces . . ."

"And talking at us very loudly and quickly . . ."

". . . and, well, *brandishing* these . . ."

". . . and sort of grabbing at you, pulling your sleeve . . ."

"*Touching* you," said Helen.

"*Right!*" said Norm. "Okay."

"*Exactly*," said Joanne. "That's *exactly* . . ."

"And then," I said, "I felt the tallest girl's hand going inside my jacket—you know—to your inside pocket . . ."

"We were so *distracted*, you see," said Helen, "what with all the talking and them pointing at the paper and waving things under your nose and being *touched* . . ."

"So anyway," I said, "when I felt *that* I realized what was happening and I hit this girl's arm away and . . ."

"Oh, it was *awful*!" said Helen. "Because *I* thought they were just beggars, you see, or kids trying to sell lottery tickets or something, and I was really horrible to Jack for hitting this girl . . . I mean, he hit her *really hard* and I thought they were just begging so I couldn't believe he'd . . ."

"But the best part," I said, "was that I probably wasn't the main target in the first place because we walked on into the station and we were buying tickets—we were in the line—and Helen . . ."

"I'd suddenly felt the weight," said Helen. "The difference, I mean, and I looked down at my wrist and the bracelet was gone. I hadn't felt a thing when they'd grabbed it. Not with all that other touching. They must have pulled and broken the safety chain and . . ."

"Of course," I said, "I ran back to the entrance but . . ."

I spread my hands.

"Long gone."

"With us," said Joanne, "it was postcards and guidebooks they were waving about."

"Where?"

"Here. In Rome."

"Girls? The same?"

"Gypsies," said Norm.

"Did they get anything?" said Helen.

"A Leica," said Joanne.

"Misdirection of attention," said Norm.

"Were they girl-gypsies?" I said.

"Misdirecting," said Norm. "It's the basic principle of illusionism."

"I was robbed right at the airport," said Nelson.

"It must be a national *industry*," said George.

"They had a baby in a shawl and I was just standing there with Mother and they pushed this baby against my chest and well, naturally, you . . ."

"I don't *believe* this!" said Norm. "This I do not *believe!*"

"And while I was holding it, the other two women were shouting at me in Italian and they had a magazine they were showing me . . ."

"What did they steal?"

"Airplane ticket. Passport. Traveller's cheques. But I had some American bills in the top pocket of my blazer so they didn't get that."

"Did you feel it?" said Joanne.

He shook his head.

"No. They just took the baby and walked away and I only realized when I was going to change a traveller's cheque at the cambio office because we were going to get on the bus, weren't we, Mother?"

"A baby!" said June.

"But a few minutes later," said Nelson, "one of the women came up to me on her own with the ticket and my passport."

"Why would she give them back?" said Helen. "Don't they sell them to spies or something?"

"I paid her for them," said Nelson.

"Paid her?" said June.

"*Paid her!*" said Norm.

"*PAID!*" said Chuck.

"Ten dollars," said Nelson.

"They must have seen you coming!" said George.

"They must have seen *all* of you coming," said Chuck.

Nelson poured himself another murky tumbler of Frascati. "It wasn't much," he said. "Ten dollars. She got what she wanted. I got what I wanted."

He shrugged. Raising the glass, he said,

"A short life but a merry one!"

We stared at him.

"I got what I wanted, didn't I, Mother? And then we went on the green and red bus, didn't we? Do you remember? On the green and red bus?"

The old woman started making loud squeak noises in her throat.

It was the first sound we'd heard her make.

She sounded like a guinea pig.

"It's time for tinkles!" sang Nelson. "It's tinkle time."

And raising her up and half carrying her to the door of the women's malodorous toilet, he turned with her, almost as if waltzing, and backed his way in.

———————

. . . not entirely without incident.

Don't mention Milan to us!

. . . except for Helen's getting mugged.

It all made quite a good story, a story with which we regaled our friends and neighbours. We became quite practised in the telling of it. We told it at parties and over dinners, feeding each other lines.

But the story we told was a story different in one particular from what really happened—though Helen doesn't know that.

The scene often comes to mind. I see it when the pages blur. I see it in my desk-top in the wood's repetitive grain. I see it when I gaze unseeing out of the window of the restaurant after lunch, the sun hot on my shoulder and sleeve. I see it when I'm lying in bed in the morning in those drowsy minutes after being awakened by the clink and chink of Helen's bottles as she applies moisturizing cream, foundation, blush, and shadow.

Chuck from Grand Forks, North Dakota, had been right. They *had* seen all of us coming. Easy pickings. Meek and nearing middle age, ready to be fleeced, lambs to the slaughter.

She'd been the first female I'd hit since childhood. I hadn't intended to hit her hard. I'd moved instinctively. Her eyes had widened with the pain of it.

I'd noticed her even before she'd run towards us. Good legs, high breasts pushing at the tight grey cotton dress, long light-brown hair. She was wearing bright yellow plastic sandals. She had no makeup on and looked a bit grubby, looked the young gamine she probably was.

I'd been carrying a suitcase and felt sweaty even though it was early in the morning. Her hand as it touched the side of my chest, my breast, was cool against my heat.

When I struck her arm, there was no panic in her eyes, just a widening. There was a hauteur in her expression. Our eyes held each other's for what seemed long seconds.

When Helen discovered her bracelet gone, I hurried out of the vast ticket hall but under the colonnade and out of sight I slowed to a walk. There is no rational, sensible explanation for what followed.

I stood in the archway of the entrance. The two small girls had gone. She stood facing me across the width of the curving road. It was as if she'd been waiting for me.

We stood staring at each other.

Behind her was a sidewalk café. The white metal chairs and tables were screened by square white tubs containing small, bushy bay trees. The bays were dark and glossy. Dozens of sparrows hopped about on the edges of the tubs. Pigeons were pecking along the sidewalk near her feet. Among them was a reddish-brown pigeon and two white ones. In the strong morning light I could see the lines of her body under the grey cotton dress. She was gently rubbing at her arm.

Sitting there in Reardon's restaurant, drowsy in the sunshine after eating the Businessman's Luncheon Special ($4.95), the cream of celery soup, the minced-beef pie with ginger-coloured gravy, the french fries, the sliced string beans, waiting for the waitress to bring coffee, sitting there with the winter sun warm through the window on my shoulder and sleeve, I walk out of the shadow of the arch and stand waiting on the edge of the sidewalk. She nods to me. It is a nod which is casually intimate, a nod of acknowledgement and greeting. I wait for a gap in the sweeping traffic.

She watches me approaching.